BROKEN!

Michael S. Kearns

and

Ronald B. Solomon

Rocky Mountain Press
Evergreen, Colorado

© Michael S. Kearns and Ronald B. Solomon. All rights reserved.

Cover design by Ronald B. Solomon.

Cover execution by Six Penny Graphics.

ISBN: 978-0-9965350-0-7

Published by Rocky Mountain Press

Rocky Mountain Press

EVERGREEN, COLORADO

Service-Connected
Disabled Veteran
Owned Business
Since 1991

RockyMountainPress@gmail.com

Dedication

For Colonel James "Nick" Rowe (1938-1989),
US Army Special Forces, father of Army SERE,
author of *Five Years to Freedom* (1984).
De oppresso liber!

<u>Acknowledgments</u>

Thank you to all those who helped with this novel, especially, Didi, Rich, Pete (the Pirate), and Phil. Hooyah!

- Michael S. Kearns

Special thanks to Neil Speer, Gordon & Kaethe Zellner, Iris, Jacob and Ethan Solomon

- Ronald B. Solomon

Chapter One

Special Agent Zellner moved into position in the D-Level nosebleed section. He had mixed feelings about the assignment. On one hand he was completely on board with what and why he was there. Damned terrorists and copycat whack-jobs were everywhere. The Boston Marathon bombing proved that. These assholes didn't care if they killed a SEAL, a cop, or the little old lady from Pasadena. Just as long as it was in the name of Allah. It was goddamned repugnant. On the other hand, it bothered him that the assignment messed up one of his favorite memories as a kid. He double-clicked his readiness to command as he recalled the first Rose Bowl game he'd attended as a twelve-year-old boy, growing up in Altadena, California.

The game had been between the Texas Longhorns and the Michigan Wolverines, both undefeated 2005 NCAA Division 1-A teams. Billed as the Rose Bowl of all Rose Bowls, to this day it is still considered one of the greatest college bowl games ever played. His father was a U of Michigan alum so Zellner was expected to root for the old man's alma mater. He'd always been a bit of a rebel though, so just to tick off his dad, not only had he rooted for the Longhorns, but he'd convinced his mother to buy him a pair of cowboy boots and a faux-Stetson to wear at the game. His dimples deepened as he recalled his dad pulling the Stetson down over his face after Vince Young threw the game-winning pass.

"You're a traitor, son," his father had laughed.

Zellner looked down. The Stetson was gone, but his cowboy boots remained. He sighed; times sure have changed. The voice of the security detail chief chimed through his earpiece, "Kickoff one. Repeat, kickoff one."

Those words meant the front gates had been opened. Within minutes, the calm of the nearly soundless stadium would be replaced by throngs of excited and in all-too-many cases, shit-faced football fans. It wasn't as crowded as the Super Bowl, but finding bad guys in a sea of 95,000 people still wouldn't be easy. Ah, well. Let the games begin.

From behind his shaded, Wiley X sunglasses, Zellner scanned the faces of nearly every fan who made it through the ground level chokepoints and up to his area. He knew for the most part that 99.9 percent of the people were law-abiding Americans. Of course, there were also gangbangers, white-collar criminals and a slew of vape pen toting, college stoners, but they weren't his concern. Not today, anyway. And even though he was fairly new at this, he knew what to look for: any and all people who looked even remotely like an Arab. Sure, it wasn't PC to profile, but for Zellner and the thousands of other FBI agents charged with protecting America, it was bloody obvious. Don't blame him. Blame Bin Laden and all the other suicide bomb-toting towel heads who'd started the insanity. When freckle-faced, red, pony-tailed schoolgirls began blowing up airliners, he'd start grabbing every ginger he could find.

There hadn't been any specific threats Agent Zellner was made aware of, but that didn't change his level of focus. He would be scanning faces, body language and looking for conspicuous bulges in jackets or the waistlines of pants that could reveal hidden handguns. He would instantly search for any relationship a scream had with what was happening in the game. Was it a signal or a cheer? Did someone else, maybe several sections, over-respond to some signal? Hopefully, there would only be cheers.

Even though there were over twenty other agents on the security detail, Zellner's concentration never wavered. Based on the mix of groans, oohs, and aahs from the stands, the game was pretty close and action-packed. But he wasn't there to watch football. He glanced at the myriad security cameras strategically placed throughout the stadium. Even if something did happen, short of it being a suicide bomber, the perp would be caught. And if the security cameras and the agents missed it, the human hive would know.

Anyone who's ever been to a major sporting event knows the sound can be deafening. That makes it extremely difficult to hear nuanced conversations. But every now and then, a hush falls over the crowd. Sometimes it's the anticipation before the snap for an attempted fourth-down conversion. Sometimes it's when a player gets injured after a bone-crushing tackle and the fans wait to see if he's going to get up or be carried off the field. And sometimes it's as if the crowd draws a collective breath while waiting to see if the perfect spiral headed toward the tight end results in a game-winning touchdown. It was in one of these moments, about eighteen minutes into the second quarter, that Zellner heard it.

At first he thought it was an insect. The high-pitched buzz of some fly's tiny, rapidly beating wings. But there was something different about this buzz. It had an odd electronic quality to it. He removed his earpiece and checked to see if the connection was intact. It was. He tapped the receiver to see if maybe the battery had somehow jostled loose. It hadn't. He looked around to see if a fly or a mosquito was buzzing around his head. There wasn't. The more he looked and tried to figure out the sound, the louder it became.

The buzz grew louder, like a swarm of bees flying somewhere in the distance. But this was January 1. Sure it was Southern California, but it was still winter, and at 58 degrees Fahrenheit, there just aren't that many swarms of bees flying around. The louder the buzz became, the more intently Zellner looked around. "What the hell is that?" he said to nobody in particular.

Agent Zellner began moving, trying to stay cool while methodically looking around to find the source of the noise. His instincts were telling him nothing except that it could be a threat. What causes that sound? Could it be feedback from a bomb detonator that's in some douchebag's backpack? Not likely. They'd searched everyone's bag before they made it into the stadium. Could it have been planted before game time? No, he'd personally swept his assigned section ten times. Then he heard a woman exclaim, "Check it out!" as she pointed upward.

Everyone near her looked up. Their fingers joined hers as they spotted the same thing. Just above the south side of the stadium a dark swarm was approaching in the sky. As it drew closer, the buzzing sound became louder and louder. In seconds it became clear that the noise wasn't from a swarm of insects, it was a swarm of minidrones. Small unmanned aerial vehicles or UAVs for short.

There were hundreds of them. Zellner knew from his experience working with surveillance UAVs that these were quadcopters. And not your garden variety, off-the-shelf hobbyist radio-controlled toys. These were highly advanced, long range, flying robots. The DOD, CIA, FBI and DHS had been using them for years. And local law enforcement was getting them for more effective, cheaper surveillance. Each vehicle had four, independent rotors that gave them incredible power, stabilization, and hover capability. Some of them could hold payloads like wireless cameras and sensors, and although the FAA prohibited it, weapons.

Zellner squinted to see if he could see any payload, but in the face of the powerful California sun, he couldn't make out any details. He had never seen so many of them together. Truth be told, it was an amazing sight. They flew above the crowd, over the field and the game stopped. Everyone in the stadium – players, coaches, fans and security guards – were transfixed, staring into the sky.

Hundreds of the miniquadcopters were flying in concert. The black, 10-inch-square drones flew around the stadium, high above the fans' heads and did circles. Like a flock of propeller-driven geese, they never broke formation. Apparently there were speakers attached to the drones because music started playing. The song came from over a hundred speakers all at the same time. It was loud enough to drown out the buzzing.

As the thrashing and metallic song, "Fuck the System" by System of a Down, blared, the drones rose and fell, dipped and soared in rhythm. Zellner had never seen anything like it. It was hypnotic. Against the harsh song, the drones were graceful. They undulated in a spectacular sky ballet. His momentary hypnosis was broken by the voice of the security chief barking over his headset.

"What the hell is that?"

"I have no idea!" Zellner shouted back over the sound of the music and incessant buzzing.

"Did someone authorize some halftime show and forget to tell me about it?"

"Nobody told me anything! And it's not even halftime," he said back.

"Well, if those things create a formation in the shape of a Coke, someone's getting their ass kicked."

There was nothing anyone could do but watch and wait to see what was going to happen. Zellner instinctively placed his hand on his Smith & Wesson. He was ready. But ready to what? Ready to start taking pot shots of quadcopters like they were clay pigeons? That wasn't an option.

"What do we do?" he asked, not enjoying the complete and utter feeling of helplessness.

Just then the music and quadcopters stopped dancing. They came to a standstill in perfect formation and just hovered. No one in the stadium moved. No one made a sound. The continuous droning of hundreds of whirling propellers was like listening to hundreds of flags flapping in the wind. An unsuspecting beer vendor entered, calling out, "Beer here! Get your cold, beer, he —" his voice trailed off as he stopped to join the already transfixed crowd.

The voice seemed to come from nowhere and everywhere at the same time. "Good afternoon, Ladies and Gentlemen!" it boomed. This time it wasn't projecting from the drones. It was coming from the stadium's sound system.

"This is the world in which you now live," the voice continued.

A digital mosaic of people appeared on the stadium's playback screen. It looked like random people, all in separate little boxes. But what people? Who were they? Then Zellner saw the face of an elderly man sitting just to his left appear in one of the boxes and knew. The drones had cameras on them and were transmitting shots of people in the stadium onto the monitor.

"What's happening? Did anybody know about this?" he asked into his mouthpiece.

"We're checking on it, but whoever is doing this has apparently hacked into the stadium's audio/video system. They're trying to shut it down."

Clearly not feeling threatened the fans began cheering and waving as they do when the cameras project them onto the screen at any other sporting event. A skinny, young boy wearing a Spiderman t-shirt stood up on his seat and began waving his arms, "shoot me, shoot me!" he yelled at the drones. A couple of blond-haired, blue-eyed sorority girls jumped up and started dancing when they appeared on the screen. Their face-painted boyfriends joined them. In seconds everyone was on their feet yelling and waving. Then, as the entire stadium was getting caught up in what was decidedly one of the coolest things Agent Zellner had ever seen, images of him and all the other security agents showed up on the monitor.

A jittery, computer-generated capture box surrounded the image of Zellner's face, then, as it was apparently being run through facial recognition software, his name flashed across his image. Information began a digital crawl upward through his box: Special Agent Gordon Zellner, FBI. Assignment: Level D Rose Bowl Security Team. Born June 4, 1990. Social Security Number 465-80-8855. It continued. The crawl listed his girlfriend's name, his bank account information, the total taxable income from his last federal return. Everything. Including the fact that he'd been getting an illegal prescription for Oxycodone filled for over a year; a fact he'd never disclosed in his security screenings. A fact that could cost him his job. Or, at the very least, make for some long and invasive polygraph sessions. The same type of highly personal information was skittering across the faces of all the other agents. Fans turned to look at him.

"That's one of them!" yelled someone. "He's a Fed!"

"We've been made," his CO barked. "We've all been made."

Zellner sprinted up the concrete steps and bolted to his left, racing to meet at the assigned incident area. Just what the threat was he didn't know, but every fiber in his being screamed that it was a threat. As he raced to join his team, the images of himself and his FBI agents dissolved into the faces of regular fans. Names, addresses, telephone numbers, social security numbers, credit card account numbers, credit scores, police histories, Facebook, LinkedIn, Twitter, Paypal, and even porn site ID's and passwords skittered across their faces.

The voice bellowed. "You are being watched 24 hours a day, seven days a week. Privacy is dead. Freedom is dead. Democracy is dead." A montage of security cameras popped onto the monitors. The video showed cameras on light posts, traffic lights, and gas stations. It showed the fans, these fans, as they shopped, as they commuted to work, and even some of them as they attended political rallies. It ended with a high-flying Predator drone that was right now 20,000 feet above the Rose Bowl. Its gimbal-mounted, high-resolution, Gorgon camera pivoting. It was watching. Watching. Watching.

"Wake up, America!" the voice boomed. "Take arms! Take back your freedom! Take back what is yours! But beware: This revolution *will* be televised!" Then the screen went black.

The drones began moving again. They formed into a circle that flew around the oval of the stadium. They were in perfect harmony. Round and round. Watching and flying. And just like that they started dropping their payloads. Thousands of tiny, egg-shaped objects plummeted toward the 95,000 fans. The crowd's hypnosis ended and panic set in.

"They're dropping bombs!" someone shrieked just before getting trampled by a mob of terror-stricken people rushing for the exit.

Chapter Two

From the ground, the Mojave Desert is mostly a barren, endless expanse of sand where scorpions, Joshua trees, coyotes, and desert tortoises fight a constant battle of survival under brutal conditions. From the air it's not much better. In the heat of summer, daytime temperatures in the high Mojave of California can reach a hellish 110 degrees Fahrenheit. The setting sun drags the air down 70 degrees along with its descent. The average rainfall is about six inches per year. Barely enough to fill a kiddie pool halfway, if it all came down at once.

One of the most uninhabitable areas of the high desert is El Mirage. Just 12.5 miles from one of the other less inhabitable towns of Adelanto, El Mirage draws thousands of tourists each year to its El Mirage Lake. Completely dry, the El Mirage lakebed is a favorite location for Hollywood film crews that want to show complete and utter end of the world locations. Designated by the state as an Off-Highway Recreation Area, or OHRA, for short, ATV riders and speedsters come from nearby Los Angeles and San Diego when they feel a need to inhale a combination of sand, carbon monoxide and adrenaline.

If there were a tourism brochure for El Mirage, it would read something like: "El Mirage. It ain't paradise. But if you want a place to disappear or a desolate location to die, we'll take your corpse."

It should come as no surprise that the towns surrounding El Mirage, namely Adelanto, Palmdale, Victorville and Barstow have been used for years by the US Department of Defense to conduct secret missions and testing. With Edwards Air Force Base located just a few miles up the road, the entire basin is filled with DOD contractors, military families and leather-skinned native, desert people.

This desolate hell on earth is also home to a myriad of well-paid engineers, security firms and unmarked airstrips that are used by the military and their overlord contractors, Lockheed Martin, Boeing and General Atomics. If you stand practically anywhere in a 20-mile radius, you can see them conducting tests of their stable of Unmanned Aerial Vehicles like the Wasp, Raven, Shadow Hawk, A160 Hummingbird, Global Hawk, and the infamous Predator. At one small, private airport in the middle of the middle of nowhere, a thumb-tacked, torn sheet of paper reads, "Warning: Unmanned Vehicle Sightings."

"What a cesspool," Chauncey thought as he looked down from three miles above the ocean of sand through the Caravan Supervan 900 jump plane's open door. He'd seen the planet through the open door of jump planes over a thousand times before, 2,265 times to be exact. He was one of the few men who'd seen the earth from three-plus miles over all seven continents. Chauncey had tasted the high-altitude air above Maryland, where he learned to jump with the US Air Force, El Salvador, Myanmar, Australia, Israel, and Lebanon. Once, in the most extreme skydive of its time, he'd sucked down the frigid air that separated the sky from the icy desolation of the South Pole. That jump had left his three fellow skydivers dead, buried face-first with shattered bones in the cold, hard ice pack.

Most of retired Air Force Captain Charles Paunce's jumps had been with the CIA as an intelligence officer and mapping expert. And they almost always ended in the death of enemy troops or the exfiltration of stranded friendlies. Nicknamed "Chauncey" after a stint with the Australian SAS Regiment that saw him return stateside with the word "mate" at the end of most of his sentences, he was now jumping from planes with cameras attached to his helmet. It was his job to document the excited, shocked and all too often, pee-in-the-pants faces of tandem jumpers looking to spice up their lives courtesy of the Desert Drop Zone School for Skydivers.

This hadn't been Chauncey's first, post-military career choice. It was no easy feat to swap a life filled with the adrenaline rush of combat and espionage for filling the Facebook accounts of otherwise play-it-safe civilians with images of the only bad-assed thing they'd ever do in their lifetime. As a matter of fact, it was a huge horse pill to swallow.

He checked the GoPro camcorder and Canon Digital Rebel XT still camera that were mounted to his Brazilian-made Rawa helmet, then fit the blow switch into his mouth as he prepared to jump. The camera flyers, as he and his mates were called, went first. They'd leap out of the plane, then ease into a back-fall position to limit their velocity enough to give the tandem masters and their flailing, human appendages time to catch up, or down, as the case was here.

For the next forty-five to sixty seconds, Chauncey would freefall above, below and all around the newly fallen to immortalize their cherished first impressions. After that, he'd break away, head down, arms to the side, and race to about 2,000 feet at nearly 200 miles per hour, where he'd deploy and be on the ground in time to immortalize the landing.

Personal history and experience aside, Chauncey still had to admit that no matter what risks he'd taken with his life, it took guts for anyone to willingly jump out of a perfectly good airplane. It definitely said something about the person.

His favorite subjects were the tough guys: men who were so full of themselves that they barely listened to the tandem master's checkout talks. The memory of one guy in particular always cracked him up. His name was "Zilla." Short for Godzilla, the infamous, nuclear-bomb created monster that attacked Tokyo, Zilla had cruised to El Mirage for a weekend of ATV's, Budweisers, and the chance to drop his big balls from 15,000 feet. According to himself, Zilla was a macho, bronco buster who did rodeos and bragged about riding bulls "whose nuts were cinched up tighter than a walnut in a pistachio shell." No wonder they bucked so hard.

Prior to the jump Zilla had bragged to anyone who would listen about his bull rides, bar fights, and the drunken escapades that ended in high-speed car chases from the LAPD. Chases in which he'd never been caught, of course. It had struck Chauncey as comical that Zilla looked like a bull. He was stocky, and had a flat head with close-cropped, black hair and a pushed-back nose that featured noticeably large, flared nostrils.

Predictably, as soon as they'd left the safety of the aircraft, Zilla turned from Generalissimo Santa Ana into Pappo the Clown. Arms flailing, legs kicking and screaming for his mama, it took every ounce of the tandem master's strength to break the bronco. Total freefall time: ten seconds. Nobody was surprised when the pale-faced Zilla had no interest in buying the souvenir CD that bore witness to his less than manly performance. But they sure as shit burned a copy of it at the drop zone office for when everyone needed a good laugh.

"Go time," said the pilot, pointing to the door.

Before he'd even heard the second word, Chauncey was all sky. Having recently passed the half-century mark in his life, he was one of the "old guys" in the otherwise youthful staff of the drop zone crew with the exception of the owner, an ex-SEAL buddy who Chauncey had done multiple missions with. Rich Killingsworth, or Killa as he'd come to be known because of all the ways he'd demonstrated he could kill a man, had opened Desert Drop Zone eight years ago. He and Chauncey had run into each other at a party at the Skydiving Museum in Phoenix, where Chauncey had volunteered to be the museum's official historian. Correctly sensing Chauncey's soldier turned dull life, Killa invited him to work the drop zone.

The job had turned out to be a lifesaver. Plagued with PTSD, depression, a failed marriage, chronic pain from heart and head wounds owing to far too many bomb blasts and bullets, Chauncey's life had become a tarnished and cracked mirror. And whenever he peered into it he saw the nothingness he'd become.

As he floated his way up, over, and around the tandem jumper, Chauncey contemplated the lyric, "how did I get here," from the Talking Heads song, "Once in a Lifetime."

He'd always been somewhat of an enigma. An enlisted man who'd grown up in the shadow of the infamous spook school at Fort Holabird, in

Dundalk, Maryland, Chauncey had fallen in love with the idea of serving his country while protecting a Civil War re-enactment site as a Boy Scout.

Endowed with the morality of his mother, a devout Protestant, the analytical mind of his electrician father, and the courage and fierceness of his Irish warrior ancestry, Chauncey really was the proverbial Boy Scout, which is exactly what the US military needed. But, as it turned out at the end, not what the CIA needed – or wanted, when it asked Chauncey to teach torture.

Sadly, a lifetime of valiant service had erupted into a scandalous finale that dumped him into military prison, then into the chaotic isolation of civilian life. Now he was branded as a disgraced U.S. government, whistleblower taking pictures of nobodies jumping from a plane in the middle of Nobodyville.

Skydiving was all Chauncey had left. It was the only thing that made him feel completely alive. The only thing that made him feel like a man again. Tragically, each time he jumped, the thought resonated throughout his body that this was the best it would ever be again. Not a comforting thought as he contemplated the rest of the road that lay ahead.

How many times had he considered ending it all? He knew firsthand how a man died, so he also knew a lot of ways he could end his own life. He knew which arteries to cut so he would die in seconds. He knew what poisons would collapse his lungs or stop his heart from beating. And he knew that if he chose that path, it would truly be "mission accomplished." No codpiece required.

Chauncey counted the growing number of his active and retired brothers in arms who'd taken their own lives in the last ten years of war. He thought of his best mate, Burton Porter, who he'd gone with into El Salvador to hunt guerillas, and how he'd lost his legs to a land mine. Porter, or "Buddy" as they called him, had decided he couldn't live without them, so he'd blown his brains out with a 12-gauge. Thom Richardson, who'd watched Chauncey's back when they'd jumped into Iran to create maps for Spec Ops to find the best places to survive in case of an invasion, had jumped in front of a bus during a bad bout of PTSD. And Sergeant Adrian Grant, who'd lost his mind during intensive resistance training at the SERE school Chauncey had run for the National Command Authority in Spokane, Washington, had hanged himself. Too many funerals. Too many color guards. Too many weeping widows crying into tight, neatly folded, red, white, and blue handkerchiefs.

Chauncey knew there was a part of him that wanted it to end. He'd even given up his own weapons to his SEAL friend, Diddy, on North Island to prevent himself from joining the growing list of his compatriots. There was something inside of him, probably the parochial teachings of his mother that kept him from taking that fatal step. And even though he was a card-carrying agnostic, respect for her carried him forward into the gray.

Maybe that was another reason he jumped so much. He told himself it was so he could feel alive. But maybe it was because the more he did it, the more the odds would stack up against him. Two years ago, to celebrate his 50th birthday, Chauncey did fifty-one jumps in five hours – the fifty-first jump being the one to grow on. With each jump he'd pushed the edge a bit more. And even though the last leaps were low-altitude deployments, they all ended perfectly. Never a cutaway. Never a scratch. Maybe he was supposed to live. For something. For what, he didn't know. But for something. Maybe.

Two days after the fifty-first jump he'd found himself at the funeral of yet another suicide. A young lance corporal who'd had the entire right side of his face, including his eye, ear, and nostril blown off by an IED in Fallujah, had OD'd on the pain pills he had gotten illegally because he couldn't get consistent appointments with the VA. That's when it occurred to him. Chauncey couldn't off himself directly, but he could place his fate into the hands of providence.

The day after the funeral, Chauncey cashed his VA benefit check and emptied his savings account to buy three high-performance parachutes. Each night since then he would carefully unpack and repack each chute. Two of them he would pack perfectly, the third one was packed to have a critical malfunction. He stashed them in a closet and each day would grab one without knowing if it was the dead-man's chute. In his heart he knew that this kind of unpredictable, risk-taking selfishness was way beyond uncool. Yet he'd still slipped into the sky 200 times since.

Although he didn't need it, the tandem instructor gave Chauncey the nod, indicating that he should breakaway. He stopped blowing into the tube in his mouth that kept snapping photographs and went into a head down position. As he sped toward the ground at terminal velocity, his skin rippled in the wind. The rushing air punched its way into his helmet and coated his ears with thunderous roaring. His heart beat like a young man with purpose and a full life ahead.

Like most parachuting masters, Chauncey loved the sensation of freefall so much that he never deployed his main canopy at the recommended 3,000 feet. He preferred low-altitude deployments. He passed 3,000 feet, then 2,500, then 2,000. Down and down, the dry, arid desert racing toward him. At 1,500 feet he finally went to release the main. But fate and the odds had caught up with him.

In order to sabotage the rig, just before the final closure, Chauncey had crossed the brake line over the folded and nearly contained chute. Now, as he released it, the switcheroo caused a line-over in the center of his canopy. Instead of fully inflating, as parachutes naturally want to do, the rigged brake line creased the center of the main canopy into a bow-tie. Chauncey went into an uncontrolled spin.

Instinctively realizing he couldn't shake the line loose, Chauncey grabbed for the cutaway cable that would free the main and automatically deploy the reserve chute. Whether it was adrenaline or the exhilaration of the moment that made him initially forget, Chauncey's memory reminded him that his sabotage had also involved disengaging one side of the cutaway release. As he spiraled downward, the ground rapidly closing in at now 1,000 feet, the main hung on and speared straight up, flapping like a flag in a hurricane.

Luckily, or unluckily, depending on your perspective, Chauncey's survival instincts kicked in. If he was going to die, it wasn't going to be without a fight. He reached into his pocket and pulled out a hook-knife. But as he frantically worked to cut away the main, his Cypres auto-altitude release computer detected it was at 600 feet and activated. His reserve deployed – right into the main. The spiral intensified as the two chutes were now engaged in a dance of death.

Continuing to hack and cut at the main, at 400 feet it finally let loose, leaving the reserve a mere 300 feet to fill with air. Chauncey surfed the ground pulling the left brake, then the right, then both, then everything went dark.

Chapter Three

"Silly Putty."

"Yes, sir. Silly Putty."

"1,984 Silly Putty eggs."

"Yes, sir. All with the exact same contents and not one usable fingerprint on any of them."

Special Agent Douglas Myles Breskin looked at the twenty or so boxes of multicolored Silly Putty eggs that Agent Zellner had toted into this office, then back down at the small, unrolled piece of paper he held open between his fingers. Short, sweet, and when coupled with the incredible drone show at the Rose Bowl, an extremely effective way of driving home your point. Breskin read the paper aloud.

"The right of the people to be secure in their persons, houses, papers, and effects, against unreasonable searches and seizures, shall not be violated, and No warrants shall issue, but upon probable cause, supported by Oath or affirmations, and particularly describing the place to be searched, and the persons or things to be seized."

It was the Fourth Amendment to the Constitution of the United States of America. These seemingly simple, fifty-four words had been the cause of wars, lawsuits, debates, and jobs, including his, for over two centuries. They epitomized freedom from oppressive government. They were the backbone of America. To many, they were the most important part of the Bill of Rights. To others, they were simply an unfortunate obstacle to keeping people safe.

Breskin imagined that if – no, make it *when* – they caught the clever, opposable-thumbed monkey who'd printed those words 1,984 times, cut them into 1,984 fortune-cookie strips of paper, then rolled and placed those strips into 1,984, weighted Silly Putty eggs and dropped them onto the heads of 95,000 Americans, that he or she would use the 44 words of the First Amendment to defend the right to do so.

Unfortunately, this high-tech stunt had caused hundreds of people to be trampled while thinking they were about to die in a terrorist attack. No doubt that was the intention. But who had done it? Were they Muslims? Homegrown anarchists? The cyberhackers, "Anonymous?" There was no "Dear Purveyors of the Persistent Surveillance State" note. Nothing to indicate next steps. Nada.

Investigators were searching for people who would have had access to so many drones and also the skill to control them so expertly. Add to that the facial recognition software and the ability to simultaneously access the personal records of thousands of citizens and you had yourself one extremely talented cyberterrorist. Hacking into the stadium's audio/video system had probably been their easiest accomplishment.

Breskin looked up from his thoughts to Zellner, who stood there with a cast on his right arm in a sling. He'd been fortunate to have gotten away with just a broken arm. Most of the other members of the security team had been standing, apparently dumbfounded, at exits, and were trampled by the panicked human stampede. It had taken the ambulances over six hours to get injured agents and fans to nearby hospitals. He imagined it would take the janitorial crew far longer to mop up the blood.

As for the quadcopters, they'd disbanded and flown away toward the East, where they'd just disappeared over the desert. Breskin's team was reviewing the surveillance footage taken during the game by the airborne surveillance assets. Between the pair of helicopters patrolling at 4,000 feet by the Customs and Border Patrol and Sheriffs, the CBP twin engine King

Air that had been circling at 8,000 feet and unseen, the DHS Predator up at 20,000 feet, there was plenty to look at. The problem was that because the drones were so small, finding where they'd gone would be akin to isolating a water vapor molecule in a storm cloud.

"I heard them coming," muttered Zellner. "Like a swarm of bugs."

"What kind of bugs?" asked Breskin.

Surprised by the question, Zellner shrugged. "I don't know. Flying bugs."

Breskin stared at Zellner. A look of disdain spread across his face. "Can you be more specific, please?"

Zellner looked back, confused by Breskin's question.

Breskin glared. "There are nearly ten million different species of bugs on this planet. Twenty-five are flying insect orders. Were they beetles? Because there are over 350,000 species of beetles. Or maybe they were in the ants, bees, and wasps order. That only has about 100,000 species."

The senior FBI agent's narrow eyes penetrated Zellner to his core. He gulped, feeling naked. More than naked, if that was possible. Breskin wasn't at all the stereotypical tall, dark and handsome federal agent who you saw portrayed in the movies. He was a bit overweight and kind of dumpy in a Joe Pesci way. Although he was Caucasian, if you looked at him from certain angles, his eyes had a thin, Asian quality. Like you were staring into the eyes of a cobra. Zellner knew that his boss wasn't someone you wanted to mess with. And he felt that he just had.

Breskin had joined the FBI's anti-terrorist division after finishing a stint as a high-level, private contractor for the CIA in Afghanistan, Iraq, Yemen, and Gitmo. Before landing there, he'd worked for the Joint Personnel Recovery Agency, using his degree in psychology to train Spec Ops troops how to resist torture. It was rumored, but unconfirmed for anyone without the proper clearance, that upon leaving the JPRA, he'd reverse-engineered the resistance techniques used in the Survival-Evasion-Resistance-Escape training to architect what became the Bush/Cheney enhanced interrogation program. So, basically, while working for the JPRA he'd towed the "torture is immoral and doesn't work" line, but as a contractor, he'd made a small fortune by taking waterboarding, pain, and fear to new levels in order to prove that "resistance was futile."

He'd studied every interrogation and torture manual ever published. Some people said he could recite the FBI's Reid Technique of Interviewing and Interrogation, the JPRA's SERE manual and the CIA's *KUBARK* Counterintelligence Interrogation manual, which copied the Chinese techniques used in the Korean War, from memory after drinking an entire bottle of vodka. If he drank vodka, that is. But he didn't.

Breskin didn't drink, smoke, commit adultery, or take the Heavenly Father's name in vain. Brought up on a potato farm outside of Salt Lake City, Utah, Breskin had learned the ways of the Latter-day Saints for his entire 55 years on earth. And as a good Mormon, he'd devoted his life to helping his fellow man. Even if it had meant "Jack Bauer-ing" them a bit on the way to meet their makers.

The only reason Breskin got the job with the FBI, which had been openly critical of the more aggressive, DOJ-approved enhanced techniques, was because when he returned from the field, he'd denounced them and espoused the more effective, rapport-building tactics used by that agency. After composing the book on the torture doctrine, he'd suddenly and unexpectedly "seen the light." Torture doesn't work. And given his degree in psychology, his vast interrogation and investigative experiences in the field, as a team player, face it, the FBI fast-tracked him to a senior level, GS-14 because they felt like they'd signed Peyton Manning.

Zellner shuffled uncomfortably under Breskin's glare. He had the sense that his soul was being scanned. With such penetrating eyes, he couldn't imagine why any prisoner wouldn't just start singing stories the moment he merely walked in the room.

After what seemed like a hundred years, Breskin loosened his look, but not his intensity. He loved staring guys down. Especially incompetent guys who thought they had all the right stuff. But he had a lot of work to do and knew there were going to be a lot of late nights after this one. He had no time to play with his food.

"How's the arm?" he asked, indicating Zellner's cast.

Zellner blew out a breath like he'd just been released from Spock's Vulcan mind meld or one of the excruciating stress positions he knew that Breskin used to employ. "It's okay, sir. A bit achy, but I'm good."

"Just achy, huh?" said Breskin. "Then I guess those painkillers you've been hooked on for, what was it the drone show revealed, a year and a half, must really work?"

Zellner stared, stunned.

"Consider yourself suspended without pay. The bureau has no place for drug addicts."

Breskin looked back down at the Fourth Amendment, as Zellner exited, completely broken.

Chapter Four

Allah was dead. For Armagan, he died exactly ten years ago. He died the day that Armagan's mother, father, sister, uncle, and over twenty others in his village had been killed by the US Army's unmanned ground bots. It had been the Americans who'd killed everyone, but it was because of the Taliban that they'd come.

Before al-Wahiri and his mujahedeen army arrived, Wajiristan had been a tiny, peaceful village in the southern desert of Afghanistan. Armagan and his sister, Lila, would wake each morning, say their prayers to Allah who was merciful, and then help their mother with the goats and chickens. After that, Lila would work at household chores while Armagan studied the Koran with his father, his best friend, Mahdi, and the village elders. They were Sunni Muslims and believed in the power of Allah. But they did not practice the corrupted type of Islam used as an excuse to murder innocent human beings.

After studying the Koran, Armagan was free to do as he pleased, so long as it also pleased Allah. He spent much of his time fixing things. From early on, Armagan was a gifted, albeit untrained, engineer. He intuitively knew how things worked. Whenever the village's well pump stopped working, it was Armagan who was called to restore the flow of life-sustaining water. If the one radio that was shared by the village went silent, Armagan would restore its voice. And if the air pump they'd found in an old junkyard would no longer breathe air into Madhi's soccer ball, Armagan would resuscitate the pump, then play soccer in the hard-packed, dirt street that ran through the village. The elders of the tribe would sit in front of the mud-packed buildings on dilapidated rocking chairs and clap whenever Armagan would score a goal.

"You are a true gift!" they would shout, pointing out that his name meant "gift."

Armagan's mother had named him after an apparent near-death delivery. Because the village had been so poor and his mother had little to eat during the pregnancy, Armagan was born premature and underweight, five and half pounds. With no doctors or medicine, and having no means of driving the two hours north to Kandahar Hospital, nobody thought he would survive. But he had. So his mother, thanking Allah for this gift, had named him Armagan.

He used to love hearing the stories of the celebration that followed his birth. Music, singing, clapping, dancing, and as much food as the tribe could muster. That feeling of shared miracle was what his village had always been. Even with the harsh desert and constant threat of death around them, the tribe celebrated life.

After the terrible tragedy that happened to the twin towers in New York, Armagan's mother and father had wept for the dead souls taken so brutally by the al-Qaeda piloted planes. Allah was about life, not death. The terrorists had corrupted his words in a sinful and, they all agreed, cowardly manner.

"This is not Allah's way!" they cried.

Armagan remembered sitting with his father and the other villagers in the months following the attack. They listened to the daily radio reports from Kandahar that reported how the Americans were blaming the Taliban for harboring Bin Laden and al-Qaeda. They demanded that he be turned over for justice. His father would scream at the radio for the Taliban to comply. But the Taliban refused and so the American War began. And, as history whispers the tale, the Taliban fell. At least for a while.

Driven from the capital, the Taliban dispersed, sending the mujahedeen, the warriors of the faith, southward into Kandahar and the desert below. They arrived in their village on Lila's sixteenth birthday. Armagan had never met a member of the Taliban and his father had always prayed he never would. He prayed five times a day, as all good Muslims do, that the mercy of Allah the Great would hide their village from the radical tyrants. But Allah's shroud was elsewhere.

The mujahedeen arrived driving Toyota Hi Lux 4x4s riddled with bullet holes from the U.S. coalition troops. In tattered manjima pants and floppy alpaca hats, the soldiers with fist-sized beards carried RPG launchers and battered Kalashnikov rifles left over from the Russian War. Alarmed that there was no proper imam or minaret, their Taliban leader, a hardened zealot named al-Wahiri appointed himself imam and required strict adherence to Sharia, the laws of orthodox Islam.

Al-Wahiri forcefully recruited all men of fighting age to join Allah's holy crusade against the infidels. He ordered that a mosque be erected immediately and forbade any singing, dancing, or even soccer playing. When Armagan's father, who was the de facto leader of the tribe, approached al-Wahiri to ask that he honor the tribe's ways, he was beaten with rifle butts and thrown into a hole dug by the soldiers to be punished by Allah's red, desert sun. That night, when trying to bring water to him, Armagan had been caught. They shaved his head and beat him nearly to death. Then his mother and sister shared the same fate for allowing him to do so.

The only thing that saved Armagan's life was his skill as a tinker. The mujahedeen who had beaten him was told to kill the boy. He leveled his Kalashnikov at Armagan's head and pulled the trigger. The only thing that the weapon discharged was a simple click, as it apparently misfired. Furious, the soldier took up a second weapon and it miraculously misfired too. Sensing an opportunity, Armagan offered to fix the Kalashnikovs. He jabbered that he was a great fixer and promised to work on their weapons, jeeps, and radios in exchange for his life. From that day forward, Armagan rebuilt engines and guns, and fulfilled whatever other mechanical needs the mujahedeen had for him.

When the soldiers would leave the village to fight, they'd warn that they would return. And, in spite of Armagan's fervent prayers that they be killed by the American soldiers, they always came back.

A year passed and the village's previous joy was replaced by the darkness of Allah's misinterpreted brutality. The tribe adapted, as they had done for hundreds of years, patiently waiting for the war to end so they could return to their peace. Armagan grew and his mother knew the mujahedeen were watching him; waiting for the day he could join them in jihad. She held him at night and prayed that the war would be over before they decided he was old enough. She whispered that she didn't have the strength to lose her gift. She prayed for this even though her husband warned that she could be beheaded for not offering a sacrifice to Allah.

On the eve of his thirteenth birthday, Armagan's parents woke him before dawn. In hushed tones they whispered prayers of love, hope, and survival. His mother gave him a small burlap sack filled with some clothing, food, water, and a knife.

"You must escape. You must not be dragged into their unjust war and die. There is no honor. There will be no paradise." She told Armagan to find the Americans and tell them the village was being held captive by the Taliban. "They will save us," she promised.

Armagan argued, "But al-Wahiri will kill you when he finds out I'm gone."

"That is no matter," said his father, in agreement with his wife. "We will be together one day in heaven. But you should make it there in your own way. These men do not speak for Allah. Now go."

It was final. Armagan knew there was no arguing. He had to honor his parents in order to honor Allah.

Armagan crept out of his home, past the well and the flowering jasmine tree under which he had spent so much time as a child, and proceeded toward the sleeping mujahedeen. To his surprise, although a passing fly would normally have made them bark, the malnourished dogs stayed silent. His father had pointed to the south as Armagan's escape route, but Armagan had other plans. The mujahedeen were sleeping and not watching their vehicles. He would remove the wires to the coils, which would make them unable to drive and catch him. Then, he would steal a jeep and drive to Kandahar to tell the Americans. But first he was going to kill al-Wahiri. He would not allow this monster to hurt his parents.

Imitating the perfect stillness of sand skittering in a slow breeze, Armagan approached the sleeping al-Wahiri. He marveled over how such a violent man could sleep so soundly. From ten paces away, he unsheathed his knife, still not knowing if he could go through with it. He prayed for strength as he knew it was the only way. Suddenly al-Wahiri's two-way radio barked, as if it were one of the village dogs realizing they'd missed something.

"The Americans are coming!" the voice warned.

Al-Wahiri and the other mujahedeen screamed awake. Without even noticing Armagan, they quickly threw their arms and supplies into their vehicles and tore away, northward, toward the mountains of Tora Bora. There they would regroup and continue their resistance. And just like that, they were gone. The Americans were coming. It didn't go unrealized to Armagan that if he'd sabotaged their jeeps, it wouldn't matter who was coming.

"We are saved!" Armagan burst into his parents' room. His father leaped up from his mat on the floor in surprise and confusion. After Armagan had explained to his parents and all the others in the village, a cheer erupted that must have shaken the gates of heaven.

"A celebration!" cried his father. "Tomorrow we must celebrate our freedom and the arrival of the Americans with the wedding of our Lila."

Armagan's sister had been betrothed to his friend Mahdi before the Taliban had arrived. But it had been agreed that the wedding would be put off until they were gone. Weddings were to be joyous. Armagan was excited to show the Americans what a true Afghanistan wedding was like.

Normally an Afghani wedding takes weeks to prepare. But in this case, plans were made quickly, hopefully to coincide with arrival of the American troops. On the day of the festive event, Armagan begged to be sent to the outskirts of the village to watch for them. Though disappointed that he wouldn't be there to see Lila and Mahdi exchange their vows, he was even more excited at the notion of being the first to see the approaching troops. As he surveilled the north, he was puzzled by a large number of approaching puffs of sand. They were coming from all sides of the village. "Jeeps?" he wondered.

He strained his ears to see if he could hear the approach of vehicles. His heart fell. Had the mujahedeen turned back? Then it soared. Are the Americans already here? Then it stopped. From the outskirts of the village came a line of unmanned ground vehicles. Made in the US by Foster-Miller, each remote-controlled Talon SWORDS had forward-facing 7.62 mm M240 machine gun bracketed by a pair of six-barreled 40 mm grenade launchers. A greater killing robot did not exist anywhere. And there were at least a dozen of them headed right toward the village.

As soon as the UGVs were close, they launched their grenades. The M240's screamed. The noise was so overwhelming that Armagan had to practically shove his fists into his ears. It was like hell had risen from the belly of the earth and was spewing fire.

Armagan ran toward the village as fast as he could. Flying rocks, heat, and shrapnel slapped at him. He kept running until a violent blast blew him backward against one of the large rocks that lined the main street. As he leaned against the boulder, his ears ringing, an object rolled toward him. At first he thought it was a soccer ball. He screamed when he saw that it was his mother's head.

That was ten years ago.

Now, on the anniversary of the death of Allah, Armagan sat on a comfortable chair in front of his new employer, General Atomics, in Poway, California. The ever-present media was there, video rolling, still cameras clicking, and long, baffled boom mics pressing toward the podium like spears.

Nels Green, the CEO of General Atomics, had called for the press conference to announce the hiring of Armagan. He stood at the temporary lectern, waiting for the applause to die down from the address that

Congressman Todd Stevens had just given. He'd said all the right things. All the things that he needed to say to make San Diego County "Drone Central." And everything he'd needed to say to keep getting GA's campaign contributions. Green knew the press was here to see Armagan. And based on the size of the crowd, he also knew that his company's stock price was ticking higher by the second.

"What a coup," thought Green. To have the miracle child from Wajiristan working for him. "This ought to shut those anti-drone fanatics down a bit."

"We all know the tragic, yet miraculous story of Armagan," Green began. The crowd quieted.

"This brave, brilliant soul was the victim of a tragic and mistaken attack on his village ten years ago in Afghanistan. Faulty intelligence caused an incursion into his village to destroy what had been reported as a Taliban base. But they'd cut and run, like the cowards they are, before the attack began and the village was destroyed. Adding to the tragedy was the fact that this mistaken attack killed his sister, Lila, in the middle of her wedding."

Armagan recalled only being lifted into a helicopter and flying. He'd thought he was going to heaven, but instead had been flown to the US Navy-run, NATO hospital at Kandahar Air Field. In the face of public outrage over the robot massacre of the wedding in Wajiristan, the DOD had gone against the wishes of the newly elected President Karzai and repatriated Armagan to the United States. "To fix what we broke," they spun.

Building on his undeveloped mechanical talents, Armagan had been educated, courtesy of the US taxpayers, at the best schools in the country. He smiled again at America's ignorance as, even though he was Sunni, they'd placed him to be raised by a Shiite family in Anaheim, California. It didn't matter to him either way as he was no longer a believer. Now one of the youngest PhDs from MIT's robotics department, the twenty-three-year-old Armagan had gotten a contract with the military's Defense Advanced Research Projects Agency GA to develop systems for some of the exact same technology that had caused him to be here in the first place.

It was the kind of story that Americans love: violence and destruction followed by redemption. Sure they'd destroyed everything he'd ever known, but they'd saved him from a lifetime in a poor village in the middle of nowhere. Armagan now had the opportunity to make something of himself. It was the American dream and, even now, all these years later, it impressed him to think about the clever Army publicist who'd concocted the public relations stunt. It had been a stroke of brilliance that dulled some of the sharp criticism of the war.

As Armagan rose to address the press conference, he heard the quiet whirring of the gyros and motors in his artificial, mind-controlled, "bionic" leg. And even though he was now part of the ever-increasing legion of robotic engineers in the country, he couldn't help but marvel at the technology that had replaced his severed leg. He habitually reached down to feel for his missing appendage, and the geek part of him thought it was incredibly cool to be a cyborg.

He got up effortlessly and approached the lectern to read his prepared speech. He knew America needed his forgiveness in order for him to get their continued support. Even though they didn't deserve it, he was more than ready to give them what they needed if it meant that he could continue working as a "tinker."

Before Armagan could say a word, someone screamed out, "Traitor!" There was a surprised gasp from the attendees as they looked around trying to see who had yelled.

"You've betrayed the memory of your parents!" the heckler continued.

Seeing that nobody close had yelled, Armagan realized the jibes were coming from outside of the security gates that protected General Atomics from the outside, taxpayer-filled world. Across the street from the main entrance stood Tom Carby with a bullhorn. At six foot five with a bald head and a fiery red goatee, Carby wasn't an easy man to miss. During the ceremony nobody had taken notice, but Carby and his ever-present, anti-drone group, "Watch the Watchers," had moved their protest movement. They'd marched from the high-traffic corner to just beyond the entrance in order to see what was happening. And, obviously, to get some attention.

Normally positioned on the corner of Scripps Highway and Kendall Avenue, Carby's group carried signs and chanted slogans that denounced the rapid advancement of unmanned vehicle systems into the world. A well-respected robotic engineer himself, Carby had served in Iraq and Afghanistan as liaison to the army's Robotic Systems Joint Project Office. It was rumored, but classified top secret and therefore completely unsubstantiated, that he'd even had a hand in the development of armed war bots.

After serving his time in the sandbox, Carby returned stateside as a civilian and became an adjunct professor at Carnegie Mellon University in Pittsburgh. In addition to teaching high-level robotics for uses in agriculture and medicine, he'd established an ethics curriculum for roboticists to help them examine the potential consequences of their work. His protest campaign was good publicity for the university, and since the money hadn't stopped coming in from private sources and endowments, they let him do whatever he wanted.

In conjunction with US Veterans for Peace, the ACLU, Code Pink, and other anti-UAV groups, Carby went around the country conducting protest rallies and educating Americans about what the new technology "really" meant. The campaign condemned the president, Congress and the growing UAV industry for not only promulgating murder and perpetual war, but for creating an authoritarian, surveillance state.

One of the more provocative tactics his campaign used was to travel the country with a miniature Predator drone. They would invite people to stand in front of the UAV and stare at its armament of powerful Hellfire missiles and gimbal-mounted, high-resolution camera. They had a real camera attached and would show people what they looked like to the drone operators on the other side of the camera just before the missiles flew.

"They killed your family and now you're helping to kill others just like them!" Carby boomed at Armagan through his bullhorn.

Armagan glanced around at the gathered press corps and GA employees as they stared back at him. It was the same question everyone wanted to ask, but didn't have the nerve. It was a fair question, and he didn't need to answer but had no problem doing so. He looked directly into the nose of Carby's Predator drone and replied in what was a dialect that betrayed his Afghani childhood.

"It is true that the United States Army killed my family. But it was an accident made in the name of freedom. In the war against oppression, there will always be collateral damage. Sometimes that is necessary in our attempt to destroy evil. The mistaken attack was caused by faulty surveillance due to technological imperfections. I see it as my responsibility to use my gift as an engineer to help limit those imperfections so tragedies like mine can be avoided in the future."

The normally jaded media burst into applause. Nels Green smiled.

Carby just yelled, "Bullshit!"

Chapter Five

Chauncey slowly exhaled a lungful of Kine Mine hashish smoke as he watched the approaching plume of sand. He cursed the brace that was tightly wrapped around his sprained ankle as he ran through the various escape routes he'd planned since buying this shithole house at the end of the end of Shadow Mountain Drive.

The weekly death threats had stopped about a year ago. To a large degree he knew they'd stopped because nobody could figure out where he'd gone. To a larger extent, he knew that as far as America's memory was concerned, the country had Alzheimer's disease. It just couldn't remember squat on its own. Most citizens relied on the media to tell them what was worth brain storage.

Over the years, the images of Chauncey testifying against President Bush and Vice President Cheney "enhanced interrogation" program before the Senate Armed Services Committee had been replaced umpteen times. The photos of Abu Ghraib had dissolved into the election of the nation's first black president which had morphed into the Arab Spring then seamlessly slid to the all-important birth of Prince William's second child. There had been plenty of new pages added to the American family album and most of them were a lot more fun to look at after dinner than the section where our country acted "kind of bad."

Still, Chauncey knew it was only a matter of time until some misinformed crazy found him and tried to shove the whistle he'd blown up his ass. Even if that happened, Chauncey knew in his heart that he'd played a part in exposing and destroying the policy that had damaged America's moral authority and put the lives and souls of America's servicemen and women in peril. He was at peace with it.

The sand cloud stopped moving about a mile out as Chauncey noted that the driver must have been trying to decide which of the three driveways to turn down. All of them led to Chauncey, as he'd intentionally created them as a way of delaying an intruder's arrival. Of course, nobody else knew that besides Chauncey and a few of his most trusted mates. The fact that the approach had stopped told him that, whoever it was, it wasn't a friend coming for an unannounced visit. And it damned sure wasn't the Avon Lady. There was always the off chance that it was someone lost, but he'd know that as soon as the sand began moving again.

Chauncey casually filled his chest with another pull from his vaporizer and waited. The hash was a mellow, caramel-tasting CO_2 extract that he'd gotten from a dispensary in Victorville. It wasn't the same kind of uber-mellow high he got from cannabis indica that helped him sleep through his night terrors. It was more of an alert, sativa buzz. Hash was much better than the long list of meds he'd been on and off of since his PTSD diagnosis. Over the past ten years he'd tried Wellbutrin, Seraquil, Prozac and all the other VA-preferred meds. The problem was that none of them mixed well with beer and tequila. Not to mention they caused a decided drop in his libido, so god knows they had to go.

On the advice of a fellow vet he'd met in therapy, Chauncey had gotten a medical marijuana card. After trying a few different strains, he met Kine Mine and had been happily self-medicating ever since. It still amazed him that there was any pushback to legalizing the stuff across the entire country.

"Ah well, the feds do like to control things a bit," he chuckled.

The sand restarted its approach to the house, so his lost motorist theory evaporated along with the hash-laden smoke. Because he'd purposely pitted the road and placed logs and rocks along the full one-mile stretch leading to his dilapidated, 800-square-foot desert house, Chauncey knew he had about five minutes to wait. Longer, he decided after hearing the engine of the approaching vehicle. Definitely not a truck. Not even a four-wheel drive SUV. More of a high-performance sound to it.

"Now who the hell would drive out to visit me in the middle of this crap in a, what is that, an Audi? A Mercedes?" he wondered. He shrugged, realizing he'd know soon enough.

Chauncey's nonchalance wasn't based on his now mollified death wish. It was just that he knew pretty much how to escape and evade anyone in any terrain. He was confident he could survive whatever the visitor had in store for him, even though his ankle had been severely sprained by the low-altitude skydive landing he'd miraculously lived through. At least he'd survived with his life. His former job was another story.

Killa had been plenty pissed after the stunt Chauncey had pulled. "I don't give a rat's ass if you want to kill yourself," he'd yelled while Chauncey was pulling pebbles out of his face and limping to the office. "But I can't have you freaking out my students. I've got a good thing going, and I'm not going to let a PTSD'd dickhead like you screw it up."

Chauncey knew that Killa would calm down after a bit. He'd go back, they'd get drunk, exchange a few war stories, and Chauncey would have the gig back. If he wanted it back.

His confidence was based more on the fact that Chauncey knew the lay of the land. His first years in the Air Force had been spent as a master cartographer with the National Geospatial-Intelligence Agency. Or as it was called at the time, the Defense Mapping Agency. An expert in mapping, charting, and geodesy, Chauncey had spent weeks roaming the high desert for five miles around his house, so he would never be stuck without an exit route.

Mapping was a practice he'd fallen in love with when he was a scout. Whenever he and his troop would be on a trekoree, tasked with getting lost and then finding their way back to camp, Chauncey was the one chosen to lead. He knew it was goofy, but he imagined that he'd been an Apache in a previous life. An Apache who'd had an unspoken connection with the land.

Fantasy aside, Chauncey was great at it and perfected his abilities years later in the intelligence community.

After working three years for the NGIA, Chauncey's work had been noticed by Nick Rowe, one of Chauncey's idols. One of his maps had helped get a squad of Army Rangers who'd been stranded on a covert op safely out of Bosnia, and Rowe had recruited Chauncey to do mapping for the evasion portion of SERE. Rowe, who'd escaped from the Viet Cong after five years as a POW, understood what men needed to protect their minds. He brought Chauncey to Fort Bragg, North Carolina, and they both trained hundreds of soldiers how to evade capture and live off the land until they were rescued by swift boats, monkey extractions, or some other means of exfiltration.

Before his assassination in April 1989, Colonel James Nicholas Rowe, the father of SERE, gave Chauncey another opportunity. Seeing his innate ability to understand the hidden connection between twigs, rocks, and a man's survival, Rowe trained Chauncey to map men's minds in the Resistance portion SERE.

Chauncey was taught interrogation techniques that had been brutally applied to American troops by the Chinese, the North Koreans, and the Russians. With the guidance of Rowe, the CIA, FBI interrogators, and others, Chauncey helped to develop a higher-level SERE resistance course for which most men didn't qualify. He shook his head as he recalled how the press had labeled his portion of the program "torturing our own troops." Another memory that faded quickly, thank God, because that's not what the program was. It had been created after the Korean War to help teach troops a way of resisting brutal interrogation techniques safely and with honor. Hopefully, to resist them long enough to escape, then evade and survive until rescued.

He knew that some of the mock interrogations had gone too far. The weeklong curriculum took place at a simulated POW camp where the troops had their asses kicked and their minds manipulated. But their students weren't regular folk. Plus they all knew it was a teaching exercise designed to save them from real-life, throat-slitting jihadis. They also knew they could use prearranged stop codes if things ever got too gnarly. After it was all over, there were debriefs to review what had happened in order to refine the soldiers' resistance better.

Sent to run the Resistance arm of the Joint Chiefs of Staff SERE program in Spokane, Washington, Chauncey kept improving. He learned things about men that most people will never know. He became an expert in body language, facial cues, and voice modulations. He learned how different personalities reacted to interrogation, stress, pain, and isolation. Mostly he learned that as a means of extracting the truth, torture didn't work.

The intense reflection of light that bounced off the hood of the now-arriving 2015 Jaguar XF nearly blinded Chauncey. He shielded his eyes with his hand.

"Damn." he thought. "I didn't consider a British car." Then, just as quickly, "What kind of doofus would drive a beautiful car like that down my driveway?"

As he squinted between his fingers to see who had arrived, Chauncey's foot slid a bit closer to a trip switch on the porch. The switch was wired to a dozen loads of C4 he'd buried under the dirt as a hidden barrier between his porch and the driveway. If the visitor was a threat, a simple tap of his toe would create a 50-foot wide by 10-foot deep crater that would take the visitor and his overpriced hunk of British metal straight down to Beijing.

"You're one tough SOB to find, Chauncey," said Special Agent Breskin, as he emerged from the silver luxury sedan.

Men like Captain Charles Paunce were difficult to take by surprise. A lifetime of training had conditioned them to always be ready and never, ever, be taken off guard. Their contingencies had contingencies. They played life like they played chess – always thinking ten moves ahead of the game. It was how they survived. But no amount of training or foresight could have prepared him to be face-to-face with the war criminal he himself had given the tools to do the harm he'd done.

Breskin saw the look in the eye of his old mentor and stayed by the driver-side door. It was a good thing, too, because Chauncey was still considering whether he should detonate the hidden charges, or simply slit Breskin's throat, then drive his corpse and his Jag into one of the 3,000-plus abandoned tungsten mines scattered around San Bernardino County.

"Nice wheels, mate." said Chauncey finally. "I didn't realize that waterboarding Pakistani goat herders paid so well."

"Yeah, well, we had a job to do," Breskin replied, having expected nothing less to come at him. "May I?" he asked, indicating that he'd like to approach Chauncey.

"Only if you came here with just enough gas for a one-way trip."

"I didn't come here to fight with you, Paunce. I know we've had our differences, but that was a long, long time ago."

"Ah, well in that case it was terrific seeing you, mate. Glad we had a chance to catch up. So good on ya' and don't let the cactus stab your bum on the way out."

Breskin and Chauncey stared at each other. Two master interrogators trying to eyeball their way through well-practiced, Kevlar veneers. Realizing that Breskin must have already mentally revisited their last meeting in Afghanistan before arriving, Chauncey now played a bit of quick catch up. Chauncey joined the war in 2002. Because of his SERE training, he'd been sent by the military to evaluate the US interrogation program. He'd visited Gitmo, Abu Ghraib, Shaikh Isa Air Base, aka Shakey's, and a dozen other black ops sites. He'd interviewed guards, interrogators, the few Red Cross observers who'd gained limited access and, of course, the "detainees." Such a nice word for tortured prisoners.

In the kindest sense, Chauncey's conclusion was that the country was caught up with fear and lost its way. America had been injured, and like a wounded animal, had emerged from the darkness worse than the beast it despised and feared. And one of his conclusions was that Breskin was a war criminal who'd reverse-engineered the techniques employed through SERE – the techniques that were deemed not only immoral but ineffective in extracting the truth – and sold the White House, the CIA, and anyone else who would listen to a bill of goods that he could break terrorists.

Chauncey's report had recommended that they stop the program immediately. He suggested they remove the troops who'd been poorly trained to interrogate and bring in the FBI to conduct proper, ethical, and effective techniques that didn't violate the Geneva Conventions, The Convention against Torture, and the moral rights of men. Above all, he'd recommended that they arrest Breskin, Bush, Cheney, Rumsfeld, Gonzales, Addington, and all the other members of the war council who'd condoned it and charge them as war criminals. That hadn't gone so well.

He recalled his final words to Breskin, "You're a disgrace, and you've betrayed the men and the country you pledged to protect." The more Chauncey thought about it, the more he liked his idea about blowing up Breskin along with his car.

"You were right, you know," said Breskin, as if he'd read Chauncey's mind. "I regret everything we did. And after you resigned your commission, things only got worse. The CIA was out of control. Even while you were back here telling the truth, they got more brutal. I still have nightmares."

"Damn. Surprise number two," thought Chauncey as he considered Breskin's contrition. "I must be losing my touch."

It didn't matter, though. He glared at Breskin, "Is that a fact? What about your whole Mormon we're-the-missing-tribe-of-Israel-so-we-need-to-Tikkun-Olam-the-broken-world-garbage?"

Breskin could see that Chauncey was becoming agitated so he ignored the bait that mocked his belief in certain Kabbalahistic thoughts. He'd done his homework and knew as much about Chauncey's post-service life as any special FBI agent could. Prison time, failed marriage, failed congressional bid, failed attempt at running a private investigation firm. There wasn't much after that. Nobody with Chauncey's CV left many traces. Breskin noted the vaporizer and hash that sat on the cheap Walmart table next to Chauncey. He also noticed that Chauncey's right foot was edging closer to a black bump on the porch. Time to turn down the heat, he decided.

"Like I said, I'm not here to fight with you. I'm here to offer you a job. I'm a senior agent with the FBI now, and we need your help."

Chauncey chided himself over being surprised for a third time. "Wow! I really have lost my touch," he thought. "I didn't realize the FBI had taken to waterboarding bank robbers these days," he said.

Breskin knew he'd completely taken Chauncey off guard. He'd been relying on it. It was a rare and extremely satisfying moment to be sure, but he didn't have time to savor it.

He continued, "I'm serious. I'm running a Special Access Program to SERE up a bunch of top-level executives with UAV Co's. We – I – need you to teach them how to resist in case they ever get kidnapped."

"Get out of here, Breskin. Now. Before I do something I won't regret later."

"Paunce, you were right, okay? A hundred percent. They should have listened to you. All of us should have. You didn't deserve what you got."

Sensing these were words Chauncey had never heard, but needed to, Breskin pressed on. "The DoD is increasing its funding to the UAS program. We've picked up a lot of serious chatter from the bad guys about grabbing the executives and torturing them into spilling their guts. We feel confident that we can protect them, but there are no guarantees. They need a chance to survive, just in case."

"Why don't you do it? Or maybe get your boy Jessings. He'll do anything for a million bucks," asked Chauncey. Jessings had been the other SERE shrink that Breskin got rich with by teaching torture.

"It can't be any of us. We're tarnished. You're clean. Still the choirboy. And besides, you're the master. You're the best man for the job."

Chauncey decided he'd had enough surprises for one day. "Get out of here, mate. As much as I realize that your hidden agendas have hidden agendas, the last time I tried to help I got burned and it ruined my life. Now I highly suggest that you drive your little piece of crap out of here before I change my mind about letting you go."

Breskin shook his head. He was disappointed, but he didn't object. He'd known it was a long shot and even more importantly, he knew he'd already pushed Chauncey close to the breaking point. Breskin took out a business card and placed it on the ground. "In case you change your mind," he said. Then he climbed back into his air-conditioned, leather-upholstered, blood money car and drove off.

Chauncey felt his body relax as he took another deep pull from his vaporizer. He exhaled, watching the business card blow away from an all-too-rare breeze.

Chapter Six

It was every jihadist's wet dream to detonate a suicide vest at a Jewish bar or bat mitzvah. On a strategic level it was because desecrating such a sacred, spiritual event would be a powerful way to sow deep, enduring fear. On a practical level it would rid the world of a Jew that would soon be capable of making more Jews. On a symbolic level it would be an even greater victory, if that ceremony was for the child of the lead aeronautical engineer who worked on the guidance systems of Predator MQ-1 UAV, the most powerful Jew-invented killing machine there was.

Unfortunately for the jihadists, the bat mitzvah of Amber Walters, the 13-year-old daughter of Leon Walters, PhD, senior-level engineer at GA was being held on Coronado Island, aka, Navy Seal Central. And even with the military deterrent in mind, the security around the historic Hotel Del Coronado was tight. Each camera on the Coronado Bridge that led to North Island, every camera along Orange Avenue, and each and every camera inside and outside the hotel had been tested and connected.

The guest list had been vetted by the FBI and San Diego's finest. And in spite of the objections and complaints by the ACLU, the employees at the hotel had been screened, resulting in twenty-three deportations and much more expensively cleaned plates. It was even rumored that the NSA had tapped the spectral phone of the hotel's most famous guest, the ghost of Kate Morgan.

Everyone who arrived for the bat mitzvah party, including Amber Walters and her giggling gaggle of pubescent friends, was patted down and wanded for concealed weapons. Indignities and hypervigilance aside, two hours into the gala everyone was having a tremendous time. Everyone except for Tom Carby.

Apparently, even after being turned down repeatedly for a license to assemble, Carby's "Watch the Watchers" campaign had still shown up to protest. The Walters' bat mitzvah guest list read like a veritable who's who of the San Diego defense contractor community. As one of the senior engineers for General Atomics, Walters was friends with some of the planet's most brilliant minds. Roboticists from GA, iRobot, Foster Miller; engineers from Lockheed Martin, Boeing, Raytheon; and professors boasting Stanford, MIT, Rutgers collegiality were in the famous Crown Room doing the hokey-pokey beneath the iconic red roof. Like a moth to a flame, Carby couldn't resist such a ripe opportunity to get into some faces.

At first, he'd pulled into the parking lot and started heckling the arriving guests. Within seconds, the hotel security staff, many of whom were retired SEALs, forced him and his liberal minions off the private property. So they loaded up their cars and perched themselves on Orange Avenue to protest from the public streets. But the Coronado PD didn't see it that way.

"No permit? No protest. Git along, Carby, git along," they said in far less nice words.

Undeterred, Carby somehow got his hands on a herd of power boats. They were now floating in the public Pacific Ocean, just off of the private, sandy beach bordering the hotel's west side. The police snickered as they waited for Carby's protest flotilla to be boarded by the Coast Guard.

Often considered weddings for spoiled thirteen-year-old Jewish children, the after-parties of bat mitzvahs were extravagant affairs celebrating one of the most important days in a Jewish child's life: the coming of age. Amber Walters was no exception. There were over 300 guests in attendance, many of whom had flown in from New York, Massachusetts, northern California, and even a few of Leon's colleagues from Israel.

Not surprisingly for the precocious daughter of the brilliant Leon Walters, the theme of the bat mitzvah party was robots. And we're not talking about the Disney movie version of robots; we're talking robots with a capital "R." Bots were everywhere. Walking, two-foot-tall Aldebaran Robotics Nao H25 Humanoid Robots and barking, tail-wagging Genibo Robot Dogs encircled ice sculptures of quadcopters and hummingbird drones.

Sitting in the center of each table was a scale model Predator. Amber had begged for a few Global Hawks, but given who was really footing the bill for this shindig, daddy endured several months of pouting over the denial.

Not wanting his beautiful, young daughter to be deprived, however, Walters had surprised the apple of his eye by talking some of his buddies at Foster Miller into lending him a few retired Talon bots. They'd reprogrammed the software so that instead of disarming IEDs, the nimble pincers and articulated arms served drinks. But that wasn't even the coolest thing at the party. For that, Walter's wife had hired the most sought-after DJ in Southern California.

Any bat mitzvah party on the scale of Amber Walters' had to have, at the very least, a great DJ. Some of the bat mitzvahs had live bands, but they had to draw the line somewhere, didn't they? They didn't want to spoil their daughter too much. So they'd hired Tony Solivan, better known as DJ Soli to his many fans.

Tall, handsome, and decorated with some very hip ink, Solivan had played some of the most extravagant celeb parties in Hollywood and was in high demand. Mostly he booked album releases or movie wrap parties, but according to his agent, he'd been eager to DJ this particular bat mitzvah. And even though the $30,000 fee didn't hurt, Solivan had another, far more compelling reason for wanting to do it. He intended to kill everyone there.

Solivan had grown up in Southern California, the son of an Army colonel. After a conflict-filled adolescence due, in large part, to his underperforming, partying, X-Box addicted ways, he'd graduated high school with few prospects. His father, naturally, wanted his son to finally grow up and let the Army guide him into manhood, but Solivan was more inclined to get stoned, write electronic digital music and play video games.

Not surprisingly, after graduating, his father kicked him out of the house and told him to make it on his own.

Unsure of where to turn, Solivan kept partying and DJing. He hadn't intended to join the Air Force, although when he did he loved how much it burned his dad up. A recruiter who'd been trolling his favorite arcade saw how amazing he was on video games. Just like Centauri, the alien recruiter in the movie, *The Last Starfighter,* the guy told Solivan that he may have the skills necessary to be a drone pilot. He promised that Solivan would be safe and sound in an air-conditioned room in Nevada, and use UAVs to kill terrorists. The guy painted a picture of James Bond on steroids. Solivan loved it.

He served for about six years at Creech AFB and in that time racked up a ton of kills. At first, it hadn't been so bad. They were evil fanatics trying to kill our troops and destroy America's way of life. But after a while, Sergeant Solivan began to like it. He would walk into work, see pictures of targeted al-Qaeda and Taliban leaders on the wall and muse, "Which one of these bastards is going to die today?" He felt like he'd become a sociopath. It became tough to reconcile the fact that he'd go to work every day, legally murder a bunch of people, then go home and party with his friends at night.

On his last day of service, Solivan's CO gave him a scorecard: 263 kills. He was beyond appalled. He could remember each strike, but the one he thought about most was the time he'd called for the launch of a pair of Hellfire missiles. Due to the nature of being a drone pilot, he had to watch the before, during, and after parts; not something that "real" pilots had to deal with. After the smoke had cleared, he could see that one of the men he'd targeted had lost both of his arms, but wasn't dead. Through the monitor, Solivan watched as the guy pushed himself along the sand with his legs, and literally bled out. As a bit of added ghoul, the IR camera on the drone feed showed the man's body grow cold as he died.

After leaving the service, Solivan moved back to his parents' home in Van Nuys. His father told him he was a hero and that he should be proud. He'd killed the bad guys. But Solivan didn't buy it. He knew for a fact that he'd killed innocents. Collateral damage, they called it. Women and children is what Solivan called it.

Solivan was a wreck. He was diagnosed with severe PTSD and suffered for over a year with headaches, insomnia, and suicidal thoughts. He spent most nights drunk, getting into fights and losing one minimum wage job after another. The final straw was when he came home, blackout drunk, and nearly beat his father to death. Apparently dear old dad had called him a pussy for whining about what he'd done. That was pretty much status quo for the level of sympathy he'd come to expect from the military.

He had no recollection of what had happened when he woke up in jail. All he knew was that his father was in the hospital, his mother had disowned him, and the other guys in his unit thought he was a loser. Finally, a halfway decent therapist from the VA suggested that he get back into DJing, something he had completely forgotten about.

Besides his dimpled smile and impeccable taste in music, one of the things that made Solivan such a sought-after DJ was an innovative hook he'd created. At all the parties he booked, he would bring out a troupe of dancing Roombas. Manufactured by iRobot Corporation, Roombas were small, round and, as much as robotic vacuum cleaners could be, they were cute. Really cute. So cute that iRobot had sold millions of them. Rather than being known for making war bots, they had a reputation as clean as the carpets their robotic critters fed on.

iRobot also sold a line of inexpensive, customizable Roombas to schools and engineers. Solivan had purchased a dozen of the little critters and put LEDs and colored lasers on them. He connected the flashing lights and motors to a simple sound modulation board so that the bots would dance and pulse with light to the beat of whatever tunes he played. They never ceased to thrill the crowds.

Today, for the bat mitzvah of the daughter of Dr. Leon Walters, one of the men responsible for the further development and enhancement of the killing machines he'd operated for so long, Solivan had given his dancing Roombas something extra special. Each one of the bots happily spinning and grooving alongside the unsuspecting folks on the dance floor contained some crystals of TATP, a small canister of water, a remote detonator and enough steel ball bearings and half-inch steel, razor-shaped triangles to tear the skin off a hundred people's bodies.

"Yo, yo, everybodaaay," Solivan screamed out through his head mic, "How about some Gomez Go?!" Amber and her short-skirted girlfriends shrieked and began dancing among the Roombas to "Come & Come Again."

Armagan had been to several bar mitzvahs since coming to the states. After the rabid anti-Semitism he'd been exposed to while living in Afghanistan, and even more while working with al-Wahiri and the mujahedeen in his village, being in the same room with a Jew had been difficult at first. After he'd been exposed to reality, Armagan came to realize that the stereotypes and hatred he'd heard were nothing more than ignorance and propaganda. Sure, in the past years he'd met some cheap, money-grubbers. Some of them had been Jewish, but the vast majority had been non-Jewish, Persian ex-pats who'd gone into business for themselves near his home in Orange County. They used hatred for Jews as an excuse for their own failures.

The first bar mitzvah he'd ever attended wasn't the lavish, keep up with the Jonesawitz affairs he was at now. It had been for the younger brother of his roommate at MIT. Barry Davidson, a robotics major had grown up in White Plains, New York. Barry wasn't your typical rich, Westchester County Jew. His family had lived on the grounds of a large, reform synagogue where Barry's father worked as the janitor and groundskeeper. So Barry grew up vacuuming carpets and mopping the floors of the temple's sanctuary, kitchen, rabbi's office, and bathrooms.

He'd told Armagan stories about the lavish bar mitzvah parties he'd gone to. He'd only been invited because of his father's job at the synagogue, and some of the kids were rich snots who teased Barry over his unfashionable shoes or clothing. But mostly, it had been a warm, inviting community. Barry's issues had always been with the wealthier members of the temple that he hated.

"We're persecuted because we're all supposed to be rich, selfish bankers, so I hate any Jews that act that way," Barry would complain. He'd gotten into MIT with scholarships and a 4.0 average in high school. "These over-the-top bar mitzvahs make us look bad," he'd complain.

Barry's bar mitzvah had been at his synagogue with his family and a few close friends. His younger brother's ceremony, the one Armagan had attended, was the same. There was no huge party, no DJs, no $5,000 checks as gifts from rich relatives. It had made an impression on Armagan for being equally as spiritual as many of the rituals he and his family had performed in Afghanistan. Parties aside, bar mitzvahs were special to Jews and represented a child's passage into adulthood by reading from the Torah. Barry told Armagan that the parties were more for the parents to show off their success than for the kids. The Walters' bat mitzvah was no exception.

Coming to America had been an eye opener for Armagan in many ways. This country had so much that it took for granted. So much freedom, so many choices, and so much opportunity. But besides the opportunity, Armagan loved the food.

Even before he'd gotten used to his newly adopted family, Armagan became a bit of a glutton and ate as much as he could. Always warned about the added stress that being overweight would put on his prosthetic leg, he still seemed to eat one extra bite at every meal. Just because he could. It wasn't only because his family had verged on starvation. It was the incredible variety of type, taste, and style. America was the greatest restaurant in the world and Armagan wanted to eat something from every page on its vast menu.

Having just finished one extra piece of poached salmon and the delicious, garlic cream sauce covered asparagus that had been served to the adults for lunch, Armagan began wandering around the party. Given his notoriety and the nature of the guests, he was stopped nearly every five feet by someone who wanted to shake his hand and tell him how horrible it was that his family had been killed. That he was so lucky to have been given such a great opportunity. He'd learned early-on how to graciously say thank you and politely move on.

"Armagan, come over here," he heard from behind him. He turned to see Leon Walters waving him over. Armagan approached Leon, who was standing with a group of other GA mid- to senior-level engineers.

"Mazel tov, Leon. Your daughter did a wonderful job at the bema," offered Armagan, remarking on Amber's Torah reading. "And thank you so much for inviting me. This is quite a beautiful affair."

Walters was dismissive. "Thank you for the compliment. And you're more than welcome for the invitation. You're a part of the San Diego brain bank now," he kidded, "so you'll be at a lot more of these."

After a few quick introductions to the other men, the group continued the conversation they'd begun before Armagan's arrival.

"I've seen the security footage and there's no way those things were programmed by anyone in the states. We just don't have that technology."

They were discussing what just about everyone in the industry was talking about: the Rose Bowl incident. One of the men, a midlevel navigation designer at GA named Bob Gibbons continued. "GPS aside, I've never seen such a sustained and uniform flight pattern anywhere. The algorithm they used is years beyond anything I've seen or heard of. It was really impressive." All of the men in the group nodded in agreement.

Another one of the men, Jim Dorning, a short, skinny roboticist with Boeing, added, "What impressed me was how they were able to swarm multiplatform so seamlessly."

"Not to mention the payload assignment. What with the speakers, the cameras, and the eggs, I have no idea how they sustained that kind of flight time, let alone got away."

Leon laughed, "The eggs were brilliant. I think Lockheed Martin's going to be at our door next month with a proposal for adding weaponized ostrich eggs to the MQ-2."

They all laughed and clapped, envisioning the meetings in the weapons design department at LM.

"Never happen," snorted Dorning. "They love those Hellfires too much. You'll never see an Eggfire missile." The men laughed uproariously.

Armagan had been in the scientific community long enough to not be disgusted by the insensitive response to what surely must have been one of, if not the most frightening moments, in the lives of the crowd at the Rose Bowl. He understood the nerd mentality and wanting to know how the quadcopters had accomplished what they'd done. Hell, he shared it. But still, a part of him was saddened by the fact that they didn't consider the human results of the event. He looked at the dance floor and saw Walters' daughter hanging with a group of friends. Had she been there she could have been trampled along with the hundreds of other injured attendees.

His eyes went from the dance floor to the DJ, who was now announcing that it was time to do the horah.

"Everyone gather around!" Solivan announced.

Armagan took Solivan's announcement as a way to excuse himself from the conversation. "So much wonderful food," he said. "I think I need to see a man about a camel," he joked. He ambled off toward the restrooms as the other men headed to the dance floor.

This was the moment that every bat mitzvah party shared. The horah was an energetic, Eastern European folk dance that had become a traditional element of every American bar mitzvah. As the familiar "Hava Nagila" began blaring, the guests converged. They formed concentric circles, each ring slightly larger to accommodate more people. Everyone held hands and the circles moved, rhythmically in opposite rotations. After a bit, they danced, as a group, forward and toward the center. Once there, they would raise their hands, shout, then dance backward.

Adding to the fun, Solivan sent in his dancing Roombas. Their sound and light sensors performed well. People clapped and pressed closer to see eleven bots spin and whirl in time to the music. The circles of people spun clockwise, then counterclockwise, and the Roombas did the same.

"They must be Jewish robots," someone cried out.

"Bring in the Bat Mitzvot," called Solivan, signaling that it was time to add the final touch to this dance. Leon Walters, his brothers Steve and Ron, along with Jim Dorning, and a couple of others, moved to the center of the crowd with Amber and a chair. Amber sat in the chair, and the men raised her above the heads of the swirling dancers. It was sea of love, family, and joy.

Calculating the Pk, probability of kill, that a pair of AIM-9 Sidewinder missiles would have when taking out a tank or a jihadist-filled pickup truck had always been challenging. The range, weather conditions, distance, and size of the targets were always different. That's one of the reasons there had always been such a high degree of collateral deaths. But as Solivan looked at the crowded, pulsing dance floor, he knew the Pk was high. Higher than any other bombing he'd caused. The bot bombs were so close to their targets and so densely packed with explosives and deadly payload that he knew the number of fragments hitting their marks would be lethal. It would be a massacre.

His training had been perfect. His ability to ignore the potential for loss of innocent life was an asset. And his desire to end the lives of these people in order to protect the lives of others was insatiable. Solivan didn't hesitate for even a second before pressing the button on his cheap, Casio wrist watch.

The initial blast radius of one of Solivan's Roombas was about thirty feet. The shrapnel radius was far greater. Multiply that by a factor of eleven, and you've got more death and destruction than the Boston Marathon bombers could have even dreamed about. The elegant crown chandeliers, designed by Wizard of Oz author L. Frank Baum, shattered instantly. Joining with the metal projectiles from the exploded Roombas, the combination of metal, crystal, and bone blasted into and through everything in an instant.

The people who'd been on the dance floor died the fastest and the least painfully. That included Amber, her father, mother, uncles, and her entire posse of eighth-grade BFFs. The guests who'd been standing around and watching the horah were torn into bits. Limbs were so flayed out and mangled that they didn't resemble body parts. Blood splattered the priceless tapestries and artwork that hung on the walls, creating Jackson Pollock-esque works of horror.

The magnificent, thirty-foot, sugar pine ceiling splintered. The massive dome collapsed and crushed anyone who was unlucky enough to have been under its fall. Steel bearings, bones, glass, wood, teeth, wrist watches, cellphones, forks, knives, spoons, shattered plates, tables, and chairs joined forces and blew through and out of the room into the lobby and out the windows.

From his floating protest just offshore, Carby saw the carnage, slack-jawed. As the signature red roof imploded, dragging the shingled crown downward, the watcher watched in horror.

Chapter Seven

Normally when Chauncey hung out with his mates at Diddy's man cave, it was a pretty crazy time. Located in one of the more industrial sections of National City, just over the bridge from Coronado Island, the man cave was one of the most testosterone-filled places on the planet. Walter Diddier, "Diddy" for short, was a retired member of SEAL Team One. Needing a place to detox after some of his more harrowing assignments, but before returning home to his wife and two young daughters, Diddy would cruise to his 1,000-square-foot fortress of solitude.

The man cave was tricked out, SEAL-style. The walls were decorated with zombie targets, and there were figurines and pictures of samurai. Ripped up, musty smelling couches and easy chairs were set up beside multiple dorm fridges that were filled with cold bottles of Sam Adams. Auto parts sat beside a half-rebuilt 1968 Chevy Camaro Z28 and a disassembled 1952 Indian Chief Special 80 motorcycle. In the back was a gun locker filled with a dozen firearms, including his brand-new, laser-sighted .460 S&W Magnum. Next to the locker was a workbench where Diddy spent many hours sucking down Hornitos tequila while bent over his Corbin Bullet Swaging machine.

His explanation for making his own bullets, for anyone with enough balls or stupidity to ask was, "Hey, if I'm going to miss the target, it sure as hell ain't gonna be because of some crap-assed, Chinese-made bullet."

Hanging out at the man cave with Diddy usually meant you were there for the night. Too drunk to drive, Diddy would grill up some brats on one of his rusted out Weber grills, and you'd be roaring until dawn. But barely 24 hours after the massacre at the Hotel Del Coronado, nobody was in a festive mood. Add to that the viscerally divergent opinions over the whole affair and you had the ingredients for a different type of explosion. The kind of explosion you get when four, extremely drunk, ex-special operations guys want to disembowel someone.

Phil, the smallest, but not surprisingly, the most ferocious of the group, had grabbed Diddy's .460, and chambered it with one of his homemade hollow points. Pissed to shit, he was pointing the weapon right at Diddy's face. Diddy, a five-foot-ten gladiator who'd done more than his fair share of damage to our country's enemies stood staring at the muzzle. His cheeks twitched with angry nerve endings while his hand held the open blade of a razor-sharp Emerson CQL-75 just below Phil's left eye.

Diddy, not one for meaningless threats, and calm under pressure, simply said, "At this point, Philly boy, I think the only chance you have is pulling that trigger. Because if you don't, I'm going to melon-ball your eye, then slice off your hand and shoot you with your own goddamned, motherfucking finger."

Even though he could see the tip of the steel blade poised at his eye socket, Phil didn't blink. "You're so full of fucking shit, you fat fuck. How the fuck can you say the guy was a pussy? You didn't fucking even know him. It's because of macho fucks like you that one of our own guys is offing himself every goddamned hour of every goddamned fucking day."

"That right? How do you figure?"

Chauncey and Killa stood to the side watching the showdown, helplessly. A hose spraying frigid water may work on rabid slum dogs, but nothing short of a claymore was going to cool down this standoff.

"Because you think that anyone, including me, who admits they got PTSD or some other bullshit mindfuck from what they did is a fairy. That's why nobody talks about it. So how the hell do they get better?"

"We got a job to do," said Diddy. "There's no draft, Phyllis. We all watched the same movies and we all signed up for the same crap. So I figure if you can't handle it, you should've got a job shoveling horseshit. 'Cause that's what you're doing right now."

Chauncey exchanged a quick glance with Killa. His mind raced; possibility after possibility of what to say or do to calm the situation sped through his mind like heated atoms. It had started when they were watching the latest CNN report on the bombing. In the hours following the massacre, Coronado had been evacuated, then locked down tighter than a chastity-belt-wearing princess. The Naval, Marine Corps, and SEAL bases that edged Coronado Island went on high alert, and the gun-toting sailors, Spec Ops troops, and law enforcement officers in a 20-mile radius went all cat-sense nervy.

San Diego-based FBI agents swooped in for a rapid assessment, and the first reports that came out of the decimated hotel claimed 79 dead, 22 of them children. The survivors would be visiting prosthetic centers when they got out of the hospital. Only one person was unaccounted for, James Temple, Ph.D. The guy was some General Atomics engineer, who the report said, like anyone cared, was one of the guys who worked on Reaper MQ-9's missile guidance system. But everyone knew the guy would turn up once they reassembled the body parts.

Chauncey, Rich, Diddy, and Phil hadn't been born in Southern California, but Coronado had been their home for years. Understandably, all four of the men felt like someone had broken into their homes and raped their families. Now with North Island locked away from their reach, they were going nuts. And for all except Chauncey, talking wasn't their conditioned first response.

Casualties and carnage were something that all of them had learned to deal with. Diddy, an underwater demolition master, had personally rigged more explosives than most SEALs. His handiwork had torn apart more boats, buildings, and bodies than he'd been able to count. Phil, a fast boat gunner, had cut men in half with the six rotating barrels and electrically-powered feed system of his GAU-17/A. One time he shot a guy's head off with a direct face shot from an MK19 automatic grenade launcher. But that was over there. Not here. Crap like that wasn't supposed to happen here.

Bodies and minds already tense from the massacre happening in their own backyard became tighter when they first found out on the news that the bomber was one of their own. One of the good guys. It was exacerbated when they learned that their buddy, Ernie, had been one of the security officers at the hotel.

Preliminary chatter coming from the bases was that Ernie had been in the hotel's security office watching cameras. Apparently only eleven of the Roombas had gone off in the ballroom. The twelfth little bot had whirled its way to the office to do a bit of cleaning up down there. Along with Ernie and another security guard, the hotel's servers, monitors, and hard drives had been destroyed. All that hard intel would have gone a long way in determining whether Sergeant Solivan had worked on his own, was part of a terrorist cell, or what.

A veteran Sig Int officer who'd started his career working with the Activity, just days before he was killed, Ernie had bragged to the guys about the cushy job he'd just gotten. No more risky missions for him. For the four men in Diddy's man cave, it was more than just a random attack. It was personal.

Phil and Diddy's skirmish started after Diddy said Solivan was a pussy who should have just slit his own wrists and not punished others with his lack of manliness. Chauncey didn't know if it would have changed Diddy's words had he realized that Phil was getting counseling at the local VA for wanting to off himself. Given Diddy's opinion about post-traumatic stress disorder being a character flaw, an opinion that was tragically shared by a lot of people in the service, it was no shocker that Phil had never mentioned it.

Chauncey only knew because he'd been going to the same center for a couple of years himself. But budget cuts and the incompetence that typified the VA had caused staff cuts and personnel turnovers that affected their care. Chauncey and Phil had ended up sharing a lot of pitchers at the Coronado Brewing Company trying to help each other. For a lot of vets, Phil included, it was a shameful way to feel.

"Guys," said Chauncey after a pair of atoms collided in his brain. "You're mates. You're both bloody pissed. And although it may seem like there's nothing you can agree on right now, I'm here to tell you you're wrong. There is something you both share. Something more important than the fact that you're brothers, more important than the fact that this country needs you now just as much as it ever has —"

Although neither Phil nor Diddy moved, Chauncey knew in an instant that he had their attention. He continued.

"Just ten minutes ago, as we watched CNN, you both agreed that you wanted to shag the shit out of Soledad O'Brien."

"In a heartbeat," said Diddy, trying to maintain his rapidly dissipating rage.

"I get her first," said Phil, gun still pointing at Diddy.

"You got it, buddy. She's all yours."

Phil lowered the Magnum and shook his head. A smile crept across his wide, still youthful face. He looked at Chauncey.

"That the technique you used to get all those Taliban sand rats to confess their sins?"

Chauncey slowly reached out and took the pistol from Phil's shaking hand.

"Rule number one of interrogation, mate." Chauncey said. "Know your subjects. And you two are without a doubt, the horniest peckerheads I know."

Killa patted Chauncey on the back and collapsed into one of the dusty sofas. Diddy stood there for a moment, composing himself. As the adrenaline subsided, he folded away his knife, then he leaned his head back and roared, "Who wants some fucking tequila?!"

Chapter Eight

The room was dark, bare, and silent. Four unadorned concrete walls, a concrete floor and ceiling, and a locked, metal door made up its main structural elements. A four-inch, corroded water pipe ran across the room just below the ceiling of the far wall. North, south, east, or west were meaningless here. Day and night were intellectual concepts that only memory could determine. But after a certain length of time, that memory became an untrustworthy abstraction. Ironically, at a mere twenty feet by twenty feet, the room could easily have been considered a luxury suite for solitary confinement.

The only thing that could provide a sensory link proving that anything outside of the room existed was the water pipe. For through this rusty metal tube, flowed the substance of life itself. To hear that sound would give a sense of an outside world. Of a lack of solitude. It could mean someone in a kitchen washing dishes, or in a bathroom brushing teeth, or even though the idea of flowing excrement could not be thought of as a soothing, reassuring sound, the flushing of a toilet could bring the mind to a place that contained fellow humans. But realizing this could be the case, the controller of the room had made sure no water flowed through the pipes. The only sound that came from them was the occasional patter of rats crawling inside of them.

The room was spartan, furnished with a cheap, six-foot plastic picnic table, behind which sat a pair of foldable, metal chairs. On the table sat an open leather case containing shiny surgical tools. Razor sharp and polished stainless steel, they would have glistened had their sheen not been obscured by dried blood.

In front of the table was a simple wooden chair, the type that was purchased as a set of four along with a dining room table. Nothing fancy, just a basic, low-end set that you might find in a discount furniture store. The carved eagle talons at the feet made it decidedly Colonial American.

In this blackened nowhere room sat James Temple, Ph.D., the man who was missing from the Hotel Del Coronado bat mitzvah. The man over whom a statewide manhunt was now being conducted. The man who was kidnapped and rendered here shortly before the massacre took place.

Short, pudgy, balding and sixty-three years old, Temple sat, naked and bound to the American Eagle chair. His hands were tied behind his back and his feet were fixed to the eagles. Temple's vision had been obscured by a pair of ski goggles with spray-painted lenses. His ears were covered with headphones that blared Red Hot Chili Peppers, Nine Inch Nails, and Metallica.

Man-made cuts and punctures ran the length of his legs, arms, and torso. The blood had mixed with his sweat so it couldn't dry. It ran down his skin in long, thin rivulets. From his toes a red liquid oozed to a drain in the floor and from there perhaps down to hell, which, in Temple's mind, was right below his chair. Attached to Temple's toes were metal clamps with wires that snaked their way to a weathered Tucker Telephone sitting beside the tools on the table.

Whatever ordeal Temple had endured in this room was known only to himself, or whatever part of the man you could still call Temple, and to whoever had the keys to the door. How long he'd been alone could only be determined by the fact that his head was still upright. Because had it listed forward, the Heretics Fork, a single piece of metal with a double set of razor-sharp prongs on both sides, was strapped to his neck and would have torn open his throat like a pit bull. And based on his weight and out-of-shape body, that couldn't have been for more than thirty minutes at the most.

Temple moaned, weakly. "Help me, someone. Please, help me," came out in a whisper. Whether his moans were soft due to pain, thirst, or the fact of the Heretics Fork were anyone's guess. Temple's body stiffened as the blaring music stopped. He involuntarily swallowed a gulp of saliva, then winced as the swallowing motion caused the sharp, double prongs of steel to cut into his fleshy neck and double chin.

The door opened, letting in a flood of light that Temple couldn't see, but revealing two men wearing plastic Halloween masks. One of the men, wearing a former President George W. Bush mask, carried a digital video camera on a tripod, which he placed to the right of the table. He pointed it at Temple, then turned it on and pressed the record button. The other man, his face obscured by the mask of former Vice President Dick Cheney, held a clipboard and plain manila file folder. He sat behind the table as GW moved to Temple. He removed the ski goggles, the headphones, then unstrapped the Heretic's Fork.

Temple's head slumped forward as Cheney opened the file folder and looked through the papers inside. After a short moment, he looked up.

"Let's begin again, shall we?" asked Cheney. "Are you James Temple?"

Temple nodded, and softly began to cry.

"The same James Temple who was born on September 5, 1952, with an IQ of 186, who graduated magna cum laude from Hackley College Prep School in Tarrytown, New York, then in six years successfully received a PhD in aerospace engineering from California Institute of Technology?"

Temple nodded again.

"Are you the same "Doctor" James Temple who earns $160,000 per year as a senior weapons engineer at General Atomics and has, for the past eight years, been instrumental in making the Predator series of unmanned aerial vehicles?"

Temple urged his head up. Looking at the man with still disdainful eyes, he mocked, "Yes. And so what? We've already established that you think I'm a murderer. Well, I make weapons because we need them to defend ourselves against an evil world. You're proof of that."

GW cranked the dial on the Tucker Telephone, shutting up Temple with a jolt of electricity that traveled through the wires and into his body via the connections on his toes. Temple convulsed with pain that coursed through every nerve ending. The current ran through his body like hot electric needles. The hair on his arms stood straight. Drool escaped from Temple's mouth as the electricity stopped. He stared at the pair of men with utter hatred.

"Your guilt as a murderer is a foregone conclusion." Cheney said, holding up the file folder. "We have the evidence. It is incontrovertible. But you are guilty of far more than the murder of hundreds of innocent men, women, and children. And for that you must confess."

Cheney stood up and walked to Temple. He lifted up his head and pointed at the Tucker Telephone. "Do you know what that is?"

Temple shook his head.

"It's called the Tucker Telephone," said the former VP. "It was a torture device invented in the 1960s that was used at the Tucker State Prison Farm in Arkansas. I'm told it's a very simple piece of engineering. Just an old-fashioned crank telephone wired in sequence with two batteries. Electrodes coming out of it were attached to a prisoner's genitals, or in more merciful circumstances like yours, the toes. The electronics of the phone are such that cranking it sends an electric shock through the prisoner's body. In prison guard parlance, a 'long-distance call' was a series of electric shocks in a row."

Cheney cranked the phone a half-turn, sending a wave through Temple's body. "That was a local call," he said, smiling beneath his mask.

"Quite clever, don't you think, Dr. Temple? A simple, yet effective bit of engineering."

Cheney then picked up the Heretic's Fork. "Here's another fine example of simple engineering. Even simpler. It's called The Heretic's Fork. Some medieval engineer figured out how to make this little beauty. I think from an industrial designer's perspective it could have been made by Apple, don't you agree? The iFork," he chuckled.

"What do these things have to do with me?" pleaded Temple. "I don't make things to torture people. Torture is barbaric and immoral, not to mention illegal."

"Is that so? You believe that torture is less immoral than collateral killing and engineering machines whose sole purpose is killing men, women, and children? Well, I beg to disagree. But that does bring up an interesting point. I didn't realize you believed in morality. Don't you highly gifted folk consider engineering to be amoral?"

"Engineering, yes. Engineers, no. What do you want? I have no information, no trade secrets. You can't torture anything out of me because I don't know enough."

"Who is your sovereign?" Cheney asked, ignoring Temple's pleas. "Do you believe in God and country?"

Temple stared at him, confused. He was so unsure of himself. Was this what was expected of him? To have a philosophical conversation in the midst of torture? Maybe it was the only way to save himself, so he tried his best to comply. "I have no sovereign but the immutable laws of the universe," he answered.

"So no God, no country, clearly you are beholden to money. How about your species? Aren't you beholden to the collective welfare of mankind?"

In spite of his desire to appear docile, Temple openly scoffed. "That's too ill-defined, not to mention it's subject to change and whimsy."

"It is an ideal!" spat Cheney, staccato.

"Maybe so, but the ideals I operate by need working definitions. And aside from your theoretical considerations, I don't agree that it's an ideal. Our species bases a lot on unclearly defined "collective good.""

"Yes, but we are all born into the same world and are therefore responsible to its collective need to sustain us. You may be limited by the immutable laws of the universe, but they are not your sovereign. Not unless you hold yourself to be separate and apart from your species.

"What you are guilty of *Doctor* Temple is being more responsible to science and engineering than you are to me. You are guilty of using your superior intellect to create technology that is *intended* to torture, terrorize, and kill human beings and our planet, and getting paid for it. You walk around with a superior, holier-than-thou persona and rationalize your actions by saying that there is evil in the world. Well, yes, there is evil in the world, and you give that evil the tools it needs to perpetrate its horror. You were born with a gift. You and all the other engineers. You are born with superior minds, yet men like you use those gifts for personal gain, disguising your weakness for money and the ego that goes with creating new, high-level technology without even considering that its intention is evil. You are a criminal against your own kind. And for that you must be punished."

Cheney began cranking the Tucker Telephone, causing Temple to go into spasms of pain. Spittle and vomit escaped his mouth. Cheney railed.

"I am mankind! I will punish you and every engineer who knowingly creates or works on devices that kill or hurt people and our world. You have a superior mind. You were born with it, yet you abuse it. Your mind holds the keys to life. It holds the answers that man sought through religion. The answers to creation! To mystery! To miracle! You possess the knowledge of all the things that make mankind gladly sacrifice its freedom and lives. And because mankind is frail, sheepish, and trusting, your misguidance brings us to the precipice of our own extinction. You must be held to a higher standard. You are quite correct, sir: Science may be amoral, but men are not. Only those of you who use your minds for the betterment of your species will be spared. You are the first, but you will not be the last."

Cheney returned to his seat behind the table and glared at Temple. Finally, he reached into a bag and pulled out a sealed glass bottle of Pellegrino water. He stared at Temple as he casually, slowly, methodically twisted the cap. He stopped turning after the sound of each metal, tearing click of the cap. Finally open, he took a long drink, loudly gulping down mouthful after mouthful. He drank so fast that some of the water dribbled from his mouth and down his neck.

"It's been two days since you've had anything to drink, Dr. Temple. Would you like some water? Surely, you know that no matter what else happens to you here, a human being can't live longer than three days without water. Surely you must know that with that big brain of yours."

Temple looked at Cheney, unsure of himself. "Yes, please."

Cheney withdrew another bottle. "It's yours for the taking. And so is your freedom. Simply confess your crimes."

"But I haven't done anything wrong," Temple pleaded. "You're insane. You're wearing those masks to make some kind of a twisted political statement, but this is wrong. What you're doing is wrong."

Cheney pondered him a moment. He slanted his head side to side and pursed his lips as if getting ready to say something. Then, suddenly, he stood up and threw the bottle of water at Temple. It shattered against his forehead, green glass and carbonated water spraying in all directions. Temple's forehead, deeply gashed, streamed blood.

"Confess!" screamed Cheney, pointing at Temple. "Confess your sins against your own kind for that is the only way to free your conscience and be forgiven. Confess and be saved. Only you can stop the pain. Confess. It's the only way that you will be free."

"Okay!" shouted Temple. "Fine! You win. I'm guilty! I used my mind to create machines that kill. They have no other purpose than the death of other human begins. I've used my intelligence in an unethical way. I am a monster!"

Cheney nodded. "And now your soul is free. Sadly, your body will not be following you."

Former President G.W. Bush picked up the blood-coated scalpel that sat on the table. He moved behind Temple and traced it along his throat. Temple's blue eyes bulged as if that was where the pain sought its escape. His body bucked and writhed as GW held him upright. At first, Temple's blood spurted far, in rhythm with his heart. But as that organ slowed, so did the force of Temple's life until finally, his head slumped forward, and he died.

Chapter Nine

All five men seated around the circular, mahogany conference table had seen the revealing photos. It was out in the open now. Abu Ghraib, Bahrain Air Force Base, Gitmo, the CIA black sites, everything. To one degree or another, each one of them was complicit in what the liberal media and leftist lawyers were calling torture. But they were also all safe. They were silently grateful to the DOJ and President Bush for the protections they extended for doing their duty to protect the greatest nation on Earth.

At the same time the men realized they'd be safe, they also realized their jobs had just become more difficult. Still tasked with getting actionable intelligence on the planned objectives, operational structures, and goals of al-Qaeda and Taliban terrorists, the men were concerned about how to move forward in a way that would accomplish the mission. For most of them, it was a sacred oath.

Sitting on the table in front of each man was a copy of a highly classified report they'd received entitled "S.E.E. Interrogation." Stability-Efficiency-Effectiveness broke down into three sections; the first part of the report had to do with the S.E.E. of Interrogation Techniques. It reviewed and commented on the various aspects of the techniques that had been employed in theater since the 9/11 attacks. The section explored and analyzed the uses of SERE, KUBARK and even the US Army Field Manual as they pertained to getting actionable intelligence from the detainees that were unwilling to provide it.

Not intended as a moral, ethical, or legal argument for or against enhanced interrogation, the report ignored those more subjective areas. After all, soldiers needed tools to win wars, not philosophical distractions. The report convincingly concluded that the current techniques were Unstable, Inefficient, and Ineffective. However, it also concluded that those failures were due, in large part, to the interrogators.

Section Two of the report spoke to the S.E.E. of Interrogators. Working backwards from its name, the report stated that no matter how experienced, educated or motivated they were, interrogators could not be "effective." There were simply too many obstacles. Cultural and language barriers made consistent, meaningful one-to-one communication impossible. Nuanced idioms, innuendos, references, social norms, etc., were all huge obstacles to the effective determination of truth. And, as these men knew, most people would say just about anything to stop pain.

Another obstacle to the effectiveness of an interrogator was the law. For all their suffering, detainees knew that eventually the interrogator would run up against a final wall that would bar them from going any further. Only so much pain and mental anguish could be placed on them. Although many had already died, interrogators would not intentionally kill a prisoner as they feared a murder charge. Therefore, most detainees knew it was simply a game of who could hold out the longest.

A third, and perhaps more obvious obstacle to interrogator effectiveness, was time. Interrogators had more than one prisoner to interrogate. Sometimes dozens. If they couldn't get the truth in a reasonable amount of time, they would be reassigned or the subject would be sent somewhere else. That was especially true in the forward stations. Then, even with the previous interrogator's notes, the new interrogator would have to start from scratch.

The S.E.E. report also stated that the use of interrogators was "inefficient." From a manpower perspective, there just weren't enough of them. This meant they couldn't spend the required amount of time with each subject. And even if they could, the entire paradigm was inefficient as it had too many moving parts. Interpreters were needed to make up for the language, religious and cultural differences. Psychologists were there to determine which phobias to exploit. Medical doctors stood by to resuscitate, if required. Analysts were required to check stories and geographical incongruities. And security forces and guards were required to keep the interrogators safe.

Finally, Section Two concluded that the current interrogators were too "unstable." Given the pressures to produce results, the stresses of war, anxieties, phobias and potential racial biases, this was an unavoidable and obvious fact.

Interrogators got little sleep and the stress caused some of them to become depressed, some to become sympathetic and others to become savage and brutal. Not to mention that many of them believed it was the detainees' fault that they were there and took it out on them.

Overall, the S.E.E. Interrogation Report was a resounding denouncement of the status quo.

Colonel Donald Brewster, a 34-year veteran of the Army, and the deputy of interrogation at Shakey's, neatly clipped his hand-rolled Monte Cristo, then lit the tip to a desired level of red. The thick, gray smoke rose and drifted around the room.

"Well, gentlemen," he began. "You've all been invited to this little party because of your role here in the sandbox. Everything we say in this room is 1,000% classified and if any of you get any ideas to the contrary you'll be damned sorry. Now you've all read the report and all agreed to its findings. What we need to do now is see if we agree on the recommendations in Section Three. I, for one, am damned tired of seeing my boys get all messed up in the head from the mind games these jihadees play on them. I got a soldier down in Oklahoma so messed up in the head and hopped up on Darvon that he's on suicide watch. And all he did was serve his country. We need to get intel. We need to get it fast. And we need to get it without hurting our boys. So I vote yes."

Brewster sat back and blew out a huge stream of smoke. He smacked his lips, savoring the taste, and looked around the table. CIA Agent Stormer, from the CIA's Detainee Exploitation Group spoke next. "Thank you, Colonel Brewster," he said. Then, indicating the report, he continued, "This is a fine piece of work. Whoever wrote it sure as hell knows their stuff. But are we sure these guys can do what they're recommending? I've read their files, but haven't had the pleasure of meeting them."

Special FBI Investigator Samuels answered for the Colonel. "They're down in Bagram. One of them is an ex-SERE shrink and the other guy's in the Engineer corps and works on the IED detection bots. I can't say that I approve of his style, but the SERE guy knows as much or more about psy ops, interrogation and the limits of what a human being can handle than anyone I've ever met. He knows when he's hearing a lie or the truth like nobody I've ever worked with. Shame we don't have more like him doing things the RIGHT way."

Samuels grabbed his copy of the report and stood up. He shook it at the men. "Because all of this is a load of crap! Of course the techniques reviewed in this report are Inefficient, Ineffective, and Unstable. That's because they're torture. And torture doesn't work! The stuff in here is immoral and illegal, and this sick idea will make things even worse."

Agent Samuels sat down and turned the report upside down. He leaned back and folded his arms across his chest. Colonel Brewster looked at him, "So we'll take that as a no vote, shall we?" Samuels rolled his eyes, then nodded.

Stormer snorted. "Well, then if my esteemed FBI colleague is against it that must mean it's a great idea. I'm in. You've got a yes vote from me."

Samuels shook his head, "You're a fucking disgrace."

The fourth man, Dr. Aldrich, stood up to speak next. An ER doc from Florida who'd been unfortunate enough to be in the National Guard when hostilities started, Aldrich had been called up to serve about three years ago. He was assigned to Abu Ghraib and had personally monitored more than two dozen waterboarding sessions. His claim to fame was that nobody'd ever drowned under his watch.

"I personally believe that what we're doing is the right thing. I take my responsibility of detainee safety very seriously. And while it makes me sick to see any human being suffer, I believe that I'm both fulfilling my oath and keeping my country safe. That being said, I agree with the report that it's an inefficient model. I'm good, but not nearly good or fast enough to protect every detainee being interrogated. I think that if they can really pull this off, Section Three is responsible and smart, and I vote yes."

Samuels applauded, sarcastically. "I believe that's the best Dr. Mengele impression I've ever heard."

"Piss off," said Dr. Aldrich as he sat back down.

The last man at the table was John Sullivan, Esq. He was Colonel Brewster's attorney. A Mormon from Salt Lake City, Sullivan had known Brewster since they were children. They'd grown up in the same ward and performed their missionary work together, riding bicycles for two years in Fort Collins, Colorado. When Brewster joined the service, Sullivan had moved back to Utah to serve the church. The two men shared the same passion for freedom and liberty, and when Brewster had shown Sullivan the report, he'd asked for his legal opinion.

Sullivan looked around the table. "I'm not a soldier. I'm not an interrogator. But I represent the men and women you all protect. I thank you for your service to the country. I've reviewed the report and its recommendations from a legal perspective and given the opinion handed down by the DOJ, I see nothing illegal about it. But what you really need to be asking yourselves is this: Forget legal. Is this moral? We're clearly already torturing human beings. That line has already been crossed. But to do this? Is doing something that could surely send everyone in this room to hell justified in the name of saving lives? That's a question each man needs to answer for himself. I, personally, vote yes."

FBI agent Samuels looked around the table. "Excuse me. Before you walk out of here thinking you've just saved the world, I have a question. What if something goes wrong? What if this plan ends up backfiring and people die?"

Colonel Brewster smiled and said, "That's the beauty of Section Three. It won't be anybody's fault."

Chapter Ten

For the most part, Chauncey loved silence. The calm that he experienced while floating down to the earth during the post-deployment phase of a jump was one of his greatest pleasures. He loved silence so much that he would take trips to Colorado in the dead of winter where he would rent a cabin about twenty miles south of Vail. Besides of the perfect tranquility of the forest at 12,000 feet, snowshoeing to the middle of nowhere to experience the absolute quiet that followed a six-foot blizzard was startling.

Chauncey also knew that silence could be a terrible thing. Most people couldn't bear it. Friends and lovers punished each other with the "silent treatment." People all around the world felt the need to fill pregnant pauses in conversations with idle chitchat, meaningless filler meant to bridge the uncomfortable void between words. Sales people and corporate executives used silence to their advantage; the best negotiators know that "he who speaks first loses."

Used properly, silence could be a powerful weapon. Well-trained interrogators would sit back and calmly gaze or intently stare at their subjects, never uttering a word. Knowing that silence was a place where the imagination did its dirty work, they knew they just had to wait. Left to their own thoughts, most men filled in the blanks with horrible fantasy. Painful, loss-filled thoughts of despair. Silence almost always made a person think things were worse than they really were.

Prolonged silence could literally drive a hearing person insane. Sensory deprivation was one of the greatest tools of torture there was. Bullying, threatening, and even waterboarding paled in comparison to its power. Starved of seeing, hearing, and touching, the human mind breaks down rapidly. Hallucinations, depression, anxiety, and paranoia set up shop within hours of isolation and grow like a psychotic cancer.

In the two days since the torture and execution of Dr. James Temple, a deafening silence had taken hold of the country. Chauncey had listened to the talking heads on FOX, CNN, and MSNBC at night. The supposed "experts" in torture, terrorism, and criminal pathology filled in the nothingness with conjecture and outrage. He'd listened to the president's speech promising that the sick, twisted people responsible would be brought to justice. He watched the cities being closed down, the surveillance cameras with footage being reviewed over and over again. And when the tortured body of Dr. Temple, his severed head bound within his arms, washed up on the shore of Venice Beach, California, he heard the silence begin to scream. After the speeches and the news broadcasts ended, no one really knew the truth of what had happened or if it would happen again. The silence left those questions to the gruesome imagination.

Whoever had murdered Dr. Temple clearly understood the power of silence. That was evidenced by the fact that the video of his execution hadn't ended with his death. Unlike the other decapitation videos that had been put online over the years, this one had continued post-mortem for another full thirty seconds MOS, film terminology that meant "Motor Only Sync." No soundtrack. No closing credits. Just an audience left to watch the blood first spurt, then stream, then quietly, gently stop flowing from Temple's neck. It was thirty seconds of silent torture. Of wondering. Of imagining. Of fear. And in this way, silence had been used as a form of terror.

Special Agent Breskin slurped the straw loudly against the bottom of his Diet Coke, trying to get the last diabetes-causing drop of soda. Then, following the hollow thunk of his empty cup being placed on the table, Breskin gave Chauncey a somewhat irritated, empty-handed gesture. "So are you going to tell me why you dragged me to a Taco Bell in Poway, or are you just going to sit and stare at me? I have work to do."

"Sorry, mate," said Chauncey. "Just enjoying the quiet. This place can be a zoo at lunchtime. That's why I usually come at 2:30ish. Anyway, I wanted to tell you that I'm in."

Breskin sat back and looked at Chauncey. Neither man spoke for several moments. An employee with a mop bucket walked past their booth toward the back of the restaurant. Like an overused shopping cart, the rusty wheel of the bucket wobbled and squeaked as he went.

Chauncey continued, "I'll SERE up your CEOs and whoever else you need me to help keep alive."

"Really," said Breskin, more as a statement than a question. "And why is that?"

"Because I saw that video online, mate. And I heard that poor bastard try to talk himself out of something he never could have."

"So you think if he'd played your 'yes, sir. no, sir, stay in the circle' stuff he wouldn't have been murdered?"

"No, I'm afraid he was a dead man before the rabbi said 'mazel tov.' But at least he could have denied that SOB some satisfaction and died with honor and dignity. Maybe I can help the next one to die more peacefully. Or, if he's lucky, maybe prolong his ordeal until you and the cavalry arrive."

Chauncey took a sip from his wax-coated cup of tea. Besides beer and water, it was all he drank. Another habit he'd picked up from the Aussies. Breskin was grateful that Chauncey didn't extend his pinky as he sipped. Although he wasn't sure if that would be the case if the tea had been in a porcelain cup.

"So you think there's going to be another one?" asked Breskin.

"That's what the man said."

"You mean his promise to punish other engineers? You think he meant it?"

"I have no reason to doubt it. And neither do you."

They looked at each other for a bit, then Breskin sighed, "No. No, I sure don't."

Breskin glanced around the restaurant. Seeing the Mexican worker mopping nearby, he leaned in and continued in a hushed voice, "The truth is we have no idea who did it. Nobody's taking credit. Nobody's denying it. We don't know if it happened here, in Pakistan, Spain, Yemen, whatever. We don't have a clue."

"It happened here," said Chauncey, matter of fact. "It was in San Diego, LA, maybe Tijuana, but it was here. That's why I'm so pissed. As much as this country turned its back on me, I can't turn my back any more. Not with something like this. Not if there's something I can do to help."

Chauncey reached into his pocket, but before he could remove whatever he was going for, the Mexican mopper was beside him. His Glock was aimed at the side Chauncey's head.

"Easy, gringo," the undercover FBI agent directed Chauncey. "Don't move a muscle."

Chauncey looked at the federale, then at Breskin and laughed. "Ooh, you brought the heat."

Breskin shrugged, "Given that the last time I saw you your foot was twitching over some kind of detonator, I figured why take chances. That plus the fact that we could have met in my nice, comfortable office instead of this rat-infested taco hut. I just figured it'd be better to err on the side of caution."

Chauncey remained perfectly still, his hand remaining in his jacket. He stared Breskin straight in the eyes. "First off, the reason I asked you to meet me here is because I didn't like the idea of being on your turf. I don't trust you, so the thought of sitting in your FBI office with your FBI surveillance cams and FBI goons got me all hinky inside.

"Second, I like this rat-infested taco hut. They have a mean ground beef and processed cheese burrito and they aren't too high-falutin to still serve Lipton tea. Unlike the Starbucks on Fifth and Olive where you go every morning at 8:37 to get your ultra-sweet latte and cranberry-orange muffin.

"And third, if I'm doing this, it's one-hundred percent my way. Now tell your mop-up man here to lower his weapon before I open a can of Guy Savelli Kun Tao on his ass."

Breskin smiled at Chauncey. "Still the same mindfucker, I see."

"Well, you had to learn it somewhere, didn't you?"

"The fact remains, Captain Paunce, that my guy here has a —"

Before Breskin uttered the next word, Chauncey had leveled a series of straight-hand blows to the agent that had him on the ground, clutching his windpipe. Chauncey, still sitting, handed Breskin the fallen agent's Glock.

"Gun?" said Chauncey, finishing Breskin's sentence. "You and I both know there are a lot more powerful weapons. So where were we?"

Chauncey reached into his jacket again and withdrew an envelope. He slid it across the booth to Breskin.

"Here's what I need to get started with the program. It's plans for the compound, materials, location, and, of course, my fee."

Breskin opened the envelope and took out the paperwork. He nodded as he scanned each page. He whistled at Chauncey's fee.

"That's a lot of Lipton tea, friend."

"Yeah, well, I figure these guys extort enough money from the American taxpayers that they can afford it."

Breskin snorted, "Like they're going to pay for it themselves? No, old friend, this tab is going to be added to the ever-swelling national debt."

He flipped another page, then looked up, confused. "A Weber grill?"

"Hey," smiled Chauncey. "Gotta' have my shrimp on the barbie, mate. Let's call it 'culinary security.'"

Chapter Eleven

Chauncey stood in the north parking lot of General Atomics, surrounded by a group of entry- to midlevel engineers. Security had been noticeably beefed-up since the press conference that introduced Armagan to the San Diego elite. Noticeably to the trained eye, that is. Chauncey spotted armed, undercover security guards at every entrance, marked and unmarked cars continuously patrolling the outer perimeter, and he correctly guessed there was an unarmed Predator B flying slow circles at 50,000 feet; its gimbal-mounted, Gorgon Stare camera was insatiably ingesting terabytes of data 24/7. Since it was above regulated national air space, GA didn't need a Certificate of Authorization, or COA as they were called, from the FAA, so the UAV took off from their base in El Mirage and flew straight up toward the realm of U2s.

Chauncey addressed the group. "I'm not one for sugar coating things, so as I said in the seminar I gave, I believe that if you get kidnapped you will be going to your execution. Therefore, it is in your best interest to escape by any means possible."

He was referring to a seminar he'd conducted the previous day for all employees of GA. Given that nobody had a clue who, what, when, where or, thankfully if, another kidnapping would occur, Breskin and the FBI were taking no chances. Breskin had instructed Chauncey to organize the DoD contracting population into groups using the SERE breakdown for training. And whether he thought they were in danger or not, he was still going to scare the piss out of them just in case.

SERE was separated into three basic levels: A, B, and C. There were higher, more intense and classified levels for specific JSOC soldiers, and although Chauncey and Breskin had both run those SV programs, they didn't apply to this assignment. In the United States military, SERE Level A was taught to all personnel in basic training. For his purposes with GA, the secretaries, mailroom clerks, accountants, and other administrative level staff were his Level A grunts. They'd attended his seminar and received a full briefing on common-sense, entry-level, personal protection techniques. Chauncey had mostly taught them low-level, anti-terrorism awareness skills. They needed to be more aware of their surroundings and to report anything that was even a blond pubic hair out of order to security. The keys were anticipation, vigilance, anonymity when traveling, and appropriate responsiveness.

The only "real" differences between his audience here and soldiers were that US soldiers lived by the Code of Conduct. And even though, in Chauncey's opinion, that had been butchered starting in Vietnam with President Johnson, it gave soldiers a common credo. These employees did not have that. Some were god-fearing, some were atheists. Some saluted red, white, and blue pasta, others merely ate it with a glass of wine. The other difference was that soldiers captured in war are protected by the Geneva Convention. Civilians are pretty much hung out to dry. Assuming, of course, that they were being captured by governments, and not terrorists. And for better or worse, from here forward, every country on earth would call captured soldiers, enemy combatants.

The bottom line to the Code of Conduct was to act with dignity and honor, and to uphold the values of the United States of America. During the seminar, Breskin and GA's CEO, Nels Green, did their best to instill a code of "corporate" conduct. They'd shown a slick, Hollywood-produced film of General Atomic's products in the field. Unmanned ground vehicles disarming IEDs, bots that watched and waited, and bots that toted heavy materials for GIs. Green had stood on the stage and read letters to his gathered corporate troops from grateful mothers whose sons had been saved by GA's war bots. When he was done, people wiped tears from their cheeks. The guy was amazing. In less than ten minutes, he not only bolstered his employees' patriotism, but he'd managed to get them teary over his corporation. It wasn't about money, it was about a sacred duty. Company equals the corps.

Given the low-level responsibilities of the seminar audience, Chauncey hadn't gone into the recommended conduct of those employees should they find themselves in detention, captive, or hostage situations. He figured who in the hell was going to kidnap and torture a mailroom clerk? But just for good measure he'd ended the seminar explaining that if they ever found themselves in a dicey situation, they should use personal optimism, faith, self-discipline, and an active mind as keys to endurance.

SERE Level B is for officers and enlisted personnel or any other military occupational specialty operating or expected to operate forward of division boundaries and up to the front lines. In DoD contractor-land, Chauncey interpreted that to be the low- to midlevel engineers. And those were the geeks, a word that Chauncey had unsuccessfully tried to purge from his mind, standing around him in the parking lot right now.

Beating his fist on the trunk of a parked Lexus for emphasis, Chauncey continued his lesson. "The bottom line here is that based on the video we saw, if any of you are captured you will need to understand what methods of coercion may be used in order to make you confess. Understand that these people do not want money, so there will be no ransom notes. They don't want information, so you could tell them your secret quantum theories on propulsion and they wouldn't care. And they do not want your reasons. In their eyes you are already guilty.

"What they want," Chauncey went on, passionately, "is your confession. And, pay real close attention to this, mates. Withholding that confession is the only thing that will keep your head attached to your shoulders.

"But since I won't have the pleasure of teaching you real-life survival, evasion, resistance, or escape techniques after you're captured, let's focus on giving you some skills to avoid that possibility in the first place, shall we? Let's keep you from getting caught."

Even though the hot California sun was beating down on their heads and also reflecting the heat from the black asphalt into their faces, the assembled engineers were pale. It was probably safe to say that, barring a few Eagle Scouts in the group, not one of them had ever contemplated what Chauncey was saying. This wasn't to say that some of them might be able to endure enhanced interrogation, but it was highly unlikely. It was difficult enough for trained soldiers and religious zealots to take the third degree, so Chauncey knew that, if kidnapped, these poor bastards wouldn't stand a chance. Still, if he could give them anything, even one tool to survive, he'd do it.

Chauncey went on, "In the initial moments of a hostage taking, both the victim and the captors are in a highly reactive mindset and prone to spontaneous actions. On the one hand, an act to resist may be seen as a threat and met with deadly force. On the other hand, the chaos of the situation may give you an opportunity to escape. Your decision to resist or comply is a personal choice you must make based on your estimate of the situation and your chances of survival."

One of the engineers, Anthony Young, a recent grad from Cornell University, was growing visibly agitated by Chauncey's talk. He raised his hand, as if he were still in school. Amused, Chauncey pointed to him. "Yes?"

Young was stymied. "I don't understand why anyone would do this."

"Neither do I, mate. But it was done."

"How can you be so sure it will happen again?"

"I'm not certain of anything other than the fact that I could really use a cold iced tea right now. But I'm still going to do my damnedest to prep you, even if it's just a little bit, for the possibility."

Young couldn't settle down. Some of his colleagues moved closer, putting hands on his shoulder. He went on, "I don't know anything. I just got here. I can't believe they would kidnap me. I didn't do anything wrong, and I sure don't deserve to have anything happen like that. This stuff is done by guys like you!" he railed. "Killers like you who don't mind shooting someone in the face or cutting their throats. It's because of guys like you that we're standing here crapping in our pants."

Chauncey had spent the last two days at General Atomics while his compound was being built for the SERE Level C training, And while Young's reaction was way over the top, it wasn't unique. Chauncey had seen and heard a mix of confusion, outrage, and borderline panic from many of the company's engineers. Proof that the massacre and torture had been effective. Only time would cool down that fear. Even so, Chauncey wasn't put off by Young's reaction. It was the proverbial "shoot the messenger" response.

Even after events like 9/11 and the recent Hotel del Coronado massacre, most Americans still felt safe and secure. So when someone tells them they're under threat and need to change their lifestyle, the one delivering the message is the easy mark. Of course, the growing concern over persistent surveillance due to the NSA's unchecked phone and email snooping, combined with the growing concerns over the approaching drone revolution, was eroding that sense of security. Slowly, but surely. Since Chauncey was the guy shoving their lack of safety smack-dab into their pocket protectors, he was naturally the one they would lash out at. And he had no problem with it.

He wasn't okay with all hostility, however. In addition to the seminars he'd been doing recon to find the vulnerabilities of GA's security. He'd told the CEO's immediate staff, as well the company's security team and other C-level executives that he was going to kidnap Nels Green and subject him to SERE Level C training. Nobody would know when it was coming, and they wouldn't know where it would happen, but they needed to know it was going to go down. He gave them all plans of response for the aftermath and assured them that nobody would get too hurt. However, they needed to take it extremely seriously, because if it happened in reality, their responses could mean the difference between life and death.

At the meeting, GA's head of security, an ex-Marine who was upset that he wasn't chosen to do Chauncey's job, gave Chauncey a world of pushback. He picked apart everything Chauncey said.

"We got that covered," he kept repeating over and over.

Chauncey had kept his cool and boosted the guy's ego by agreeing that he could probably do a much better job. However, it was Chauncey's gig, so he needed cooperation. He repeated that he was confident of pulling this off with no issues, but didn't want to take any chances with stray bullets. And even though Chauncey had decided that the guy was going to get a mean concussion when he nabbed Green, he wouldn't get shot in the ass as he would have liked. Probably.

One of the best meetings Chauncey had had at GA was with Armagan. Because of who he was and what he'd gone through as a child, Chauncey had approached that meeting with a high degree of sensitivity. God knows that Armagan had already experienced more terror as a child than most human beings would in a lifetime. But given Armagan's top-secret contract with DARPA and GA, his vulnerability was high. That was the reason Breskin and Green had approved the meeting.

They'd met in Armagan's office. Surprisingly, the place had been decorated in pure Americana. There was a full-sized American flag standing in one corner, and the yellow "Don't Tread on Me" flag hung in another. It exuded a live free or die mentality that Chauncey hadn't expected. Other signs of America were present as well, from framed Norman Rockwell and Remington prints to photos of the High Sierras taken by Ansel Adams.

Armagan's scientific sensibilities were reflected in various ways. There was a framed Albert Einstein prominently hanging behind his desk, revealing Armagan's sense of humor. It was the photo of the genius poking out his tongue at the photographer. There were white boards with mathematical equations scrawled across them on the wall to the right of his desk. At least Chauncey thought they were mathematical equations. For all he knew, they could have been a recipe for making moo goo gai pan.

Perhaps the most noteworthy decoration was a perched, glass-encased robotic hummingbird. A joint venture between DARPA and Simi Valley-based AeroVironment, the hummingbird was a nano-arial vehicle that had been modeled after the real-life bird. Because of its natural speed, maneuverability, and hovering abilities, the hummingbird had been chosen as an ideal subject. The bot bird they'd made flew nearly as well as the biological hummingbird, with the two main differences being that first off, the bird was a robot, and second, its eyes were cameras. DARPA had been interested in developing it for surveillance and reconnaissance missions.

As he stared at one of the most sophisticated bits of technology he'd ever seen, Chauncey couldn't help but think that the Tom Cruise movie, *Minority Report*, was coming true. He shuddered when he recalled the scene in the film where the police had released spider-like robots that skittered through a building scanning people's retinas in order to find the "bad" guy.

Although he didn't know squat about the science behind the invention, Chauncey had read about it and seen videos on YouTube. So he knew that he was looking at a rare slice from the cutting edge. If it were real, that is. And he'd be learning more about it soon because after he finished at GA, he was headed to AeroVironment to SERE up their CEO and top-level engineers.

Following Chauncey's eyes to the nano-drone, Armagan said, "It's real. It is one of the earlier prototype shells. When everyone was bidding on my concept, AeroVironment was very determined. They sent me this as an enticement to show what kind of brain power and innovation they had. I've always loved the idea of blending robotics with the animal kingdom and they knew that. Similar to the NFL sending a Super Bowl ring to a college athlete, I suppose."

"So why'd they let you keep it if you went to GA?" asked Chauncey.

"They said they wanted me to be reminded of my bad decision every day. And to see it as a key to their door at any time."

Chauncey leaned in and peered closely at the bird's eyes.

Armagan sensed his question and answered without being asked. "GA's security checked to make sure there were no cameras. The mechanics have been completely gutted. No sense in giving away trade secrets, right?"

The only thing in Armagan's office that had anything to do with his home in Afghanistan was a thin, corked test tube filled with sand from his village. Armagan picked the test tube up and turned it from side to side, watching the sand go from top to bottom, then bottom to top.

While he did this he said, "I'm sure you were told that I was at the Walters bat mitzvah. I was friends with many of the guests and knew Dr. Temple well. He and I were working together very closely. Such a brilliant man. I hope they hunt down the dogs that did it and kill them. It's the only way their families will ever find any peace." Armagan put down the sand and sat at his desk.

Chauncey hadn't known what to expect when he found out he'd be meeting Armagan. Certainly he knew his story and had heard he was a genius, so he expected to be impressed. But he hadn't expected to like him. Not this much, at any rate. Chauncey was now disappointed that Breskin had told him not to run Armagan through his SERE course. He would have liked the chance to get to know him under any circumstance. But although he was a likely target, Breskin had explained he wouldn't need any training because he'd already had it.

From the first day he'd stepped foot into the United States, The FBI had been concerned that Armagan would be a target of al-Qaeda and every other Muslim fundamentalist group. It made perfectly good sense for them to want to take back what had been used as propaganda against them. As a result, Armagan had been trained in resistance techniques since he was a boy. One leg and all, Armagan was a third-degree black belt in Hapkido and an expert sharpshooter.

"It's one thing that this kind of thing can happen in my native country, a place trapped in the stone age with tribalism, misogyny, and ignorance of science, but here? That's simply not acceptable," Armagan concluded.

As much as he would've liked to spend more time with Armagan, Chauncey had to excuse himself to meet the engineers in the parking lot. Because he had no business cards he wrote his private cellphone number on a sticky note and gave it to Armagan. "Call me any time, mate." Chauncey shook Armagan's hand. In his gut he knew they would meet again.

Chauncey now stood in the sweltering parking lot, looking at Young with a bit of pity and a whole lot of concern. It was up to him to calm the guy down and more than that, to teach him how to calm himself.

"Try to relax. You're a very low-level guy, so there's no reason to be concerned," he said. "There's very little chance that you'll be targeted. I'm just here to give you a few pointers." What he'd wanted to say, but didn't know how, was "get a job reinforcing our country's crumbling bridges."

Getting back to why the guy was probably freaked out in the first place, Chauncey tried to give him an out. "This exercise is completely voluntary. You don't have to try escaping from a trunk if you don't want to."

Chauncey was referring to the fact that he was teaching the engineers some basic escape skills. Groin and eye jabs for close abduction and, in the event that they ended up in the trunk of some terrorist's car, how to keep cool and escape. It was probably how they'd gotten Dr. Temple from San Diego to wherever they'd killed him, so it was a good idea.

He'd explained that all cars were now made with inner trunk releases that glowed in the dark. If they were being transported in a car, they just needed to keep cool, wait for the car to slow down or stop, then pop open the trunk, jump out, and run like mad. Simple. That is, if they weren't hogtied, blindfolded, and gagged, but he didn't mention that. He'd purposely left that out for the benefit of guys like Young. But even unbound, it was a great confidence builder that would help these guys to at least walk the streets feeling they had some small chance.

Suddenly, something, or someone, began banging from the inside of the nearby car trunk. Chauncey knew that the trapped engineer who was attempting to escape from the locked trunk would have been screaming the entire time had Chauncey not taped his mouth shut with duct tape. "Just for reality," he'd said.

As the banging became louder, Chauncey explained what was happening. "If Professor Chang in here listened to my instructions, then he tried to use the auto release. But I broke that and didn't tell him. His next move would have been to try pushing the back seat forward to escape into the car itself. But I broke that, too," Chauncey smiled.

The banging was now reaching a fever pitch, possibly a result of claustrophobia. Chauncey didn't make a move to open the trunk. He explained to the group that if they listened carefully they could hear that the trapped man had torn off the tape, chewed through the tape binding his hand and was now full-blown screaming. Although from the outside it was soft and muffled. "They really make these things pretty sound proof, don't they?" Chauncey asked the others with a grin.

"Get me out of here!" Chang yelled from the trunk, louder.

A couple of the engineers exchanged glances with muted smiles. Several of them even began to snicker a bit.

"This is not a joke," Chauncey snapped. "Your associate in the trunk went in there willingly and now he's starting to freak out. You need to keep your wits. You are all thinking men so never, ever lose your capacity for cool, calm reason."

Chauncey banged his fist on the trunk and yelled to it, "Think! What else can you do? What else did I tell you?"

The banging and screaming stopped as Chang apparently became still again. A moment later the right taillight of the car popped out, and Chang's hand emerged waiving.

"Splendid!" said Chauncey to the flailing hand. Then, to the group, "Others may see the hand and alert the police." Then, back to the hand, "All good in there?"

Chang's hand stopped waving and gave Chauncey a thumbs up.

"That wasn't too hard was it? Care to try it again in a smaller, older car?"

Chang's extended thumb was quickly replaced by an extended middle finger.

"Good on you!" said Chauncey as he popped open the trunk and helped the sweaty engineer to painfully unfold his body and exit. He then turned to the group and asked, "Who's next? Mr. Young?"

Chapter Twelve

Eyesopen.org was one of the many, growing, Internet-based news organizations that's emphasis was on exposing the government's encroachment on civil rights and privacy. It didn't matter that they had a small staff of passionate do-gooder reporters with solid investigative skills. Like most nonmainstream media outlets they didn't have nearly enough capital to spread their word in traditional ways like the New York Times. Fortunately, they had a loyal pool of foot soldiers who donated money and then helped spread the word virally.

Every article published on its website or emailed in its weekly newsletter got forwarded, liked, pinned, and all other manner of digital distribution. The eyesopen.org messages could be found on Twitter, Facebook, LinkedIn, and other social media sites. Hundreds of comments were posted by readers along with each article arguing the pros and cons of the message against the new status quo.

While many critics called the website and its followers a den of un-American whistleblower lovers, eyesopen.org maintained its right to free speech protection under the First Amendment. Just as members of the NRA loved their guns, members of eyesopen.org loved their free speech. And many of them swore they would die to protect it.

This belief hadn't stopped the "true" patriots of America from creating disinformation campaigns, relentless computer hacking, and even throwing bricks through the plate glass window of the organization's office in downtown San Diego. The police had recommended they install CCTV surveillance cameras outside of the office, but eyesopen.org always declined as it was hypocritical. And based on the fact that their homepage sported the Benjamin Franklin quote, *They that can give up essential liberty to obtain a little temporary safety deserve neither liberty nor safety,* they were being consistent. The police merely shrugged, said there was nothing they could do, then proceeded to spy on the office with their Qube quadcopter drones and CCTV cameras. Not to protect them, but to find, follow, and intimidate potential terrorists.

The founder and lead reporter of eyesopen.org was Marcella Kraner, a thirty-eight-year-old journalist who'd been fighting for civil rights since the day she was born. The daughter of Harry Kraner, a political science professor at Columbia University, Marcella had attended more political and civil rights rallies than most NASCAR fans had attended county fairs. And while she'd garnered both a solid reputation as an investigative reporter and a large fan base, she'd also been beaten, stalked, arrested, and spat on more times than she could count.

The FBI had a slew of suspicious activity reports, aka SARs about her and, had the current administration wanted to, they could have caused her a lot of trouble. That's not to say they hadn't tried. After spending three weeks sleeping in downtown Manhattan in the early days of Occupy Wall Street, the TSA had issued a no-fly certificate on Kraner. Working with her attorney and the ACLU, it was revoked quickly, albeit reluctantly. But given that the FBI, the DHS, the CIA, and the DOD knew where she was, what she was doing, and who she was doing it with virtually every minute of every day, they weren't that concerned.

In the years following 9/11, Kraner had found it fairly simple to book people for her interviews. Even with her nickname, "The Spiderwoman," earned because she was an expert at weaving an inescapable web of words around people, then metaphorically devouring them on camera, she could get bankers, lobbyists, and truth-tellers, now called whistleblowers, to speak with her.

While most of her sources agreed to talk because of solid ethical concerns, the fact that Kraner was a five-foot-ten, auburn-haired bombshell with the loveliest pair of 34C breasts around, didn't hurt either. Desirable and very single, Kraner had a smile and hazel-eyed twinkle that made men believe they had a chance get her in the sack. The right wing, cowboy-types especially viewed a sit-down with her as an opportunity to break her progressive independence and take her home with them as a trophy. Until she completely neutered them on camera, that is.

Her allure aside, over the past few years subjects for interviews had been slowly drying up. The vilification and prosecution of men like Julian Assange, Bradley Manning and Edward Snowden, men she considered to be heroes, had had a chilling effect on people's willingness to expose the awful truths they knew about the US government and their corporate financiers. And when you combined the newly fabricated, anti-whistleblower legislation and blatant NSA spying on journalists' emails, phone calls, and computer files, the will of today's truthsayers had been withered.

Ever since Tom Carby had called Kraner to ask for an interview, she'd been curious as to why. It's not that Carby was a difficult man to find. All you had to do was go to General Atomics on the first Thursday of every month, and you'd see him and his mock-Predator drone watching the watchers. It was just that he was a mainstream media guy and didn't usually grace the smaller, web-based news outlets with his presence. He'd been at every Occupy Movement in the country, been on Good Morning America, and even did a stunt where he placed David Letterman in the crosshairs of his drone to simulate targeting him as a terrorist.

Her best guess as to Carby's motives for calling her was that beside the whistleblowers being scared to admit the truth, her brethren at CBS, CNN, and NBC were not only afraid of being prosecuted for complicity, but their sponsors would back out of advertising agreements, and thus, cause a drop in revenue. The thought of that was repugnant to her. Journalists report the truth. Often called the fifth estate, journalism and freedom of the press was so important to the founding fathers that it was mentioned, by name, in the First Amendment. And the current climate being created was casting an Arctic chill that bordered on authoritarianism.

Kraner and her cameraman pulled their news van up to Carby's house on a tree-lined street in La Jolla and found him in his perfectly-tended garden. He beckoned them over with his hand and trademarked, impish smile. Kraner's cameraman, Ethan Michaels, grabbed his camera, a pair of Sun Gun lights, a battery pack, and a mic set and emerged from the van with Kraner.

Michaels considered himself a true crusader. His camera, which he called "the Eye of Truth," was his proudest possession. He viewed it as an extension of his desire to capture what was wrong with the world and broadcast it straight into the wrongdoers' living rooms. A photojournalism major from Emerson College in Boston, Massachusetts, he'd been embedded in Iraq, Afghanistan, Libya, and many other violent hotbeds. After he was hired by Marcella one year ago to do a piece on London's surveillance network, they became a team.

"Turn that thing on," said Carby, indicating the camera as they approached him. "You'll want to get this on tape. It's really cool!"

Michaels dropped his cases, swung the Eye of Truth onto his shoulder and said, "We're rolling."

Kraner had met Carby several times and knew that he had a flair for the dramatic. Even so, she admitted to herself that if he was excited about something, it was probably something worth exploring.

As they got closer, Carby pulled aside one of his mulberry bushes and revealed a small, knobby-wheeled garden gnome attached to a hose.

"Meet Gnomy, my garden bot," said Carby. "This little guy is the world's first AGV, autonomous gardening vehicle. He's equipped with sensors that detect different types of plants. Then with other sensors, he measures the soil for moisture content, and if a specific plant falls below its optimal needs, he waters it to perfection. No more overwatering, no more dead roses, just the perfect garden all the time. It's going to be huge in England."

Carby disconnected the hose and stood back.

"Observe."

To his delight, Gnomy began moving from plant to plant, analyzing leaves and soil, then watering them through a sprinkler built into his crotch. It was not only an amazing bit of technology, but it was really funny. Kraner and Michaels were entertained and amazed at the same time.

Carby beamed as his latest invention went on its merry way down the rows of bushes and flowers. He winked at Kraner, "It's the good side of bots. Gonna make me a fortune." Then he turned deadly serious. "Let's go inside. We have some things to discuss."

Kraner and Michaels exchanged a look, then followed Carby inside. While the outside of his house was a typical Southern California Spanish ranch house, the inside was a shiny, new-age technological wonder that would have made Bill Gates and Steve Jobs jealous. Automated lights, music, and climate control sensors changed the environment as you moved from room to room. Roombas vacuumed, and other gadgets wheeled around freely cleaning, dusting, and keeping the house immaculate.

"Let's do the interview over here," said Carby, pointing to the living room.

He sat down and flicked a switch on his glass coffee table. Instantly, the wall opened up revealing an array of thirty high-resolution monitors. As Michaels raced to light the room, put mics on Carby and Kraner and lock off the Eye of Truth on a tripod, Kraner composed herself to do what she did best. Rather than spend time on pleasantries, she got right to it.

She looked at Michaels, he gave her the thumbs up, and Kraner looked at the camera.

"This is Marcella Kraner for eyesopen.org. I'm in the home of Dr. Thomas Carby, noted roboticist and leader of the well-known 'Watch the Watchers' protest group. An avid proponent of privacy, civil liberties, and ethics in robotics, Professor Carby has invited us into his home to reveal something that he says will be shocking to us all. Professor?"

Carby slid a pair of sensor straps onto his hand and began to type on the tabletop as if it was a keyboard. For a moment it seemed like he was either blind or crazy, but either conclusion would have been wrong. The straps were a powerful combination of electronic components, sensors, proprietary algorithms, and artificial intelligence. So even though there was no physical keyboard, as his fingers typed, the monitors obeyed. Each screen came to life, playing back different legs of Kraner's drive from her office in San Diego to Carby's home. As the playback showed the different legs of her travel, Carby explained.

"This is a montage of your drive," said Carby. "You have been recorded by over a hundred closed circuit televisions in the 27.3 minutes that it took you to get here."

While she was a bit taken aback by the high resolution and seamless, complete documentary of her trip, Kraner wasn't blown away. She wasn't new to this stuff.

"We all know how pervasive the surveillance state is Professor Carby. We've reported the growing security matrix for years. I assume they planted some kind of an illegal GPS tracking device on me somewhere in order to keep tabs of my whereabouts, right?"

"Not device. Devices," corrected Carby, his face becoming a bit grim. "You have been infested with smartspecks."

Kraner had heard of smartspecks but wasn't sure what he was talking about. She instinctively looked at herself and brushed off her shoulders.

Carby continued, "You won't find them, and there are too many to brush off. They're smaller than the width of a single hair, and there are hundreds of them on you right now. Mostly in your hair."

Fighting off the urge to run for the nearest shower, Kraner kept her cool. "I'm familiar with them," she said. "They're tiny, wireless networked sensors. But I was under the impression that they were still experimental."

"Not at all," said Carby. "The US Army has used them for years. Soldiers in Afghanistan use the little "nodes" to keep an eye on things when they're not around. They're a technological tour de force. Depending on what kind of batteries and sensors are in the little buggers, they can be dropped into an area from minidrones and monitor for chemical weapons, changes in geological force to detect tanks, conversations, whatever. And now they are being prepped for surveillance by the DHS."

Kraner thought she'd seen it all. Her mind raced through the possibilities, both good and bad, that this type of technology brought to the table. It would be a boon for agriculture, forest preservation, wildlife control, and more. But, as was her job, she instantly assessed the dark side. She imagined protest rallies where attendees got showered and tagged by drones dropping this nanotechnology. Once infested, they would be profiled as agitators and dissidents and tailed indiscriminately for being enemies of the state. If the government had had this in the 1960s, African Americans would probably still be sitting in the backs of buses.

"Christ," she said, softly. "But how did they get on me? How did you know?" Her paranoia was beginning to show a little more than usual.

"I had them put on you," said Carby. "Remember the homeless guy who asked you for money when you walked out of your office?"

Kraner thought back and nodded.

"He sneezed all over me," she said, reliving a bit of disgust.

"He sneeze-bugged you," said Carby.

"That's freakin' crazy," said Michaels without realizing he was speaking. Then, "Oh, sorry. My bad."

"That's only the half of it," said Carby. "I love technology, that's a fact. Just look around. It's going to make the world a better place, no doubt. But we need to control it. We need to show the world what's being made before it's too late. This has got to be regulated before it's out there."

Kraner had regained her composure and realized that Carby had spoken in future tense.

"You mean this smartspeck stuff isn't on the market yet?" she asked.

"Not yet," said Carby. "But they're getting close. And they're not going to stop with *watching* us. They're focused on *stopping* us, too. Not only will they track us, they'll subdue us. Here's the shocking part."

Carby pressed an unseen return key on his virtual computer and all of sudden Michaels went into a spasm and dropped to the floor.

"He was doused with some of the motes too," said Carby. "And they just emitted enough electricity, in tandem, to take him down. Like little, networked nano-tasers. Cool, huh?"

Michaels groaned a bit and began to get up. He wasn't happy about the demonstration, especially given he hadn't been forewarned. Carby didn't apologize and kept on going.

"A lot of people will say this stuff can prevent terrorist attacks. Maybe if they'd been sprinkled around the entrance of the Hotel del Coronado with explosives sensors, the massacre never would have happened."

Carby stared ahead, clenching and unclenching his jaw. His cheeks moved in and out. "The truth is that nothing could have prevented an attack. Not smartspecks, drones, nothing. And I'm not surprised. We've moved the trigger."

"I don't follow," said Kraner.

"In warfare, you must shoot the trigger to stop the firing. You have to aim at the shooter. Early on it was easy. It was a club or a sword; the guy was right there in front of your face. But technology has moved the trigger farther and farther away. Spears, then bows and arrows, guns, missiles on gunships, and now drone ground stations in the United States. The trigger is here. They have to come here to stop it. It's their only hope.

"I saw the tape of that engineer being tortured," he continued. "And while I know it won't be a very popular thing to say, that terrorist was a harbinger. We have to get engaged. We have to establish a moral compass for our technology and our technologists or we'll have more 9-11's than we can count. I don't want the trigger in my backyard."

"Sounds a little Ted Kaczynski-esque," said Kraner, referring to the still imprisoned Unabomber.

"Kaczynski was a theorist. I'm not. I was in Iraq and Afghanistan," said Carby. "I saw some of the diabolical things that robots did. A lot of it is good, yes. But a whole lot more of it is bad. I'm just saying that Americans need to engage and see that their tax dollars are being used in ways that aren't exactly, American."

Realizing that this was his final statement, Kraner looked at the Eye of Truth and signed off. "This is Marcella Kraner for eyesopen.org with Professor Thomas Carby. You've just had your eyes opened."

Chapter Thirteen

Breskin didn't like surprises. He kept a well-arranged schedule, his Culver City house was always clean and uncluttered, and he even planned his vacations two years in advance. While that mentality may have seemed to run counter to being an investigator, it made sense. Although crimes were often messy, as a special agent, a psychologist, and an interrogator, he was an expert at finding patterns. Patterns were neat, taut, and predictable.

That personality trait was just one of the reasons he'd been dreading his current trip to the nation's capital. It was mid-February, and the temperature could fluctuate between the low twenties and high fifties. It could snow, it could rain, it could be dry, it could be humid; you never knew. And although it may have been a bad career move, politically speaking, it's also why he'd decided to live in Southern California where it was always warm and sunny.

So while it was a short trip, he'd packed gloves, an umbrella, a medium-weight and a heavyweight coat, and even a pair of galoshes because he didn't like getting his shoes wet. Thankfully, whether it was global warming or cooling or whatever, the city was experiencing an unseasonably mild winter. The only unpredictable thing Breskin would have to contend with was the mood shifts of the politico who'd summoned him.

It was a closed door meeting in Senator Todd Stevens' office in the basement of the Brayburn Building. Breskin had been guessing what it was about for a full day. He hadn't even been told who was going to be there. But when a congressman like Todd Stevens invited you to a meeting, you went.

Stevens was an old-school Republican right down to his Buzz Aldrin crew cut and black bifocals. At sixty-seven years of age, he was on his fifth term as a congressman from San Diego County. As such, his constituency was pretty much the Navy, the Air Force, and the dozens of DOD contractors that employed the citizens who controlled his re-elections. His coziness with the CEOs of top defense contractors like Lockheed Martin, Northrup Grumman, General Atomics, and others was well known, and he'd been sharply criticized for taking excessive campaign contributions from most of them. That, plus the fact that he was chairman of the House Armed Services Committee and co-chair of the Congressional Unmanned Systems Caucus, aka the Drone Caucus, made him one formidable politician.

Stevens' position in the DC power elite aside, Breskin had been pretty put off by the fact that he'd had to leave his Hotel Del Coronado massacre investigation to attend this meeting. Especially given the fact that Stevens was about to return to San Diego for one of Congress's many vacations or, as they liked to call them, state work periods. Breskin figured it was just the guy's way of throwing his weight around.

However, given that after two weeks the investigation had hit a roadblock, and Breskin still had no idea how the kidnapping and torture tied in with Solivan, he knew the break might be a good thing. Stepping back from the trees to see the forest could be helpful.

Breskin had a hunch that Stevens was going to grill him about the massacre. On the flight from LAX to Dulles, he'd prepared his response about the investigation's progress. He was basically planning to say that they were following up on some solid leads, but there was nothing that he could report yet. That hunch had turned out to be wrong.

Also gathered in Stevens' office were Nels Green, the CEO of General Atomics; Jim Sorrentino, the president of the AUVSI; and Doug Golden, the FAA's Unmanned Systems Integration Executive. After the obligatory niceties had been exchanged, coffee, soda, and iced tea were served by Stevens' extremely beautiful, extremely young, and, Breskin was sure, extremely ambitious, aide. After the distraction shook its way out of the room, the meeting got started.

Like Breskin, Stevens was matter-of-fact and to the point. But surprisingly, rather than ask about the hotel massacre, the kidnapping, or the ensuing torture/execution, Stevens started by asking about the mini-UAV incident at the Rose Bowl.

"Agent Breskin," Stevens began, "I know that you're still investigating that stunt in Pasadena, so I'm curious about any progress you've made."

To be sure, Breskin was more than a little taken aback by this. Not to diminish its importance, but the Rose Bowl drones were the least of his worries. For all he knew it could have been a publicity stunt by Jeff Bezos from Amazon to promote his Prime Delivery scheme. He wasn't even heading up that case. He'd assigned it to one of his junior agents. The country had just experienced a horrendous terrorist attack, and this didn't seem as high on the totem pole.

Besides, everyone in the room knew there was no possible way to track those mini-UAVs, or MAVS, as some people called them. As soon as they'd shown up, the FAA had been called to see if they'd granted any temporary COAs for the Rose Bowl. They hadn't. And by the time the Sheriffs and Customs and Border Patrol had coordinated their choppers, the UAVs had dispersed over the desert.

Breskin replied, "To be honest, there isn't a whole lot we can do. The police couldn't follow them because they were so small and flying too low. Not to mention they had no way of tracking the GPS signals." Not to mention who gives a rat's patootie, he thought, but didn't say.

Undaunted, Stevens continued, "Did you review the video? Can you track the purchases? There were what, a hundred of them? You must have seen who the manufacturer was."

"There were a hundred and twenty of them and the video showed that they were DIY drones. Probably made with parts bought at Home Depot and hobby shops like Radio Shack," said Breskin.

"UAS," interjected Sorrentino with a bit of attitude. "They are not drones, they are unmanned aerial systems. Let's get in the habit of calling them what they really are, okay?

Sorrentino, the head of the Association of Unmanned Vehicles Systems International, aka the AUVSI, led the largest robotics industry lobbying group in the world. He'd been on a campaign to not only show people all the positive uses of the flying, swimming, and crawling bots, but thought the word "drone" was one of the reasons that Americans were so afraid of them in the United States. Never mind that the television and Internet news showed drone attacks on a nightly basis.

Remaining on his soap box, Sorrentino added, "When the average person on the street thinks of the word 'drone,' they think military. They think hostile. They think large, autonomous, and lethal. The term doesn't accurately reflect how UAS are being used domestically. They assessed the flooding of the Red River in the Upper Midwest. They helped battle California's wildfires. They're helping to study everything from hurricanes in the Gulf to tornadoes in the Great Plains and volcanoes in Hawaii. And the more the public is afraid, the longer it will take to add tens of billions of dollars to our economy and protect our country."

Breskin looked at Sorrentino in disbelief. If the guy wanted to delude himself that it was the word *drone* and not the idea of a low-cost technology that could open the gates to the most pernicious public surveillance in history, then there wasn't a helluva lot he could do. Beyond that, if Stevens had called him here to somehow assist in Sorrentino's PR campaign to save the drones, he was going to be cranky.

Breskin continued, "I stand corrected. There seems to be no way of tracking who built and deployed the *UAVs* at that Rose Bowl."

Stevens looked at Golden, who nodded that he agreed.

"The FAA did not review or approve any COAs for minidrones," said Golden, smiling at Sorrentino, "at the Rose Bowl. And Agent Breskin is correct. There was no way to track them. That's one of the reasons we're trying to be so thorough in fulfilling our mandate."

Golden was referring to the FAA Reauthorization and Reform Act of 2012. Passed by Congress and signed by President Obama, the act had directed the FAA to create regulations and a streamlined process to safely integrate unmanned systems into the national airspace by 2015. It was multi-tiered legislation that had set milestones governing testing, reviewing, authorizing, and monitoring the safety and integration of the new technology. So far every milestone had been missed.

As Golden spoke, Breskin could see Sorrentino's body language shift. He clearly didn't like Golden. He correctly figured it was probably less personal and more a result of pressure Sorrentino got from the UAV makers to let them sell their products with as few regulations as possible.

Nels Green, who'd been characteristically quiet to this point, interjected. "That's not entirely true, Doug, and you know it. Our new Nightshade system could not only have followed those MAVs and helped the FBI figure out who was responsible, they also could have activated ground bots to move in and make an arrest."

Breskin had no idea what Green was talking about, but intuitively realized they were coming to the meat of the meeting. The dynamics went from pseudo-friendly to a witch hunt as Stevens, Sorrentino, and Green leaned forward toward Golden. Golden, predictably, crossed his legs and arms across his chest.

"Nels," said Golden, "We've approved your SAC-EC, now you'll just have to wait until we've reviewed the systems. This isn't Iraq, it's the United States, so you can't just toss whatever you want in the sky. If we find it to be safe you'll get your COA. There's nothing I can do about it. It takes time."

Stevens jumped in, but not to calm things down. "Doug, unfortunately, time is running out. The more things like this Rose Bowl incident that happen, the more the public is becoming nervous."

"Unjustifiably nervous," added Sorrentino.

Stevens went on, "We've got states passing anti-UAV legislation. Hell, one town in Colorado passed a local ordinance that permits people to shoot them down on sight. We've got to fast-track this. It's for the public's own good."

Now it was Golden's turn to lean in. "Gentlemen, I'm on your side. I love the technology, and quite frankly, I'm sick of investigating crashes that are almost always due to pilot error. Unmanned systems *are* the future. But they're not ready for domestic prime time. The FAA's job is to protect the manned aircraft, the people in them, and the people walking beneath them. Leaving the privacy issues on the side, the lack of an effective sense and avoid system of UAS is the biggest problem. And we're working on it. NASA's working on it, MITRE's working on it, MIT's working on it. For all I know the Campfire Girls are working on it."

"An enhanced NexGen ADS-B is on every single Nightshade. It's got autonomous sense and avoid that works, Doug. You've seen it," said Green.

Golden sighed and leaned back. "My hands are tied. I cannot expedite your COA. Especially since you're asking to put thousands of those things in the NAS at the same time."

With those words Breskin looked up. He'd been listening, somewhat distractedly, but it simply wasn't his fight. He'd obviously been asked to the meeting as a way of getting Golden there without suspecting he'd be bushwhacked. And if the weather had been nastier, he would have been plenty pissed. But the thought of thousands of those things in the sky made him take a bit more interest.

""Would you guys mind bringing me up to speed," Breskin asked. "I'm a smart guy, but I'm clearly lacking some intel on this issue."

"No problem," said Green. "General Atomics has developed an unmanned system that we're calling Nightshade. It's an MAV —"

Golden interrupted. 'Seventy-five pounds is hardly an MAV."

Green nodded. "You're right. According to the current definition it's twenty-one pounds too heavy to be an MAV. That being said, Nightshade employs a very sophisticated cooperative technology. DHS, FBI, and local law can launch hundreds of them in strategic areas in a city. Like a squadron of flying robocops they can hover and do intelligence, surveillance, and reconnaissance of specific, GPS-defined grids for up to eight hours. If the ground operator or the UAS itself spots any suspicious activity, it automatically alerts the others. They all converge and swarm to neutralize the situation."

"And just how do they neutralize that situation?" asked Breskin.

"Pepper spray mostly, but we're nearly finished developing a smartspeck dispersion system that will emit incapacitating electrical shocks."

The implications blew Breskin away. If they'd been deployed in Pasadena, they'd have been able to follow the Rose Bowl drones and knock them down, providing the evidence that Breskin needed but didn't have.

Golden was on his feet. He gestured to Stevens to Green to Sorrentino and back with each point. "A. They're too heavy to be classified as MAVs, which is why they're not being deployed right now for law enforcement. B. They're weaponized and the president says that's a nonstarter. C. The sense and avoid hasn't been fully tested. And D. They're a disaster waiting to happen. Sure they could help law enforcement, but they present a huge safety risk as well."

Stevens could see the wheels turning in Breskin's head. He leapt on it, addressing Breskin, "Can't you see how having these things at your disposal would help more than hurt? It'd give you 10,000 eyes in the sky."

There you had it. The true reason Breskin was at the meeting. If he endorsed a system like this it would be the FBI's seal of approval. He was there to put additional pressure on the FAA. Breskin felt his cheeks getting warm. He felt unprepared and setup, two things he hated feeling separately, let alone at the same time.

"I can definitely see how helpful something like Nightshade would be but –"

Sorrentino cut him off, "But what? Hundreds of people got hurt because of those UAVs at the Rose Bowl. For all we know they might have even stopped the San Diego and Boston bombings before they happened.

The FAA is dragging its feet. The more support we have, the faster we can get them to move."

"Mr. Sorrentino, you don't know me at all, so, for your edification, I have the dubious distinction of having conducted many interrogations in Afghanistan, Iraq, and other undisclosed places. Very intense interrogations. That experience has taught me that having patience is not only a virtue, it's a necessity. Some things just take time. So without more information, I'm going to err on the side of caution."

"So we're just going to let the greatest technology for law enforcement sit in a closet while terrorists destroy the will of the American people with fear tactics?" said Sorrentino throwing up his hands in disgust. "Whose side are you on?"

Breskin ignored the question and placed his hands around his cup of coffee to warm them. Nobody spoke. Stevens' grandfather clock's ticking was the only thing anyone could hear. Green ran his finger around the rim of his glass of Diet Coke, thinking. After a moment, Stevens looked at Golden.

"You know that I can get the act amended. We changed the bill once, we can do it again. And if we do, whoever is heading it up, might not be you," said Stevens.

Golden was used to being bullied and threatened. People were angry at regulators all the time, from the Wall Street banks, to the oil and gas industry, to law enforcement, and more. But it didn't really matter what he thought. His mandate was clear.

"Sir," he said. "You may do whatever you please. The fact of the matter is that the FAA has always been a tombstone agency. We warn, we recommend, we're ignored, people die, then our recommendations are taken — etched as a footnote on the tombstones of the dead. My position is firm. I will not endorse your new system without the proper steps, nor will I recommend to the secretary of Transportation that we change anything. You feel free to propose any fast-track legislation that you want. But rest assured that I will fight it. And the day your bill crosses my desk is the day I resign."

Chapter Fourteen

A small wave of relief washed over Green as he felt the wheels of his prized, Hawker-Beechcraft 4000 touchdown at Lindbergh Field in San Diego. Unfortunately, an even larger wave of nausea washed over him at the same time and he dry-heaved into the air sickness bag that he'd been clutching since wheels-up in D.C. five hours ago.

Green had been vomiting pretty much nonstop since about ten o'clock the previous evening. Whatever was rotting in his stomach had started after he'd returned to his hotel room from having dinner with Senator Stevens and Sorrentino. He'd figured it was a bad lobster tail and hoped it would ease up after the bad crustacean was purged from his body. No such luck. His bodyguard, Joe Reicher, ran to a nearby Walgreens to get Pepto-Bismol, Tums, and Gatorade, but nothing had helped. The stuff just kept coming out. All night long.

After enduring such a miserable and sleepless night, Green would have stayed in DC until he felt better, but a frantic, five a.m. phone call from his wife, Iris, put the kibosh on that possibility.

"She's missing!" Iris had shrieked into the phone.

"Who's missing?" Green groaned.

"Stacey! Our daughter!"

Through a mix of tears and hysteria, Iris had explained that their fifteen-year-old daughter hadn't been home since the previous day. Yes, she'd called her friends. No, none of them knew where she was. Yes, she'd called the police; they were sending someone over. And no, damn it, she would not calm down. She wanted him home immediately. Now. Yesterday. She became even more upset by his insensitive line of interrogation.

It was a fight they'd had many times. In Green's mind he wasn't interrogating her, he was just clicking into CEO mode and gathering information to solve a problem. It was his way. Gather, interpret, decide, then act. He'd negotiated and closed many high-level deals using that strategy. But before an argument started, Green reminded himself of what their marriage counselor had told him: His family wasn't a business deal.

"I'll be home as soon as I can," he said. "Try to stay calm until I get there. I'm sure she's fine. We'll find her." He hung up, then sprinted to the john for the umpteenth time of the night.

Being the CEO of a billion-dollar Warco had its perks. While Reicher contacted Green's private pilot to get his personal jet fueled up and ready for an early morning departure, Green called the mayor of San Diego. After waking him from a sound sleep, Green got a personal assurance that all assets would be devoted to finding his daughter.

Other than dealing with his bad case of food poisoning, Green figured getting home would be pretty straightforward. He'd sleep on the flight, then by the time they landed he'd feel better, and Stacey would be home. But as the John Lennon song put it, "Life is what happens to you when you're busy making other plans." And in this case, Green's plans had nothing in common with what life had in store.

They'd gotten to the FBO at Dulles and then onto the plane without incident, but once they'd taxied onto the tarmac, the pilot was called back to the hangar to check a potentially faulty fuel line. Rather than wait inside the terminal, Green opted to stay onboard and try to do some work. The continued nausea made it impossible to concentrate, so he tried calling Iris to tell her he was on his way, but his phone couldn't get a signal. Neither could Reicher's.

Reicher remarked, "It's amazing. We can remote-pilot drones from Creech and push buttons to have them launch smart bombs at terrorists in Pashtun, but we can't get a damned signal on a cellphone." That got a smile from Green.

Several uncomfortable hours later, the plane was wheels up. As anyone can imagine, turbulence and food poisoning don't mix very well, so Green bounded to the head as soon as they hit twenty-thousand feet. Still surprised that there was anything left inside of him, he filled the bowl with vomit. He flushed and turned to return to his seat, but before he could take a step, the apparently malfunctioning toilet, violently ejected his foulness. It spewed onto the walls, the ceiling, mirror, and all over Green.

The stench quickly filled the cabin, which only served to intensify his nausea and make the flight attendant and Reicher queasy. Making matters worse, while the crew attempted to clean the mess, the cabin's air recirculation system broke, preventing any way to filter out the putrid smell. Even if Green had a sense of humor, he wouldn't have laughed at the comedy of errors. He was far too worried about his daughter, felt like crap on toast, and was stuck in a twenty-million-dollar private jet that smelled like a Grand Central Station toilet.

Every time Green closed his eyes and attempted to drift off for a moment, he got the dry-heaves. Adding to the stress, besides the plane mechanics missing the faulty fuel line and plumbing problems, the ground crew had failed to provision the galley, so there was nothing to drink. Not even bottled water.

As he gratefully accepted three Altoid mints from Reicher, his only solace was the fantasy of putting the owners of the restaurant and the ground crew in a building together and firing a railgun at it. That joy was short-lived because Stacey's face kept popping into his mind. In spite of himself, his imagination was running rampant with terrible thoughts.

Reicher tried his best to calm Green by explaining that before leaving the hotel he'd made some calls to his San Diego security team. They weren't just going to trust the police. Members of his team were searching all of her haunts. And although he was an ex-Marine who'd been trained to always plan for the worst, for Green's sake, he tried his best to diminish the threat.

"She probably got a little too buzzed at a party, lost her cellphone and fell asleep on a friend's floor or something," he offered. The words felt insincere coming out of Reicher's mouth, yet he felt better saying it all the same.

Green understood what Reicher was doing and was grateful. But he knew his daughter. Although she was a spoiled, only child in the thick of her teenage rebellion, she was still respectful and responsible. She knew that if she ever got too drunk, she could call home and get a ride. No questions asked.

"If anything bad happened to her," Green said. "I don't know what I'd do."

"We'll find out soon enough, sir," said Reicher stifling a gag from the odor coming off of Green's soiled clothing.

The midsize luxury jet taxied in and came to a stop near the terminal. The crew immediately opened the door to get some fresh air into the compartment. Reicher helped Green unbuckle and stand. As the clean Pacific Ocean sea air swept inside, he began to feel a bit better. He was still exhausted, but at least the nausea had subsided.

Green pushed Reicher away. "I'm fine," he said. "Let's get to the house. Iris must be eating the furniture by now."

He emerged from the doorway, squinting into the light and immediately put on his Oakley sunglasses. As he descended the steps, he looked around for his limo. Not seeing it, he threw a look at Reicher.

"Didn't want to tell you onboard; stuff was bad enough. Jim got a message to the pilot. He got a flat tire and for some reason there was no spare. They're sending a different car. Should be here any second."

"Holy hell," said Green. "What else can go wrong?"

As they walked the hundred feet to the terminal, Reicher scanned the area to make sure the answer to Green's rhetorical question was "nothing." Whatever his well-trained eye saw – or more to the point, didn't see – put him at ease. Reicher breathed an unnoticed sigh of relief when, seconds later, he spotted a black Lincoln Town Car approach. He and Green stepped toward the curb as the limo pulled up.

"Thank God for small favors," said Green as he grabbed his briefcase.

"Let me check it out first," said Reicher as he went to open the car door.

It was too late. The rear, curbside window opened and the electrified tips of a pair of Taser darts hit Reicher in the center of his chest. The initial fifty-thousand volts of electricity, followed by multiple 1,200-volt shocks stopped his muscles from working and turned him into a quivering marionette. A second set of darts hit Green and he crumpled. Before he hit the ground a pair of hands grabbed his falling body and dragged him into the limo through the window.

Green hadn't even processed what was happening before the rear door opened and he was yanked into the car.

"Hola, Senor Green. Greetings from your daughter," said a Spanish-accented voice behind a red bandana mask. Then he received a stun baton jab in his chest.

The jolt that Green received was a much shorter duration shock intended only to stun. He grabbed his chest in pain and attempted to speak, but couldn't. As the Town Car sped away, the masked man snapped open a spring hinge in the back seat and shoved Green into the trunk.

Green's body slammed around the cramped compartment as the Town Car raced west on Airport Terminal Road. To make sure he experienced the maximum level of discomfort, the driver made frequent sharp turns and short stops as he turned on and off Harbor Drive to West Grape and finally onto Interstate 5, headed south. The jerking turns brought Green's nausea back with a vengeance. Combined with the residual effects of the stun baton shock, he could barely think straight. If it hadn't been for all the hours Green had logged as the pilot of small, private prop planes, he could have added claustrophobia to his list.

He tried as hard as he could to clear his mind. To make sense of what has happening to him. "Greetings from your daughter?" he recounted. "What the hell was he talking about?" Yet each time he attempted to complete a thought, the car would hit a pothole slamming his head against the hood. As the car drove past the Barrio Logan and onto the Coronado Bridge, one thing did solidify. His daughter had been kidnapped. *He* had been kidnapped. But by whom? Why?

Green quickly dismissed the "why" question. There were lots of folks who wanted him dead. His corporation was feared and hated by people all over the world. That's why he traveled with a bodyguard and had security forces surrounding his home and offices. For heaven's sake, that was why he'd agreed to go through the advanced SERE training from Captain Paunce. But he'd thought that was a farce from the beginning. Sure, his employee had been murdered by terrorists, but they only went after easy marks. He was anything but that. Or so he'd convinced himself before learning, now, that he apparently was.

But his daughter? As naïve as it was, the thought that his actions might have put her in real danger suddenly eclipsed everything else. It was something he'd contemplated many times and was the source of constant tension between him and Iris, but he'd never allowed himself to believe it.

Once over the bridge, the Town Car reached Orange Avenue and made a left turn, heading southbound toward Silver Strand Highway and the beach. Green tried his hardest to clear his head. He was no good if he couldn't get it back together.

How the hell had he been kidnapped, he wondered. How the hell did this happen? Green knew this wasn't the time to contemplate. It was the time to act. He recalled what Chauncey had taught him when it came to surviving a kidnapping.

"Stay inside the circle," Chauncey had said during his briefing. "No matter what."

The circle was D-C-S. Distrust: Don't accept things at face value; they're not always what they seem to be. Contest of Wills not a Battle of Wits: Don't engage in dialogue with your captors. Just wait it out as long as you can. Help would eventually come. And Shield: Stick to your cover story and give them no way of entering your mind. It's what they taught SEALs, Rangers and Delta Force so it sure as hell was valuable information, but only if Green could use it properly.

At a point just north of the naval amphibious base where the Navy SEALs trained, the limo turned off the road toward the ocean. It took a narrow roadway in between a pair of large east-west running berms that separated two sections of the beach. The car kept driving west until it finally stopped near the water's edge where the sand got harder from the surf.

Green had done his best to follow turns and stops, but it hadn't worked. He was too off-balance and his adrenaline was pumping hard. By his estimate they hadn't been driving for more than fifteen or twenty minutes, so he figured they were still somewhere in San Diego. He could feel the blood rapidly pumping through his jugular vein. He clenched his jaw repeatedly, painfully gnashing his teeth. He felt around the trunk for anything he could use as a weapon and was rewarded by the hard steel of a lug wrench.

"Sloppy. Must be amateurs," he allowed himself to muse.

Just as he was trying to figure out what he'd do when the trunk opened, it did. Momentarily blinded by the sun and unable to see anything, Green lunged from the trunk, screaming and swinging the lug wrench. Someone he couldn't see rabbit punched him from behind. He fell to his knees and someone else grabbed the wrench.

"Que paso, Senor Green?" the man in the bandana asked, avoiding Green's flailing attempts at freedom. Then he added, "Scream all you like. Nobody's around to hear you."

The man expertly zip-tied Green's hands, then dragged him by the scruff of his neck toward the water, screaming all the while, "You're a murderer, gringo. I'm going to drown you!"

Once at the water, the man forced Green's head into the churning surf. His face crushed into the sandy bottom, and his cheeks were scraped by broken shells. The salty water stung. In spite of his efforts to hold his breath, he inhaled and swallowed mouthfuls of briny seawater. Just when he thought he was going to drown, the man yanked his head up. "You're one real tough hombre, ain't you? You like killing innocent homies," he said, then shoved Green's head back into the water again.

As Green's head was submerged, an old, white refrigerator truck backed into the section of beach where they were. The truck was twenty feet long with the words "Cool as Ice" printed near the mouth of a smiling cartoon polar bear on the side. The masked driver emerged and opened the hinged door to the rear of the truck. The cold from inside the compartment escaped into the warm California air in a white mist.

Another man ran toward the water to help drag Green back. He was pleading, "You've got the wrong guy. I've done nothing to upset anyone. Please, please, tell me what's happening?"

"Silencio!" barked the man who was apparently in charge. He pulled out a ball gag and roughly forced the strap over Green's head and the ball into his mouth. The man from the truck snapped open a box cutter like it was switchblade. He smiled and moved the edge of the razor toward Green's neck. Green's eyes bulged, but instead of slicing his throat, the man slit Green's clothing from top to bottom, then ripped them off of his body. All three of the men lifted his naked body and threw him into the ice truck.

The air inside felt frigid on Green's wet body. Especially in comparison to the warm San Diego heat. The men lifted him and clipped his tied hands into a hook that protruded downward from the center of the roof. His feet barely touched the ground so he had to stand on his tiptoes in order to not hang from his wrists. Green struggled, but one of the men punched him in the solar plexus. He vomited, but the ball in his mouth prevented it from escaping. The bile burned his throat as he swallowed it back down. Next, the men clamped a brace around his neck. The brace was also connected to the ceiling.

"This is so you don't break your neck on our trip," said the head guy.

His hands bound, his neck secured, and his mouth gagged, one of the men shoved a dirty burlap sack over Green's head. They were about to leave when one of the men snapped his fingers. "Damn. Almost forgot," he said. Then he pulled out a wireless, rectal thermometer and shoved in into Green's sphincter. Satisfied, the men jumped out of the truck.

The door still open, Green heard them outside discussing what to do with Reicher. "What do we do with the bodyguard?" asked one of them.

"Matalo. Kill him," came the calm, easy reply.

Green cringed three times. One time for each shot he heard. Then the door to the truck closed and he was surrounded by cold blackness. As the truck began moving, speakers in the rear began to play. It was Green's daughter, pleading. "Help me, daddy. They're hurting me. Help me, daddy. I need you!"

The refrigerator truck drove, nonstop, for over two hours. Freezing and shaken to his core, Green had no idea where they were going. For a brief moment while they were dragging him from the water, he thought he'd recognized where he was. But within minutes of leaving he was lost. His worst nightmare was that they were headed to Mexico. The thought of being out of the country and away from any help brought him to near panic. Still, he considered what he knew of Tijuana. He spoke fluent Spanish and had friends there. If he could escape, he would find his way to the United States consulate and get help.

Every time Green moved, the plastic zip-ties dug into his wrists. Whether it was a bump in the road, a turn, or a minor adjustment on his part, the pain was excruciating. He had to remain on his tiptoes for stability, and the cramps in his calves soon became unbearable. Switching from toe to toe alternately, he gave each calf a rest. When that became too much he would endure the horrendous choking caused by the neck brace as it accepted his full weight.

Perhaps worst of all, the entire time, ceaselessly, torturously, the recording of his daughter's pleas filled the cold truck. In spite of himself he imagined horrible scenes of Stacey in a similar situation as him. Maybe even worse. She was his light. His shining beacon of innocence. He fought it off. "Distrust everything," Chauncey had said. This was only her voice. It could have been someone else? Maybe an actress?

His mind recalled how close they'd gotten in the days following the massacre at the Hotel del Coronado and the torture-execution. His long work hours and frequent business trips, coupled with her teenage angst, had created a lot of tension between them. But after the horrible events, she'd come to him worried about his safety.

"I don't want that to happen to you, Daddy," she told him. "I don't want to lose you."

Warm tears streamed from his normally dry eyes as he realized that his choices had put her in harm's way. The sadness quickly gave way to indignance. Nothing he had done could justify this. She was innocent and didn't deserve to be mistreated.

Ironically, it wasn't the uncontrollable shivering that made Green realize how cold it was inside the truck. It was the fact that the tears on his cheek instantly turned cold. He was shivering intensely. His entire body was trembling. His teeth were chattering uncontrollably. Having spent a lot of time skiing in Aspen, he realized it was the beginning of modest hypothermia brought on by his naked body's inability to retain any heat. He knew that if he stayed in there for much longer he could die.

Fighting the fear, Green tried to keep his head clear. All was lost if he couldn't think straight. Through it all, "Help me, daddy. They're hurting me. Help me, daddy. I need you!" played over and over again through the truck's speakers. Green tried to focus on Stacey's voice. Not for self-pity but because the longer he heard it, the longer he reckoned she was alive. He listened intently to the tone and words. Were they forcing her to say it as a way of getting to him, or were they recording her while they tortured her? He couldn't tell, but still he listened.

He loved the sound of his daughter's voice. For him, it was one of her best qualities. He loved hearing her talk. He loved her laugh. And he especially loved to hear her sing. His mind filled with memories of Stacey playing guitar and singing her favorite songs. He recalled watching her perform in school musicals. She was incredibly talented and wanted to be a famous actress. So beautiful. So talented. So graceful.

The truck jerked to a stop and Green barely noticed. Seconds later the door opened, and two of the men jumped up into the frigid compartment.

"Wakey-wakey, pig," they screamed at him. "Time to meet your maker."

They roughly undid the neck brace and lifted him to remove his hands from the hook. Green immediately collapsed, his legs so cramped they were unable to hold his weight.

"Let's go, pussy," one of the men barked. He pushed Green out of the truck with his feet. Green fell to the ground into the heat. His legs were worthless and his arms completely numb from cold and lack of blood. He curled into a protective ball. His limbs tingled as the fluid and warmth shot their way back through his veins and capillaries.

"Yo, I ain't carrying you, bitch," said one of the men, forcing Green to his feet. He summoned some strength and staggered forward, being prodded by the machine gun muzzles of the kidnappers.

Green squinted and instantly realized that they were in the desert. Saguaro cacti and Joshua trees pushed up from the hot, dry sand.

"Welcome to Tijuana, gringo."

After only a few steps, Green collapsed again. The heat from the sand both soothed his cold body and burned his skin at the same time. He tried to get up but the exhaustion ran too deep. He hadn't eaten or slept in nearly twenty-four hours and his body was dehydrated from all the vomiting.

"Agua," he pleaded. "Por favor."

The men laughed and grabbed Green's zip-tied arms. They dragged him toward a small, adobe house. The pain of his bare legs being dragged across the course, hot sand, and pebbles was excruciating. With his last bit of strength, he stood up. He wobbled into the house and was shoved into a small room with two chairs. One of them was occupied by another man wearing a tied, bandana mask. The men forced Green into the chair directly across from him.

Save the two chairs, the room was practically empty. There were no windows. Cheap, faux-wood paneling covered one wall, and the other three were bare plaster with cracks and what appeared to be bullet holes in them. A single speaker was mounted in the far corner of the room, and a video camera was fixed in the high corner to the left of the door. Focused on Green, the camera's red record light beamed a steady red.

The man seated across from Green waved his compadres away. They exited, closing the door behind them. After a moment, the man asked Green, in a calm voice, dripping in a thick, Pakistani accent, "What have you been up to, Mr. Green?"

Green was utterly confused. The other men had Spanish accents, but this man was Middle Eastern. He'd heard that al-Qaeda had moved into Mexico and was working to raise gun money by helping the cartels, but he'd only thought it was a rumor. If it were true, he was in worse trouble that he'd originally thought. His only hope now was to endure whatever they had in store for him. Someone would notice he was gone. Iris would tell the police when she found out he'd landed but not returned home. They'd find Reicher's body. Something.

He opened his mouth to reply when the man leaped to his feet and screamed into Green's face. "What have you been up to, you murderous dog?!"

Shaken to his core, Green's mind floundered. He clutched at Chauncey's words, praying the lessons would keep him alive long enough to be rescued. "Courtesy costs you nothing, mate." Chauncey had said. "Contest of wills, not a battle of wits."

"Sorry?" Green replied weakly, falling into his training. "I don't understand the question."

"I said, what have you been up to, Mr. Green?" the man repeated.

"Well, I was kidnapped by some men and now I'm here. Is that what you mean?"

"No, that is not what I mean, and you know it. Are you playing games? Are you trying to provoke me?

"No, sir. My apologies. I want to cooperate with you."

"Good. Then tell me what you were doing in Washington, D.C.? Why did you have a meeting with Senator Stevens?"

"It was just dinner. A little lobster."

The man screamed at Green. "Why do you insult me?! I have your cellphone! I have your calendar and your briefcase! I know you had a meeting with Senator Stevens and some other men!"

"Just dinner. I had dinner," Green said, giving away as little information as possible, yet still sticking on the side of truth.

"So you went to Washington, D.C. to have dinner?

"Yes."

The man pushed some buttons on Green's iPhone then shoved it in his face. "Then why does it say on your cellphone that you had a meeting 're: integration?' What does this mean, integration?"

Green had no idea how they'd gotten the personal code to his phone, but they clearly had. While he ran through the short list of people who knew it, he continued playing dumb. "I'm not sure what you mean."

The man yelled in Green's face, spit spraying from his mouth. "Your calendar says you had a meeting, then dinner!"

"I don't understand. I just said I did have dinner."

"And what about the meeting?"

"I, someone must have put that in my calendar. I don't know anything about it."

"So then you were not at the Brayburn Building yesterday having a meeting with Senator Stevens, the executive director of the AUVSI, someone from the FAA and FBI Special Agent Breskin? If that's not so, why did you sign into the building at 2:55 p.m.?"

The man threw the sign-in papers from the Brayburn Building at Green. He was utterly lost. How did they have that? The Brayburn was a government building. They had a secure entrance with armed guards. How could these people have gotten the registration forms? Who was this guy?

"I, I, I only met Senator Stevens there. We went to the restaurant from his office."

"You clearly take me for a fool, Mr. Green. I know what you did. I know who you met. I know everything. Everything. Don't make matters worse for yourself and your daughter by lying to me."

"No, sir. I won't, sir."

"Do you really expect me to believe you went to D.C. to have a dinner, then go home again. Why do you want me to hurt your daughter, Mr. Green?"

"Pardon?"

"Why do you want me to hurt your daughter? You do know we have her?"

Green's mind raced. The man had just admitted he had his daughter. Was she safe? Was she here? He had to stay calm. He told himself not to betray his feelings. Keep them silent. "My daughter is here?"

Green asked, feigning confusion.

"What have you been up to, Mr. Green?"

"Nothing. I told you I only had dinner."

"What was your meeting about? Did you discuss killing more of my people? You're a murderer, Mr. Green."

"What? I, who are your people?" Green asked, trying to remain in the circle and still get information at the same time.

"The people you kill with your company's robotic flying assassins."

"I don't kill people."

"Of course you do. And you started a long time ago. In Nicaragua, yes?" asked the man.

"Nicaragua?" repeated Green, now genuinely confused.

"Yes. Long ago. Before you bought General Atomics. When you were building your fortune on the backs of peasants on your Nicaraguan cocoa and banana plantation."

"What about –?" asked Green, completely taken off guard by the sudden change of direction and nearly stepping outside of the circle that Chauncey had taught him never to leave. He recovered. "I don't recall," he answered, not as convincingly as he would have liked.

"You don't recall Olga Sacasa? The poor thirteen-year-old girl that you raped, got pregnant and then had your despot friend, General Samoza, murder?"

Green stayed in the circle, applying the shield. "I don't know what you're talking about. I don't know what my company does. I just sign checks. That's all I do. I sign checks."

The man stopped and looked at Green. He smiled and nodded as he sat back down in his chair. "He only signs the checks," he said to himself then took a sip of cold water.

After a moment, he looked up. "Clearly you have been coached. And you are doing a remarkable job. But this is not a training exercise. Nobody is coming through that door to pat you on the back, say 'good job,' then hand you a cold Diet Coke to nurse your nausea. This is real, Mr. Green. We have your daughter, and we will kill her just like you killed my family. Yes, Mr. Green, my children are dead. Thousands of children are dead because of you!"

The speaker in the corner came to life with his daughter's pleading. "Help me, daddy. They're hurting me. Help me, daddy. I need you!"

The man screamed even louder and faster at Green over the recording of his daughter. "You are a murderer. Your drones kill my people every day. Now we will kill your daughter to show you how it feels."

Green struggled to maintain his composure. He breathed harder and harder as he thought of what he could do. Maybe they don't have her, he thought. And if they do, why kill her? She's the only leverage they have on me. He reasoned that the longer he fought them, the longer she would stay alive.

"What have you been up to, Mr. Green?!" the man screamed.

"I only write the checks," Green said.

The man jumped up and screamed into Green's face, "This is not a game."

He walked to the door and punched it hard. Green realized that he was getting to the guy. Frustrating him. He was glad because when one party gets emotional, that's the side that makes the mistakes. A moment later he realized he was wrong as another masked man entered wheeling a video cart with a monitor. The extension cord trailed out the door. Green's breathing became faster as he considered making a break for the door, but before he could even complete the thought, another man with a Kalashnikov moved into its frame, blocking any hope of exit.

"What was your meeting about, Mr. Green?" the man yelled.

"Dinner. It was just dinner," said Green out loud. Then to himself, "I can do this all day if I have to."

"Fine. Have it your way." The man flicked on the monitor instantly revealing that they not only had his daughter, but his wife as well. Stacey was in a small, dog cage and Iris was kneeling on the ground. Her hair was disheveled and her face was streaked with dirt. A man stood beside her with a machete. Both of the women were whimpering.

Green's mind went blank. He blinked fast, trying to take in what he was seeing. His breathing intensified and his muscles tightened. Without thinking, he lunged from his seat toward the man.

"You bastard!" he screamed. The man at the door grabbed Green from behind and held him tight.

"Yes, we have your wife, too. We will kill them both if you don't cooperate. Their lives are in your hands. What have you been up to, Mr. Green? Why do you kill my people?"

Green didn't know what to do. He began to cry. To plead. He croaked, "Please, they're innocent. Let them go."

"So too was my family innocent! They never even had a chance to beg like your precious wife and daughter. Slaughtered! Blown to pieces so small by your dishonorable missiles that there was nothing left to bury!"

"I'm sorry!" pleaded Green, weakly. "I'm sorry for your family. I didn't know. Please. My wife. My daughter. Let them go."

"You are sorry? For what? You just said 'I only write the checks.' Wrote the checks for what? To build a fleet of flying robots to rain bombs on my people? To bribe politicians and generals to keep an illegal war going so you could make money?"

"No," said Green.

"No, what?"

"I didn't."

"You didn't? Then shall I kill them?" he turned to the door and screamed in Arabic, "Kill them now."

"No, I did! I did!" yelled Green.

The man wheeled around. "Did what?"

Green ranted without any thought to what came out of his mouth. "Everything you said. I built unmanned assassins. I paid politicians to keep the war going. The meeting was about Panopticon!"

"And what about Olga Sacasa?"

"Yes. I raped her. I had her killed so that nobody would find out. I'm a murderer." I'm sorry. I'm sorry. Please don't kill my family. Please don't kill them. Please don't –" his voice trailed off weakly.

And just like that the man pulled off his mask, revealing it was Chauncey. He looked at Green and said the phrase he'd explained would mean a time out from the lesson. "It's time to see the dentist, mate. This has been an exercise."

The man at the door also removed his bandana, revealing it was Diddy. The man by the monitor was Phil. They were straight-faced and knew from personal experience how shaken up Green was feeling. Having gone through Chauncey's program years ago during their SEAL Team Six/JSOC training, they knew it well.

Phil turned off the monitor and wheeled it out of the room. Diddy remained at the door just in case Chauncey needed him. He had been completely broken, but some guys who were in Green's delicate position still freaked. Nobody knew how Green would react now that he knew the entire thing had been staged.

Chauncey spoke gently, yet firmly to Green. "Your family is safe. Your wife and daughter were never in any danger. They volunteered to do the tape because they understood it was being made to save your life. To help you stay strong."

Green remained silent. He blinked his eyes rapidly as his brain screeched and reversed, trying to comprehend what he'd just learned. His breathing was slowing down, getting under control. Phil returned with a blanket and a plastic cup filled with iced Diet Coke. He handed the soda to Green then covered him with the blanket.

Green nodded his thanks and took a small sip of the soda. The sweet, carbonated syrup coated his stomach. He looked at Chauncey, "Reicher –?"

"He's fine, mate. If you recall, you didn't see him get shot. You only heard the gunshots. He knew about the entire exercise. He wasn't crazy about it, but he'd signed an agreement like you had, so he went along. He's the one that gave you the ipecac in DC to get you vomiting."

"Even that was a setup?"

"Yes, sir. Everything that happened to you since you returned to your hotel from dinner last night was part of the exercise."

Chauncey gave Green a bit of time to soak in the reality. He knew that it was tough for most men. But for a man with Green's power and success, to know he'd been duped was especially difficult. Green shook his head, "It was so real. So real."

"Not as real as it could have been, mate. You could have been dead. And your family would have been dead for sure. You killed them as soon as you stepped out of the circle. Now let's review the past twenty-four hours, then get you ready for phase two of the exercise."

Green was visibly taken aback. "Phase two?"

"Now we get to the rough stuff."

Green shook his head. "Uh-uh. I'm done."

"I'd advise against that, Mr. Green. You did well in certain areas, but overall, you failed the exercise."

"I don't really care what you think, Captain. I said I'm done."

Chauncey took it in then said, "Okay. Well, at least we know one thing. You need to improve the security around your wife and daughter."

Chapter Fifteen

The 210-foot Coast Guard cutter "Baywatch" sliced its way through the Atlantic at a steady cruising speed of fifteen knots. Headed back to Boston after completing a stressful sixty-five day, multi-mission patrol in Florida, the one-hundred-member crew had earned a bit of well-deserved, shipboard unwinding. For Seaman Cassie Carroll, however, a movie and some beers didn't constitute sufficient unwinding. After spending over two months at sea, she was craving something more substantial. Something a bit more satisfying. Something to give her a smile that would last until they pulled into port. And she knew just how to get it.

Cassie had been sexually sparring with Gunner's Mate PJ Manning for at least six months. She knew he was attracted to her. That fact was no secret to anyone on the ship. Anytime Cassie walked near Manning, he would slap her butt, call her a whore and tell her how much he wanted to "do her." One time, while she was swabbing the mess hall, he approached her from behind and shoved his pants-constricted erection against her ass. He bit the back of her neck and panted, "I want you so bad." The surrounding crew, including Cassie, had laughed at his playfulness.

In uniform, most women weren't very attractive. The military establishment had intentionally designed the clothing with that in mind, and Cassie was no exception. A tomboy growing up, she had somewhat hard, masculine features with a chiseled jaw and high cheekbones. As per regulations, she wore her hair stuffed up inside a standard-issue watch cap. Her unflattering, operational dress uniforms weren't exactly found hanging in the "Come Fuck Me" section of Victoria's Secret. And the work boots definitely didn't exude that Sheena, Amazon Sex-Goddess feel. Still, some guys don't care what surrounds it. Pussy is pussy. PJ Manning was one of those guys and Cassie knew it.

After dinner, a raucous screening of "Captain Phillips," and some beer pounding, Manning had gone on duty patrolling the flight deck. Cassie knew that because he'd invited her to join him and patrol more than the ship. Nudge, nudge, wink, wink. She'd swatted his hand away from her tits for the hundredth time and said "no.' Verbally, that is.

As soon as Manning left, Cassie had beelined it to her room. She'd grabbed a special bag, then locked herself in the head. Ten minutes later, she stood on the flight deck behind the HH-60 Jayhawk looking like the whore Manning knew she was. Her blond hair had been set free and, although she still wore her Coast Guard cap, it now spilled out the back and sides. The moonlight reflected off of it, increasing her allure.

She'd put on a lacy, black push-up bra and kept the top three buttons of her shirt undone to accentuate her cleavage. Instead of tucking it in, Cassie had tied her shirttails around her very sexy, very flat stomach like a halter top. Below the shirt she wore only panties; Coast Guard blue, of course. And on her feet, she'd slid into a pair of shiny, patent leather pumps that DSW could have advertised as an alternative to Viagra. She was about to get the satisfaction she craved.

Manning was standing at the stern, smoking a Marlboro Red as Cassie approached him from behind.

"Your whore is here," she said in a silky voice.

Manning turned, and instantly a horny grin spread across his face. For a moment, in the strange night light, Cassie noticed that his pale skin and fat, red lips made his face look like a clown. He was practically drooling as he reached out to grab her. Before he could get a handful, Cassie spun him around so he faced the ship's frothing wake. She shoved her barely covered mound against him, then nibbled at the back of his neck. He shuddered.

"Stand on the rail," she whispered. "I want to grab you from behind."

"I knew you were a slut," he panted, as he eagerly complied.

The two steps up onto the rail were the last two steps that Gunner's Mate 2nd Class PJ Manning ever took. Once he was there, rather than reaching between his legs, Cassie simply shoved him overboard. She leaned over and watched as his screaming body slapped the water. A moment later, it was regurgitated by the cutter's massive propellers. Manning was now human chum. She began to laugh uncontrollably as she imagined his mangled body parts being ingested by sharks, then excreted all over the Atlantic.

Cassie's near maniacal laughs gave way to an explosion of tears as she repeated over and over, "It felt so good, it felt so good, it felt so good."

Dr. Kay Adams, MSW, sat and watched as the women in her military sexual trauma group jumped to their feet, screaming and clapping. They roared like female gorillas having a moment of primal catharsis to celebrate the victory of a member of their shrewdness. The women grabbed Cassie and hugged her screaming, "Hoo-ah!" "You go, girl!" "Dismissed that boy but good!" and other supportive chants. After a moment of celebration, the group settled down and retook their seats.

Cassie looked up at Dr. Adams, "So was that a good dream, doc?"

All the girls laughed as Dr. Adams nodded. "It was a very good dream, Cassie. You finally took control of your fear and embarrassment. You punished the man who violated you, and now you can begin healing."

This particular group had been coming to Dr. Adams' small office in Van Nuys, California, for nearly a year. All of them except for Cassie were living in shelters. Cassie was living at home. It was an improvement given they'd all been homeless when they'd first come to work with her. Every one of her patients was a veteran who had been raped or sexually assaulted by men in their units while serving in the US military. And while an outburst like they'd just had would never have happened in a civilian's sexual trauma group, these women were ex-soldiers.

Everyone in Dr. Adam's groups was a female vet who had signed up to fight for their country. They weren't prisses. They were tough, strong women who'd been betrayed by their fellow soldiers, their superior officers and in some cases, even their chaplains. Unfortunately, deemed by many to be an "occupational hazard," rape, sexual assault, and sexual harassment happened to over thirty percent of women in the armed services. And that was only the number of women who reported it; most didn't. Fear of retribution, recurrence, or dishonorable discharge deterred honesty. And those who did report it rarely got any satisfaction. As a matter of fact, the DoD's desire to keep it in the corps made the aftereffects worse.

Called MST, or Military Sexual Trauma by the VA, once out of the service, victims were given mind-numbing medications rather than therapy to help deal with it. That sweep-it-under the-rug mentality had led to suicides and thousands of homeless, drug, or alcohol-addicted female veterans. It was a national disgrace.

Dr. Adams looked around the room. Sabrina Ortiz had been raped by a serviceman in a latrine on a base in South Korea. When she'd gone to her commanding officer to report it, he raped her, too. Dichonte Johnson was raped in the shower by several other sailors while on patrol in a submarine. Jana Wayne was raped in her sleep while on post in Alaska. Joan Samson had been slipped a mickey, then gang-raped on her way to the infirmary.

Cassie had been raped while on a mission in the Coast Guard by PJ Manning. When she reported it to her CO, he reprimanded her for sleeping with a married man and accused her of adultery. Refusing to reassign her, the CO made Cassie work side-by-side with Manning for six more months. He raped her several more times during that period. When Cassie went to her chaplain, he'd told her that the rape was God's way of getting her back to Christ. Finally, she was discharged for being too unfit to serve.

Dr. Adams knew hundreds of stories like these, including her own. She was an expert on MST because she'd been raped in the service as well. She understood Cassie's dream because she'd had similar ones many times herself.

She'd grown up in Panorama City, California, a small city in the northern part of the San Fernando Valley with a large number of gangs. Her father, a single dad who had worked in explosives ordnance disposal for the Navy during the Vietnam War, now did demolition consulting for a construction firm. He couldn't stand the idea of his daughter falling in with a bunch of gangbangers, so he decided to give her a future by teaching her his craft. She was a natural, and by the time she graduated high school, did him proud by enlisting in the Navy to be an EOD technician herself.

In September 2003, Adams was sent to Iraq as part of a Joint Improvised Explosive Device Defeat Organization, or JIEDDO, unit to help with the increasing number of IEDs that were killing US troops during the growing Iraqi civil war. Stationed at Uday Hussein's palace in Adhinaya, Petty Officer Adams survived random firefights, RPG attacks, and snipers in her unit's mission to find and dispose of roadside bombs. She could never have anticipated that it would be one of her own that she should have feared the most. Although in hindsight, staying at the infamously brutal Hussein's palace was a harbinger of bad things to come.

Sergeant Skip McGovern was a mean bastard who had probably been a bully since birth. Everyone knew that he was a sadistic mother and his constant insults of women showed he was a misogynist to boot. There had been rumors that McGovern had raped and beaten several female recruits in basic, but as he was still in the Army and had been promoted several times, most everyone thought the stories were fiction.

To be on the safe side, Adams avoided him as much as possible. Even though she always dressed "ugly" and made it clear to him that she was a lesbian, he still made weekly, unwanted advances. Now that they were in one of the hottest, most deadly sections of Iraq, his advances seemed to stop. Until Thursday, October 12, 2004.

Their unit had returned from a grueling patrol where they'd found an IED near a mosque. They'd sent in the unit's PackBot to investigate the device, but the articulated arm had jammed when an unseen pothole caused it to roll on its side. Sergeant McGovern sent one of the grunts in to see what was wrong, but the bomber had been watching from a nearby building and detonated the bomb by cellphone as soon as the guy got close. He was dead and the PackBot was mangled.

Later that night, McGovern had gotten shit-faced drunk and started ragging on the dead soldier for being too slow.

"I'd give up all of you pukes to have a dozen of those bots," he slurred.

Still shaken from the incident, Adams had screamed at McGovern to shut his hole for being so insensitive. She got a fist in her face for her trouble. He looked down at her and spat, "I should've taken care of your squiddly dyke ass a long time ago."

He then dragged her to his quarters where he raped her. Adams had struggled but McGovern was much stronger, so she couldn't move. After he finished, he puked on her and passed out.

The next day she reported the incident to her unit commander and he suggested she was flirting with McGovern and, while inappropriate, he was probably just blowing off some steam from the horrible day. Adams didn't accept that and insisted on pressing charges. Her CO told her flat out to drop it.

"He's one of the best EOD guys we have. Not only that, he's a goddamned genius at rebuilding those PackBots. I need him, so just drop it."

Adams seethed, but realized there was nothing she could do. Especially since her CO had finished the conversation with a threat that if she took the incident anywhere else, she'd be hunting IEDs in parking lots all by herself. If the bomb didn't kill her, the snipers would.

Feeling betrayed by her commander and her fellow battle buddies, she tried to put it behind her. She could barely sleep and soon became more afraid of creaking floor boards than approaching explosions. She became a loner and refused to hang out with the unit after patrols. After about a month, she woke up in the middle of the night to find Sergeant McGovern on top of her in her bunk, raping her again.

Being a sailor, Adams did what she had to in order to survive. She'd grabbed her knife and sliced him across the face. Apparently McGovern nearly beat her to death because she woke up in a military hospital. She'd been physically mended, but less than honorably discharged.

Back in the states, with the help of her father, Adams tried to go through the proper channels with the DoD and the VA in reporting the rape. She got nowhere. The CO had never logged her complaint and when questioned about it, he'd stated that she was unstable and a trouble-maker. She was unfit to be in the Navy.

For six years Adams lived in a car or slept on the streets or under the Santa Monica pier. She couldn't sleep near people, including her father, because the trauma was so deep. Her father finally found her in an ER with extreme alcohol and cocaine poisoning. He got her into a newly formed VA program called Renew. In Long Beach, Adams lived with a dozen other women with MST for a twelve-week, intensive program that employed psychotherapy, journal writing, and yoga. When she came out of it, she enrolled at Cal State Northridge University and earned a master's degree of social work. She successfully got her less than honorable discharge reversed and began counseling disabled vets.

Dr. Adams looked at Cassie, then around the room at the group. Even though the session was ending on an all-too-rare high note, she knew the girls had a lot of work to do. She also knew that the odds were not in their favor. Of the 300-plus women she'd worked with personally, only a handful could hold down a job. Most of them would never have intimate relationships with their husbands or partners again.

Before she could close the session, the door opened and Special Agent Breskin entered. Like Osama Bin Ladin walking into a mess hall filled with Army Rangers, he quickly realized he'd made a mistake. The glares of the women were beyond unnerving.

Breskin defensively whipped out his badge. "Hi. Uh, I'm Special Agent Breskin, FBI. I called? Is Dr. Adams here?"

"Of course," said Dr. Adams. "I'll be with you in a moment."

Without missing a beat, the girls all stood up and hugged as a unit. The promise of family they'd been cheated out of by the armed services was here. They were sisters in pain. Sisters to the core, not the Corps.

"I'll see you all next week," said Dr. Adams. "Don't forget to journal and do yoga every day." Then she shot a wink at Cassie.

The girls left the office, parading past Breskin with harsh glares and a few hard shoulder shoves. Once gone, Breskin walked toward Dr. Adams.

"Well, that was awkward," he said and extended his hand to shake. Dr. Adams ignored the outstretched hand.

"I believe you wanted to discuss the drone pilot who committed suicide at the Hotel del Coronado?" she asked.

"I wouldn't exactly say that we're investigating a suicide, but I suppose we could add that to his list of transgressions," Breskin replied.

He quickly brought Dr. Adams up to speed on their investigation and what he knew about Solivan up to this point. Dr. Adams was being brought in because, besides being an expert in treating PTSD, she was outside of the VA system. She wasn't beholden to them and would therefore be able to lend the bureau her expertise in revealing information about broken veterans. Perhaps she'd even worked with some of Solivan's friends. Breskin hoped she could review the case and give him some insights as to places to look.

"We found a guy who might know him. He works for AeroVironment, a UAV manufacturer in Simi Valley. Since Solivan used robots to do his dirty work, there may be a connection," Breskin said, handing her a sealed manila envelope. "Some of his known associates will be at a get-together next week. Here's some information about the gathering and the guest list. Please go and interview some of them to see if you can get any information."

Breskin extended his hand again, but Dr. Adams didn't accept it this time either. Realizing the meeting was over, Breskin left without another word.

Dr. Adams' breathing became a bit more intense as she stared at the envelope. The sounds of cars driving on Balboa Boulevard melded with the droning of her struggling window air conditioning unit. She opened the envelope and pulled out an eight by ten photograph of a man with a long scar across his right cheek. She shuddered and as she continued staring at the picture of Skip McGovern. A single tear rolled down her cheek.

Chapter Sixteen

Many of the SERE instructors Chauncey had met and worked with over the years were excellent at what they did. Like him, they viewed themselves not as interrogators or torturers, but as teachers and, in many cases, lifesavers. The darkness in which they forced their students was only done so they could hold onto the light through the worst possible enemy situations. That was something handed down from the program's creator, Nick Rowe, a man who'd been through five years of the worst torment the Viet Cong could throw at him.

Unfortunately, the sad fact was that there were also a lot of interrogators who were sadists looking to take their rage out on anyone they could. In part that was because holding the power of life and death over human beings brought out the primal part of most men. It was also because the DoD, in its infinite lack of wisdom, had allowed ex-POWs to take the helm of many SERE programs. The reasoning was "who better to teach the techniques than those who'd been exposed to them, and survived?" It was the term "survived" to which Chauncey took exception, though. Survival entails a lot more than just living and getting home with a still beating heart.

Whether it was us or them, the victims of torture, or enhanced interrogation techniques as most Americans call it when *we* do it, never come out unscathed. And no dosage of SSRIs or antipsychotic drugs could reverse that. Time, perhaps, was the only hope. But few survivors lived long enough; many of them choose a fast gun in the mouth or a longer, more self-destructive path to liver failure as their fates. Hopefully, thought Chauncey, the ones who lived wouldn't bring their pain with them to the next life, whatever that might be.

It was even hard on the interrogators. The incidence of PTSD among the agents at Gitmo, Abu Ghraib, and the other places where they'd plied their inquisitional skills was among the highest in all of the armed services. Guilt, nightmares, drug abuse, and alcoholism were forever pinned to their chests, the only lasting medals they'd received for their mostly futile efforts.

The effects hadn't been that much different for Chauncey. Having trained six CEOs in two weeks, he was a wreck. And he had one more to do starting that evening. It didn't matter that his goal was to teach survival. Once you've slithered into the asp-filled pit of human despair, no amount of light could help you shed its dark, scaly skin. That may have been one of the reasons he loved skydiving so much. The jump plane brought him closer to heaven, both literally and figuratively.

While Green's interrogation training session had been one of the most painful to watch, none of them had done particularly well. Chauncey wasn't surprised. They weren't soldiers, much less special ops troops who'd signed up and trained to endure the worst that mankind could dish out. They'd never truly been subjected to SERE levels A through C, so they were destined to fail from the start. Chauncey knew that Breskin was aware of the risks. They'd taught SERE and been field interrogators together. They'd shattered a lot more than bones. Even though he'd argued that more time and finesse were needed, Breskin had vetoed him. Time was mission critical.

"Just give them whatever skills you can, and fast. Internet chatter is increasing," Breskin had said.

So Chauncey had done his best, which was saying something. But after each session he would go skydiving to cleanse himself. He hoped the 120 mph wind would wash away some of the memories of their shared pain.

"More tea, hon?" asked Deb, gesturing to Chauncey's empty cup with her silver pot of boiling water.

"Oh, yes. Love some," Chauncey smiled back.

The "Devil Drone" coffee shop at El Mirage Airport was one of thousands of dive restaurants where small plane pilots hung out to swap flying stories, mechanical ideas, and inside aviation jokes over greasy eggs and hash browns. Most of them had names like "The Bent Prop," "The 49th Aerosquadron" or, Chauncey's favorite, "The Hard Landing." Recently renamed because of all the UAV activity in the area, the Devil Drone's walls now sported framed prints of Predators alongside B-52s and F-16s.

"It's a different goddamned world, for sure," said George, who sat at the counter to Chauncey's left. An old Korean War, Naval F2H Banshee pilot, George had achieved the ripe-old age of ninety-two. He was one of those guys who never seemed to slow down. It had to be good genetics because he still ate fried foods, loved to ogle women, and poured bourbon in his coffee. Because of his poor eyesight, he wasn't allowed to fly anymore, but he still loved being around the veteran's community and venting to anyone who'd listen. Chauncey had heard some of his racist rants before, and because of his respect for George's service, never quarreled.

"Drones replacing bombers and fighters? It's not right," George spouted, pulling at his still full head of once black, but now white, hair. "And give me a break. How the hell can those drone operators claim to be pilots? They're just goddamned video gamers who don't know nuthin' about nuthin'."

George was referring to an article he'd just read about giving medals to drone pilots. He was one of a dying breed of Air Force pilots and didn't like it one bit. To him and many others, pilots were the crème de la crème. Officers and gentlemen. They were elite, educated soldiers who understood the repercussions of what they did. Above all, rather than sitting safe and snug in some stateside trailer, they risked their lives.

"But they sure as shit are great for killing the enemy. I just don't know what we're doing with all this pinpoint strike crap. Just strap a few nukes on those robot birds and take out all the Arabs at once. Then wait a couple of years and go take the oil. No muss, no fuss. Just don't give a medal to the trigger puller who squeezes off a round, then goes home for dinner, and call him a pilot is all I'm saying. Goddamned video gamers don't know nuthin' about nuthin'."

"Give it a rest, George," said Deb with a slight nod of her head toward Chauncey.

"Ah relax, honey." he spat back. "Chauncey's a vet. He knows what I'm talking about."

"He's just too polite to tell you to shut up. Not everybody wants to hear the pollution that comes spewing out of your mouth."

Chauncey liked Deb a lot. An overweight blond with a beautiful smile, she'd been a waitress here for over twenty-five years. She was poor, but not bitter about it and was a great listener. Great because she heard more than just the words. Deb had known George for as long as she'd been waitressing and even though they weren't what you'd call social friends, they were both locals and had definite opinions about the massive changes that had taken root in their "white" desert town.

Deb's main complaint was that crime was getting worse. And although he never ran out of things to complain about, George's main gripe was that the valley was being overrun by "towel-heads," "jiggaboos," and "crack-headed gangbanger wetbacks." While it was mostly a racist rant, he wasn't too far off. Over the past decade the UAV boom had created a lot of new jobs. Aerospace and the military were drawing engineers and more "pilots." It was also creating employment for minimum wage workers, thus the influx of Mexicans and other minorities. Surprisingly, there had also been an increase in the number of Syrian immigrants. Hookah shops, convenience stores, and Mediterranean restaurants were widespread.

"Thanks, Deb," said Chauncey as she gave him a fresh bag of Lipton tea to dip into his now steaming cup of water. Then, regarding George, "Everyone's entitled to their opinion."

"Damned right," snorted George. "I was shot down over The Iron Triangle! Put a survival knife through a chink's eye who was fixin' to capture me. Saw a hundred guys get shot right around me. I earned the right to speak my mind."

"Absolutely," said Chauncey.

"So what kind of gear you got there?" asked George, changing the subject. He was pointing at Chauncey's repacked chute. "I'm guessing it's one of those square chutes with girly colors. When we dropped into Inchon we were just fine packing a round parachute. We didn't need no reserves."

Knowing that George was trying for the hundredth time to goad him into a fight, Chauncey gave him a grin. "Well, you know what we say, mate: Round will get you down, but square will get you there."

George made a face, not knowing how to retort. Not wanting to give up, however, he said, "'Mate'? What are you some kind of a goddamned kangaroo —" but before he could get out the words, he stopped cold. As he stared at the front door, a look of abject hatred crossing his face. "Aw jeez, here's one of those American Talibans that are infesting us like fleas on a camel."

Chauncey looked toward the door and was very surprised to see that Armagan had walked in. Wanting to spare him any indignities from George's racist rants, he stood up.

"Excuse me, mate. Been nice chatting with you, but I'm going to hippity-hop myself to my friend over there." And with that, Chauncey quickly moved away from a slack-jawed George and shook Armagan's hand. He knew he'd hear about it the next time.

"Fancy meeting you here," said Chauncey. "Probably the last place I'd have expected to see you."

"Greetings, Captain Paunce," said Armagan, a warm smile filling his face. "I live in Adelanto. GA has set me up with a sweet lab, and I use their airstrip at Gray Butte for my testing. I like the solitude of the desert. People leave me alone here." He nodded toward the counter where George and Deb were staring at them. "Will you join me for a cup of tea?"

"Absolutely," said Chauncey. "But first, all of my friends call me Chauncey. And second, I think we'd be more comfortable at a table."

"As you wish, Mr. Chauncey. I'm not such a huge fan of George, myself."

The two men moved to a table near the long, panoramic window overlooking the airport's single runway. As soon as they were seated Deb was there with a clean teacup for Chauncey, a glass for Armagan and two metal containers of hot water. She gave Chauncey a white dish filled with Lipton tea bags, then turned to Armagan.

"You all set, as usual, hon?"

"Yes. Thank you, Miss Deborah."

"You're welcome. Milk's in the container," she added before turning and walking away.

Before Chauncey had a chance to open his teabag, Armagan pulled out a small, beautifully etched, teak box.

"I see you're a tea man, Mr. Chauncey. Would you care to try a blend I've made?"

"You've made?" asked Chauncey.

"Oh yes. One of the few things I brought with me from Afghanistan is my love of tea. Everyone drinks tea there. I'm not a genetic scientist, but I would not be surprised to learn that Afghanis have a 'tea' gene."

Armagan slid the top out of the box revealing a mixture of dried herbs and tea leaves. The smell of cinnamon and cloves enveloped the table. Chauncey watched as Armagan then opened a small, mesh tea ball and filled it with a couple of pinches of the mixture from the box.

"It's a traditional masala chai," he said. "Cinnamon bark, cloves, crushed cardamom seeds and Darjeeling tea. Some people like to add jasmine, but I find that makes it too perfumy." He closed the ball, put it into Chauncey's cup then filled it with hot water from the silver container. "At home I would make it differently, but for here this should suffice."

Chauncey knew from his time in Afghanistan how large a part of life chai was there. Afghanis drank tea all day long, generally, molten hot from a glass while sitting on the ground. They were one of the most polite cultures he'd ever experienced. Afghanis treated strangers as honored guests in their homes, offering them a seat at the head of the table, giving them their best, and sometimes only food, and filling their cups with tea until it was turned over to say you'd had enough. As an interrogator, he had needed to understand the culture of those he'd questioned, and of the hundreds he'd studied. Afghanistan's culture was one of his favorites.

"So what brings you to this place in the middle of nowhere?" Armagan asked while the tea steeped.

"Well, coincidentally, I happen to live here."

"Really? What a small world. And are you a pilot? Is that why you're here at the Devil Drone?"

"I am a pilot of sorts. But I just got dropped off by a friend." He patted his rig and pointed up. "And I mean *dropped off*."

"That's wonderful! You must be the reason that I had to circle the desert for fifteen minutes. I heard the NOTAM about someone skydiving and wondered. Do you know, I've always wanted to try it."

"I'd be more than happy to teach you," said Chauncey.

Armagan shook his head. "Wanting and doing are very different things. I'm not so sure I could ever bring myself to leap from a perfectly functioning aircraft. Not to mention that I would be afraid of —" Then patting his prosthetic leg with a smile, "having trouble with my landing gear."

Chauncey laughed. He knew from the moment he'd met Armagan in San Diego that he liked him. "What about you? Are you a pilot?"

"Yes. I've just returned from meetings in San Diego. I have a small plane for commuting. It was one of the conditions of my deal. She's right out there."

Armagan pointed out the window to a parked Cessna 206 Caravan. Chauncey was amazed. The 206 was a high-altitude, turbo prop plane extremely popular for small skydiving schools. Besides being able to seat six passengers, the 206 had a jump door on the side. His buddy, Killa, owned two of them.

"You have a jump plane but you don't jump?" asked Chauncey.

Armagan explained that because of his leg, getting in and out of small cabins was awkward. He'd had the 206 modified by removing the middle row and co-pilot seats so he could get in and out more easily.

"I consider it my air limousine," he smiled.

Armagan plucked the tea ball from Chauncey's cup. "I drink mine with sugar and milk, but you may drink it as you'd like."

"Hey, when in Adelanto," said Chauncey.

As Armagan prepared another cup for himself, Chauncey tore open a white packet of sugar and poured the crystals into his cup along with some milk. He stirred the tea then lifted it up and inhaled before taking a sip.

"Delicious, mate." Then, "Cheers."

Armagan nodded as he watched Chauncey take a sip. The steaming, sweet chai coated his tongue and warmed his throat and stomach as he swallowed.

"I'll never be able to drink Lipton again. Thank you."

"I'm delighted that you like it. I'd be honored to make some for you to take."

Chauncey took another slow sip as he considered the gentle man sitting across from him. In his wildest imagination he couldn't fathom how someone who'd met with such tragedy could be so warm and gracious. Especially to the people who'd killed his family and continued to decimate his homeland with drone attacks. He noticed that Armagan was studying him as well. Neither man spoke. It was an easy, comfortable silence.

"So do you like living in America?" Chauncey finally asked.

"Yes, I like it very much. Your country has so much to offer. So many opportunities for someone willing to embrace them. I must say that most of you Americans take this for granted."

"You're a remarkable guy, Armagan. No disrespect, but to forgive us after what we did to your family – amazing."

"For me, the past is the past." He closed his eyes and paused for a moment before continuing. "Certainly I miss my family and my friends," he then said. "And I will say that there is probably some anger still alive inside me somewhere. But my adopted father taught me that dwelling on things that cannot be undone is unproductive. So I choose to focus on the present."

"Good on you, mate," Chauncey smiled.

"But what about you? Do you like America?" asked Armagan. "It may have murdered my parents, but this country certainly destroyed your life as well, no? Actually, given that you are a citizen, it would seem to me that you have endured an even larger betrayal."

Chauncey's pale Irish face turned beet red. This guy cut right to the chase. He knew that Armagan was talking about his fall from grace within the defense and intelligence communities. But he was surprised that Armagan possessed the knowledge. Of course it wasn't exactly secret information. Chauncey's revelations were all over the Web. Even though it had happened over a half dozen years ago, his interviews could be seen and read on the sites of CNN, *The Guardian, The New York Times,* and the one that started it all, Eyesopen.org.

Depending on whom you spoke with, being a whistleblower was either a badge of honor or a scarlet letter. He'd given going public with what he knew a lot of thought. It meant losing his rank, his pension and two years of his life in a military prison. Branded a traitor by the country he'd done his best to protect was more than heart-breaking. It was a total destruction of the soul.

Destined to share the history books' pages and websites with the likes of Edward Snowden, Bradley Manning, John Kiriakou, and the other truth-tellers was something that would be Chauncey's fate. Yet he'd known that and still decided that the things he'd seen and been asked to do were wrong. Criminally wrong. Oaths and time-tested codes had been broken. Laws ignored. People's lives destroyed. Although it had cost him dearly, the secrets that he brought to the public were vital. Yes, he'd suffered for bringing them to light, but the truth had set him and many others free.

Whether he would do it again was a question he tortured himself with every day. He wanted to believe the answer was a resolute "yes." The fact that he'd never told George or Deb about it, however, showed his mixed feelings.

"When I got out of prison," Chauncey explained, "most of my mates understood that what I said was true. And most of them agreed that it should never have happened. Sadly, most of them disagreed with me for coming forward. They hold to the belief that 'we're paid to do a job, then shut the hell up about it.' We all make decisions that we have to live with. Until recently, the ones I made were destroying me. But I'm happy to say that things are looking up."

"Agreed," said Armagan. "Sometimes the things we do for the right reasons turn out to be very painful to us and to those around us. Nevertheless, in the end we must be true to our own inner sense of justice."

"I admire you, Mr. Chauncey. I look at your country and see that its phenomenal past is at risk of being wiped out by its horrendous present and uncertain future. People like you are rare heroes and should be celebrated for making difficult choices."

Chauncey nodded. They were kindred spirits. He lifted his teacup. "To difficult choices."

"To doing what you have to do," said Armagan.

He wasn't sure why, but something about the way Armagan said those last words made the hair on Chauncey's neck prickle. He contemplated the man as he took another sip of the chai.

Chapter Seventeen

Thirty-six hours later Chauncey found himself standing on the helipad of Palmdale Regional Medical Center watching the medevac chopper leave with the CEO of AeroVironment. He shielded his face with his arm as the propeller wash pelted him with gravel and dirt. After the bird had moved away, Chauncey went to shake Dr. Craig Shalmi's hand.

"Thanks for taking such good care of him, mate. He's got you to thank for getting him in that chopper alive."

Dr. Shalmi shook Chauncey's hand back. "You're welcome," he said. "But your triage was more responsible than anything I did. Without your actions, he never even would have made it here."

Chauncey walked with Dr. Shalmi and the two hospital orderlies toward the elevator. Shalmi stared at him as one of the orderlies pressed the button to summon the car. He hadn't had a chance to ask any questions since going into surgery over three hours ago. He knew a sixty-seven-year-old Caucasian male had arrived at the emergency room in a white freezer truck after having a massive coronary. The man was wearing an adult diaper, had bruises, cuts, and scrapes over most of his body, and was muttering, "I just sign the checks. I just sign the checks." Chauncey and two other menacing-looking men had rushed the patient into the ER on a makeshift stretcher and demanded a cardiac surgeon stat.

As soon as Dr. Shalmi and his surgical team had stabilized the man, he'd been informed that the patient was to be transported to Cedars-Sinai Medical Center in Los Angeles. Everything else had been shrouded in secrecy.

The elevator doors slid open and the men stepped inside. Chauncey knew that the doctor and the others who'd been involved had a thousand questions. He also knew that none of them would be answered. Not by Chauncey, at any rate. The orderly hit the button marked M and the door closed.

Dr. Shalmi considered Chauncey for a moment. His cheekbones pulsed as he nervously clenched and unclenched his jaw. He hadn't said anything the entire time they'd been together other than the recent show of gratitude. And even though it was completely against hospital protocol, he'd stood in the operating room watching the procedure from start to finish. Nobody had even objected. He'd just had a look that said he wasn't someone to be messed with. Shalmi considered asking Chauncey who the man was and what had happened, but resigned himself to his ignorance. The elevator car moved downward as the four men listened to the gnashing metal gears that controlled its descent.

When the doors finally opened on the main floor, Chauncey said, "Thanks again for your good work. Good on you, mate."

He started for the lobby exit, but before he got there a half-dozen Palmdale police officers moved in from around the corner. One of the men, a tall, neatly shaved man, stood directly in front of Chauncey. They surrounded him, hands touching their still holstered, yet unstrapped weapons.

"I'm Captain Dan Brown, sir. Palmdale PD. Are you one of the men who brought Mr. Paulson to the hospital?"

Chauncey looked around, taking in the situation. "So they figured out who he is," he thought to himself. "So much for a graceful departure."

Even though it was a desert hospital, Palmdale Medical Center still had its fair share of action. Mostly minor accidents, babies being born, strokes, and other routine procedures. Anything serious got referred to San Diego or Los Angeles hospitals. Right now the lobby was filled with families, patients, nurses, and others. They were staring at Chauncey. Not only staring, many were aiming the cameras on their smartphones to document the excitement.

He figured that whatever the outcome with the police, within minutes his face would be plastered all over the Internet. They'd be texting, posting, and tweeting him all over the cyberworld.

He'd never quite gotten the social media bug. Chauncey couldn't understand the fascination that people had with publicizing their most intimate moments. Technology was bad enough when it came to gathering data and invading people's privacy, but to give it up willingly? That was just nuts.

In addition to the six officers who were now sharing his present five minutes of fame, there were another half-dozen outside. Six squad cars, lights on, were parked in the traffic circle leading to the front door. Officers stood behind their cars, weapons drawn.

Chauncey looked at Captain Brown. "So his name is Paulson, huh? I didn't know him. My friends and I were driving along and saw him lying on the side of the road. We just figured he needed some help."

"He sure did," said Captain Brown. "You guys apparently saved his life. Good job."

"Glad I could help. Bye now," said Chauncey and tried to walk away. The officers quickly drew closer, blocking him in. Two of them drew their sidearms, keeping them low and close.

"I'm afraid I'll have to ask you some questions for my report, sir. Sorry, I didn't get your name," said Captain Brown.

"That's because I didn't give it to you, mate. Am I under arrest for something?" Chauncey remained polite, but he wasn't thrilled that now there were guns out.

"Not yet, you're not. Mr. Paulson had some other injuries that the hospital staff noticed which is why they called us. His wrists were badly bruised and cut from what looked like very tight handcuffs. And he had a couple of Taser darts stuck in his chest. You wouldn't happen to know anything about that would you?"

Chauncey sized Captain Brown up. He seemed like a good sort. Blond, late thirties, in good shape, solid posture, and steady, cold, blue eyes. Definitely a formidable kind of guy. He was also staying calm, outwardly, at any rate, which was the best thing to do given that he didn't know who Chauncey was or what he was capable of doing. With a hospital lobby filled with civilians, calm was the order of the day.

"I'm afraid not," Chauncey shrugged. "Like I said, we found him on the side of the road and just did that good Samaritan thing. Now if that's all, I'd really like to go home."

He didn't want any trouble. All he needed was for the media to find out that the FBI had hired him to kidnap and torture CEOs. What with all the revelations of NSA wiretapping, the constant fear of domestic terrorism, and the still unsolved massacre in San Diego, the country was already on a thin edge. He looked at some of the cellphone cameras and figured that right now this was still a tiny, local thing. Going national was unacceptable.

"That is not all, sir. Not by a long shot." Brown quickly stepped back and withdrew his weapon. "Cuff him," he said to one of his officers.

Chauncey really did just want to go home. He wanted to chill out with some Kine Mine and chai because torturing people really gave him a headache. Instinctively, his subconscious played out a number of high-risk escape scenarios. He could easily grab the officer's weapon and use him as a hostage to escape. He could grab Dr. Shalmi, who was standing way too close for his own good. He could run through the crowd of visitors and patients to the door in the back of the lobby, knowing that no shots would be fired. Or he could simply let them cuff him and then get away en route to the police department. Spying a little boy peeking at him from behind his mother's leg, he calmly extended his wrists.

"That won't be necessary, officer," said Breskin as he entered the lobby, his badge displayed in its leather case. "FBI. Tell your men to stand down."

Nobody moved as Brown examined Breskin's creds. "He a good guy or a bad guy?" he asked, gesturing to Chauncey.

Breskin casually folded up his badge and returned it to his jacket pocket. He looked at the other cops then leaned into Brown's face. "He's a none-of-your-business guy. Now you and your men just go back to chasing tarantulas or whatever it is you do here. The situation is under control," said Breskin, displaying his uncanny ability to forge instant lifelong friendships.

Brown bristled at the insult, but nodded to his officers who then secured their weapons and started toward the exit. He took a last glance at Chauncey who indicated himself with his thumb and mouthed the words, "good guy."

Breskin turned to Chauncey, "We need to talk."

"Indeed," Chauncey shot back.

Breskin led Chauncey out of the lobby's main doors toward the parking lot. Chauncey could feel the smartphone cameras struggling to keep him in frame. Breskin stayed a couple of feet ahead as they approached his parked Jag. The doors unlocked with a chirp from his remote key lock.

"Get in," he said, as he opened the driver's door and slid into his leather seat.

"Nice ride," said Chauncey as he closed the door. "I've never been in such luxury."

"Yeah, whatever," said Breskin. "I want to know what happened. Why is Neil Paulson, the CEO of the drone maker that supplies 85 percent of the DOD's mini UAVs on his way to Cedars?"

"He had a heart attack, and I didn't think that letting him die was part of the plan. That's what happened."

"Thanks. How'd he get it?"

Chauncey shrugged. "I tasered him at the SAFE spot during recapture. Nobody told me the guy had a pacemaker. That information would have been nice."

"Great. Just great," said Breskin, clearly perturbed.

"Hey, you know the program better than anybody. You got this car because you repackaged SERE and made beaucoup bucks selling it to the Bush White House, so don't act like a shocked schoolgirl."

Chauncey proceeded to brief Breskin on the session. He explained how they'd abducted Paulson while he was mountain-biking in the canyons by his house in Agoura Hills. They'd put him through the paces like the other CEOs, but even though he had no military training and was the oldest of the group, he'd held strong. He was the only one who figured out it was Chauncey, and that it was part of the exercise from the beginning. He'd kept saying that they needed to "step it up" if they wanted to get anything out of him. So they had.

He'd spent twenty-four hours in solitary with sensory deprivation gloves and blacked-out goggles. Chauncey had threatened to rape his wife, his sons, and even his granddaughter. They'd used stress positions and exploited his phobia about fire by piping in black, acrid smoke, but nothing fazed him.

Finally, they'd chained him to the ground in the basement and made him watch preparations for his own waterboarding. The guard, played by Phil, had assumed the role of a Mexican drug dealer whose own family was going to be executed if he failed to break the man. Phil had slowly and meticulously set up the bench, chains, and buckets of water. He'd described how they were going to strap Paulson's body down with straps so tight they'd cut off his circulation, tilt him backward, and shove a filthy sack in his mouth. They were then going to pour an ocean of water over his face. That he would inhale the water into his lungs, and it would slowly begin to shut down his nervous system. While Phil prepared, they'd even forced Paulson to watch the hundred-plus waterboarding sessions of Abu Zubaydah at Gitmo.

Paulson had stayed in the circle the entire time, never giving an inch. Just when Chauncey was going to call the exercise over, he'd escaped.

"How'd an old man get away from you and two ex-SEALs?" asked Breskin, truly fascinated.

"It was impressive," said Chauncey. "He was the only guy who picked up the paper clip that I dropped accidentally on purpose from my paperwork during one of the interrogations. He picked the lock while Phil wasn't looking, then when he was being led to the bench for waterboarding, he knocked Phil out with a stool."

By the time Phil had regained consciousness, Paulson was gone. Chauncey followed his trail to one of the SAFE spots they'd briefed all the men about in their initial sessions. Whether it had been panic, adrenaline, anger, or what, when Chauncey arrived, Paulson attacked him with a huge rock. So Chauncey zapped him.

"Jesus," said Breskin, uncharacteristically invoking the name of the Heavenly Father outside of the LDS sanctuary. "I'm going to get an earful over this one."

"Can't help you there, mate. But as Bush II so famously and inaccurately put it: Mission Accomplished. Your CEOs are SERE'd. Now there's a small matter of my final payment."

Breskin gestured to the back seat where there was a plain brown briefcase. Chauncey grabbed it, snapped open the gold hinges, then lifted the cover. He'd never seen a million dollars before, but there it was: a million bucks, neatly stacked, and wrapped in one hundred dollar bills. There was so much of it, the scent filled the car. He sat back and whistled. "There really is money in torture," he thought to himself.

"May I take it that my record has been cleared? That my dishonorable discharge has been reversed and my pension reinstated? Not that I need it now," he added looking at the cash.

"As far as the FBI and the Department of Defense are concerned, you are a new man."

Chauncey closed his eyes. This moment had been a long time coming. But just as he started mentally planning how he would skydive his way around the world, Breskin continued.

"Unfortunately, as far as the DoD's *contractors* are concerned, you're a problem."

"A problem how?" asked Chauncey, snapping the briefcase closed.

Breskin casually explained that the CEOs who had worked with Chauncey were nervous about what he now knew about them. That with all the personal and professional information he possessed, he posed a serious threat.

"I suppose they'll just have to trust that I'm a professional who got paid to do a job. Now that job is over."

"I told them that. Unfortunately, you're also a convicted whistleblower so it wasn't good enough."

Breskin pulled a red, wrapped candy from the pocket of his sport jacket. He casually untwisted the cellophane that covered it. For Chauncey, the obnoxious crinkling was like chalk on a blackboard. Breskin clacked the candy against his front teeth a few times then popped it into his mouth.

Every sinew in Chauncey's body twitched. So much of his past troubles had emanated from the man sitting beside him. His brain tracked back to the day Breskin drove down his driveway. He should have killed him then and there. He looked at Breskin who sat calmly to his left. He noted the easy thumping of his pulmonary artery in his neck. It took the summoning of every tool he'd ever learned to squelch the fury that was trying to bulldoze over his better judgment.

"I only spoke the truth," Chauncey finally said.

"That, my friend, is precisely what they are worried about. So I asked myself what they possibly could have revealed to you that would make them so anxious. As a group, I mean." Breskin looked at Chauncey, expectantly.

"To be honest, I don't really know what they're worried about," said Chauncey. "They didn't tell me anything other than some fairly twisted sexual stories." But in his mind, the word "Panopticon" took on a greater significance than ever. Each one of the CEOs had said that word just before they'd broken off their sessions. Chauncey had expected to hear it from Paulson during his interrogations, but hadn't, so he'd dismissed it. That is right up until the man's heart attack. While Chauncey had been delivering mouth-to-mouth and CPR, Paulson had said that and more.

"We're killing them. Panopticon," he'd mumbled.

"So now what?" Chauncey asked looking down at the briefcase. "You arrest me on some trumped up charges and stick me in a Supermax for the rest of my life?"

"I know you'll find this difficult to believe, Paunce, but I'm on your side. I brought you into this, so I don't want to see you get hurt. But I would highly recommend that you give me the tapes from the interrogation sessions just in case."

"In case what?"

"They're powerful men who make powerful weapons. If they know the FBI has the tapes, then you'll be insignificant."

Breskin smiled at Chauncey. His teeth were red from the dye in the candy.

"If I give you the tapes, then I am a whistleblower because no matter what you say, I still don't trust you one bit."

"I'm just trying to protect you, Paunce. If those guys decide you're toast then there's nothing the FBI or that million dollars will be able to do. I highly recommend you reconsider."

"I'll take my chances," said Chauncey. "Good on you, mate," he said, not really meaning it. He got out of the car with the briefcase and strode away.

Chapter Eighteen

Al-Wahiri and his mujahedeen drove through the Afghanistan countryside, the white mountains of Pakistan rising in the near distance. They'd been called to join a large group of freedom fighters to attack the invaders near the caves of Tora Bora. It was their sacred duty to save The Sheik from the infidels.

Because they knew the roads were being closely monitored by the satellites and American drones, the band drove northward across the barren valley that had once been fertile farmland. None of the men held weapons, and some of them even wore burkas just in case they were spied from above. Their Toyotas bounced over the dirt and rocks that once were thriving wheat, potato, and melon farms, the glory of Afghanistan's farmers.

The Afghani agricultural community had been all but destroyed by over two decades of drought, wars, and Moroccan locusts. But of those three, al-Wahiri knew that the most nefarious by far was the locust. When that 1,000-year-old plague descended, day turned into biblical night and every plant in its path was consumed. A swarming cloud of locusts could devour a field of potatoes or melons in less than four hours. Flying and hopping as if a single eating machine, they were like a moving carpet that consumed the very earth itself.

During their occupation, the Russians had given the local farmers technology and powerful pesticides to deal with the insect hordes. It had helped, and during their brief reign, farms, at least, had flourished. As their grasp on power had been worn down by the relentless onslaught of freedom fighters, the Soviets withdrew both their armies and their assistance. With their retreat, the hungry locusts returned.

The farmers did their best to combat them, but they were ordered to stop. Once again in power, the Taliban had forbidden the farmers from killing the locusts. "They are God's creatures," the mullahs had said. "These are living creatures created by Allah and should not be killed; for Allah alone is charged with giving food." So for many years, the insects were the only ones with full bellies.

Al-Wahiri's cellphone chirped, alerting him that it was time for afternoon prayer. He signaled the others with a single beep of his horn and they all parked beneath the quasi-shelter of long-dead trees. al-Wahiri and the others ritualistically unfurled and cleaned their prayer rugs. They said their ablutions and knelt down, facing Mecca.

As he recited his praise of Allah and touched his forehead to his rug, al-Wahiri felt the ground stirring beneath him. Thinking that perhaps it was a sign of approaching vehicles, he lifted his head and looked around. Relieved to see no approaching clouds of dirt, he looked back down to resume his prayers.

Before he restarted, he saw that his prayer rug was rippling. It was undulating as if something beneath it was moving around. Just then, one of his men began to scream. He looked to his left and saw the man covered from head to toe with locusts. He was running and screeching in panic. Within seconds, the man succumbed and fell under the heavy blanket of insects. Simultaneously, all the other men in his company were covered with insects and screaming.

Al-Wahiri looked back at his rug and cautiously lifted a bit of the front edge to see what was there. A rush of locusts leaped out from beneath it and covered his body. Like a swarm of bees or ants converging on their prey, the locusts coated every inch of al-Wahiri's body like a new layer of flesh. They bit and stabbed. They clawed and sawed their legs against his skin.

He jumped up to run, but quickly fell to the ground as hundreds of locusts forced their way into his nose and mouth. The locusts crawled down his throat into his lungs. The swarm ate al-Wahiri and his men from the inside and the outside. And within minutes, nothing remained in the field but jeeps, prayer rugs, and skeletons.

Armagan lurched awake, screaming and covered with sweat. He instinctively jumped to his feet, swiping to rid nonexistent bugs from his body. After a second or so, he realized that it had been a nightmare. The same horrifying dream had recurred since his childhood. After he calmed down, he saw that he'd fallen asleep at his desk while working. His cup of tea sat cold in front of him.

At first Armagan had hated the nightmares. Locusts were a fear he'd had since he'd seen the devastation that the voracious insects had caused to his uncles' farms as a child. He could still feel their crunching under his feet and bouncing against his legs as he walked through fields, still visualize the clouds of insects that moved across the horizon.

His psyche had apparently merged his fear with his hatred and caused it to create a nightly catharsis. He had understandably hated the nightmares. But with time, he'd not only came to realize it offered him the vengeance over al-Wahiri that he would never know, but it had also given him a direction in life. Obsessed with the power of swarming insects, while his friends in Anaheim had spent their days playing soccer and cruising to the beach to body board and surf, one-legged Armagan had stayed inside, studying bugs and growing angrier at his fate.

He'd read every book he could get his hands on that explained the power of swarming insects. He'd studied the complex group behaviors of nature's most pernicious bugs: fire ants, yellow jackets, army ants, Africanized honey bees, and, of course, locusts.

That obsession had melded with his love of engineering, specifically robotics, and he became interested in finding ways to make technology imitate and maybe even improve on nature. Fortunately for Armagan, the field of nanorobotics, led by DARPA and the DoD, was equally obsessed.

Now, ten years later, Armagan was the head of General Atomic's top secret research arm called "Hornet's Nest." While many of his peers at Stanford, MIT, and Carnegie Mellon had focused on creating microbots that could help pollinate fields or cure disease, he'd focused on harnessing that power for revenge.

Armagan picked up his teacup and took a sip. Grimacing because it was cold, he got up to fetch some hot water. Before he took a step, his secure cellphone rang. Although it looked like a regular Samsung Galaxy, this phone had encrypted voice, text, and data storage. Made by the German company GMSK in answer to the phone-hacking revelations, his CryptoPhone was as secure, if not more so, than a satellite phone. In part because the $3,600 unit had been designed from the ground up to be secure, in part because the person who was calling him was one of just three others who had the same, off-network device.

"Armagan," he said into the phone.

"Yes," he replied to an apparent question. "The system is ready. We can deploy at any time. What's the target?"

He leaned over to grab a pen and paper, then scribbled down a series of GPS coordinates.

"Who is the target?" he asked, ready to write that down as well. As he listened, his back straightened and he put down his pen. Even though it was a Sensitive Compartmented Information Facility and nobody could possibly be eavesdropping on the conversation, he unconsciously looked around his office to make sure nobody could hear. Nobody on his side of the SCIF, that is.

As he typed the latitude and longitude into his computer, he asked, "Are you quite certain this is necessary? Is there no other alternative?" After hearing the obviously snippy reply, Armagan obediently said, "No. There's no problem. It's just, well, he seems like a decent sort, and I —"

Moving the phone away from his ear a bit as the voice of the caller became agitated and louder, he sighed and closed his eyes.

"They will be ready for launch in thirty minutes." He studied his monitor then added, "As this is apparently very close, it won't take long to execute the mission. I'll call him when they're set, so he can run the op remotely."

Armagan hung up the CryptoPhone without saying goodbye.

The first thing Chauncey did when he'd left Breskin at the hospital was to grab a cab and go to his medical marijuana dispensary, "Buds N' Suds." It was so named because the owner also had a liquor license and sold beer, and Chauncey went there to get his monthly supply of medical marijuana and hash.

With the cabbie waiting, he went inside and bought several grams of their most potent hash. While he knew exactly what he wanted, he still enjoyed looking at the rows of closed masonry jars behind the counter filled with the best pot grown anywhere. As a guy who'd grown up looking over his shoulder every time he lit up a joint, it was an amazing thing. He moved to the section of the store where they sold paraphernalia and picked up a brand-new glass paddle to smoke it with.

After leaving the shop with a bag and a smile, he directed the driver to drop him off exactly 1.1 miles from his house, in an abandoned lot outside a housing complex. The guy thought it was a bit crazy, but accepted the $100 tip with wide eyes and drove away, no questions asked.

Chauncey proceeded to walk for a half-mile through the desert over rocks and sand. He barely noticed the scorpions and lizards that fled his path as he was thinking about the mission. The last seventy-two hours had been more exhausting than the preceding three weeks. The SERE sessions had taken a huge toll on him, both physically and mentally. Recovering from the physical part would just require sleep. Unfortunately, the nightmares that would come in that sleep would prolong the mental healing.

Still, he was done. He had just been given a rare midlife do over, and that was incredibly relieving. The fact that he had enough cash to do pretty much whatever he wanted was icing on his cake.

As he walked across the sand, the sun beat down on the back of his unprotected head and neck. It may have been spring, but it was still in the high eighties. He ruefully wished he'd bought one of the pot leaf hats sold at the dispensary. The leather handle of the cash-filled briefcase grew damp in his now perspiring hand. Finally, he came to a clump of tumbleweeds that sat beside a large group of boulders. After a furtive look over his shoulder, Chauncey lifted the tumbleweeds that were apparently secured to a metal grate. The grate had been covering the entrance to an old, tungsten mine shaft.

Chauncey entered the mouth of the mine and slid the grate back in place, once again obscuring its existence from anyone who happened to be hiking or ATVing nearby. He'd discovered the entrance to the long-abandoned tungsten mine several years ago when he'd mapped the area around his house. It had taken the better part of a year and most of the disability money he received from the VA to extend the tunnel to his house. This was the first time he felt the need to use it.

The shaft started down steeply, then straightened out before him into darkness. He unclipped a flashlight from the buckle of his belt and proceeded down the claustrophobic tunnel. As the height and width of the tunnel changed, he alternated between duck walking, crawling on his knees and slithering on his belly. He proceeded the 2,692 feet to the other side of the tunnel and emerged from an equally well-obscured exit next to his house.

Two hours and a cold shower later, he sat alone on his porch with a cup of tea, his hash, his new paddle, and a lighter.

Six miles away, in the ghost town that used to be home to hundreds of families stationed at George Air Force Base in Victorville, a stray cat stalked a mouse. The mouse scuttled down the street, sticking to the corner between the concrete and the curb. From time to time it passed something that could have been food, but as it was on an escape path, it didn't stop. The mouse scurried past houses that had been left untouched by the Air Force after the base had closed in the early '90s. It was an eerie, still, graveyard of memories. Rusted cars, dilapidated baby strollers, and even flattened and rotting soccer balls were as they'd been for nearly twenty-five years.

The neighborhood was surreal, like the movie set of a town that had been wiped out by an incurable disease. All the houses were still standing, but nobody lived in them anymore. And whether it was due to the severe climate, two decades worth of marauding bands of bored, spray paint-wielding teenagers, or the military's periodic urban warfare exercises, block after block was filled with uninhabitable, half-destroyed homes.

The cat followed its prey down the main street that looped through the town, past the movie theater and the playground that had once been alive with laughing and screaming children. The rodent turned a corner and scurried up the pitted driveway that led to the abandoned high school. The cat followed, knowing it was close to a meal. Then it stopped. The cat froze, its whiskers twitching as if it had sensed something it didn't like.

Suddenly it shot off down the street in the opposite direction, away from its hopeful meal. It had been scared off as the roof of the high school gymnasium slid open on huge runners. Once fully opened, twenty-five quadcopters flew straight up from inside the building.

When all of the twenty-five drones were together, hovering at 1,000 feet, they buzzed westward toward a specific GPS coordinate. Within minutes they passed over the tumbleweeds that had obscured the entrance to Chauncey's mine. Another minute later they stopped and held their position on the periphery of his compound.

The quadcopters slowly descended. When they were ten feet above the ground, each of them dropped four eggs onto the dirt. These eggs were different from the ones at the Rose Bowl that contained the words of the Fourth Amendment. They weren't plastic, but rather, a strong, yet lightweight composite, clearly designed to protect whatever was inside them. The flying carrier bots quickly rose and followed a reverse path back to the high school.

As the quads returned home, the one hundred composite eggs "hatched" their offspring. From inside of the now open eggs emerged one hundred, small mobile robots that looked remarkably like scorpions.

Biomimetically inspired, the scorpion-bots combined the most advanced robotics, optics, and computer technology with the million-year evolution of the hardy desert arachnid. If you asked their inventor, Armagan, he would have told you that he'd left nature in the dust.

At approximately five inches long, the bio-bots had lightweight polymer shells to protect them from the desert environment. Rather than patterning their locomotion on the eight-legged spider, which was far less efficient, the movements of a cockroach had been their inspiration. That meant they could not only run and walk, they could also jump onto and over most obstacles.

Armagan had improved on the WHEGS technology developed by the roboticists at Case Western University. Rather than just having six legs, they used a wheel/leg combination. The flattened bottom of the WHEGs gave them the capability of compressing loose material beneath each foot. Getting through the desert of El Mirage would be no trouble at all.

In the iconic tail of each bot was a high-resolution, mini-FLIR camera. Each shell was packed with uplink and downlink transmitters so they could be tracked and, if necessary, operated remotely. Those features alone made these tiny robots fantastic for surveillance, but when you added an explosive payload, they became weapons. Powerful weapons.

And that's what these were. Each of the lethal, mechanical critters carried a payload containing seven grams of Semtex. Multiplied by one-hundred, that equaled one-and-a-half pounds of one of the most powerful explosives known to man. A half-pound was enough to blow a hole in the side of a 747. Three times that would do far worse.

Automatically sensing one another's presence, the mechanical swarm activated. Their tails moved upward, cameras on and scanning on behalf of the remote operator. They began crawling over the desert terrain in the direction of Chauncey's house. Traveling at an average speed of three mph they would arrive in no time at all.

Chauncey casually flicked his lighter and placed the flame beneath the flat part of his brand-new hash paddle. After about thirty seconds, he put down the lighter and placed a slice of hash onto the heated glass. The hash quickly melted and turned to vapor. Chauncey slowly inhaled through the other end of the glass tube. He held the smoke in for as long as he could, allowing it to expand in his lungs and absorb into his bloodstream. Unable to contain it, he burst into a coughing spasm that lasted for a full minute. When he finally stopped, his eyes were bloodshot and glazed. He sat back with a smile and a contented sigh.

"Good stuff, that!" he said aloud. "Now what the hell am I going to do with all that money?" he laughed.

As his buzz intensified, the scorpion bots crawled their way closer. The preprogrammed GPS coordinates would have them arrive within ten feet of where he was sitting. The trenches and rocks he had placed around his house might have been good for slowing down cars, but they would be useless in slowing down the tiny, robotic hit squad.

The scorpions had been programmed to approach the designated coordinate, keeping at least five feet apart. When they got closer, they would increase speed and swarm. That was the only way there would be enough collective Semtex to do the job. Even if two-thirds of them failed to arrive, there would still be more than enough explosive power to complete the job. To make sure there were enough of them before detonating, like insects, they'd been embedded with sensors that would help them detect each other's presence. Once enough of them were there, the Semtex would be triggered by the clicking of their pincers.

Chauncey took a sip of his tea and silently thanked Armagan for introducing him to the tasty brew. He made a mental note to send him a proper thank-you card. Not an email thank you as so many lazy people had taken to doing. A real Hallmark card in an envelope sent via the good old USPS. Maybe he was a softy, but he believed it was more sincere that way.

He grabbed his lighter and began to reheat the paddle for another hit. A slight breeze shoved the flame into his finger, causing him to get burned and drop the lighter. As he leaned down to pick it up, he noticed some movement on his driveway. Chauncey sat up and scanned; his senses heightened. He saw one of the bio bots approaching, but thought it was a regular scorpion. Then he noticed several more of them.

Stoned as he was, he knew something was up and stood to assess the situation. Just then his cellphone chirped. He looked away from the driveway and saw a text on his screen.

"Get out now," it read.

Survival was in Chauncey's DNA so he didn't think, just reacted. Like the cat in town, he sprang off the porch and lunged toward the hidden tunnel entrance. As he scrambled to lift the rock-covered grate and dive into the shaft, the scorpions began reaching their target. One, two, ten, fifty, one hundred. All of them had made it. They circled and climbed over and around each other attempting to reach the center of the swarm. Once enough of them were touching, they clicked their pincers and exploded.

Chauncey's hash pipe melted into a slag of molten glass. Then the glass bubbled. Then it evaporated, along with his house, in the heat of the inferno.

Chapter Nineteen

The unreality of his situation fluttered through his mind like tiny flecks of dust floating in a beam of sunlight. Abdullah, or "MAID Subject #1" as his captors referred to him on the protruding tab of his file folder, had no dependable memory of how long he'd been strapped to the table, when he'd last eaten, slept, or even how he'd come to be wherever it was that he was. The rapid strobing of white light against the even whiter, sterile walls of the room in which he was incarcerated, combined with the thunderous screeching of AC/DC's "Highway to Hell," made even the concept of sleep something akin to leaping off a building and flying away to freedom; a fantasy in which #1 liberally indulged.

He cursed himself for being weak and dishonoring Allah, but no matter how deep his spiritual beliefs, #1's prayers for strength were no match for the biological effects that gripped his body in the face of his situation. To Abdullah he was being tortured. To his brain, the continuing trauma to which he was being subjected was increasing his levels of stress hormones, especially cortisol. The rapid excretions had the short-term effect of reducing stress. The long-term effect, however, was that of decreasing the tissue volume in his hippocampus and prefrontal cortex, thusly vanquishing his desire and previous ability for memory, concentration, and rational thought.

Simultaneously, heightened levels of stress hormones were flooding his amygdala, the part of his brain's primitive limbic system. The effect was enlargement. Free will be damned; the hormonal tsunami caused an involuntary and intense increase in his fear and anxiety. His fight or flight instincts were running amok. The prolonged state of physiological hyper arousal he'd endured was provoking his brain to release a flood of adrenaline and glucose that were increasing his blood pressure and heart rate, pushing him perilously close to death.

Sensing that #1 was nearing the point of no return, the sensors in the purple electrode-laden cap he wore sent out a signal, which automatically shut off the music and strobes. His blood pressure and pulse slowed, returning to near safe levels.

Strapped upright to a modified, stainless steel field surgical table, Abdullah's breathing slowed. His head would have drooped had it not been held in place by clamps on the back of the cap. His body was equally immobile as his arms, waist, and feet were secured to the polished, metal bed that held him captive.

"Are you alright, Na'wasey?" said a concerned, elderly female voice from somewhere he could not see.

Abdullah looked up, surprised at the sound of the voice and the fact that she'd called him grandson in his native Pashto tongue.

"Anaa?" he asked, squinting to find his beloved grandmother. "Is that you? How can you be here?" His blood pressure and heart rate quickened in response.

As his vision adjusted to the lack of strobing, his eyes bulged in astonishment.

"Can this truly be you?"

"Yes, my darling Abby," she said. "Please tell the Americans what they want to know so you may come home."

Memories slowly returned. Apparently no permanent damage to his hippocampus had occurred yet. The patrol had cut him off as he'd returned home from the meeting with Muhammed Nunari, head of the local al-Qaeda cell. Nunari had told him something. What? He strained for the memory, reaching deep inside in search of it. There it was! Nunari had told him that they'd put something in the trunk of his car. That it was for the mujahedeen. He recalled protesting, but Nunari had threatened to kill his family. His sons. His wife. His anaa.

"Park it in front of your house and leave the car keys inside," Nunani had said. "They will take the contents when you are inside."

#1 was not political. He'd agreed to what they said only to save his family. But he'd never made it home. The Americans had stopped him in on the way back. They'd interrogated him, and even though he'd told them the truth, they didn't believe him. So they'd beaten him, starved him, and subjected him to sleepless, pain-filled days. Now he was here. On this table. His usual interrogator was nowhere in sight. What was his anaa, his grandmother, doing here?

"Why did you have those weapons in your car trunk? When did you join al-Qaeda?" she asked. "Tell them what you know."

Still foggy from the increased levels of cortisol, he worked the question through his mind. His brain scanned itself looking for the correct place where the memory was stored.

"I don't know," he said.

As he spoke, the newly designed, functional magnetic resonance imaging, or fMRI, component of his cap sent powerful waves of magnetic energy through Abudullah's cranium. Nearly 100 percent more effective than a standard polygraph, the fMRI measured the blood oxygen dependent levels in the neurons connecting the lobes of his brain. Unseen algorithms rapidly detected an increase in oxygen-saturated, red blood cells racing through the neural connections to fourteen areas of his brain, including the anterior cingulate cortex and the hippocampus. The conclusion was instantaneous. Abdullah was lying.

"That's not true," his grandmother said. "They know you are lying. Why do you shame Allah by speaking falsehoods?"

"You are not Anaa!" Abdullah yelled, finally realizing what he was looking at. Then he screamed upward, to the people he knew must have been listening, "I am telling the truth!"

Again, the fMRI detected elevated levels of oxygenated blood in his prefrontal cortex. The more vigorous the activity, the greater the conviction of his dishonesty.

"You are lying," she said, disappointed. She then became sympathetic and nurturing. "Allah expects you to obey him, but he will not send you a burden that

is greater than you can handle. You have done that. Your resistance has freed your soul, and now you may speak without fear of hell."

"They cannot know what is in my mind! Only God knows this and they are not God!" he yelled.

"Oh, but they are," said his grandmother. "You are no longer in control of your destiny. You are in their hands. They have complete control. They know if you speak the truth. They control everything: your sleep, your food, your air. Even your body."

"No one has that power," he said, trying to convince himself.

"They do," she replied. "They will show you."

The coils that were inside his cap silently clicked. The transcranial magnetic simulation sent magnetic pulses into the primary, pre-motor and supplementary motor cortices that sat in the rear portion of the frontal lobe of his cerebral cortex. The powerful and pinpoint signals converted to electricity and sent signals through the neurons, down his brain stem, and directly to the appropriately targeted nerves that controlled his muscles.

#1's body parts moved against his will as if he was a marionette. He was horrified as he witnessed the involuntary twitching movements of his feet and hands. He tried willing them to stop but could not. As he attempted to voice his outrage, the TMS clicked again, sending even more magnetic pulses into his brain. Now, the only sound that escaped from his mouth was gibberish.

The hydraulics built into the table on which he was strapped were activated as if by some unseen hand. The section that held his arms to his sides rotated outward, then above his head. The part on which they were tethered expanded and extended, stretching his body upward. When he was fully extended, the shackles on his head, waist, and feet unclamped. #1 dangled by his wrists, screaming unintelligibly.

Chapter Twenty

There are moments in life when everything changes in a split second. Mostly, they are insignificant moments, like when you cut open your hand while slicing a bagel the wrong way and have to get stitches to close it up. Or when you hear the car door click closed just as you realize you've left the keys in the ignition. Sometimes those moments are far more serious. Like when your doctor announces that you have lung cancer and you know deep down that you should have quit smoking but kept putting it off. In these instances you wish you'd done something differently, but it's too late. An impenetrable steel door has sealed you from your past, forcing you forward against your desires.

Chauncey recognized this moment in all of its stark violence as he stopped crawling halfway down the tunnel to catch his breath. Someone had just tried to execute him in a particularly high-tech way, and no amount of wishing it hadn't happened could change that. He'd gone against his better judgment and made a deal with a man who'd already destroyed his life. "Fool me once," he thought. No matter; there was no turning back now and the future was very unclear. At the same time, he realized the past hadn't been much better.

As he stifled a cough from breathing in the copious amounts of dirt that the explosion had blown through the grate covering the tunnel entrance, he attempted to gather his thoughts. He wanted to go back to whatever was left of his house to gather evidence and see what was left, but he dismissed that thought even before it had fully formed. There was no sense in escaping, then getting shot in the head by a mop-up crew.

It was time to click into survival and evasion mode. The survival part was more or less straightforward. That was mostly about understanding and working with the elements, a skill Chauncey had honed in his years of humint work for the JPRA. He'd been dropped into Iran multiple times, with Spec Ops teams of no more than six, to chart exfiltration points and escape routes. His evasion and escape maps were in the bug-out bags and cockpits of every Delta Force member, SEAL team, and fighter pilot in the US military. He knew how to survive and thrive better than just about anyone.

Evasion, however, was another story entirely. That was all about staying ahead of the enemy and, unfortunately, right now he didn't know who that was.

He did a quick body pat to make sure no shrapnel had hit him while diving into the mine. Checking for the feel of damp blood was the best way to do that because right now his other senses couldn't be trusted. Normally pain was the best way to know if you were injured, but it wasn't a good barometer when you had gallons of adrenaline pumping through your veins. Satisfied that he'd miraculously escaped without a scratch, he continued his crawl to the other side of the tunnel.

Once Chauncey got to the opposite grate, he fell silent. Working against his stress to still his breathing and his heartbeat, he listened for any potential threats outside of the exit. He had to move fast because even if no mop-up crew came, the police would be arriving soon to see what had happened. There was no doubt that the explosion hadn't gone unnoticed, even if it had occurred in the middle of nowhere.

He waited for about five minutes to make sure nobody was there. In that short time he thought a year's worth of thoughts. His mind wandered through itself, unrestrained, in an attempt to make an evasion plan. There'd be time to figure out who had tried to kill him after he got away from the desert, so for now, escape was his highest priority. As he calmed down, a plan formulated. He went over the map in his head a hundred times, looking for flaws, backups, and contingencies. The more times he went through it, the clearer it became.

For the moment, it seemed that whatever had happened at the house had stayed behind him, so Chauncey slowly pushed the grate away. He opened it just enough to squeeze his body out and no more. First, he stuck his head through and scanned in all directions to make certain he was alone. Then he crawled out, keeping his body flat on the ground. As soon as he'd cleared the hole he reached back in and grabbed the briefcase that he'd gotten from Breskin. He was grateful that his paranoia had told him to leave it in the mine.

Chauncey crawled around the side of the boulders that bordered the entrance to the mine. He quickly located a marker and pushed a few large rocks aside. The rocks were on top of a six-foot-by- six-foot sheet of desert camouflage netting that obscured a half-dozen eight-foot-by-twelve-inch plywood planks. He gathered up the camo net, and then moved away the planks, revealing a five-foot-deep hole in which he'd stashed a gassed-up ATV.

Listening for anything that would signal someone approaching, he cautiously slid into the pit and opened the front rack that contained his bug-out bag. He grabbed it and slithered back to the flat area by the opening of the mine to make sure everything was still there. Although he checked it every three months, since he was only a half-mile west of the El Mirage OHV recreation area, he had to be sure some weekend warriors hadn't stumbled on it and stolen the contents.

Surviving without a bug-out bag would be possible, but it would be much more difficult. Chauncey had set his up to meet most any possibility. He went through the contents and found it all there. Not expecting to be on the run for that long, he focused on the essentials, which for him were a button compass, a rescue whistle, a signal mirror with aiming screen, MilSpec cord, and a disposable handcuff key. There was also a small first-aid kit with Band-Aids, lip balm, sunscreen, insect repellent, and lots of other things he hoped he wouldn't need. Lastly, he had six prepaid cellphones and ten, plastic liter bottles of water.

Before closing the bag, he grabbed two of the prepaid, Samsung S125G TracFones. Heavily used by drug dealers and terrorists who wanted anonymity while conducting business, these devices were also called "burners." He'd bought them at Walmart with cash and given a fake name and address. Once they'd served his purpose, Chauncey could just "burn" them, or otherwise destroy them, to get rid of incriminating evidence. They could still be traced by triangulating cell towers, but that took time.

Chauncey also kept out his Model 26, 9mm Glock. It may have been the smallest handgun they made, but it was, hands down, his favorite sidearm. Although it came standard with a ten round magazine, Chauncey had bought a larger capacity magazine that held 33, 9mm rounds. He loaded the Glock, then shoved it behind his back before putting the bag back into the ATV's storage compartment along with his money.

After another quick scan of the area, Chauncey activated one of the burners and punched in a number. "Please be there," he said to himself as he wiped his face with sunscreen. The grit on his skin felt like sandpaper as he smeared the liquid across his face and forehead.

"Hello," answered the voice of Killa.

Chauncey looked around as he spoke, keeping his voice only as loud as necessary to be heard. "Killa, it's Chauncey. Don't ask any questions. I need an exfil at 34 dash 117, number 12 at 20 hundred hours. Bring my BASE rig."

Sensing Chauncey's tone, Killa simply said, "Roger that."

Chauncey hung up the phone then pulled out the battery to make sure the GPS that was a chip inside all cellphones – burners or not – was dead. He then closed off the entrance to the cave and used some creosote bush to hide his tracks. It took up precious minutes, but he knew from experience that it was a risk worth taking.

It was 1700 hours. The explosion had happened approximately twenty minutes ago. The fact that there had been no choppers told him that his would-be assassins probably weren't coming. He made a mental note that whoever had tried to kill him was over-confident. The police, on the other hand, were a completely different story. They would absolutely come. There were still two hours of sunlight left, but he couldn't risk waiting for nightfall. He had to get gone now.

By his calculations, it would take two-plus hours to reach the exfil spot where he was meeting Killa. That was fine. He had another call to make, and he knew where he'd make it from.

The Yamaha Grizzly 450 4x4 roared to life with the touch of the starter button. A quick turn of the throttle and it leapt out of the hole like a mechanical bull. Fighting his desire to just flee, Chauncey dismounted the ATV and recovered the hole. He then jumped back on and sped north, flanking Shadow Mountain Road. After about a quarter of a mile, he turned the off-roader west and headed toward the eroded igneous peak of Shadow Mountain.

Movement felt good. The more distance he put between himself and his house, the safer he'd be. Even though the ATV was loud, about five minutes into the ride Chauncey heard the sounds of police sirens headed down Shadow Mountain Road. He assumed they were headed toward his house but didn't take the time to look over his shoulder for confirmation.

The flat playa of the Mojave was hard-riding terrain with lots of loose scrabble and dirt. Whenever possible, Chauncey dipped into the deep, dry washes to keep the dirt plume to a minimum. He pushed the 421cc, liquid-cooled Yamaha hard and bounced over rocks and crags for miles. He almost tipped several times, but he managed to pull out before going down.

As he drove, he fought off the persistent desire to analyze what had happened. There was no sense in mind-buggering himself now. He had a plan and he was sticking to it. But he couldn't stop it; he pinned dots on people he'd met and places he'd been, then connected those dots into a map comprised of motive and opportunity. The beast was back. All of it: The Special Operator, Targeting Officer and the Air Commando. The near-death experience and realization that he was being chased brought back the confidence, passion and energy of his youth. Good or bad, Chauncey realized that even though he was being hunted, he felt great!

Green, Paulson and the other CEOs were clearly on the top of his list of potential hit men, but there was no way he could sort that out now. Better to let the shadows of thoughts work their way through his subconscious without any interference. He called it "musing." Letting the mind work a problem on its own. In his experience, he found it was always best to stay out of his own way. Sometimes the mind worked best on autopilot.

One hour later, Chauncey crested Silver Peak. From his perch at 4,000 feet he now had an ideal view of the desert and would be able to see if anyone was following him. He switched off the ignition and massaged his jaw. He hadn't realized he'd been clenching his teeth ever since he'd dived into the mine. The bumps of rocks and other debris he drove over for the past hour hadn't helped either. He'd clamped down so hard that he had a raging, tension headache. Ignoring the pain, Chauncey downed another liter of water and scanned 360 degrees with his binoculars.

From his vantage point he could see that there were at least six police cars and a fire engine at whatever was left of his house. Their lights blazed a continuous, swirling, angry red and blue. Chauncey wondered what they would find left, if anything. He looked around with the binoculars and was grateful that nobody seemed to be following. Of course, given why he was there, to think he was lucky would have been a ridiculous overstatement, yet he was grateful nonetheless.

With an hour to wait until his rendezvous with Killa, Chauncey decided to make his second, and last, call of the day. Burner or not, he knew that the call had to be quick, given the person on the other end had the wherewithal and the equipment to trace the call. Still, he'd made up his mind that the risk was worth it. The results of the call would tell him which way to go.

Chauncey activated the Samsung and dialed Breskin's private cellphone. It would take longer to trace the call by calling that number instead of his office line. Breskin answered in the middle of the second ring.

"Breskin," he said, sounding officious.

"Okay, mate" said Chauncey. "You can tell whoever the hell it was that tried to off me that it didn't work. I am alive. I am unhurt. And I am really pissed."

Breskin's reply was fast. "Paunce? What are you talking about? Who tried to kill you? How? What happened?"

Chauncey considered Breskin's response. He seemed to be genuinely taken off guard. There wasn't the "overly surprised" response Chauncey was listening for that would have revealed he was full of it. Still, Breskin was a skilled interrogator, so he'd been trained to be a better actor than Sir Laurence Olivier.

"I'll tell you what happened. Someone just sent a whole bunch of exploding robots into my yard. I barely made it out without becoming Chauncey on the barbie."

"Where are you?" Breskin asked. "I'll send some of my people to get you. We need to get you safe in a hurry."

Chauncey laughed. He couldn't believe that Breskin thought he would actually answer that question. "I'm in China," he said. "I'm going to jump on a rickshaw, find out who it was, and take care of business myself, Rambo style. And I'd better not find out that you had anything to do with it. Because if I do —"

Breskin cut him off, bristling, "I already told you I'm on your side. Why would I have given you the money if I was going to kill you? I had nothing to do with this. And even if I did want you dead, we both know that I've already had plenty of opportunities."

"Maybe," said Chauncey. "I have a pretty good idea who did it. I'm guessing it was one of your CEO buddies. I'm just not sure which one."

"Don't go rogue on me, Paunce. Let me help. We're not enemies anymore. Afghanistan is too many years behind us."

"I'll be in touch," Chauncey replied. Then he hung up. He opened the back of the phone and pulled out the battery, then grabbed another bottle of water. He sat back against a rock and sipped as the sunset exploded across the western, desert sky in colors more exquisite than any manmade explosives could ever equal.

Chauncey checked his watch as the sun finally dipped below the horizon. 7:15 p.m. Killa would be picking him up in 45 minutes and he had to be there waiting. He stowed his gear and drove the Grizzly down the other side of Shadow Peak, heading northeast toward Sun Hill Ranch Airport. The whole way down the word "Panopticon" churned through his subconscious.

Chapter Twenty-One

When Tom Carby decided to settle in La Jolla, he'd done so in spite of his utter disdain for the opulence and wealth of the city, and its uber-rich one-percenters. He despised his neighbors because he believed they used their money and power for personal gain and didn't give a rat's ass about anyone else. Rather than volunteering their time or donating their money, the trophy wives took tennis lessons, had spa treatments, and teased their gardeners and pool boys with personal-trainer perfected bodies, Botox-injected lips, and surgically enhanced breasts.

Their chief executive hubbies played golf, flew private jets, and bitched that the growing number of homeless people was destroying their country. The irony of this, of course, was that many of them were working tirelessly to create greater automation, or offshoring their labor, which in turn, was creating even more homeless Americans. California may have been a blue state overall, but from Los Angeles down to the border the colors were green and red.

Carby hadn't been handed a damned thing. Born poor, he'd worked his ass off to get ahead. His father, a Costco cashier, and his mother, a hairdresser, did their best to give him good things, but when it came time for college, it just wasn't in the cards. And because Carby had spent his high school years playing third string quarterback and drinking beer, there were no academic scholarships in the offing. So Carby had taken a commission in the all-volunteer Army to get an education. Luckily for him, his COs saw his innate engineering brilliance and put him into the technical corps where he'd become one of the best bot docs anywhere.

He took that learning to heart and figured out a way to capitalize on the coming robotics revolution. Now, a decade after his discharge, Carby was preaching ethics and raking in big bucks from patents he'd licensed to the companies whose bots he'd repaired in Iraq and Afghanistan. He had enough money to live anywhere and do whatever he pleased. Right now it pleased him to be a thorn in the side of the military-industrial-political complex.

He'd chosen to live in La Jolla because it was next door to Torrey Pines, the corporate home of General Atomics. That proximity made it a simple matter of driving ten minutes to harass anyone going in or out of the company's unassuming, bucolic headquarters. Although his expressed reasons for hating the company so viscerally were that they helped to kill innocent men, women, and children, the true reason laid buried deep inside of him.

To say that Carby was a little paranoid would be an understatement on the same level as calling a level five hurricane a pretty girl's fart. There were days when he would be startled by his own shadow. And the more time that passed with no arrests over the torture session that followed the Hotel Del Coronado massacre, the worse his paranoia became.

But as paranoid as he was, Carby's fears of personal safety never dented his self-righteous stance over the government's wanton and illegal use of surveillance on its own citizens. Because of that, he couldn't justify attaching cameras all over the place as a way to keep his house secure. Besides, he rationalized, if someone was going to break in, then the omnipresent hive of CCTV cameras already in place would identify the intruder without his having to exert any effort whatsoever. If the powers that be refused to share those images with him, he'd simply hack into their servers and take what he needed.

This wasn't to say that Carby hadn't taken some precautionary measures to keep safe. He had sturdy locks on all of his doors and windows, had motion sensors attached to floodlights, and his Beretta 92A1 was always loaded and close at hand. In reality, none of those things would probably be required because just in case anyone did decide that they wanted to come enter his house uninvited, they would have to get past a highly advanced team of armed and dangerous sentry bots that patrolled his property 24/7.

It didn't hurt that his backyard butted up to the high cliffs separating Cali from the Pacific Ocean. Besides the obvious aesthetic, it was, in his words, "a security thang." If they were coming to get him, they'd have to fly in with choppers because the crumbly, sandstone edifice was unscalable even for the elite troops that were stationed to his south. And since choppers made quite a racket, Carby would know they'd arrived. What he hadn't considered was the more finessed approach that Captain Charles Paunce had decided upon.

From Chauncey's current position approximately 3,000 feet above the Pacific Ocean and rapidly approaching Carby's backyard on a tandem paraglider, he had no idea what to expect. All he knew for certain was that his mission required a stealthy breach, a brief and hopefully informative parlay with Carby, then an equally surreptitious retreat. If all went as planned, he'd be there and gone in less than fifteen minutes. Even though he was nearly 100 percent certain that Carby's home was being watched, it was a risk he had to take. Carby was the only guy he knew who had a chance of knowing what had attacked his house.

Chauncey tapped Killa on the leg and pointed to the open space that was Carby's backyard. As Killa adjusted his course, Chauncey recalled how many times he'd seen Carby repair bots in Afghanistan. Repair them? Hell, he built them from the ground up. The guy was a veritable Tony Stark, taking scraps from blown up IED detector bots like the Talon and creating smaller, smarter UGVs that could detect and deactivate terrorist bombs, then serve up some cold brewskis to the guys on post an hour later. He was so obsessed with robots that he named them and even cried when one of his favorites was blown to smithereens by a jihadist roadside bomb.

They'd gotten along fine until Carby turned to the dark side. Chauncey had seen it coming and begged Carby not to go down that particular rabbit hole. His efforts fell on deaf ears. Carby's love of gadgetry had compelled him and others to go the way that many men before them had gone. Chauncey knew that war was to blame. Its power and violence were seductive and drew many good men in a direction they could neither resist nor, for many, escape. That dark side existed in all men; it just needed the right trigger to be released. For Carby, that trigger had been bots.

Chauncey checked his Glock, tightened the Gemteck signature suppressor one last time, then switched on his second generation, Soviet-made night vision goggles. He liked the monocular NVGs because they were lighter and easier to fix if something went wrong. Not to mention they were readily available on eBay. Killa banked the prop-driven paraglider south, Carby's yard now just 1,000 yards ahead.

It had been Killa's idea to use the tandem parasail when Chauncey sketched out what he needed to do. Killa had picked Chauncey up at the Sun Hill Airport nearly six hours ago. Rather than rant and rave about Breskin, the first thing Chauncey had done was to give Killa the money he'd gotten.

"There's a million dollars in this suitcase. I want you to give $100K to Diddy, a hundred to Phil and keep $200K for yourself as payment for helping me with those douche bag CEOs."

"Why do I get twice as much?" Killa had asked.

"It's the least I could do for almost getting your DZ license revoked after my suicide jump," Chauncey smiled. "If I don't turn up within forty-eight hours, split the rest of the money between Veterans for Peace and Wounded Warriors."

As he flew, Killa completely ignored the fact that he'd just been handed four years of salary. Money had never been his M.O. Instead, he focused on the conditional ending of Chauncey's request.

"If you don't turn up from what?" he'd yelled over the roaring sound of the Cessna's twin props.

Chauncey merely handed him a piece of paper with some GPS coordinates on it.

"That's my target," he said. "I need to land within five feet of that mark and I need to do it real quiet."

Killa recognized that the drop was somewhere on the coast, SSW of where they were. As the sparse lights of small desert dwellings passed beneath them, he considered Chauncey's request. He didn't question the fact of it, nor did he ask for motives. He did, however, suggest that he had a way do it sneakier.

"You in a hurry?" Killa asked.

"It's got to be tonight," said Chauncey.

"I got an idea that I think you're going to like."

Killa banked to the south and flew to his drop zone. He landed the plane and taxied to the hangar. Without a word the two men hustled inside. Killa unlocked one of his six "secret" storage containers and pointed to a unique looking paramotor and tandem paraglider. Chauncey smiled and nodded. He'd known that his friend was resourceful from their work together in a handful of classified DoD "black" programs. But he didn't know that he'd illegally kept a bunch of the unconventional warfare gear he'd worked on. The programs were defunct and no longer of interest to the DoD, so he'd held onto as much of the shit-canned equipment as he could. Killa was basically a high-tech war toy hoarder. It would make one crazy-assed reality show for sure.

The paraglider that Killa had was special. While most of them used all-metal components, this one used composite carbon fiber. The engine was housed in a radar absorbing and deflecting material that could avoid any air traffic control systems in the world. Even the rigging and fasteners were made of indestructible, nonradar reflecting nylon. The engine had an oversized muffler for enhanced noise reduction. And last, but not least, the entire thing, glider included, was painted a dull, flat black. Basically, it was a one-off, silent, flying stealth machine that even Batman would have envied.

"Nice, huh?" Killa grinned.

Five hours later, they were soaring above the Pacific Ocean. The night air was calm and soundless and gave Chauncey the peace that he needed to review his plan. It had been a long, long day. From losing Paulson to nearly being arrested at the hospital, getting paid by Breskin, then nearly getting blown up, it had been challenging. As they soared southward along the coast, the only sound they could hear was the wind and crashing waves 750 feet below. A quarter-moon painted La Jolla's sunset cliffs with speckles of light that hit protrusions in the sandstone facade.

Killa and Chauncey watched as Carby's yard came in view. Killa gently squeezed Chauncey's shoulder, signaling they'd hit their mark. Without so much as a thumbs up, Chauncey unbuckled his harness and dropped. Unburdened by the weight, the paraglider jumped fifty feet into the air. Killa easily regained control and flew down the coast to rendezvous with Diddy and Phil at Bird Rock. He watched Chauncey disappear, hoping it wasn't the last time they'd see one another.

The BASE rig that Chauncey wore was a special parachute used by expert jumpers who could land in the center of a dartboard bull's-eye on a moving rowboat. An acronym for Building-Antenna-Span-Earth, his BASE rig was light and packed small with a seven-cell canopy. As it was meant to be deployed under 1,000 feet, there was no reserve, meaning Chauncey had no room for error. After a mere two seconds of freefall, the canopy deployed, slowing his descent.

Through the queer, green light of his NVGs, Chauncey scanned the ground for the shape and size he'd memorized from Google Earth. He took a spiral turn around the house and did a quick assessment of defenses and possible targets that could mess things up. There was nothing like people taking their dogs for late-night walks or husbands sneaking home after late-night affairs to screw up an op. Satisfied that all was clear, Chauncey guided the chute over Carby's roof to the back of the house. He landed at an easy trot, stopping three feet from the edge of the cliff.

His pulse beating like a racehorse, Chauncey tore off his rig and threw himself behind one of several palm trees that served as a natural fence between the cliff and Carby's house. He'd been ready to remove his NVGs if motion detectors had set off any floodlights. It wasn't necessary because, as he'd hoped, by landing fifty feet from the house he was out of their range.

Backyards in towns like La Jolla tended to be extremely small. Apparently the super rich preferred to have more house than yard, which was something to which Chauncey could never relate. As he pulled in the canopy and rolled up the chute, he took a quick visual of the yard. He figured rather than beeline to the back door, he'd run a zigzag pattern. The north side of the yard was bordered by a long row of close-packed cypress trees. Along the south side ran a stained pine fence.

Chauncey noted that the lower portion of the wood was faded, which meant there was an in-ground sprinkler system. He'd have to be careful not to step on one of the heads. And since the neatly mown Bermuda grass was dry, he had a fleeting thought that the sprinklers could turn on at any second. He allowed himself the pun that it would put a damper on things.

Although he knew that whoever had tried to kill him would know that he'd escaped by now, Chauncey forced himself to go slow. In spite of his need to get the information fast, he'd been trained to have patience. As an interrogator, he knew that taking his time was the most effective means of extracting useful intel. So even though he didn't have a ton of time, he wasn't going to make a mistake by rushing; this was Thomas Carby, after all. In his arena, there were bound to be things that bumped and buzzed in the night.

Chauncey did one more long scan of the yard. There were no obstructions, no leaves that would crunch under foot giving him away to the sensitive ears of neighboring dogs. No lights on inside the house meant that Carby was sleeping. Chauncey knew he was home as he'd called from the parking lot where he and Killa had landed the Cessna to load their equipment into Diddy's van. Carby had answered, cranky about a late call, and Chauncey apologized for a wrong number, then hung up.

Chauncey checked his watch. It was 3:30 a.m.: go time. He switched off the NVGs and removed the helmet on which they sat. He stashed the helmet beside the rolled up gear, drew a breath, and then stepped out from his cover. He stepped lightly, feeling the grass give way beneath his feet. As exhausted as he was, all of his senses were hyperaware, which is probably the only reason he heard the innocuous sound.

It was as if someone was walking toward him, crushing the grass as they approached. He looked toward the noise, but there wasn't a person, a dog, or even a rabbit in sight. He lowered his gaze and noticed a round, bowling ball-sized object rolling across the yard in his direction. He froze. So did the ball. He did a quick study of the dark object, but in the darkness it wasn't easy to make out many of its features. It was a jet black sphere with two, plastic-encased cameras protruding like ears from each side. Modified by Carby, the Rotundus GroundBots' sophisticated motion detection sensors had discovered Chauncey's approach and rolled in to investigate. Chauncey knew he couldn't just stand there. He had no choice but to keep going, so he decided to move faster and more directly to the house.

He took several quick steps toward the back door, and the GroundBot immediately rolled to intercept. Unnoticed by him, one of the cameras projected an IR beam onto his chest. Seconds later, a swarm of tiny, buzzing, DVD-sized quadcopters emerged from behind the house. They lined up and formed a flying wall, blocking Chauncey's path. He gulped. He didn't know if they were armed or not. It looked like they were just acting as a barrier between him and the house, but all the spinning rotors made it like a spinning lawnmower. Without a doubt, it would scare the crap out of any would-be burglars.

Remaining as quiet as possible, Chauncey jinked to his left. Hell, even if he didn't move, the pounding from his chest would probably have been enough to keep the ball's attention. As he stepped, the Rotundus followed and, like a mother ship directing a fleet of alien spacecraft, the quadcopters adjusted, reforming the barricade between him and the house.

Seeing no other option, Chauncey pulled out his Glock and took aim at the Rotundus. He fired off a quick, muzzled shot, but the sphere easily rolled out of the way. He pulled the trigger again, but the ball dodged the second shot just as easily.

"Jesus," he thought. "This is insane."

It was a technological Mexican standoff, and Chauncey didn't speak this particular dialect of Spanish. He felt like the Road Runner being pursued by one of Wile E. Coyote's crazy ACME contraptions, only this wasn't a cartoon. He considered running toward the cliff and stopping short. Maybe the ball wouldn't stop in time and would roll off the edge, taking the quadcopters down with it like a bunch of robotic lemmings.

Realizing it was his only viable option, Chauncey sprinted back toward the palm trees. The Rotundus and the drones pursued. He hit the ground and slid to a stop, just inches away from the edge. The GroundBot wasn't fooled. It stopped easily and the drones reformed their flying wall.

Unaware of whether the device had wirelessly sent a signal to Carby or, worse, the ADT of the future, Chauncey had to either shut it down or grab his paraglider and abort before accomplishing his goal. Failure was not an option. But what was? He couldn't shoot it, he couldn't outrun it and nothing in the bug out bag strapped to his chest would help him, but maybe —

Chauncey sprang for the tree where he'd stashed his equipment. He grabbed the BASE rig and dove at the Rotundus that was rolling toward him. He caught the bot in the unfurled canopy like an animal in a trap and swung it with all his might against the tree. The Rotundus shattered. Instantly, the quadcopters lost the signal from mama and casually returned to their hidden posts.

The immediate threat apparently passed, Chauncey sank down against the tree, panting. He knew Carby was a smart guy, but holy crap! He'd somehow enhanced existing technologies to the point where they were more capable than ever. Chauncey had seen a lot but nothing like this stuff. He looked out at the water and recomposed himself. The ocean made sense, so he soaked in its calming rhythms while realizing he had to take another stab at getting to the house.

He took a deep sigh, then got to his feet for another go. Before he could take a step, the backyard lights switched on, and Carby stepped out of the house in his robe. He directed his Beretta at the tree line.

"Chauncey?!" he called. "Where the hell are you, boy? And what'd you do to poor Walter?"

Chauncey pulled out his Glock and stepped out from behind the tree, leveling it at Carby.

"Hey there, Tom. Who the hell is Walter?" asked Chauncey.

"My bowling ball security bot. I named him after Walter Sobchak from the *Big Lebowski*. He loved bowling, you know?"

"Sorry, mate. Didn't realize he was a friend of The Dude's. Anyway, helluva a drop zone you got here. How'd you know it was me?"

With his free hand, Carby pointed to his eyes. "Walter was outfitted with some infrared, retinal scan, and facial recognition hardware. He sent the information to my iPhone. I got dressed as fast as possible when I realized it was you. Figured if anyone could take him out, well, whatever. What's so important that after ten years you couldn't just call or maybe even ring the doorbell?"

"Ten years is a long time, Tom. I had no idea if you still harbored a grudge."

"Chauncey, you did what you did because you believed you were right. I'd never blame a man for standing up for his convictions. And even though it caused me a world of headaches, I came out of it fine. Besides, you're the one who went to the hoosegow, not me. So if anyone's got a reason to still be pissed, it'd be you."

Chauncey considered what Carby had said, then, "So we're good?"

"Other than your killing Walter? Nada."

Chauncey lowered his weapon, leaving his finger in the trigger guard. Carby put away his Beretta and walked over. They shook hands as Chauncey pointed to the crushed bot in his parachute.

"Sorry about that, mate. I didn't realize he was family. And I would've discussed this over the phone, but I'm trying to stay under the radar."

"Radar's pretty low these days, my friend," replied Carby. "You'd have to be some kind of fancy limbo dancer to get beneath it."

Chauncey nodded.

"Let's go inside and have a sit-down," Carby offered.

Chauncey considered the invitation. Besides the fact that he was already outside and that given what he'd just seen, Carby probably had even more high-tech gizmos that could be used to keep him there if he wanted, he politely declined. "Thanks, but if it's all the same to you, I just have a few questions, then I'll get out of your way."

Leaving out the SERE and CEO details, Chauncey proceeded to tell Carby about the scorpion bots that had attacked his house. He described them in as much detail as possible. Carby pushed Chauncey's observational skills to their limit by asking him questions about size, speed, mobility, color, composition, noise, and other seemingly benign things. Chauncey didn't object to any of the queries because he knew they were specific for a reason.

Carby wiped his hand over his bald head and pursed his lips in thought.

"A lot of Warcos, with the help of our buddies at DARPA, are working on developing minis as fast as possible. Talking about bot infantry, autonomous jets. Not just for use in the theater, mind you, but for law enforcement and spying in the good old U.S. of A."

Carby sighed and looked at the water as he thought about what he considered to be an approaching nightmare. Finally, he said, "You might want to ask your Afghani tea buddy Armagan. He's working on minis for GA."

Chauncey was surprised and said so. He thought Armagan had been developing algorithms for NexGen sense and avoidance. Giving those capabilities to drones was the last real barrier against the FAA opening the national airspace to widespread UAV use.

"Nope," said Carby, matter of fact. "He's developing killer biomimetic minis. Pretty cool ones from what you just told me." Then, he added, "Much has changed since you, Breskin and I went all loopy in the sandbox. Things are even more out of control now. The lunatics are running the asylum, if you know what I mean. You managed to stop some of us crazies by going public – thank you by the way, it took bull-balls and you were right – but there's other stuff that's going on. Bad stuff."

It wasn't so much what Carby had said, but how he said it that gave Chauncey a chill. He stuck out his hand to shake.

"Thanks, Tom. I appreciate the information and the forgiveness. You know it wasn't personal." He turned to walk away, then turned back. "By the way, I saw your interview with Marcella on eyesopen.org. How is she?"

"Still hot as a furnace, buddy. You're the only guy I know who ever tamed that filly, and I admire the hell out of you for it. Might even say a bit envious. When's the last time you saw her?"

"At the divorce signing," said Chauncey. "Thanks, Tom. If anyone asks, I wasn't here."

"Who wasn't where?" Carby smiled.

Chapter Twenty-Two

Skip McGovern Jr. was a prick. But like his father, former Sergeant Skip McGovern Sr., he was a smart prick who knew that with the right amount of charm and cunning his despicable actions would either be ignored or get blamed on someone else. Skip Jr. had learned that lesson from his father who blamed anything that ever went wrong on Muslims, the Democrats, crackheads or the easiest target, his wife, Dolly. And given that she'd never divorced the elder McGovern, even after over a decade of verbal and physical abuse, Skip Jr. had all the parental modeling he needed.

Tall, dark-haired, handsome, and with the same dimpled chin as his father, Skip Jr., or JR as Mr. McGovern called him, was a successful seventeen year old. He was a straight-A student, captain of the Thousand Oaks High School varsity baseball team, and now, as of thirty minutes ago, an Eagle Scout. How he'd become an Eagle Scout was a wonder to most of the people who knew him. His chief tactics had been bullying, threatening, and stealing credit for the accomplishments of his fellow scouts. The fact that his veteran father had joined the scouting leadership had helped them to overlook many of the son's pronounced anti-scouting personality traits. In all honesty, they just wanted JR to be done and gone.

Armagan didn't know any of this as he smiled at Dolly McGovern and indicated JR, who was across the room of the prestigious Sherman Country Club's Fairway Room. Dressed in his Boy Scout uniform, he was currently holding court with some fellow scouts and making fun of how certain guests were dressed.

"You must be very proud of him," Armagan said to Dolly. "I've heard that becoming an Eagle Scout is very difficult."

Dolly smiled and touched the miniature Eagle pin she'd received from Skip Jr. during the award ceremony. It was a strange, self-conscious sort of smile. Not the happy look that Armagan would have expected. She kept her lips firmly together, showing no teeth, and her eyes clicked from side to side looking for something that Armagan would never know. She reminded him of some of the Muslim women he'd met while still in Afghanistan. Under Sharia, women were not allowed to speak with men and were afraid of doing things that would displease their husbands.

"Thank you," Dolly said to him in a cottony voice, apparently sensing she was safe enough to speak. "His father helped him a great deal. Even when he wanted to quit, Skip Sr. gave him the motivation to keep going. To be honest, I'm not sure who it was more important to, Skip or JR."

Armagan raised his eyebrows and nodded a small bit. Then Dolly added, "I'm sorry, but how do you know my husband?"

"We nearly worked together at AeroVironment. Mr. McGovern was one of several employees who attempted to get me to work there after I'd graduated from MIT."

"Attempted?" she asked, an imperceptible glimmer entering her eye.

"Yes. They brought Mr. McGovern as a representative of the sales team to tell me about the company's customer list and tempt me with promises of untold clients with insatiable technology desires. Not to mention that during his military service he'd spent time in my country. I suppose they hoped our mutual distaste for certain enemies of America would make me feel more comfortable on a personal level. When I ended up elsewhere, your husband was apparently rather disappointed."

"I should say so." Dolly breathed. "That man is used to getting whatever he wants."

Although in a deeper sense she was referring to their relationship and the fact that her husband was cruel, right now she was thinking of how she'd wanted a smaller, more intimate setting for JR's Eagle Scout ceremony. Her son had taken on many of the same qualities as her husband, being rude and dismissive of her among them, yet she was still proud of what he'd accomplished.

She had framed his merit badge-filled sash in a tall, handcrafted shadow box. She'd planned to hang it beside a dozen smaller shadow boxes, which were filled with all of the badges he'd earned, right from his first Tiger Cub Award all the way to the present day. Because Skip Sr. wouldn't allow Dolly to get a job using her nursing skills, she'd become a scrapbooker and quilter. The family's Simi Valley house was filled with her crafts. There were dried flowers, framed photos, and idyllic Norman-Rockwellian prints throughout. Crafting was her way of disappearing into a place where she was creative and safe. Not to mention a blatant attempt to dilute the raging testosterone that surrounded her at all times. Even their pet bulldog, Patton, was a male.

When Dolly had told her husband that she preferred to host a small gathering of close friends and family for the pinning, he'd rejected it out of hand.

"JR's a man, Dolly," her husband had barked. "It's time you stopped trying to make him into some kind of cocksucking queer bait. You're like those fag hags who want to let homos into the scouts. Well, it's not going to happen on my watch. We're going to have a blow-out party at the club to celebrate and that's that."

In a rare and reckless moment of self-advocacy, Dolly had objected and reiterated her desire for a small party. She'd wanted to create an intimate affair with close friends. She would cook tummy-warming campfire foods like beef stew and chili and serve them in rustic, wooden bowls. The décor would be comprised of scouting colors, faux-campfires as table centerpieces, and a podium constructed of lashed wood. Skip had exploded. Not only had he refused, but he'd taken all of the shadow boxes and run them over with his Hummer. In one fell swoop, he pissed all over her pitiable attempt at happiness and his son's badges at the same time.

What Dolly hadn't really understood was that her husband needed to make a grand show of his son's accomplishments to cover his own lack of recent success. It had been seven years since he'd retired from the Army to work at AV as a salesman. The company had hired him to be a living testament to the power of its mini UAV force. His firsthand accounts of leading an elite EOD force were impressive testimonials to their products. His stories about using AeroVironment's Wasp and Raven systems to locate IEDs in theater had led to sales wins with not only the DoD, but annual bookings in Australia, Italy, Denmark, Norway, NATO, Spain, The Netherlands, Thailand, the Czech Republic, France, and others that could never be disclosed.

Because the occupations had ended, and the governments of Afghanistan, Pakistan, and Iraq had curtailed the US's use of drones to kill insurgents, the demand for UAVs had declined. Besides the fact that McGovern's anecdotes had long stopped being entertaining and had become exaggerated to keep them fresh, over the past three years sales had plummeted by over 40 percent. He was close to losing his job. Even though the family could no longer afford their membership at the club, he'd insisted the party take place there for appearances. It was a stroke of luck that April saw low bookings, so it wasn't as costly as it could have been.

McGovern had invited the world, and a large portion of it had come. He'd invited Paulson and the AV Board, his colleagues in business development, the nerds in engineering, the Boy Scout troop, the mayors of Thousand Oaks and Simi Valley, and all of their neighbors. Paulson wasn't there, nor were any of the other C-level folks from AeroVironment, but most everyone else had shown up. It wasn't that they liked McGovern that much, but the company was, after all, an extended family of sorts.

He'd rented out the $3,000 a night ballroom and catered it at $50 a plate times 200 people. Rather than making Dolly happy, he'd hired a party planner whose client portfolio read like a who's who of celebrities. Now, a half-hour after the award ceremony and dinner had ended, the party was in full swing.

"Well, again," said Armagan to Dolly. "My congratulations to you and your family. Your son has accomplished something wonderful. I have no doubt he could not have done so without your help and support." Dolly blushed. A part of her wished that he'd accepted the company's offer because in her opinion, many of the men at AV were arrogant, self-important warmongers.

Neither Armagan nor Dolly had seen his approach, but McGovern was at their side to hear Armagan finish his thought.

"What a bunch of garbage," McGovern started. "Dolly had nothing to do with any of this. If she'd had it her way, JR would be wearing skirts and playing with Barbie dolls."

Armagan was taken aback by the harshness of McGovern's statement, not only because of how disrespectful he'd been to Dolly, but because of the blatant inappropriateness. He remained silent.

McGovern continued, "I'm glad you called me, buddy. You weren't exactly on my favorite people list, but when you mentioned you weren't happy at General Atomics, I figured I'd get you here to have a quiet convo with Shane Huffle, our director of business development. He can talk more specific engineering things with you and maybe convince you to switch sides. Come on."

McGovern failed to mention that had it not been for Armagan's presence, his boss would not have come to the celebration. He took Armagan by the arm and led him away from his wife without so much as a cursory adieu. Over his shoulder, Armagan nodded a goodbye to Dolly as McGovern led him to Shane. In his heart McGovern hoped that Armagan would bring his work to AV so it would give the company a much-needed technological shot in the arm. Plus, getting the golden child would be a job-saving feather in his cap.

McGovern reintroduced the two men and launched into his own theory about how AV's electrical energy systems wouldn't ever return them to their glory days. Maybe if Armagan came onboard with some fresh ideas, they'd be okay.

As Armagan and Shane began speaking, a commotion erupted from the round, glassed-in area of the room where the award ceremony had taken place. They looked over and saw an apparently inebriated woman tripping her way to the podium. A couple of guests were trying to help her as she stumbled and knocked over the American flag. McGovern scowled and grumbled something about how people who couldn't hold their liquor should be shot. Then, as he looked closer, he turned pale. Armagan noticed the change in his pallor instantly.

"I need to take care of something. You gentlemen carry on," said McGovern.

Armagan suggested that he and Shane take a walk outside to talk, and the two strolled out. As soon as they left the room, Armagan closed the door behind them. Unnoticed, he deftly flicked a switch that locked the doors from the outside.

McGovern strode toward the section of the room where the drunken woman was yelling and rolling across the splayed Stars and Stripes. Spying his father's approach, JR and two of his scouting friends stopped snickering and gallantly assisted her to her feet. The guests had all stopped their conversations and were watching with confusion, concern, and some amusement.

"Petty Officer Adams!" bellowed McGovern. "Just what in the name of hell do you think you're doing?!"

Doctor Kay Adams shook off the Boy Scouts and stared at McGovern. All of the Vicodin and vodka that she'd taken in the week since Breskin had handed her his photo seemed to evaporate, their effects no longer apparent. Even though she'd contemplated the possibility of confronting her rapist for years, she was still stunned by her response to seeing him. As urine dribbled down the legs of her pants, Adams straightened her shoulders and saluted McGovern.

"Sergeant! I wish to report there is an IED on the premises!"

McGovern didn't know what to think, much less what to say. It was true that he hadn't seen her for many years. Not in the flesh, at any rate. She was, however, still a frequent, albeit unwelcome visitor of his dreams. She looked terrible. She'd probably put on at least fifty pounds and her face was lined with deep crevices that you found on much older people. He instantly knew that he was responsible for her horrendous state. In the same instant, he didn't care one bit. She was a bitch then and apparently a fat, drunken bitch now. And she was ruining his party.

"What the hell are you talking about?" McGovern screamed. "Are you insane? We are not in Iraq, Adams. We are in goddamned Thousand Oaks, California. You are not welcome here, and you must be crazy because you do not salute me. I am not a goddamned officer!" McGovern screamed. As he became more agitated, his face grew redder, except for his scar. That remained the same dead, white color and even more pronounced from his face in contrast.

Adams held her salute. As much as the sight of McGovern made her want to vomit, she continued to stare at him. The guests moved closer to see what was happening.

"Sir, I know that. But as much as it may be true that we are not in Iraq, there is still an IED on the premises."

McGovern searched her face. As he looked in her eyes, a small spark of fear lit up a long dormant room in his mind. It was a place that had been dark for nearly a decade. A place that had once blasted blinding strobe lights and klaxon alarms on a daily basis. A place that held dread and hate and fear and smells of Semtex, C4, TNT, blood and memories of death.

Dolly stepped up behind her husband. "What's going on, Skip? Who is this?"

Without breaking his eye-lock with Adams, McGovern said, "This is someone who used to be in my EOD unit in Iraq. She's clearly having some kind of episode. Now don't ask me any more questions, just get everyone out of this room as –"

Adams cut him off. "I wouldn't recommend that, Sergeant. Not a good plan. If anyone attempts to leave this room, the bomb will go off."

The word "bomb" was instantly repeated two hundred times as it sped like a lit fuse from guest to guest. The fear that McGovern had felt spread, and the guests began to rush for the doors.

"Halt!" commanded McGovern in a voice he hadn't used for a long time. Without even realizing they'd submitted to his order, the crowd froze.

Adams lowered her salute and looked around the room. The once nurturing and compassionate part of her was a mere whisper being drowned out by her shrieking need for revenge. She pointed to a long table to the side that was piled high with gifts.

"There is an improvised explosive device inside one of the presents for your, no doubt, piece of shit son. It is on a timer. If you cannot find and diffuse the device in ten minutes, it will go off. There are also radio-activated triggers on the device, so if anyone makes a cellphone call, a text or even a Facebook post, it will go off. And, lastly, if anyone tries to leave the room or rush me, I will detonate the bomb myself." She looked at the CCTV cameras and added, "That includes any security or police intervention from outside." She held up her cellphone to accentuate her point.

The word "why" never crossed McGovern's mind. He knew damned well why. Without a word, he bolted for the gift table. Sitting on a round table, covered by the Eagle Scout quilt that Dolly had knitted, were nearly eighty gift-wrapped boxes. All eyes were glued to McGovern's back as he surveyed the table, trying to figure out which box contained the bomb. Realizing that he'd never have enough time to unwrap each one he gently picked out the top gift and held it above his head.

"Who is this from?" he screamed.

Nobody said a thing.

McGovern turned to the guests and repeated his question. "Who brought this fucking present?!"

The meaning of his query dawned on the stunned group. The scoutmaster's wife, Louise Cullen, a fiftyish woman sheepishly held up her hand. "That's from us," she said in a voice filled with terror. "It's a Coleman camping stove."

McGovern threw the gift to the side and lifted another one.

"Whose?!" he yelled.

One of his co-workers, Chad Isaacs a lead avionics hardware engineer yelled out, "Mine!"

McGovern threw that gift to the side as well. The repeated cadence of "whose," "mine," then a box crashing to the floor was repeated seventy-two painful times. Finally, a gift that was lifted received no claim.

"Very good, Sarge. You now have seven minutes to save everyone in this room," said Adams.

McGovern slowly lowered the box onto the table. He gingerly removed the wrapping paper revealing a plain brown box closed with a single strip of scotch tape. He peeled back the tape and looked inside.

On first look, the IED was a surprisingly simple and weak device. Through a clear, Plexiglas cover McGovern saw that Adams had connected a 9-volt battery to a detonator cap through a digital Casio watch, the favorite timer of terrorists. The watch face showed six minutes and ticking. Once it hit zero seconds, the circuit would complete, detonating the bomb. And true to her word, there appeared to be a secondary detonator; an antenna was hooked into the system that could receive wireless signals.

McGovern looked closer to see what kind of charge the blasting cap was connected to. He felt a momentary twinge of relief to see that the explosive was a single stick of TNT. Any damage from that explosive would be minimal, especially if everyone stayed as far away as they were. It was kind of ridiculous to have gone through this much trouble for such a lame bomb. The thing was as basic as it got and probably would be a snap to disarm. So why do it? Was Adams so nuts that she'd forgotten all of her expertise? Maybe she just wanted to scare him. Then again, maybe there was more to it.

As he scanned, McGovern noticed that below the dynamite was a pair of glass orbs. They were filled with some type of clear liquid. He tilted his head a bit to one side to look for any kind of markings. There were. In black ink, each of the orbs bore the initials GB.

He spun to look at Adams. "This is a chemical device!"

Adams merely nodded. "Sarin," she said. "Already mixed."

McGovern knew what sarin could do. Syria and Iraq had used it on their own citizens, killing thousands. But those were done by the military with armaments. Missiles containing the deadly brew were shot into cities to basically melt their citizens. That didn't mean it had to be military strikes.

His mind played back the scene of sarin attacks by the Buddhist terror group, Shoko Sakaraha, in 1987. There, sarin had been concealed in lunch boxes and soft-drink containers and placed on three different subway train floors. It had been released as terrorists punctured the containers with umbrellas before leaving the trains. The incident was timed to coincide with rush hour when trains were packed with commuters. Eleven people died and over 5,500 were injured in the attack. The low body count was only because the attacks had been poorly executed. Experts agreed that if a more effective means of dispersion has been used in such an enclosed area the body count would have numbered in the thousands.

Recalling the effects and amounts of nerve gas made McGovern feel like a retired NFL player trying to remember the playbook of games he'd competed in ten years ago. Except these were deadly plays. He remembered that sarin is colorless and odorless with a lethal dose of 0.5 milligram for an adult. It is twenty-six times more deadly than cyanide gas and twenty times more lethal than potassium cyanide. Just 0.01 milligram per kilogram of body weight, a pinprick sized droplet could kill a human. Within a minute of exposure, people experience runny noses, tightness in the chest, and pupil constriction. After several minutes, they have difficulty breathing, become nauseated, and start to drool. They then lose control of their bodily functions, begin twitching, and ultimately suffocate in a series of convulsive spasms.

When he'd known her, Adams had been one of the best chemical EODs there was. How she'd gotten the sarin was incidental. She definitely had the skill set to make this work.

McGovern looked back down at the open box before him. He removed a small case that she'd apparently placed inside the box for him. The case contained a screwdriver and a pair of wire cutters. He realized that Adams was giving him a chance to disarm it. He didn't stop to think of her reasons; she was clearly out of her mind and screwed up by making a device that almost anyone could disarm.

The timer now read three minutes. McGovern lifted off the Plexiglas cover, making sure not to jostle the IED. It was then that he knew Adams hadn't faltered. The entire package, including the charge, had been placed into a clear epoxy compound that had solidified around the bomb components. He could see all of the internals but was unable to reach them.

Her device suddenly went from basic to brilliant. Since sarin, the most powerful nerve agent made by mankind is highly lethal in even tiny doses, by containing the orbs in the epoxy compound, Adams had assured that no harm would occur unless the device exploded. He figured that she'd probably injected the chemicals into the orbs as the compound was curing to mitigate any danger to herself. Plus, if the package dropped, accidentally breaking the glass, no liquid or vapor would escape. Dispersal through an explosion was a horror story that made *Apocalypse Now* look like *Goodnight Moon*.

Unless McGovern could diffuse the bomb, the explosion would vaporize the liquid and break apart the containment unit. The gas would dissipate through the room, killing anyone who inhaled it – basically everyone. It could even kill people outside of the room if the gas filtered into the ventilation system and under cracks beneath the doors.

The fear that had started as a spark erupted into a full-blown inferno. He knew that given the circumstances, it was impossible. She'd given him the illusion of success just to give him a feeling of false hope.

"Please," he said back to Dr. Adams. "Kay. I'm sorry."

"You're sorry?" she spat. "Sorry? That's the best you can do? Because of you I lost everything. I couldn't have a family. I couldn't even have friends. Look at this?" she said, indicating the room of family and friends.

Adams became unglued. "You're fucking sorry?! Fuck your sorry! Fuck you, fuck you, fuck you! Now diffuse the bomb, you abhorrent piece of shit, or everyone dies."

He looked back at the device, completely lost. He had no effective tools. No way of cutting through the epoxy that housed the device. Hell, even if he'd had a shield to guard against the explosion, the vaporized nerve gas would spread through the room and kill everyone.

Adams continued, "Impossible, isn't it? Just like it's been impossible for me to erase you from my mind. I've tried to diffuse the horrible memory you planted inside of me for that past ten years. No tools could do that, Sarge. Every day, every night, it sits inside ticking away, rotting me, eating me up, waiting to explode."

Sensing a sort of twisted kinship with the woman, but not knowing why, Dolly looked askance at her husband. "What did you do to her, Skip?"

"None of your business," he replied with hate.

Dolly's eyes blinked rapid-fire as she attempted to contain herself. "What are you talking about? Of course it's my business. She's going to kill me because of something you did. She's going to kill all of us. Now what did you do to this woman?" "Shut the hell up!" McGovern screamed. "I have to think. I have to focus."

"Tell her," said Adams. "Tell her, tell your son, and everyone else in this room what you did. And you tell them right now," she held up her cellphone as a threat.

McGovern looked at his shaking hands. He looked at the guests. At his family, his friends, and associates. Then he looked at Adams.

"I raped her," he whispered.

"You did what?!" Dolly screamed, mortified.

"I raped her," he said. This time more audibly.

"That's right. He raped me. Six times!" said Adams. "You started a timer inside of me that has been ticking off the seconds for ten years. Ten years of torture. Ten years of drugs, booze, and failed therapy. I always knew that it would go off one day, but I never knew when. I guess the timer's done. I'm ready to go boom now."

Dolly stepped toward Doctor Adams, her palms out to show she wasn't a threat. She said that she understood the rage over Skip. She shared it. She'd been Skip's prisoner for nearly twenty years and had secretly wished he would be killed by a car or get cancer or some other painful, lethal disease. She asked, quite simply, if it would be possible to let go the innocents.

Doc Adams shook her head. She trembled as she looked at the pleading faces of the guests. "I would have been satisfied with just killing your husband, but killing all of you is what they wanted in exchange for this. It was a tradeoff I was willing to make to rid myself of this damned bomb inside of me."

"Who are 'they?'" asked Dolly.

Her question was never answered. As Doctor Adams lifted the cellphone into the air, everyone in the room rushed for the door but it was too late. Adams was finally at peace.

Chapter Twenty-Three

Through the plastic slits of his George W. Bush mask, Armagan looked at the man wearing the Cheney mask, awaiting his instruction. Cheney sat behind the table of the same grim room where Dr. Temple had been executed. His eyes were closed as he listened to the soft sobs of Shane, whose utterances, rather than sounding like those of a man in his prime, came out like those of an old man. This was due to the fact that his teeth had been crushed together and painfully shattered by the increased and intense pressure of the Head Crusher that was attached to him. To Armagan it was merely ambient, white noise.

Cheney opened his eyes and looked at Shane. On the table before him was a plain file folder that contained the man's résumé and charges. On top of the folder was a large, polished piece of granite that served as a paperweight.

"Right now you only need some dental work, Mr. Hoff. I could give you a card for someone," said Cheney. "But one more twist of the vice grip and your eyes will literally pop from their sockets. I don't know any ophthalmologists who could help you after that."

The Head Crusher was a simple, yet horrifying machine. A convex, metal skullcap fit over the top of Shane's head. The cap was connected to a flat, thick, metal strip that ran along the bottom of his chin. The cap and plate were connected to a frame by long screw arms that were attached to a wooden handle above the skullcap. If the handle was turned clockwise, the cap pushed downward, compressing the skull into the jaw.

Cheney continued. "Here's an interesting sidebar; some of these devices had little cups on them to catch the eyeballs. Some neat-nick inquisitor, I suppose. Nevertheless, right now your jaw is broken, and your teeth have been pulverized. One more twist and your eyeballs will come out. One twist beyond that and your cranium will shatter. The bones will tear apart your brain, and you will be quite dead. So. You have the power here. Does the pain stop because you admit your guilt or because the circuits in your delicate gray matter cease sending out signals?"

He gestured to Armagan, who wordlessly turned the screw handle counterclockwise. The relief could be felt simultaneously by all three men as the cap loosened. Shane felt the least relief. While the immediate physical pain had subsided, the surreal Escher-meets-Picasso-meets-Coltrane moment was beyond comprehension. He felt as if his very soul had been raped. Nothing in his life had prepared him for the absolute insanity of his predicament. People didn't do this. All the rules he'd learned in his life were completely obliterated, so there was nothing for him to grasp.

He had no idea how long he'd been tortured. Time wasn't something he could fathom. And he saw no way of appeasement. He had no information for these men. Nothing he'd done, knew, or ever would conceive of doing could justify this. There was no word in any of the dozen languages he spoke to describe the savagery.

Armagan stifled a yawn beneath his mask. In part it was a yawn caused by fatigue. In the beginning, he'd thought the execution of their plan would take no toll on him. He didn't care about Shane or anyone else in the crosshairs. He believed in the mission with all of his heart. But nights had become increasingly restless. He didn't realize the cause fully, but the violence was robbing him of sleep, among other things. He hoped the brutality of this session would speed things along.

On another side, he was finding it tedious. While he believed that the tactics they were employing were in line with the ultimate strategy, he just wished they were there already. Surprisingly, he suffered little guilt over the torture. In his mind, he was simply the button pusher and didn't view himself as a barbarian. In fact, he considered his role to be a bit noble. He was the executioner. An ender of pain. A deliverer of justice, freedom, and peace. The Reaper did not judge. The Reaper simply reaped.

As Armagan watched the blood flow from Shane's mouth, the fallibility and fragility of man swirled through his mind. Barely twenty-four hours ago, Shane had been prominent and powerful. A wealthy, highly respected part of the engineering community. Now he was nearly nonexistent. It had been so easy to lure him away from McGovern with the promise of more domination. Like a western sheep to the slaughter, he thought. So sad they had no honor.

Armagan recalled how they'd left the party and went out the doors of the country club discussing ways to build better military mousetraps. As they strolled through the croquet court, the party in view through the windows, Shane had noticed what was happening inside. Just as the explosion went off Armagan had pricked him with a tranquilizer. With all the attention now fixed on the massacre, he and several other well-paid men had shoved Shane into a van, then drove to the Simi Valley airport. They'd then stuffed his body through the side door of Armagan's jump plane and flown him to his current situation.

Cheney stood up and walked toward Shane. Armagan moved away to stand beside the video camera that was capturing the brutal ordeal. Cheney moved behind Shane and gripped the smooth, wooden vice handles. He gently rocked the Head Crusher forward and back as he leaned over and spoke into the man's right ear.

"The device sitting upon your head was created by engineers like you to help elicit confessions during the reign of Torquemada, the Grand Inquisitor. But unlike you, this barbaric machine was created for moral reasons. And while those men, who ironically were mostly in the clergy, were equally guilty of devising evil, they were still your superiors because those deeds were done from a misguided sense of moral responsibility. You, my friend have used your intellect to create and sell evil without any moral cause. You are a blight on mankind. And you owe us an apology."

In spite of the intense downward pressure that was still being exerted on his head, Shane's bulging eyes moved side to side as he racked his brain for a response. He licked his torn-up lips with what was left of his tongue. He barely recognized his own dry and poorly enunciated voice.

"I was responsible for my role only. You can't punish me for creating a situation I had no say in."

"Wrong!" spat Cheney. "You have general responsibilities as well as causal responsibilities. You're not an idiot. You were not coerced. You knew what you were doing and you could have refused. My God, I'm sure you saw what we did to Dr. Temple. Did you not take us seriously?"

In his heart, Shane knew that appealing to the man's humanity would be useless so he didn't even try. Besides, as a man of science, he didn't believe in any of the emotional arguments he could have made. His broken jaw throbbed, and even moving it a little bit caused him excruciating pain. He summoned his strength and fought through it, realizing he had only one chance left. At this point he knew that no matter what he said or did he would probably be executed. He was already maimed beyond repair, so who cared if he antagonized the man. He painfully began his defense.

"So your view is that good guys make no weapons, and bad guys produce lots of them, and it's that simple? What happens when the bad guys decide to be bad with their weapons by using them on the unarmed, defenseless good guys? Or maybe some people should work in the weapons industry, but feel really, really bad about it. And then, of course, those of us who have nice jobs are the better people, since we took the high road by forcing someone else to be bad. Maybe we could have a lottery to decide who is bad so that our good lives can continue safely. Then we can all sit back and bask in the shiny, sunny warmth of just how good we all are, unlike those bad, bad people who make weapons that we can defend ourselves with."

Cheney walked around and stared at Shane. He shook his head, sadly.

"You engineers betray your big brains by being so simple-minded. Use your imagination. Get creative! Design something that defends without killing. The shield protects us from the sword. Umbrellas keep us dry without blowing up the clouds. Hats shade us from ultraviolet rays. If killing is bad, then killing to end killing is even worse because you employ that which you deem evil to rid the evil. It is more unethical if you believe it's wrong, then do it anyway to justify it. Defend us, then let the diplomats resolve the differences with words while we parry with your technology."

Realizing that he was losing and that this time it meant more than not getting a purchase order, Shane put on his best sales pitch. "When an engineer designs a weapon, he's not causing the pain and suffering. And even if I agree with you, there are ten thousand others out there who would gladly step in to do the job."

Cheney grabbed Shane by the face and squeezed. His eyes bulged and his body spasmed from the searing pain.

"Once you worm away from 'complete responsibility,' the rest is easy, isn't it? Well I don't buy it. You don't get off the hook. I've heard all of the excuses: If I don't do it, someone else will. I need to feed myself and my family. It'll only be used on the bad guys. It helps protect my country. It's the user's responsibility not mine. The boss thinks it's a good idea. It has significant, non-evil uses. No one will ever know it was me. Well, that's not true. We do know it was you. And you need to be held accountable."

He let go of Shane's face and began parading around the room. He was dancing and singing to a sprightly, upbeat Tom Lehrer tune:

"Don't say that he's hypocritical,

Say rather that he's apolitical.

Once the rockets are up,

Who cares where they come down,

That's not my department,

Says Werner Von Braun."

"You're insane," Shane moaned, incredulous.

Cheney sighed. His reply was calm.

"You who understand technology need to make value judgments. All of you. It's a simple matter of ethics. Do you willingly take money to sell weapons whose sole intent is to kill human beings? Do you agree to create systems that transfer wealth from middle-class to rich folks? Do you write codes, like the NSA's, that violate the constitution, the law, and common decency? I say you do. I also say you may not. Not anymore!"

He walked back to the table and slid the rock off of the folder. Its apparent weight scraped the table roughly. He opened the folder, and as he read from whatever papers were inside, Armagan walked to Shane and removed the Head Crusher. Shane's head instantly slumped forward, a torrent of red drool spilling onto his legs.

Cheney read the charges against Shane aloud, in an officious, self-important manner. "Director of International Business Development for AeroVironment, Senior Project Manager for Strategic Products, consultant for multirole UAV weapons carriage systems on MQ-1 Predator A's and MQ-9 Predator B's, Technical Presenter for Smart Weapons and Miniature Munitions, etcetera, etcetera, etcetera."

Before he put down the folder, Cheney withdrew a single sheet of paper. He shook it at Shane.

"This is your confession. If you sign it, you will purge your soul and you'll head to wherever you are bound in a white cloak accompanied by the Lord's angels."

He took a pen and walked toward Shane.

"It simply says, 'I knew it was wrong but I did it anyway.'"

Broken, Shane took hold of the pen and painfully signed the document. He didn't believe a word of it, but he wanted the anguish to end.

"Very good," said Cheney. "Your eternal soul is now free. You are still guilty, but you are cleansed."

Cheney nodded to Armagan who picked up the rock that was on the desk. Because of its weight, he needed both hands to lift it. As he moved behind Shane and hoisted it above his head, Shane looked at Cheney.

"Is God guilty of murder for creating the stone you'll use to kill me?"

Cheney stared Shane in the eyes, the right side of his lip lifting into a sneer.

"An excellent question. Feel free to ask Abel when you see him."

Chapter Twenty-Four

0900 Hours – Torrey Pines, California

San Diego was a mob scene. The normally quiet and secluded street leading up to General Atomic's massive 120-acre compound on Torrey Pines Mesa was packed with news vans, protestors, San Diego police, and surprised GA employees going to work. In spite of their efforts to keep the crowd on the sidewalks, angry protestors easily sidestepped the outmanned police force and beat on the employees' car hoods and trunks as they tried to pass through the company's security gate. They glared at the drivers and, even if it was just a secretary, called them "murderers," "baby killers," and "traitors!"

It was no surprise to anyone that, in addition to protestors from groups like Code Pink and Veterans For Peace, stood Tom Carby. His bald head and red beard reflecting the morning sunlight, he stood on the sidewalk and screamed into his bullhorn, "End the military industrial complex! We don't want your war machine!"

Today, his normally booming voice melded with nearly a thousand others. Cries of "Stop the lies," "We reap what we sow!," "Stop the drones," "Kill the engineers!" and worse were chanted louder and louder.

While the police attempted to maintain calm in the street, the National Guard had been activated to keep protestors from entering the company grounds. Called to duty because of hundreds of threats made by anarchist groups, the soldiers were stationed at strategic points armed with M-16s. Their orders were to subdue, not shoot. But as the crowd and intensity increased, the possibility of some fear-induced mistake mounted. Keeping order in this situation was a task akin to digging a hole in water.

General Atomics was by no means the only defense contractor to become the target of public outrage. Barely twenty-four hours after the videotaped torture and execution of Shane Hoff went viral, similar scenes were taking place all over the country. Boeing, General Dynamics, Raytheon, AeroVironment, Teledyne, Lockheed Martin, and other death merchants were experiencing the same level of outrage.

The protests were swift and had happened organically. There had been no warning, no lawful assembly applications, and no websites announcing dates.

In spite of YouTube, Twitter, and Facebook trying to keep the video of Hoff's execution offline, it was unstoppable. Like cutting off the head of a hydra, every time one instance was blocked, a hundred more were uploaded. In less than twelve hours the videos had been viewed over a million times. In twenty-four, that number had swelled to over fifty million worldwide. Finding the source of the initial upload was frantically and unsuccessfully being investigated.

Why Doctor Temple's torture and execution just a month ago hadn't prompted the same reaction was anyone's guess. It was probably because the Twitter revolution that had engulfed the Middle East didn't seem to affect Americans the same way. Americans were jaded and complacent. It apparently took more than a couple of potentially doctored torture videos, lies to the UN Security Council about WMDs in Iraq, or revelations of Torture Memos from the president's office to make college students look up from their sext messages.

What had prompted the outcry was plain and simple. Fear. Just prior to the viral distribution of the video, the dead body of Shane Hoff had been found hanging from the Hollywood sign. Around his neck was a placard that read, "You're not listening America. We are here and we are not finished." There was a QR code on the placard that led to the video. His suspended and mangled body had been Go-Pro'd and wirelessly transmitted to the Internet.

Marcella Kraner had been to a lot of protest rallies, but never one like the one in Torrey Pines. Other than terrorized citizens looking for someone's head, it was uncentered and chaotic. The possibility of it turning into a riot was extremely likely. In spite of her courage, Kraner stayed close to Ethan Michaels whose Eye of Truth camera greedily chronicled the happenings. She looked around for an entry point, a place to start her story. There were too many.

Rather than yell over the noise, Kraner patted Ethan's shoulder to get his attention. She pointed to herself, then across the crowd to Carby. He nodded, and then pointed to himself to see if he should follow. She shook her head no and left him to shoot as much B-roll as possible.

Kraner worked her way through the crowd, getting bounced and squeezed from body to body as she went. When she reached Carby, he looked down at her and smiled.

"Lovely day, ain't it?" he shouted.

In spite of herself and what was happening, she smiled back. She yelled over the din, "You love this stuff, don't you?"

"What? Civil unrest?" he boomed back. "Absolutely. It's the only way to keep a superpower super!" Carby looked up and sniffed the air. "I love the smell of revolution in the morning!"

Kraner shook her head, then pointed to a blocked-off parking lot about fifty feet away. Carby understood that she wanted him to follow her. Rather than let her navigate the crowd, he gallantly took the lead and cleared a path. She easily followed in the wake of his long-legged strides. He lifted one side of the blue police barricade and gestured for her to go first. Although there was still a smattering of people in the lot, it was a much quieter place to talk.

"What's up, pussycat?" Carby asked.

Worn on some men, behavior like his was as chauvinist as it got, and Marcella Kraner would have bristled. From Carby, it came across as polite and protective. It was just his way.

Kraner gestured to the crowd. "What's your take on all of this?" she asked. Sensing her tone, Carby immediately became serious.

"Which part of 'this' are you referring to, Ms. Kraner? The 'this' that's about terrorists torturing and executing engineers on American soil? Or the 'this' that we just found out they slaughtered a few hundred folks to get at 'em?"

He was referring to the second wave of viral videos that followed Hoff's murder. After local law enforcement had responded to the chemical attack at the Sherman Country Club, the FBI had ordered a media blackout to keep them in the dark about the sarin. In addition to setting up a wide perimeter, the FAA had ordered a temporary flight restriction in Thousand Oaks to keep the press helicopters away. They'd blocked anyone carrying a camera who wasn't a fed or a coroner from getting within a mile of the scene.

That meant the skies normally filled with news-choppers would remain empty while the pros took stock, mopped up, and figured out their talking points. For all of their efforts, the FAA, the FBI, FEMA, and the SWAT crews hadn't prevented the terrorists from buzzing in a drone with a mounted GoPro.

While the psy-ops teams fed a line of bull to the local press and concerned citizens about a minor incident at the club, the drone was capturing footage of dead bodies in the croquet court and the first tee of the golf course. They were the corpses of guests who'd apparently been in the back of the banquet room and thrown chairs through the windows to escape the sarin. The brew had been extremely potent so even though they'd escaped fast, they'd still inhaled enough to kill them. It had just taken a bit longer for their neural transmitters to malfunction.

Flying above the stiff, foam-mouthed carcasses, the minidrone captured WMD techs in orange, level-A hazmat suits taking readings with mass spectrometers and swabbing the insides of people's cheeks for samples. In the parking lot where the command station had been set up, firemen in bunker gear conducted gross decontamination of the club employees and survivors with fire hoses. They were trying to wash off whatever trace amounts of sarin may have still been on their bodies before bringing them in for triage and evaluation.

The terrorists, whoever they were, had allowed the fear from the Hoff torture video to take root, then blasted the net with a virtual secondary device. This time, edited over the eerie night footage of the massacre at the county club was a voice-over proclaiming, "People of America, you are being lied to. We killed the people in Thousand Oaks with sarin. We killed the people at the Hotel del Coronado. We kidnapped, tried, and executed Dr. Temple and Shane Hoff. We demand that all engineers and scientists cease their work on weapons and weapons systems immediately or there will be more killings."

The media threw gasoline on the fire. All day Sunday, reports filled the airwaves with conjecture about this group or that group. Rebroadcast images of the massacre at the Hotel del Coronado, the dead bodies of Dr. Temple and Shane Hoff, and provocative graphic segment titles like, "Is Anyone Safe?" "Who's Next?" "War on Engineers" fed the public's anxiety.

Kraner didn't know how to respond to Carby's question. His gaze was condescending and made her feel like a child. She gulped and looked away.

"I guess all of it," she said. "Who did it? You're a drone guy. Who could it be?"

"You disappoint me, Ms. Kraner," he said. "You may not be as guilty of fear-mongering as the other members of the Fifth Estate, but you are guilty of asking the wrong questions to the wrong people. Now if you'll excuse me, little lady, outrage and anger are in my wheelhouse so I got to roll." With that, he turned and strode away, his fists lifted skyward and pumping the air.

1100 Hours – Thousand Oaks, California

When it came to bombs and massacres, Special Agent Mark Guerke had been around the block more than a few times. In his previous position as director of critical incident response for the Jefferson County, Colorado, Sheriff's Office, he'd handled over a hundred calls a year for nearly a decade. He'd handled pipe bombs in malls, insane gunmen in movie theaters, white supremacists with huge arms caches and, perhaps his most dubious claim to fame was being the lead officer in the Columbine High School shootings.

Now in his early sixties, with barely a wisp of hair left and bit of a well-earned paunch, Guerke was the FBI's lead counterterrorism agent in the Ventura County office. His specialties were EOD and hostage situations. Really, though, he was a bomb guy. As a cop he'd trained in Israel and at the FBI's Huntsville, Alabama, facility. The DoD and other special agent bomb tech's had been impressed with his expertise and forensic skills. When the position in Ventura came up two years ago, Guerke's name was at the top of everyone's list.

He wasn't a cowboy or a hothead. Rather, he was patient and looked at situations like a tactician. He knew that investigations could be tedious and time consuming. Not that the lag wasn't frustrating, he just understood the need for thoroughness.

Some of his peers, the ones who didn't know him, sometimes made the mistake of confusing his easygoing manner as a sign that he was a pushover. He was anything but. Guerke was a hardheaded, old-time beat cop who gave you just enough rope to hang yourself. The agents in Ventura quickly learned to respect his style. And they loved his self-introduction, "If it stinks, glows, burns, or blows, I'm your man." *Stinks* referred to chemicals, *glows* to nukes, *burns* was arson, and *blows* was for bombs.

Guerke was currently the SAIC, or special agent in charge, of the sarin attack in Thousand Oaks. His main parking lot command post was getting up-to-the-minute reports from all of the three-letter professionals from EMS, FBI, WMD techs and more. "Alphabet soup" is what he liked to call it. The order of the day was containment and decontamination.

Right now he was standing beside Special Agent Breskin, who was finishing up an interrogation of the security guard who'd witnessed the situation develop on CCTV in the Fairmont room. From Guerke's perspective, the guard had done his job well. He'd listened to Dr. Adam's instructions and not risked entering the room. After calling in the hostage situation to local law, he'd evacuated all nonparty guests to a safe distance and kept them calm and together while they waited for the police and SWAT teams to arrive.

The guard, Neil Kopit, was in his late thirties. He had thick, curly, black hair and was as thin as the wire rims that held the eyeglasses on his face. Breskin had instructed him to sit on a round, glass-topped end table on the south veranda of the club. Kopit was sweating profusely. Not only because of the heat and the stress of being interrogated, but because he was scared his weight would shatter the glass tabletop. He was doing a sort of half-sit, half-crouch to keep that from happening. His legs were getting fatigued.

Breskin, in stark and intentional contrast, sat in a comfortable patio chair just in the shade created by the roofline. He stared at Kopit, unblinking, as he methodically unwrapped a piece of candy. As intended, the crinkling was unnerving. After he finished slowly and noisily unwrapping each side, he tapped the candy against his front teeth three times, then tossed it into his mouth. He then neatly folded the clear, square sheet of cellophane in half several times, until it would get no smaller. Breskin looked around for a garbage can or an ashtray. Finding neither, he placed the small square into his shirt pocket.

"I hate litterbugs, don't you?" he asked Kopit.

Kopit nodded, eager to be done with this ordeal and, hopefully, go back home. All he wanted was to get as far away from this place as possible. The images of dead and dying party guests would haunt him for the rest of his life. He'd known the McGoverns for years. The question of whether he could have done more would never leave his thoughts.

Seeming to read his mind, Breskin said. "You did a great thing by clearing the guests out of the club. If you'd tried to break into that room a lot more people would be dead."

"Thank you," said Kopit. "I was just doing my job."

Breskin sucked his candy loudly. "Was it also your job to erase thirty minutes of the party, including the section where Mr. Hoff left the room?"

Guerke, who up until this point was thinking Breskin was a bully, perked up. This was the reason he'd been asked to set up the field interrogation. He hadn't been told anything other than a bigwig from LA was coming. He'd figured it was just another case of a bigger office trying to pull out its bigger dick. Over the past few hours he'd heard a lot of uncomplimentary things about Breskin, but in spite of that, he was beginning to admire the man's technique.

Kopit answered, "What? No way! I didn't touch the footage. I called the police, then got everyone the hell out. That's all."

"You used to be a pretty good videographer, didn't you? Back when you were in the corps. Did anything ever happen with your work? Anyone ever tell you it sucked or anything like that?"

Kopit was completely taken off guard. "No. Everyone liked what I did. They thought I was great. I could've been a Hollywood guy."

"Then why weren't you?"

"Hey listen, can I please sit on a chair? I feel like this table is going to crack under my ass any second."

"Soon," said Breskin. "And if it does, crack under your 'ass,' Special Agent Guerke here has enough EMTs examining dead bodies to stitch you up. But since you mentioned it, why aren't you a big time Hollywood guy?"

"I got PTSD from sitting in a tank, so I can't stand being in one of those cramped editing bays anymore. Happy?"

"Ecstatic. I just find it a lot of bit odd that you were the guy at the security station who saw what went down, but when the hard drive got to my office, the one section where the kidnapped man left the room was missing. Don't you find that odd?"

Without warning, Breskin abruptly stood up. His heavy metal chair slid back, loudly scraping the deck. Surprised, Guerke's hand instinctively moved to his holstered sidearm. Kopit shifted his weight so fast that the glass beneath him shattered. His bottom went down into the hole, scraping the glass and cutting his hips. He howled in pain as he and his stuck ass fell sideward.

"Get him out of here," Breskin said to nobody in particular. Then, back to Kopit, "And don't think I believe that was an accident."

As an agent helped Kopit to painfully extract himself, Breskin and Guerke walked off. Until today they'd never met and if it hadn't been for the missing footage, they probably never would have. Breskin had called after he'd gotten the computer drive to make sure Kopit was there. He'd been brought in on the case because of the torture aspect.

"I hope you don't think I'm trying to piss on your investigation," Breskin said after a moment.

"Not at all. Another set of eyes is always good," said Guerke. "So you see some tie-in with the video editing?"

Breskin didn't normally like discussing cases, but given Guerke's background he figured it might be helpful.

"No. I see a tie-in with vets. What's your take?" asked Breskin.

"I'm not sure yet, but on the surface it's pretty straightforward. That gal was psychotic from being raped by McGovern and not getting justice from the DoD or help from the VA."

"Agreed," Breskin replied. "But it's a bit too straightforward. She had a grievance and went over the top. DJ boy had a grievance and went over the top. So what do we have? A couple of prime-time massacres pulled off by veterans. Both of the vets had axes to grind with the DoD, but neither of them lived to be considered accomplices to the kidnappings, right? So I have a theory. Some terrorist group is manipulating broken vets against Defense to get their hands on the engineers. They couldn't care less who gets killed in the massacres, but that's where they do the grab. Net result is total paralysis, maybe if they scare enough engineers the machine will grind to a halt."

Guerke ran his hand over his head, taking in what Breskin was suggesting.

"Seems pretty elaborate. Why not just grab the engineers at their homes or on their way back from work?"

"Because killing their family and friends at parties will scare hell out of anyone who even knows an engineer. The community will become a bunch of Typhoid Mary's."

"Interesting theory. But there's a shit ton of messed up, angry vets out there. Saying you're right, how do you see 'em coming?"

Breskin shook his head. "Don't know. Maybe go through all the VA's records."

"Then what?"

"Like I told Senator Feinstein on the phone this morning, GW had the guts to take off the gloves in Iraq. Let's take off the gloves here. They're whining that the Patriot Act needs to be pulled back, but I don't think it's enough. We need to constitutionalize the Patriot Act, get rid of FISA and untie NSA's hands. And we damned sure need to tell the FAA to deregulate

UAVs. Those things are the best surveillance tool ever invented. I'd have one of them tailing every messed-up vet in the country."

"Scary thought," said Guerke.

Breskin pointed to the Fairmont Room. "Any scarier than that?"

1400 Hours – El Mirage, California

Besides a handful of highly trusted mates like Killa, Diddy, and Phil, Chauncey was pretty much on his own. For a man who'd spent most of his adult life in military intelligence, the isolation was crippling. And if he was going to figure out who'd attempted to kill him, he was going to need access to information. Tradecraft was just one part of being an effective intel officer. To be successful you also needed a network of well-placed, high-level informants. He didn't have that anymore.

Not long ago, Chauncey had had a worldwide network. He'd started building it the day he'd joined the Maryland Air National Guard, 175th Tactical Airlift Group, as an Intelligence Operations Specialist AFSC 20170. Because his subspecialty was in evasion and escape, he did E&E planning at the 175th. After graduating intel school and getting his top secret clearances, he got "read into" the 175th war plans, and used national imagery, HUMINT, and tradecraft to research and develop escape routes from hostile territories.

At one point he'd had thousands of contacts all over the world. After he'd lost his clearances, it was like he was a shark plucked from the ocean and dropped into a goldfish bowl.

As the prepaid cellphone in his hand completed his call, he had no idea if the man on the other end would pick up. He hoped with all of his might that he would answer, but it was a crapshoot. To most of his old comrades he was persona non grata. Helping him could be a career ender.

Nothing put a red stain on a person faster than being labeled a whistleblower. It didn't matter that Chauncey had been officially exonerated, he'd still been stripped of his access, security clearances and few, if any, of his old associates would even take his calls.

He impatiently waited as the phone on the other end rang and a part of Chauncey wished that none of it had ever happened. He rubbed his temple to sooth his non-stop headache and contemplated how different things would have been had he been a different person who'd made different choices. Hang that! He was a commissioned officer and had sworn an oath to defend the Constitution of the United States. It sickened him now, as before, to watch the uber-rich and powerful selfishly raping the founding fathers' vision with illegal and immoral actions.

Ten years ago when he'd been sent overseas to train CIA interrogators, he had no idea what he'd find. He'd boarded a plane at Fairchild AFB for Bahrain, ostensibly to oversee the interrogations of some al-Qaeda detainees. When the flight landed, rather than jump into a jeep and heading for the prison, MPs shuttled him to a private charter Gulfstream IV.

The plane was small and cramped and he was only one of three passengers. One was a CIA agent named "Charley," and the other was a detainee who was wearing a diaper, blacked-out goggles and handcuffs chained to the floor. Every time the prisoner tried to stretch his cramping muscles, Charley would kick him in the jaw and bark for him to sit still.

When Chauncey asked what the guy had done, Charley snorted and said, "We'll find out soon enough." Things went downhill from there.

Several hours later the plane landed in Rabat, Morocco. There they were greeted by the Moroccan Secret Service and Breskin, who six months ago had worked at SERE as a psychologist. Now, apparently, he was a civilian employed by the CIA to help with interrogation training that he'd learned under Chauncey. Breskin shook Chauncey's hand excited and told him how great it was to see him.

They hopped into an HMMWV and drove several hours to Temara Prison, one of the CIA's black ops sites for high-level detainees who'd allegedly been involved in planning the 9/11 attacks. During the drive,

Breskin bragged to Chauncey how he and another ex-SERE psychologist, Jack Sway, had started a company and were consulting with the CIA. They'd gone to Rumsfeld and told him that when it came to interrogation, they knew what worked and what didn't work. Now they were making a lot of money and wanted Chauncey to join them.

At the prison Chauncey witnessed some of the most inhumane and gruesome enhanced techniques he'd ever seen.

"GW wanted the gloves off," Breskin said nonchalantly.

Breskin showed Chauncey around the prison. In addition to the reek of sweat, vomit and decaying flesh, he saw detainees in isolation chained naked to walls and floors. Many of them had bruises over their entire bodies, and several had deep, oozing contusions on their chests and genitals. Red-stained cricket paddles leaned ominously outside of each cell just in case they needed to be quieted down. He sat in on several interrogation sessions where the only thing they did was spit on the prisoner and beat him.

Not only was he unimpressed, Chauncey was mortified. This wasn't even close to what they did at SERE. They taught US forces that torture didn't work. They preached that it was immoral and illegal. That only the bad guys did it. And they taught it because it was true.

Breskin asked him to teach the interrogators at Temara how to do it right, but it was apparent that nobody believed in his tactics. All they wanted to know was how to exploit phobias and how much water a prisoner could be forced to inhale before they drown. The CIA and military intelligence agents had been instructed to get intel fast and they didn't want to hear about the slow, methodical relationship-building techniques used by the FBI. They just wanted to know which methods would leave the fewest external marks.

Chauncey refused to cooperate and was quickly labeled a *faggot sympathizer* by the guards and interrogators. He recalled how Charley had sat next to him during dinner one evening, sharpening his knife.

"You might want to reconsider falling asleep tonight," Charley warned.

"I'll just do that because you'll need someone to take you to the hospital to get that blade out of your ass," Chauncey had replied.

Over the next seven days Chauncey and Breskin argued over the tactics that were being used. Chauncey pleaded with Breskin to reverse course. He appealed to his sense of reason and justice. To his ethical pledge as a psychologist to heal not injure. He even appealed to Breskin's Mormon beliefs. Breskin responded that he was doing the Lord's work through *Tikkun Olam*, the Kabalistic belief that God was once a vessel of light which had shattered. It was mankind's responsibility to gather the broken shards and rebuild the Lord. In his warped interpretation, the terrorists represented evil shards that had to be fixed before God could be reassembled.

It was bad with a capital B and Breskin had clearly convinced himself that he could get information – actionable intelligence – the way they were going.

After a week of stubborn non-compliance and a few fights that left some hurt guards and lots of purple bruises on Chauncey's knuckles, they packed him up and shipped him back to Spokane. Before he left, he was sternly reminded of his NDA and told that if he revealed what they were doing he'd be court-martialed.

"Chauncey?" a voice on the other side of his burner phone answered, mercifully shaking him back to the present. "Jesus, man, we all thought you were dead. Those sensors picked up some serious seismic shit and then nada. What happened?"

Relieved that his friend was still taking his calls, Chauncey didn't waste any time with pleasantries. The man, Myles Bradley, was a Measures and Signals Intelligence, MASINT, analyst at the JPRA facility in White Bluffs, Washington. They'd become close friends during Chauncey's stay at SERE and, after he'd gone public about the enhanced interrogation techniques he'd witnessed, Bradley was one of the only people who'd sympathized with Chauncey's public revelations.

Following Chauncey's court-martial, stint in prison, and subsequent move to the desert, he'd planted a number of unattended ground sensors around the house. He'd told Bradley about them and explained that if something should happen to him, they'd most likely hold the key to what had occurred. So when the scorpions vaporized his home and the entire MASINT community was thrown into a state of confusion over the signals coming from unlogged domestic sensors, only Bradley knew what it was.

Chauncey spoke quickly. "I'm fine, mate. Just need to know if you can ID any acoustic UAV signatures prior to the event."

"Give me two hours," came the reply.

Chauncey hung up and felt a small ray of hope. As he dropped the phone to the ground and crushed it with the heel of his boots, he watched the continuing news coverage of Shane Hoff's torture.

The local news broke off to go to the Oval Office where the President was about to address the nation about the massacres and tortures. "Breskin was right about one thing," Chauncey said. "This country is shattered."

1600 Hours – Van Nuys, California

Sam whistled as he hurriedly swept up and threw away the long brown strands of hair that he'd trimmed from the head of his last client. He lifted the garbage bag from the container and twist-tied it, then tossed it into the garbage bin behind his salon. As he returned inside and began wiping off the counters, he smiled, recalling how the woman, Bonnie Covelli, a long-time customer had teased him about his rush to close up early.

"Don't you mess up my hair because you decided to go on your first date in seven years," she'd teased.

Like most of his customers, Bonnie was family so Sam didn't mind her joking with him about his upcoming date. He had been cutting her hair ever since he'd emigrated from Lebanon and opened Sam's Salon in 1985. He'd cut her hair, her children's hair and just one week ago gave her first grandson his first haircut. The kid had been so hyper that Sam gave him an apple to make him sit still. Bonnie cringed as her grandson happily licked his own hair off of the fruit.

It was true he hadn't dated in seven years. Eight actually, because he'd been stood up by one of them. But that had suited him fine. She'd been a wealthy, uptight Persian divorcee from Hidden Hills. He'd met her at the Venture Boulevard Hooka Bar he managed at nights when she drove up in her Mercedes 500 SE. As she impatiently waited for her teen-aged son, Sam proudly told her that he owned a hair salon and he'd love to cut her hair.

Once she saw the small, dingy place in a Reseda mini-mall, she'd decided Sam wasn't "relationship material." Black men call it TSS, or Typical Sister Syndrome. For men of Sam's persuasion it was PPS, or Persian Princess Syndrome. His ex-wife had it as well, which is why she was his ex-wife.

There was some truth to the snobby attitude, though. Reseda wasn't exactly the center of the Southern California elite. There were some good pockets, but mostly it was comprised of lower class Mexicans, Vietnamese donut shops and, of course, old-guard, working-class white people. If Sam's Salon had been located less than three miles south, in Encino, he could have been charging five times what he normally made his customers pay.

Sam was well aware that if he'd relocated the salon, he could have been financially better off. It wasn't an option. Living in a rich Persian ghetto like Encino just didn't interest him and it certainly wasn't why he cut hair.

Born and raised in Beirut, Sam Bedein was the nephew of the owner of the famous Salon Khalil, aka Mike's Barber Shop on Bliss Street. Taught to cut hair by his father's brother, Khalil Bedeir, Sam had fallen in love with the intimacy and storytelling aspects of being a barber. He'd always been taken by how his uncle could get people to open up and tell them their deepest secrets. The daily conversations about politics, family, religion and other matters had been addictive.

Sadly, when he'd lived in Lebanon, and even now to a certain extent, it was an unstable and dangerous place embroiled in a deadly civil war. His father's and uncle's brothers were fleeing the daily car bombs, kidnappings and unfettered violence to move to Canada and Khalil encouraged Sam to follow them.

Once in Toronto, his uncles settled into a Lebanese community and did well. Canada had a high Muslim population and even though they were Christians, they still fit in. Sam had stayed there for several years, but he'd always dreamed of living in the United States. So he borrowed money and moved to So Cal to open Sam's Barber Shop. Now, nearly thirty years later, it was still there.

Besides the up and down economic times, there had been some extremely turbulent political moments where Sam worried whether he'd survive, not only the business, but his life. Being Lebanese in America after the Marine Barracks attack, the first Gulf War, the 9/11 attacks and the Boston Marathon bombing had led to death threats and shattered windows in his shop.

His survival, however, hadn't been due to his diplomatic nature. He was outspoken and opinionated. And it certainly wasn't because Americans were tolerant; they weren't. It was, quite simply, because most people thought he was Mexican, and if he felt the slightest bit threatened, Sam didn't go out of his way to correct the error in identification by speaking Spanish.

Standing with straight shoulders, Sam was about 5'8" tall. However, after stooping to give haircuts for so long those straight shoulders were a thing of the past. Time and plenty of good food had pushed his flat belly outward, while his mop of coarse black hair had thinned, he still sported the same bushy, black moustache that he hadn't shaved off since puberty.

Most of his clientele didn't like talking politics. For them, Sam was only too happy to give advice on relationships, retirement planning and anything else they cared to discuss. Some people came to the salon to discuss politics, even if they didn't need haircuts.

When people were in Sam's court, he was an ambassador, a teacher and a poet rolled into one. He did his best to extinguish the ignorance that most

American's had about the Middle East. To the majority of Americans, there were Arabs and Israelis. Period. Israelis were Jews and Arabs were Muslims. Period. With his non-threatening, gift of gab, Sam loved to educate them and then have deep conversations about the problems in the region. He also had no problem discussing America's xenophobic leanings. It was only because of his obvious love of his adopted country that it didn't get him into any trouble.

He was proud that he'd weathered the racism and political storms and could make true claims to opening people's minds. Sometimes he would leave the television on and let the news stories prompt conversation. Today, the television was off. The recent massacre in Thousand Oaks and the ensuing torture worried him like no other event had. Nobody was officially blaming "Arabs," but he knew what most Americans were thinking, and it frightened him.

Sam shook off his concern and focused on more pleasant things, namely, his upcoming date. Just one week ago, a stunning, middle-aged Syrian woman named Nitsana Akrouk had come into the salon for a manicure. As she sat having her nails French-Tipped, she listened with amusement to Sam's ranting about the Islamic Revolution, specifically his belief that Al Assad was a tyrant. Once Sam noticed that she was listening, he spoke louder. He gesticulated with his scissors and became more passionate and animated. At one point, the man whose hair he was cutting begged Sam to chill out because he was afraid of getting stabbed.

He was undeterred. Once Sam had an audience, especially one as beautiful as Nitsana listening to him, nothing could still the storm. To his delight, she engaged him from her chair and the two of them spent the better part of a half-hour verbally sparring. Everyone in the salon fell silent and watched the Sam and Nitsana show. At the end of their argument, Sam had a telephone number and a date.

1700 Hours – San Diego, California

Normally Marcella was involved in every aspect of a story before it went on air. From choosing the subject, to writing the copy, to selecting the footage, to completing the final edit, her thumbprint could be found on every element. So to say she was a micromanager would have been a gross understatement with which she would have agreed. She might even have upgraded the characterization of herself to absolute control freak.

"My face, my message," she would say with a smile that was part cute, part threat.

She was unfortunately unique in this, as most of the new-era journalists just wanted to create provocative entertainment that would make them popular and thus, increase their chances of anchoring network or CNN. To the better reporters, like Marcella, stories were like their children. They developed and then released them to the world to stand on their own two feet. Not so different from parenting really.

Tonight's broadcast was different because Marcella hadn't seen any of the footage shot by Ethan at Torrey Pines. Unlike their usual workflow, she hadn't spent hours in the editing room with him comparing the final visuals with the final broadcast copy. No battles had been waged over even a single frame of footage, a bare 1/30th of a second, which might hold the key to the factual or emotional truth of a piece.

It wasn't that she'd had some epiphany and suddenly decided that delegating would not only show her trust in Ethan but dramatically reduce her stress. She would have worked on the piece if she hadn't spent the past four plus hours in the emergency room getting eighteen stitches in her head. Ethan had followed the ambulance to the hospital from Torrey Pines and offered to wait for Marcella, but she'd told him to go edit the story footage without her. She would write the copy in the waiting room with one hand holding the bloody bandage to her head, the other holding her pen to her pad of paper. She'd text him the narrative as soon as she could.

As Liz Bass, the hair and make-up stylist did last minute, pre-broadcast touch-ups to her face, Marcella absent-mindedly fidgeted with the bandage on the back of her head. Liz gently slapped Marcella's hand away.

"No touching. You'll infect it," she advised like a doting mother.

Marcella smiled, gratefully, and checked her kneejerk desire to tell Liz to mind her own damned business. She knew that she was really pissed at whoever had thrown the rock, but since she'd passed out, she'd had nobody to vent on. A twinge of guilt raced through her mind as she recalled calling one of the hospital interns, a pre-pubescent twerp who was just playing doctor. Ah, well. Another potential viewer down the drain.

Liz applied some powder to Marcella's face for what felt like the thousandth time and got pushed way.

"That's great, Liz, thanks," Marcella said. She then spoke into her Lavalier mic to Ethan, who was sitting in the control booth. "Are you sure it fits the copy?"

"You're good to go, Marcella. I would say *trust me*, but I know that you never trust people who say that," came his tinny reply through her earpiece. Then, "I had pretend fights with you while I was in the edit bay. I even let you win a couple of them."

"Wise ass," Marcella retorted.

This was an important story. It had to be right. Even though it went against every fiber of her being, she had to trust that Ethan had done a good job. She knew in her heart that he had.

She lifted her hand and massaged her right temple. Not only did the wound hurt, but the concussion was giving her a headache that had taken root behind her eyes. It just wouldn't go away. She fought off the pain like a trooper as the crew manned their cameras. When the studio lights came on, the heat level shot up by ten degrees.

The more Marcella thought about what had happened, the angrier she became. Not as much at the protestor who'd thrown the rock that hit her, but at that damned smug engineer, Adrian Gerard. He'd been so arrogant that a part of Marcella was happy his Porsche had gotten pelted by rocks. But it was only a tiny part of her. The larger part realized the incredible disconnect and saw its dangers.

The stage manager cued Marcella that they were ready to go on air. He did the three-two-one countdown to quiet everyone on the set, then pointed to Marcella. Staring into the camera with her well-known, grace, charm and charisma, she began:

"Good evening America. This is Marcella Kraner from eyesopen.org reporting from our studio in downtown San Diego. As many of you know, in the wake of the horrific and cowardly murders and tortures that have struck our nation, a groundswell of public protest has sprung up all across our land.

"This morning I joined an impromptu protest held outside the headquarters of General Atomics. The irony that this company, which creates the aptly-named Predator and Reaper killing drones is located in the beautiful sanctuary of Torrey Pines, would be comical if it weren't such an affront to nature.

"By now you've all seen the images of law-abiding citizens gathering to voice their dissent. Many of these lawful assemblies were subjected to increasingly militarized law enforcement who were called out, no doubt, to protect military contractors. Another irony, that the very people whose tax dollars go to pay for the companies and soldiers are treated by them as threats.

"But that's nothing new, is it? We've seen this institutionalized debasement of free speech and the desire for open government time and time again.

"As I stood in this growing river of discontent I heard something I've never heard before. It wasn't fear. It wasn't helplessness. And it wasn't directed at the purported terrorists who took credit for the recent horrendous acts. It was anger. Anger at science. Or to be more precise, anger at the scientists and engineers who created the greatest large-capacity killing technologies ever known to mankind.

"As I walked through the sea of outraged and concerned protestors, my cameraman and I spotted a road that was a seemingly innocent patch of black tar. We thought it was for delivery trucks to bring supplies into the back of the sprawling complex. But when we walked down a few hundred feet, we were surprised to see a lone guardhouse. Like a guard house posted on some hostile border crossing, its windows were blacked-out and large, metal gates barred both entry and exit. Tire spikes ran along the ground on each side of the tower. I was curious why the same kind of spikes weren't at the main entrance.

"I knocked on the glass to see if the guardhouse was manned and as you'll see, was not greeted with friendliness. The story that follows will speak for itself. "

Marcella sitting at the news desk dissolved into video footage of Marcella tapping the window of the guardhouse on the side street at General Atomics. As Kraner had stated, it was a small, one-person structure. Built out of thick, stacked cinder blocks, the structure has windows that were completely blacked-out, intentionally obscuring whatever was inside.

Marcella tapped the opaque glass with her microphone a few times and called to see if anyone was there. Getting no response, she walked around the side and disappeared from frame. A moment later, she returned, walking backwards, away from the booth. Her hands were raised skyward in the universal gesture of surrender.

"You're trespassing on private property, ma'am," said a tall, pistol-wielding security guard who was apparently the reason for her retreat. "You and your cameraman need to leave right now or you'll be detained and held for the FBI."

"Stay calm, officer," Marcella responded. Her voice was even and conciliatory, without any hint of emotion. "We didn't mean to trespass. We thought this was a public street."

"No ma'am. This road belongs to General Atomics." Then, turning to Ethan, "Sir, please turn off the camera and remove it from your shoulder so I can see your face."

The camera moved backward shakily, as Ethan apparently took a few steps back. He did not stop taping as ordered.

Marcella continued, "Maybe they should post some no trespassing or private property signs. That way nobody will wander down here."

"Yes, ma'am. I'll mention that to my boss. Now the two of you need to go."

As Marcella turned to walk back up the street, the tire popper beside the guard booth lowered and the barring arm pivoted upward. A black, 2015 Porsche Boxster drove out. Its license plate read, "IOfMordr," a reference to the dark lord in J.R.R. Tolkien's "Lord of the Rings" trilogy.

The car drove straight at Ethan, who had apparently decided to stay put. As the Porsche stopped, his lens zoomed in. The glare of the sun from the windshield obscured the driver's face. Before the guard could reach Ethan, the driver-side window lowered. The face of a fifty-ish year old, well-tanned man appeared. He had a salt and pepper goatee, thin, piercing brown eyes and the hair that had once covered his head now shifted back and into a short, pony-tail.

"Excuse me, pal, would you mind getting out of the way? I'm trying to drive here. Been kind of a stressful day what with those moronic protesters out front and all," Gerard said.

Marcella quickly stepped into frame and approached the car.

"Aren't you Adrian Gerard" she asked?

"Yes, actually I am," he responded. "Who's asking?"

"Marcella Kraner with eyesopen.org. I've seen some of your interviews," she said. "As head of the engineers that designed the optics for the Predator targeting systems, how do you feel about what these supposed terrorists are doing?"

"'Supposed' terrorists?" Gerard shot back at her. "Are you serious? I'll tell you how I feel. I'm pissed off. These psychopaths are killing my friends for no reason. My wife and kids are terrified."

"How do you feel about their cause?" she asked. "Do you think there's any credence to their assertion that engineers are being irresponsible to society?"

"Are you serious?!" said Gerard, raising his voice. "Listen lady, I don't know what mail-order school you got your journalism degree from, but without us you'd all be human sushi for mountain lions."

"So you're saying that you have no responsibility to me or the rest of our world? That you can just create anything that pops into your head even if it's destructive?"

Gerard was visibly anger. "That's your take on this? That I'm the criminal? Now listen to me. I'll even talk slowly and use small words so you can understand. The church put Galileo away because he said the earth wasn't the center of the universe. Well, the *sun* is the center of our solar system, the earth is *round,* and there's no white-bearded guy on a cloud judging everyone. So let's get real before we do a quick step back to the dark ages."

"And you're not scared at all?"

"I didn't say that. Of course I'm scared. I said I was pissed. But if those losers think I'm going to all of a sudden stop my work because they've got a fear of science, then forget it. Remember that *we're* the smart ones. Your meager little lives depend on geeks like us to survive. So instead of attacking us, you'd better protect us. Otherwise we might just move to an island and keep all of our "spooky science" to ourselves. Let's see how long you last with no indoor plumbing or email."

Before Marcella could say another word, a rock hit Gerard's windshield. It was followed by another and another. His car was being pelted. Ethan's camera whipped around 180 degrees to see a group of masked protestors approaching. They were shouting and throwing rocks. Ethan's eye of truth spun back to see the guard fall back fast and the Porsche screech backward through the gate. The camera also caught Marcella falling to the ground, blood spilled from her head where she'd been hit by an errant rock.

1730 Hours – El Mirage, California

Chauncey clicked the cursor of his mouse on the upper right corner of his TOR web browser. The program obediently closed before he heard Marcella's signature sign-off. The fact that she'd just delivered the story told him she was alright, so he didn't need to hear it. Besides, he knew it by heart because he'd heard it a hundred times.

He'd heard it before he approached Marcella ten years ago to help him reveal the truth about the country's use of enhanced interrogation on detainees in the war. He'd heard it following the fateful interview she did with him where he informed American citizens about what its government was doing in their name. And he'd heard it a hundred times following that, from behind the cameramen as he waited for Marcella to finish a broadcast, so they could go have dinner then make love in her apartment for the rest of the evening.

His mates had all been extremely happy for him, although not one of them believed he didn't have something on her. For months Killa had hocked him to reveal what naked photos or piece of ass-getting intelligence Chauncey had that would have put her away for years. Chauncey couldn't blame them. He hardly believed his luck in landing such an amazing woman either.

No matter how many times she'd assured Chauncey that she was attracted to him, he'd never quite believed it. Women like her dated famous actors or powerful media moguls. They had their pick. But Marcella Kraner wasn't only attracted by Chauncey's boyish good looks, she was attracted to his character; specifically to his courage. Not the bravery of his deeds in the clandestine world he'd inhabited, the strength of conviction and character that came from acting on his beliefs. Even when those convictions would and did destroy his life.

Most people who'd witnessed egregious wrongs remained silent. They would rant and rave in private and talk about how they would do this or do that, but the more their voices risked for them on a personal level, the more tightly bound their lips became. To Marcella, Chauncey wasn't a whistleblower, he was a hero who'd had the inner strength and valor to do the right thing.

He'd been equally impressed by her. Not just because she was fearless — she'd been willing to go to prison before giving up important sources for her investigative stories — but because of her integrity as a journalist. She was a rare breed in this day and age of news as entertainment. While most of her peers were just pretty talking heads worried about their TVQ and parroting whatever came across the teleprompter, she knew what the story was really about because she'd constructed it.

Once while he lay in bed watching her follow up with a source, Chauncey told her she'd make a great HUMINT officer. She'd leapt back into bed, feeling like a journalistic Mata Hari and asked him to explain himself. To him, Marcella, like the greatest reporters and the most effective spies in history, worked from refined gut instincts, but then verified everything before drawing conclusions. They both came up with multiple theories, then gathered information. They then checked, double-checked, and triple-checked that information for reliability and validity. It was the cornerstone of practically everything that required solid intelligence: the best scientists, engineers, educators, journalists, detectives, military commanders, and spooks all knew that those two factors were essential. Reliability and validity.

Marcella and Chauncey made a good team because they thought alike. Both of them believed it was important to work and substantiate the reliability of sources in order to get to the truth. Personal biases and desires for certain conclusions had to be identified, so if they polluted the truth, they could be shelved. Chauncey had been impressed with her honor as well. When he'd first gone to her with his story, she'd spent over a month fact-checking him and his information. To help her become better at it, he taught her the grading methodology used in the worlds of HUMINT, GEOINT, SIGINT, and OSINT.

First there was reliability of source. It was a letter system that went from A through F. "A" was given to a source that was completely reliable. It was only assigned if there was no doubt of that source's reliability, trustworthiness and competence. Next came validity, which was assigned to the accuracy of the information provided. It was a number system that went from 1 through 6. A value of "1" meant the information had been substantiated or confirmed by independent sources or agencies. The information had to be logical unto itself and agree with other intel on the same subject. An "A1" was the most reliable and verifiable, while an "F6" was the least.

These time-tested metrics had proven effective tens of thousands of times. Not only in their successes, but by revisiting the failures that had come about when they were ignored. It still made Chauncey want to throw chairs and tables out of windows when he thought about the invasion of Iraq based on the unchecked reliability of "Curveball's" assertion of WMDs. No US intelligence agents ever met or even spoke with him to see if he was a credible, reliable source. Nor had his information been vetted for validity. In Chauncey's book, you didn't invade a sovereign nation, bomb a purported terrorist camp, or even take the milk and cookies away from a kindergarten class based on an F6 rating. It was unconscionable.

Not only had the Bush/Cheney administration's hard-on for war ignored this with Curveball, but its desire for revenge had allowed it to disregard the unreliability of information gathered through the use of torture. It had listened to men like Breskin who created false positives and pretended that history didn't exist. Any investigator worth his or her salt knew that people would say anything to stop pain. He'd personally witnessed a man profess to be the Queen of England to stop the unbearable treatment he was getting. Intel gathered through the use of torture was an F6.

To his mind, there were only two things that could never be successfully subjected to the reliability/verification matrix: Religion and Love. Religion, because it required faith and trust in an idea that could neither be seen nor proven in any tangible way. In his world, religion was an F6.

Then there was love: the ultimate in unreliability. In Chauncey's mind there were too many non-provable variables involved to make it trustworthy.

It was pure emotion and subject to biases, fears, hopes, desires, unspoken needs and jealousy. If there was anything that fell under the Rumsfeld statement of "unknown unknowns" it was love. Another F6.

Tragically, because both Chauncey and Marcella were empiricists, their relationship was destined to fail. They both had been too uncomfortable with faith and doubted the dependability of the feelings they had for one another. As they got closer, Chauncey found himself looking into her past to see if she'd ever burned other lovers. Marcella had been doing the same. So when Chauncey had gotten arrested for revealing state secrets, they let their romance die. They hadn't spoken since.

Before he plunged too deep into the memory, the timer on Chauncey's phone chirped. It pulled him back from the wish that he could have a happy relationship and reminded him that it was time to call Bradley back. He punched the number into the prepaid phone and hoped his MASINT mate had some good news.

"Hey Chauncey," came Bradley's voice through the speaker. "Your hunch was a good one. Your sensors were all still online and recording strong signals. All of them picked up the exact same acoustic signatures just prior to the blast. They were UAVs all right."

Chauncey silently thanked the gods of technology and DARPA that had helped mankind to create the SenTech Compact Acoustic-Seismic UGS devices. Each one of the rugged little units was about eight and a half by five inches and weighed less than five pounds. They had built-in radios, triple-axis geophones, GPS, five-microphone conformal arrays, and long-lasting, internal batteries. Their intended military use was for detecting, identifying, locating, and tracking vehicles and dismounted personnel in the field. They would sit wherever they'd been hidden for days or even years, collecting information and intermittently pinging it through a separate communication gateway up to an Iridium satellite.

Chauncey also silently thanked Killa for stockpiling the high-tech inventory the two of them had illegally stashed in the DZ's hangar. Years ago, they'd placed the arrays all around the perimeter of his house just in case he ever got murdered and someone wanted to run some forensics after the fact. Well, this was after the fact, to be sure. It was just a different fact.

"What'd you find out? Could you trace it to a source?" Chauncey asked.

"Yessireebob," said Bradley. "I ran 'em through the FAA and DIA databases of acoustic drone signatures, and the UAVs are registered to AeroVironment."

The news pulled Chauncey to his feet. He paced through the hangar like a man ready to run a death race. He was both surprised and not surprised at the same time. Thoughts and theories began gushing through his mind against his will. There were too many to process all at once. Above all, Breskin's warning that the CEOs were concerned about him bounced through his brain like a super-ball.

As he marched to the door to go find Killa, he asked, "You certain about that, mate? Absolutely certain?"

"A1," was the response.

2100 Hours – Encino, California

Sam didn't usually valet park. Besides thinking it was a waste of money, he thought that unless you were handicapped or old, it was just something people did to show off or feel rich. And he was neither wealthy nor did he have the need to pretend he was just to impress Nitsana. If she couldn't like him for the simple barber that he was, then as attracted to her as he was, she wasn't worth the effort.

Intuitively, Sam knew that she wasn't that kind of a woman. He prided himself on having great instincts, and once again, they'd proven right. Not only had Nitsana not made any comments or rolled her eyes about his dented-up 1978 Toyota FJ40, but she'd fawned over it.

"My Uncle Faraborz had one just like it when I was growing up," Nitsana had crowed when Sam picked her up in his classic mustard-yellow clunker. "My sister and I loved playing inside and pretending we were driving around Damascus."

Another thing she'd done to endear herself was offer to split dinner. Something no true Persian princess would ever do. Customarily, a man from Sam's macho world would have been offended by the offer. Just the implication that he couldn't afford it questioned his manhood. Maybe he hadn't been offended because he'd lived in America for so long, or maybe it was that he had no pride. Either way, he just laughed and playfully slid the check over to her.

"Split it?" he replied. "No way. You should pay the whole thing. I drove. That truck of mine is a gas guzzler."

Of course, he grabbed it right back and insisted that he'd invited her out so it was his obligation to pay.

"In that case," she kidded, "I will make sure to never do the inviting."

That's how the night had been. They were simpatico from the moment they were together. It was wonderful. So wonderful, in fact, that Sam hadn't paid too much attention to the looks they'd been getting from the other diners in the small Studio City Italian restaurant. Maybe it was that they were laughing a bit loud. Or maybe, he figured, they were just looking at Nitsana. God knew he couldn't stop. She was a storied beauty. Thick, shiny black hair framed her deep-set, mysterious almond-brown eyes and high-cheekbones, pointed chin, and long, thin, kissable neck. And then there were her perfect breasts. Breasts he hoped that other men were looking at and envying Sam for being with.

Unfortunately, her looks and their good time couldn't stop Sam from finally acknowledging the disproportionate looks they were getting. The more he noticed, the more uncomfortable he became. It wasn't just other customers, it was the wait staff as well. It had been people they'd passed on the street as they walked to the restaurant. Every time he would catch someone looking at them, they would avert their gaze quickly.

Sam hadn't felt paranoia like this since 9/11. He corrected himself because that hadn't been paranoia. Those fears were well-founded as white Americans had turned their pain and outrage onto anyone who looked even remotely Arab. In the weeks and months that followed the attack, Sam had kept his head low and eagerly fostered the misperception that he was Mexican. He'd even toned down his rhetoric at the shop, fearing someone would misconstrue his monologues with sympathy for al-Qaeda, a group he despised.

He wondered if it was happening all over again. Were people thinking that the executions on YouTube had been conducted by Muslims? Clearly, the torturer had spoken with a clear western dialect. And the slayings had been conducted by American veterans. *White* American veterans. There was no tie to the Middle East at all.

Yet in his heart, Sam knew that didn't matter. In times of great stress, reasonableness was an ability most people didn't possess. When people needed a scapegoat, they pointed to the lowest-hanging boogieman on the tree.

Sam opted to skip dessert even though the restaurant was famous for its homemade tiramisu. He paid the check, making sure to leave a hefty tip, then grabbed Nitsana's hand and practically dragged her out. Sensing his mood shift, she asked him what was wrong, thinking she'd said or done something to upset him. He put on a good face, and, as they walked through the San Fernando Valley heat back to his truck, told her that he'd simply forgotten the time. The show he'd gotten tickets for was starting soon, and he wanted to be in their seats before it started.

It wasn't a complete lie. He had gotten tickets to a show. They were going to see Fetanah Validi, the famous Iranian songstress perform live at Club Tehran in Woodland Hills. On any other night being a bit late wouldn't have mattered to him, but given the inexplicable dread that was creeping up his spine, he felt the desire to be surrounded by "his kind." For safety, if nothing else.

The valet at the club snickered at Sam's old FJ as they pulled up to the curb outside of the opulent Club Tehran. Sam might have said something, but the man's face changed to such a pleasant shade of envy when he saw Nitsana step out, he didn't need to. Sam tossed his keys to the guy like he was leaving a Maserati and went to take his date's hand.

Before they'd taken two steps away from the street, Sam's fears were confirmed. A beaten-up, white and beige, Dodge Ram raced up and jumped the curb, nearly hitting him and Nitsana. The suddenness of the truck's appearance forced them apart onto opposite sides of the vehicle. The truck screeched to a stop, nearly hitting Nitsana who fell to the ground. As the newly vilified, Confederate flag attached to the Ram's antenna flattened, a tattoo-covered, bald man screamed from the driver's seat.

"Go back home, you fucking sand niggers! We don't want you here!"

As Sam was heading around the truck to help Nitsana, another man jumped up from the truck bed.

"Well, looky, looky," he said. "We got an oily Arab bitch. Here! Have some towel head cum."

He shoved a hose that was connected to a large drum out from between his legs and pressed a nozzle. Thick, black, motor oil spurted from the hose and coated Nitsana. She tried to get up to run, but the ground had become so slippery from the oil that she slipped and fell. The skinhead in the back howled with laughter.

"That's for all of our dead buddies," the driver screamed.

The man in the back pulled out a Zippo lighter with a swastika emblazoned on its side. He lit it, then tossed it at Nitsana's head as the truck peeled out and drove off honking its horn. Nitsana screamed at the approaching flame just as Sam jumped in and caught the lighter. But he'd gotten some of the oil on his arm, and it lit up like a torch. The valet and the bouncer pounced on Sam and, with their bodies, extinguished the fire with their bodies before it spread any further. As he attended to a weeping Nitsana, Sam wondered if the real fire was just getting started.

Chapter Twenty-Five

Chauncey and Diddy turtlebacked the last fifty yards of chop to the rendezvous point and signaled with a waterproof LED that they'd arrived. They tread water, silently waiting, moving with the tide, each man lost in his own thoughts. Even from a mile offshore, the ambient light from Santa Barbara skipped across the surface like a flat stone, making them able to see one another slightly. A moment later, the soft splashing of the whitecaps was drowned out by the approach of a small outboard motor, indicating that Phil was approaching in the Zodiac.

The cold Pacific Ocean water was refreshing as its salty waves splashed against Chauncey's face. As cold as the water was, it did nothing to cool his anger. It'd been bad enough that he'd found out Paulson used AeroVironment's technology to try having him killed. He hadn't asked to work with the man. He'd been perfectly content with his new life as a desert person. Getting fried on hash while he fried in the sun was almost okay. Besides, he'd done his best to help the bastard and his undeserving peers. A part of him now hoped that they got kidnapped by real bad guys so they'd appreciate how much he'd taught them.

Although his anger at Paulson hadn't subsided, his overall level of pissed-off-itude had grown exponentially by the conversation Bradley had played for him before they hung up the day before. The men he was ready to execute after the call were lucky that Killa had been around to chill Chauncey out.

"Better to live in fear than to not live at all," Killa had said.

Now they just needed to inject the fear.

"There's more," Bradley had said before Chauncey hung up, ready to trigger Paulson's pacemaker again. "After the bombs went off, your sensors switched to SIGINT mode and picked up a cellphone call that was made from the vicinity three hours later. You need to hear it."

"Go for it," Chauncey had said, pacing through the Desert Drop Zone hangar where he'd been holed-up.

Phil pulled up to the water-bound men and cut the engine. As Chauncey and Diddy clung to the boat, Phil hoisted their Draeger onboard. They handed him their masks and fins, then climbed onto the topsy-turvy raft.

"All good?" asked Phil, once they were seated, backs to the side.

Diddy smiled and pulled out a Limpet MK146 Acoustic Firing Device.

"Will be in a few seconds," Diddy said.

He ceremoniously handed the unit to Chauncey. "You may have the honors, sir," he said.

"Thank you, mate," said Chauncey. He carefully took the unit from Diddy's extended hand and looked toward the shoreline. In a moment he would be declaring war on an extremely powerful enemy. He opened his mouth wide as if to stifle a yawn. The bones in his jaw cracked audibly as they violently slammed back into place. Diddy and Phil stared at him.

"Damn," said Phil. "Clench your teeth much?"

Chauncey nodded, then opened his mouth wide again. His jaw cracked once more.

"Hurts even worse than it sounds," he said to Phil.

It only happened when he dove in a stressed-out condition. And since that phone call he'd been as stressed as he'd ever been. He'd been chomping down too hard on his regulator mouthpiece for the better part of the last two hours. That's how long it had taken them to swim around the Point Castillo breakwater into the Santa Barbara Harbor Club to plant the limpet mine on Paulson's multimillion dollar luxury yacht, then swim back to the rendezvous site.

Finding Paulson's 106-foot Ferretti Navetta 30 had been a piece of cake. Not only was it the biggest, most jaw-droppingly gorgeous yacht there, but just to be sure, Killa had painted it up from his perch on Stearns Wharf with an infrared laser. Moored to an end-tie close to the harbor entrance, Chauncey used a pair of waterproof NVGs to get a positive ID. Once they got to the side of the ship, he bounced a nonvisible laser off the windows to hear if there was anyone onboard.

Confident that the captain hadn't returned from a night on the town, he and Diddy had submerged and begun the process of attaching the limpet. Thanks to the Draeger LAR V's they'd used, their underwater approach to the yacht had been sans bubbles and completely stealth. Plus, by using front-mounted UBAs, they were able to transport the limpet components on their backs.

Even though it was two in the morning, they were still concerned about being discovered. Harbors were notorious for the live aboards. All they needed was some insomniac boat dweller to notice the sound of them placing the mine on the vessel's hull. They figured that the tourists, drunken UC Santa Barbara students, and the police would be somewhere up near Isla Vista or in The Funk Zone, so they wouldn't be a problem. In spite of that, these were extremely careful men.

To make sure that nobody approached Chauncey and Diddy, Killa had donned the guise of a late-night fisherman. He sat on the wharf with a beer, a line in the water and a Winchester Model 70 .300 WinMag sniper rifle in his duffel bag. If anyone had gotten close to his friends, a spate of .300s would have hit the nearby fuel dock, creating an effective distraction.

Diddy was the underwater demolition expert, so Chauncey assisted as they located the exact right spot on the hull that would sink the vessel. The default limpet mine is the MK 36 Demolition Charge (D.C.) containing 3.5 pounds of H6 High Explosive (H.E.). But setting it up and then detonating it required more than just slapping it on the hull. It was going to take some work.

The MK 36 DC was just one of four components in a limpet mine series. First was the explosive charge, second, an out-of-line safety and arming device known as the MK 39 S&A device, third, a back-up firing device called an MK 24 Demolition Firing Device, and last the primary Demolition Firing Device. The first three components were always the same for any configuration in the MK1 Limpet series. The fourth component, the primary firing device, was the only thing that changed depending on the requirements.

Working underwater, each man removed the limpet components from each other's backpacks. The default attachment device is a ring of powerful magnets running around the face of the demo charge. Unfortunately, the hull of Paulson's yacht was built with Composite/GRP, so the magnets weren't any good; they needed a different attachment method. Rather than risk the noise from using the MK 22 Stud driver to attach the limpit to the hull, they opted for the MK 84 kit. The kit included four adhesive padeyes. Each padeye had a layer of epoxy ampules on the face in a ratio of two to one epoxy/hardener. Diddy pressed a pair of padeyes against the hull and rotated back and forth until the epoxy ampules were crushed and the liquid contents mixed. After a couple of minutes, the padeye supported the mine's weight.

Diddy checked that the limpet was secured and gave an a-okay signal. Chauncey then removed the arming pins. As they swam back to the exfil spot, Chauncey clenched his jaw over and over again. He couldn't stop his mind from replaying the telephone conversation.

"I've only got a few minutes so I'll play the feed over the phone," Bradley had said to Chauncey back at the DZ.

At first he hadn't realized who the voices belonged to, but it didn't take long to identify the unique and irritating nasal twang of Breskin. Chauncey knew it had taken place at his house after the attempt on his life. Breskin was apparently the cleanup crew. They'd probably waited until dark to avoid any local police interference.

"It looks like he wasn't here," Breskin had said.

The second voice belonged to Paulson, the CEO of AV who'd performed so well in Chauncey's SERE class.

Paulson replied, more than a little miffed. "What the hell does that mean? He sure as shit was there. We had a positive visual."

"I'm aware of that. But there's no sign of him now. And I mean 'any' of him." The implication of body parts hung in the air like a lob pitch.

"He was sitting on the goddamned porch. We saw it on the Predator feed."

Chauncey had instantly made a mental note that AV built minidrones. The Predator's belonged to General Atomics. How did AV get a hold of one?

Breskin responded with his trademark condescension. "And again, I'm aware of that. The fact remains that there are no remains. Maybe he wandered off in a hash glaze, maybe something spooked him, and he got away at the last second; maybe it was a mirage. The fact is that he wasn't here."

The candor of the men's conversation had stunned Chauncey. You just didn't speak so plainly about attempted murder. Clearly the men had encrypted telephones and were overconfident that there was no way they could be overheard. That's one of the reasons Chauncey was such a huge fan of overconfidence. Not in himself, of course, in his enemies.

"Well, what about the primary objective," Paulson continued. "Did we at least get that?"

"Yes. All the computers in the house were fried by the secondary EMP. You and your associates don't need to worry about any embarrassing secrets."

Chauncey knew that Breskin was lying to Paulson. He had no computers in his house. The laptop he'd used to record the sessions had been locked up in a safe place ever since they'd ended. He'd never intended to use them for anything, but it was always good to have a "get out of jail free" card somewhere.

Paulson clearly believed Breskin, and his voice took on a relieved tone.

"So that's good. We should be all right."

"Not exactly," Breskin said. "We found a pad of paper in a fireproof safe with the word 'Panopticon' written on it about a hundred times."

"What the hell does that mean?!" Paulson spat, his relief dissolving away in an instant.

"Well, I wasn't there so I can't be sure, but my guess is that during interrogation at least one of you guys mentioned it."

"Christ. That's not good. Does he know what it means?"

"I doubt it. But the guy's a genius. He knows you're all in the surveillance field. The sad fact is that he probably wouldn't have cared about it. Until now."

"What the hell does that mean? Bringing him in was your idea. So was this botched assassination attempt. This is all on you. So you make it go away."

"Not a problem."

"We can't afford to get derailed. Things are moving too fast."

"I'm on it."

"Make sure that you are. Otherwise you may end up in one of those black sites you loved so much. And I don't mean as one of the good guys."

The line went dead.

Chauncey opened his mouth wide, filling the dark, night air with yet another loud crack of his colliding jaw bones. He'd had a hunch that Panopticon had some serious undertones. Now the hunch was confirmed. These guys were up to some serious no good and he was damned-well going to figure out what it was before they tried to kill him again.

Diddy tapped Chauncey on the shoulder. "Let's do it, Man-O. I'd like to get out of these togs, and I'm damned sure Killa's already caught a bucket load of fish."

Chauncey looked at the Limpet Acoustic Firing Device in his hand. He knew that nobody was on Paulson's yacht. But he wasn't there to kill anyone, yet. For the time being he was just sending a message. And he knew that destroying the custom made $10 million Italian yacht would an expensive message.

As the Zodiac rocked back and forth, he activated the hand-held acoustic transponder and turned the switch. The unit obediently sent a coded acoustic signal 1,000 yards to the limpet mine. The HD blew, puncturing an eight-foot hole in the yacht's hull. It belonged to the bottom of the Pacific Ocean now. A moment later, Phil's walkie-talkie clicked two times. Killa had signaled "mission accomplished."

Chapter Twenty-Six

MAID Subject #3, Karama Khamisian, was secured upright on the table, facing the interrogator. Other than the purple fMRI cap, the only things covering his body were a soiled diaper, a thick black beard, and a layer of orangeish liquid, the ingredients of which were saline, bile, and blood. It was the same brew that had pooled on the floor where he'd spent the last hour and a half being waterboarded by the table's sophisticated EIT functionality.

The table was so high-tech that throughout the course of enhanced interrogation session, it had continuously monitored MAID Subject #3's heartbeat, respiration, and blood/oxygen levels in order to make sure the mock executions remained mock. If a life-threatening change in his condition was detected, the table software would automatically inform the MAID which would stop the session and initiate whatever lifesaving measures were required.

Today's session had stopped abruptly after #3 had begun choking and coughing up blood. Violent gags and vomiting were expected when a person undergoes waterboarding; after all, there's just too much water being forced into the body for someone to swallow it all. In order for the procedure to work properly, the excess water had to aspirate into the lungs. That was what created the desired drowning effect. The yellow, digestive juices that were regurgitated were also expected given that #3 hadn't eaten in over twelve hours. Besides the water, it was the only thing in his stomach. The blood, however, was cause for the MAID to stop the table from continuing treatment.

Subject #3 looked outward, trying to recompose himself after the treatment. He wasn't sure why, but it seemed more difficult than it had in the past. His face, beard, and chest were still covered with the orange-colored excretion, but because his arms were still secured by his sides, he couldn't wipe it off.

"I don't feel well," #3 whispered. "My stomach and my back hurt more than they have before. And why am I throwing up blood?"

"It's most likely a Mallory-Weiss tear," answered the MAID in an even, matter-of-fact voice. "You vomited quite violently during this session so you've probably torn a small hole in your esophagus where it meets your stomach. The blood is coming from the tear."

Subject #3 wasn't happy with the answer and was clearly concerned. In spite of himself, he thanked the MAID. He did so even though he knew had he not been waterboarded in the first place, there would have been nothing to stop.

"Can I die?" he asked.

"If left untreated, yes," answered the MAID.

Subject #3 swallowed hard at the response. He was so groggy and in so much pain that his normal reaction was muted. He spat a bit to see if his saliva was red. Though relieved at seeing no blood, his concern ebbed only a tiny bit.

"I want to be treated right now," he said.

"Soon," was the nonplussed reply.

After having experienced the MAID's past responses to anger, #3 knew better than to yell. There were no conversations. No warnings. Only pain, darkness, and deafening rap music would result from that. Pain that was far worse than what he felt now, physically, at any rate. There was nothing the MAID could do to increase the psychological pain he was in. At least, he hoped there wasn't. Personal experience had taught him that just when he couldn't conceive of anything else they could do to hurt him, something even more evil was found. What he'd experienced since the day he'd been turned over to the Americans by the Pakistani police was beyond compare.

"Man kharam," he said softly in Farsi.

He moaned the words through squinted eyes and clenched teeth because those were the only things on his body that weren't restrained. He spat again to make sure there was no more blood.

"Man kharam, man kharam, man kharam," he repeated in an almost wailing tone. It was a voice of despair, helplessness, and self-recrimination.

"Yes," agreed the MAID. "You are quite an idiot. People don't usually just stroll in the door like you did. Especially not 'innocent' people." The only thing missing from the statement was a sardonic laugh.

Subject #3 ceased his mantra and lifted his head. "Not from 'innocent' people?'" he quoted, barely able to contain himself and praying that he'd heard right. For a moment all of his pain subsided. He was fully clothed and warm. His body was clean, and he smelled the fresh air of his beloved Pakistan. "Then you believe me?"

There were two truths happening concurrently. The first one was his undeniable innocence. Prior to his arrest, #3 had been nonpartisan with no ties to any terrorist group anywhere in the world. He was neither a threat nor did he possess information that would be helpful to the American War on Terror in any way, shape, or form. The second truth was that he was, indisputably, an idiot. A huge idiot.

His entire situation had been of his own making. He was an uneducated, twenty-five-year-old taxi driver from the outskirts of Islamabad. Like most Pakistanis he eked out a feeble income and still lived at home, a small, dilapidated apartment, with his family. When he and his two brothers had read a leaflet about Americans giving rewards to people with information about the Taliban or al-Qaeda, they saw an opportunity to get rich. He had read it so many times that he'd memorized the document. He'd repeated it hundreds of times, verbatim, to the interrogator in an attempt prove his story:

"Get wealth and power beyond your dreams. You can receive millions of dollars helping the anti-Taliban forces catch al-Qaeda and Taliban murderers.

This is enough money to take care of your family, your village, your tribe for the rest of your life. Pay for livestock and doctors and school books and housing for all your people."

After Karama had drawn the short straw, which made him the one to "have information," he and his brothers had made up the story that he had used his taxicab to deliver kidney medication to Osama Bin Laden, and that he was a trusted courier. Never mind that they had no idea where Bin Laden was or whether the man needed medication. They just knew that if the Americans believed the story, they would pay a fortune.

Since the Americans had begun dropping their psyops leaflets throughout Afghanistan and Pakistan promising bounties for information, many of their neighbors had cashed in on it. Some had turned in their enemies to settle tribal conflicts. Some had turned in rival suitors for women just to get them out of the way. Even the government had falsely accused criminals of terrorism so the Americans would take them. Everyone knew the United States was horny for informants. They had no idea how much they were being taken advantage of, or, more tragically, of the innocence or guilt of their growing herd of detainees.

Karama remembered how he and his brothers had howled with laughter as they contemplated how easy it would be to fool the idiot American troops to get a high bounty with such a story. And they had. To add authenticity, they'd had Karama darken his eyes with makeup. He'd spent three months growing out his beard, then oiling it like the Taliban so he would look the part. And although he was a nonbeliever, he'd learned to recite prayers and perform religious ablutions.

When his brothers told the Americans their story, they'd agreed to pay $10,000 US dollars to get their hands on Karama; nearly two times the highest bounty ever given. While it may have been twice the going rate for bounties, it was nearly ten times the annual salary of any of them. They had naively figured it would be a simple affair. They'd turn over Karama, get the money, then after a few questions it would be obvious he'd been falsely accused, and they'd let him go. He and his brothers would split the money and live happily ever after.

Their plan had worked too well. It had now been nearly two months since Karama got renamed MAID Subject #3. Sixty days of horrendous interrogations had ensued. So now, after the MAID had admitted he was innocent, #3 was desperately hopeful that his torment would end.

"If you believe me, why do you continue to treat me this way?" he asked. With his eyes, he indicated the room, the table, and the orange liquid all over the floor.

"We had to be sure," was the reply.

"And are you?"

"Yes."

Subject #3 was beginning to feel more like Karama again. He imagined himself eating a lamb gyro, driving his taxicab through Islamabad, cursing at pedestrians to get out of the way. He grew defiant. In spite of the rising nausea and pain in his stomach, he struggled against the table's inescapable grasp, half-expecting that the shackles would pop open and he would walk out the front door of wherever he was.

"Then free me. Free me this instant," he demanded.

"Perhaps," said the MAID, ignoring # 3's outrage.

"Perhaps?" he asked, his eyes widening in disbelief. "You just said you know that I'm innocent. Why is it 'perhaps'?"

"If only you would work for us," came the response. "It would be helpful to have a cab driver to get us information and mark targets."

The swagger-fed wind that had momentarily filled #3's sails dissipated. The seas went from choppy to glass. A cold sweat broke out as he contemplated what the MAID was suggesting. A new wave of nausea rose up and he swallowed. This time it tasted like blood.

"I cannot," said #3. "You know I am innocent. Now release me. Please. Please release me. You know I am just an idiot."

"You are innocent of the story that you and your brothers concocted, yes," said the MAID. "But you are still guilty of a crime. By your own admission you stole from us. Ten thousand dollars is a lot of money. I believe that stealing is still a crime in Pakistan."

"I will pay you back," he stammered. "When I get home. I will get the money from my brothers and give it to you. All of it. I swear!"

"That's a promise you can't keep. Your brothers have already spent the money."

"How do you know this? It's a lie," said #3 in an attempt to remain indignant. But his energy was waning. He was fading in and out of unconsciousness.

"We know because we have arrested your brothers."

#3 fought against the approaching twilight to stay present, but it was becoming extremely difficult. "For what?! We made it up. I have been punished. My brothers are also innocent."

"We only know that you are innocent. We will find out the truth. Of course, we could just set all of you free. If you agree to help us."

"They will kill me if they find out!" #3 pleaded.

The MAID was unmoved. "We will arrest your father next. And then your mother. How do you think your mother would like the table? Does she like water?"

The more the MAID spoke the more agitated #3 became. Had the esophageal tear been smaller, it might have been easier to maintain his composure, but it was large. He hurt more and more with every passing second. His agitation only increased the amount of bleeding and the production of digestive acids. His stomach was nearly filled to capacity.

#3 did his best to stay present, but the pain in his back and the nausea was becoming unbearable. The monitor inside of the IB detected a sudden spike in his heartbeat.

"*Calm down, number three. Your heart rate is climbing very fast,*" *the MAID said, its voice softening and taking on a sweet, female, Afghani regionalism.*

"*I. Cannot. Breath.*" *IB #3 gasped.*

"*Yes, you can. You're just upset.*"

The blood that had pooled in his stomach for the past fifteen minutes chose this moment to race upward. It escaped the stomach through his esophagus, causing him to vomit a liquid projectile of red. He screamed in fear. He vomited again. His stomach went into spasms, sending waves of blood upward to escape. As he gasped for air, he swallowed the blood back. It burned his throat and he gagged uncontrollably. He swallowed and gasped and coughed all at the same time. The blood went down the wrong tube. It aspirated down his trachea into his lungs, which increased his gasping even more.

Heavier and more gelatinous than water, the blood clogged the alveoli in #3's lungs preventing him from getting any air. It was a death sentence. His coughing and gasping slowed down as the blood filled his lungs. He turned blue as he drowned in his own blood. Only this time it wasn't a mock drowning. And this time there was nothing the MAID could do to stop it.

Chapter Twenty-Seven

Approximately three hours after destroying Paulson's yacht, Chauncey was back in the desert. Dawn wasn't far away, so he had to act fast if he were to make his next move while it was still dark. Unfortunately, he hadn't counted on dealing with a pair of armed sentries stationed outside of Armagan's house. It made sense though. Armagan was a valuable asset and General Atomics needed to keep him safe. Safe from what, or whom, was the question Chauncey didn't know the answer to.

He'd thought about what Carby had said and considered just calling Armagan on the phone for an invite, but he doubted the bulldog sentries posted outside of his house would agree to the guest list. There was also a high likelihood that Armagan's calls were being monitored, so it didn't make any sense to let whoever was listening, most likely Green, know his plan. He'd ultimately decided to take the direct approach. The direct approach, "Chauncey-style," that is.

After he, Diddy and Phil had rendezvoused with Killa at Point Loma, they drove to Brown Field and jumped in Killa's waiting Cessna. Since Armagan's small, desert house was in the middle of ten barren acres just east of Shadow Mountain, they'd thought about landing in his backyard. The fact that the area was riddled with unmapped mines made a safe landing iffy, so they'd changed the plan to land at the Desert DZ and drive to Armagan's house.

However, after Chauncey and Killa had spotted the guards during their recon pass of Armagan's house from 8,000 feet, Chauncey changed that plan as well.

"Let's keep this simple, mate," he'd said.

He asked Killa to drop him near the Adelanto Sheriff's Department, then go back to the DZ alone. Killa had merely said okay and changed course. He knew that Chauncey would do whatever he wanted no matter what argument he made regarding recklessness. After all, this was the guy who'd cut his secondary release line on purpose and lived to jump again.

To Chauncey, the direct approach was to skydive into a parking lot across from the sheriff's department, hot-wire a squad car, then drive right up to Armagan's house like a desert Dudley Do Right. He'd reckoned that the goons would think he was a cop and wouldn't draw their weapons. By the time they realized who he was, it would be too late. And he was right.

"Evening, gents," Chauncey had said to the security guards as he stepped into the still hot, early morning desert air from the sheriff's car.

To make it look real, he brandished a badge that he'd gotten in Colorado as a brief stint he'd done as a deputy sheriff. Too dark to see anything but the glint of metal, Jim Aberbach, one of the tough, leathery looking mercenaries, assumed Chauncey was legit.

"Evening, officer," came the casual reply. "What can we do for you?"

Chauncey quickly sized up Jim and the other man. They were big. Much bigger than they'd been from 8,000 feet. And the way they approached him, one on either side, hands relaxed and at their sides where their weapons were probably close at hand, told him that they were pros. He surmised they were ex-special forces. Probably worked for Academi. He'd heard the Warcos were hiring the private security firm for domestic protection.

It made the situation both more dangerous and more exciting at the same time. It was dangerous because Academi, previously Blackwater, only hired well-trained, ex-military for their assignments. He had no doubt they would be formidable, so he'd need to be on his game.

It was exciting because Chauncey hated mercenaries and would love nothing more than to wreck these guys. To him mercenaries were just criminals with badges. Unlike officers, they didn't answer to the Constitution. They answered to the almighty dollar, poor justification for killing. Blackwater had gotten away on technicalities after killing innocents in Iraq, and they'd never been convicted for being the CIA's private army when it came to kidnapping and extraditing possible terrorists to their black sites. Whoever they were, it was clear to Chauncey that after being so easily grabbed by him, Green had brought in the big boys.

Moving slowly and in a nonthreatening manner, Chauncey looked at the two men. He leaned against the hood of the car and pointed to the house with his chin.

"You two live here?"

Aberbach and his partner, Dan Hammer, exchanged a look as they moved a bit closer to Chauncey. One on either side, they maintained their distance.

"Yeah," said Aberbach. "Just moved in about a week ago. Doing some security work up at Edwards Air Force Base."

"Nice," Chauncey replied. "I hear they pay well. I've considered doing some moonlighting myself."

The men smirked, clearly thinking Chauncey was a lame desert cop. As they deluded themselves, he noted their clothing. Both were in standard issue fatigues with desert boots. Over-sized pockets probably held knives, and pistols were most likely holstered in the small of their backs. They wore matching black T-shirts, the sleeves of which bulged from their well-developed arms. He thought how amusing it would be to make a gay joke about them living together in the middle of nowhere, but decided it wouldn't be prudent. It made him smile inwardly, nonetheless.

"Welcome to the neighborhood," Chauncey said.

He looked at the house and around the sides for any movement that would indicate a third man. There was no light on inside, so he assumed Armagan was sleeping. As the men drew even closer, Chauncey stared harder at the house, focusing his energy and relaxing into a Zen state.

"Something wrong, officer?" asked Hammer, trying to determine why a sheriff had driven out at this ungodly hour. "We just got back from work and were about to call it a night."

Before the man could say another word, Chauncey straight-handed him in the chest with a fierce, Dim Mak strike. He executed the blow to leave no external scarring, but to wreak havoc on the insides. Hammer was out before he hit the ground. And even if the blow hadn't knocked him out, his head bouncing off the car's bumper would have finished that bit of business.

Taken by surprise by the sudden blow, Aberbach stepped away and drew his weapon, aiming it at Chauncey's head.

"What the hell kind of a cop are you?" he asked.

"The kind that doesn't like seeing two gay mercs in his town."

Chauncey jumped up and executed a perfect roundhouse that knocked the weapon from Aberbach's hand. Before the pistol hit the ground, Aberbach dropped and leveled a sweep kick that knocked Chauncey off his feet.

Cursing his age and slowed reflexes, Chauncey rolled to his side just in time to avoid a chop kick aimed at his head. The first kick was followed by several more, in rapid-fire succession. On the fourth attempt, Aberbach's heel struck Chauncey on the side of his face. Chauncey was grateful because the pain lit up his brain. It ignited his chi, his energy.

As Aberbach moved in to finish him, Chauncey rose to his knees. He leaned to his left, supporting his weight with his elbow and delivered a savage side kick to Jim's knee.

The popping of the man's ACL was loud in contrast to the silent night air. He winced as Chauncey propelled himself off the bumper of the car and rolled over the top of the Aberbach's head. Coming to rest behind him, Chauncey grabbed Jim in a carotid choke.

Aberbach bucked against Chauncey, repeatedly slamming his back against the car and into the side-view mirror. He used every move in his arsenal to get free, but Chauncey held fast. After a moment Aberbach sagged to his knees, and then fell to the side like a tree.

Wasting no time, Chauncey hog-tied the two mercenaries back-to-back with zip-ties. Still breathing hard, he then dashed up the four short steps and entered the house. No sooner had he closed the door behind him then he was greeted by the sound of a shotgun chambering a round. The light clicked on, and he saw Armagan aiming a fully automatic AA-12 shotgun at his face. If there'd been any doubt in his mind that the guys he'd just knocked senseless were with Academi, they evaporated instantly. The AA-12 was the weapon of choice for Blackwater.

"Easy, mate," Chauncey said, immediately raising his hands into the air.

"Mr. Chauncey?" Armagan said, completely taken off guard. "What are you doing here? I thought, I thought you were —"

"Dead?" said Chauncey, finishing his thought.

"Well, yes," said Armagan.

"Who told you I was dead?"

Chauncey was equally taken aback. How would Armagan have known he was supposed to be dead? Armagan became flustered. He stammered and backed away from the door.

"The news," Armagan finally spat out. "A week ago the local news showed pictures of your home and photos of you. They said there had been a fire and an explosion. Caused by a stove that you'd left on when you went to sleep. They said they found your body."

Chauncey was impressed. Breskin and Paulson had even gone to the length of putting a dead body on the scene. In a way, they'd done him a favor. Now that he was dead, he might be able to move around more freely.

Satisfied with Armagan's explanation, Chauncey relaxed a little. As much as a man could with a shotgun leveled at him.

"Well, if you're not happy that I'm alive, pull the trigger. If you are, then how about pointing that thing toward New Jersey?"

Armagan scraped his upper teeth across his lower lip as he studied Chauncey and considered his options. They'd tried to kill him because Chauncey represented a threat to the success of the plan. But he clearly didn't know of Armagan's involvement – yet. Maybe he never would. Besides, he liked Chauncey. If he shot him, he would lose the only friend he'd made.

Lowering the weapon, Armagan said, "Those kidnappings and tortures are horrifying. I'm an engineer, you know. They told me I was a target."

"Yeah, I know," said Chauncey. He moved to the window and looked out to make sure the men were still unconscious. "That why your friends were outside?"

"Friends? Good gracious, no. I objected when they told me they were coming. They are nothing more than paid killers. Racist ones at that. But because of my work, GA insisted."

Armagan grabbed his cane and hobbled toward the kitchen.

"Would you like some tea?" he asked. He'd evidently been roused from sleep and hadn't had time to strap on his high-tech artificial leg. He was understandably feeling vulnerable and scared. Chauncey took in the room. It may have been small and simply furnished, but the aroma of Afghani spices filled the house and his senses.

"I wish I could stay, but given that in a few minutes there are going to be a couple of very pissed-off guys looking for me, I need to make this brief. I was told that you're really working on nano-drones and swarms. I need some information."

Armagan turned back and shook his head.

"I'm very sorry but I can't talk about my research. I've signed documents."

"I understand," said Chauncey, not happy with the reply. If he'd had more time, he would have tried to convince Armagan otherwise, but that commodity was something he was rapidly depleting. He went on, "I just wanted to see if you knew anyone who was working on biomimetic insects. My house didn't burn down by accident. It was an assassination attempt. They sent in some weaponized robotic scorpions."

"Whoa," said Armagan. "That's amazing. I might even say kind of cool, if it weren't for the circumstances. I'm not aware of anyone who has done such sophisticated work. But I will see if I can find something out. And since we're exchanging favors, I have one to ask of you."

"Name it. But name it fast," Chauncey said as he peered out the window again.

"I'd like you to check on my adopted father. He's an imam at the Muslim Center of Anaheim. I'm concerned that with the anti-Muslim sentiment being caused by these terrorists, he is in danger. Did you see the attack that happened in Encino?"

Chauncey nodded. "I completely understand. What can I do?"

"Please find him and tell him that I sent you. Please give him some of your SERE training so he can protect himself should someone come after him."

Chauncey nodded in agreement.

"You got it, mate. In the meantime, please check on those bots. I need to know who made them."

Chapter Twenty-Eight

Agent Breskin looked at what was left of Paulson's yacht and let out a whistle. Now out of the water and strapped on a boat trailer at the Santa Barbara Harbor Marineworks, there was a ten foot by ten foot hole in the port side of the hull. The jagged gash exposed what was left of the decked-out master bedroom. Inside was a mix of shattered Murano glass, mulched Corinthian marine carpet, splintered teakwood and a veritable forest of stinky kelp.

"I guess it's a good thing you weren't cheating on your wife last night, isn't it?" Breskin asked.

Paulson decided to disregard Breskin's instigating remark and replied calmly, "Yeah." His clipped tone gave evidence of a man doing his best to control an on-edge temper. "And that bastard Chauncey knew I wasn't onboard."

"Paunce?" asked Breskin, a single eyebrow shooting upward. "What makes you think he had anything to do with this? Not that I'd be surprised."

"Do you really think I would have asked you to meet me here if I thought it was just an accident? That SOB is a pain in the ass and unless we stop him, he's going to do a lot more than just damage a ship."

Breskin shrugged and added, "I agree that he needs to be taken care of, but why are you so adamant that it was him?"

"Because the smug bastard left me a voice mail," replied Paulson. Then, doing his best Chauncey imitation, recalled, "Ahoy there, mate. I know that you and your human mistress shack up onboard every Thursday night, so I decided to have my way with your other mistress last night."

Green pulled his head out from the hole in the hull and looked at his associate.

"So you're saying he somehow dog-paddled into the harbor and set up a charge at exactly the right spot where you get laid? He's a disgraced spook. He doesn't have those skill sets."

"Whoever he is, he's got more skills than you think," said the unanticipated opinion of Pete the Pirate, walking toward them across the yacht's deck. Having just come out of the engine room, he wiped his hands on an oily rag. Breskin, Paulson, and Green exchanged a look; they hadn't realized anyone in the parking lot was within earshot.

Pete "The Pirate" Carolan was the owner of Frogman Salvage, a wreck salvage company based in nearby Ventura. Carolan was a sixty-four-year-old ex-SEAL turned businessman. He'd graduated from BUD/S Class 47 in 1968 and had been a Navy Frogman with Underwater Demolition Team 13. After serving two combat tours in Vietnam, he'd been the swim team leader in the recovery of the famous splashdown of Apollo 13. He loved telling the story about how he'd been the guy knocking on the capsule door.

Still extremely fit with a full head of thick, salt and pepper hair, Pete The Pirate was a mix of Jack LaLanne and Jacques Cousteau with a bit of John Wayne sprinkled on top. While most of his veteran friends hadn't been able to cope with civilian life, Pete had done well using his knowledge of the sea and the mechanical beasts that tried to tame it. Besides his ship salvage company, he owned a dive shop, used his underwater cartography skills to lead occasional treasure hunts, and was renowned in the SEAL community for his artwork. His Freddie the Frog illustration was iconic.

Knowing full well that neither his opinion nor his presence would be well-received, Pete marched up to the men and continued. He didn't really care what they thought, but since he loved the sound of his own voice, he told them what he wanted.

"Whoever did this to your ship used a directed limpet system. They don't use 'em much anymore, but back in the day they were the shit. This guy knew exactly where to place the unit and exactly how much charge was needed. To be honest, it looks like he went out of his way to keep this junker intact. It would've been much simpler to place the charge by the fuel tanks, so I reckon they didn't want to destroy the harbor or risk hurting civilians. No, sir, what you've got here is a bona fide warning shot."

"How much did you happen to overhear?" asked Breskin. His hand moved slightly toward his Glock.

Pete casually stuffed his oil rag into his pocket and pulled out a can of Smithwick's beer. Even though it was only ten thirty in the morning, he tapped the top a couple of times, then popped it open and sucked down the suds in a single breath. He wiped his mouth with his hairy forearm and let out a well-practiced belch before looking into the gaping gash that had once been the ship's hull.

"Enough to know that you're going to let me take this yacht and sell it as is, scrap it for parts, or fix it up and change my lifestyle."

Paulson was incredulous. "And why would I do that?

Pete sucked his nose and spat out a perfect wad of spit. He then explained, "Because judging by the damage, it was done by some of my fellow SEALs, so you must have pissed off one my friends pretty good. Secondly, on the other side of this gate here is the Harbor Patrol and the Coast Guard. They're waiting on a report from me to say what caused this floating turd of yours to sink."

Paulson sighed, "Fine. What do I need to sign?" He looked at the yacht ruefully.

Pete handed him a clipboard and a pen. Barely glancing at the paper, Paulson signed it then handed the clipboard back. Pete gave him a business card that had the name of his company and a hand-drawn frog on it.

"Let me know when you get the next one blown up," Pete smiled.

He then calmly turned and walked back toward the Harbor Marineworks. As soon as he was gone, Green looked at Breskin.

"How the hell did Paunce do this without your knowing?" Green asked Breskin. Then to Paulson, "And how could he have known about your, uh, personal indiscretions?"

Breskin popped a candy into his mouth and simply shook his head. He glared at Paulson and said, "He probably blabbed about all kinds of stuff while Chauncey was teaching him how to not blab about all kinds of stuff."

"Is that right?!" stormed Paulson. "Well let me tell you something. In ten wars, you couldn't sell the CIA enough of that torture crap of yours to pay for this goddamned ship."

Breskin positioned the piece of candy between his front teeth and sucked in slowly. He stared at Paulson with a look that was both threatening and condescending at the same time. He then bit down, splitting the candy in half with only his front teeth.

"You know the old expression, 'those that can't do, teach?'" asked Breskin. "Paunce didn't have the stomach to 'do,' but I did. So mind your tone, or you may just end up in a place where the goal is not education."

"Gentlemen," said Green, stepping in between the two angry men. "I didn't risk coming up here and being seen together just to referee a fight. We are in the middle of something, so don't blow it now. The FAA is getting pressured by the president right now. Let's keep our eyes on the ball."

Breskin considered Green as he leaned against a nearby car. He wasn't happy with this turn of events one bit. Not only because it put a chink in his reputation, but because he genuinely didn't like the fact that Chauncey was still out there. A fact that he intended to change. "Point well taken, Nels. I obviously underestimated Paunce. I brought him into this so I'll take him out."

Still stinging over his loss, Paulson commented, "That's what you said the last time. What makes this so different?"

"Because now I know where he's headed. After taking down a couple of Green's security guards last night, Paunce had a chat with Armagan."

Paulson's eyebrows shot up. "What the hell?"

"It seems that they've struck up a little friendship. Somehow Paunce found out that Armagan is really working on biomimetic robots, so he asked him to help figure out who created the scorpions. Armagan agreed to look into it if Paunce agreed to go check on his adopted father. Up until now we didn't know where he was going. Now we do."

Green added, "I've got a Predator circling the imam's neighborhood right now. I don't care how clever this guy is, we'll know when he shows up."

"And when he does, we'll be waiting," added Breskin.

Chapter Twenty-Nine

Chauncey carefully traced his finger along the spine of the exquisite, handbound Koran. He felt the raised gold letters and gilding of what was clearly, even to an infidel like himself, an ancient and valuable volume. This particular Muslim holy book sat on a shelf surrounded by other Islamic works, including a full set of Hadith, the books of sayings of Muhammed, the prophet. To his surprise, there was also a copy of the Old Testament.

He didn't read Arabic, nor had he ever picked up a translation of the Koran, but he imagined the bumps that gently fired up the nerves in his fingertip as Braille. By some interpretations he'd heard, the words' meanings were sublimation, devotion, and obedience. To others they meant love, mercy, and forgiveness. But to many they meant manipulation, jihad, and suicide bombs. If he'd been caught touching the holy book in certain mosques in Saudi Arabia, Iran, or even in homes somewhere else besides Anaheim, California, it could have resulted in the removal of his fingers, or worse.

Right now, though, Chauncey was in the home of Armagan's adopted father, the Imam Sheik Ayman Hama. More specifically, he was in the imam's home office. He'd surreptitiously worked his way to the small California bungalow in the heart of the southern California city, avoiding the web of CCTV cameras that were spread throughout Anaheim. It hadn't been easy because the city was heavily watched; in part it was because of its large Muslim population. However, it was also because Anaheim was home to Disneyland. And when it came to keeping the happiest place on earth happy, the tourists weren't the only ones snapping pictures.

Once he'd arrived at Armagan's childhood home, Chauncey had made sure nobody was there, then picked the lock to gain entry. As he walked through the modest home, sweeping for wireless security cameras and microphones, he'd noted the many framed photographs of a happy, smiling Armagan standing in between Imam Ayman and his wife, Claudia. He had clearly been loved.

Imam Ayman was a Syrian-born cleric who'd immigrated to the United States over twenty-five years ago. He'd assimilated deeply and happily into American society. Because of his vocal, anti-fundamentalist, anti-terrorism stance, he'd even spent some time as a chaplain at Edwards Air Force Base. He'd met his wife, Claudia, a converted blond UC San Diego world history teacher while on Hajj in Mecca. Considered liberal Muslims, or as Americans called them, "good" Muslims, Imam Ayman and Claudia were viewed as non-threats, so it made perfect sense that Armagan had been left in their care.

In spite of the fact that Chauncey knew this particular imam and his brand of Islam were peaceful, he couldn't help but feel a bit uncomfortable in his home. Like a Jew in the presence of a German, an American servicemember in the presence of a Muslim caused the hairs on the back of his neck to stand at attention.

It wasn't as if he'd never met Muslims before. Unfortunately, most of them had been military detainees who'd be labeled "terrorists," but he'd also met a fair amount of interpreters and peaceful locals. They'd always been extremely warm and courteous. Not all Muslims were bomb-wearing boogiemen. Chauncey was embarrassed by his bias, but the military's brainwashing had been effective. He ratcheted back the undue racism by reminding himself of the fundamental difference between the message and the messenger.

Chauncey wasn't what you'd call a religious man. Truth be told, he thought religion was a complete crock. Contemporary religion, that is. As a pre-science, pre-centralized government concept for demystification and crowd-control, he completely got it. As with any mythology, it explained the unknown and gave humans a set of laws to follow. Only humans had evolved a great deal in 3,000-plus years. At least, in its understanding of the world, it had.

Where mankind hadn't evolved was in its pathological craving for power and control. So since religion provided both, it had survived. If people believed that you had God's ear, the ones who desperately needed to find meaning would give you anything: money, power, and even children to molest. And innocents that could be sent to slaughter had always been one of organized religion's most valuable commodities.

Unlike other atheists he knew, Chauncey respected that some people needed religion as a crutch. Blind faith helped people to cope with some of the toughest challenges life could mete out. One of his best mates growing up, Bill King had been a raging alcoholic. He'd gotten married to a drop-dead gorgeous model and had three incredibly beautiful children. Unfortunately, the toxic stew of stress and genetics had pushed him to the Altar of Alcohol, the Reverend Ronrico Rum presiding.

No matter what or how Chauncey and others had tried to pull Bill out of the liquor-filled abyss, nothing worked. He beat his wife and daughters and ended up in jail. Inside he met the Lord and hadn't taken a drink since. He'd exchanged one crutch for another, but at least the one he leaned on now was somewhat healthier. So as Chauncey closed the glass door that protected the imam's book collection, he mused that while rare in his estimate, uncorrupted religion could be a good thing.

From inside the dense row of cypress trees lining the fence in the imam's backyard, Jim Aberbach and his partner, Dan Hammer, watched and waited. Using a thermal night-sight goggle, Aberbach monitored Chauncey's body heat as he moved through the house. Once he'd entered, they'd radioed Breskin to get the green light to execute.

"Target is in position," Aberbach had said. "Shall we launch the bird?"

"Negative," responded Breskin. "We wait until all targets are assembled."

Aberbach was taken aback. He'd been told his only target was Chauncey. Breskin had just thrown a curve to a man who preferred fastballs.

Shoving the thick, itchy cypress branches away from his face, Aberbach whispered, "What other targets?"

"I'll tell you what you need to know when I'm ready for you to know. Until then you just sit on the bird," said Breskin.

Aberbach clicked off and petulantly resumed his surveillance. He'd done this type of mission before and knew that you went when it was ready. You didn't change the plan in the middle unless it was absolutely one-hundred percent necessary. When you had the shot, you took the shot. Of course, he had to temper himself because he knew that not so deep down, a part of himself just wanted to kill Chauncey. His bruised ego from losing their desert fight had torn more than his MCL.

Taking his frustration out on the foliage, Aberbach tore off the clump of cypress branches that had been brushing his face. The sticky layer of sap that now coated his hand just aggravated him even more. He told Hammer they were supposed to wait. He didn't know why, but those were the orders.

The men exchanged a disbelieving look. They'd been in hiding in the cypress fencing for several hours, ever since the Predator had spotted an unsuspecting Chauncey on the move. They were understandably anxious to get things done.

Hammer unhappily looked at the enhanced, AeroVironment Hummingbird drone that sat beside them. It didn't matter to him that the nanoair vehicle had been made by AV through DARPA funding. It was creepy. The thing looked just like a real bird and had tiny cameras in its eyes. It could fly, hover, go through windows and do just about anything it was commanded to do via its iPad remote control. That they'd just packed the damned thing with 100 grams of Semtex made it even worse.

"This is bullshit," Hammer said.

"Hold," said Aberbach suddenly. "They're here."

He pointed out that the imam and his wife were entering the house. Then, speaking into his headpiece, he told Breskin, "More company has arrived."

Breskin spoke back and said, "Hold tight. Wait until they are all in the kitchen."

"How in the name of hell do you know they'll end up in the kitchen?"

"Let's just say I'm a lot smarter than you," said Breskin.

Chauncey heard the front door open and knew the imam and his wife were home. He walked out of the office and crept down the still dark hallway toward the entryway. There was no way he would be able to reveal himself without startling too much, so he had to be as mellow and non-threatening as possible.

"Asalaam Alaykem," Chauncey said gently, as Imam Ayman tried unsuccessfully to turn on the foyer light.

Chauncey knew the light wouldn't go on. When he'd broken into the house, besides performing advanced, technical countersurveillance measures as part of his operational security, he'd removed the light bulb in the ceiling lamp by the front door. It would be less startling to hear the words that meant "peace be upon you" than to see a complete stranger who'd broken in approaching. They were still alarmed, as Claudia screamed and frantically turned back to the door.

"Armagan sent me," Chauncey added, quickly. "I'm a friend."

The imam said something to Claudia in Arabic that apparently soothed her. He then turned to Chauncey.

"Wa'Alaykum Asalham," he said, completing the traditional Muslim greeting. Although he'd been in America for over half of his life, the imam still had a fairly thick Syrian accent. "Why has our son sent you? Is he safe? We have been very concerned. These killings have been terrible, and he does not return our calls."

Chauncey silently noted that the imam didn't ask why he hadn't called in advance. Or even why he hadn't just knocked on the door after they'd gotten home. He must have understood on some level that their adopted son was working on top secret projects that contained an element of risk. Chauncey reached out to shake hands.

"He's fine. I'm Captain Paunce, but please call me Chauncey. I've become mates with your adopted son and he asked me to see if you were safe."

Claudia breathed a relieved and nervous laugh. "Isn't that just like Armi! He's the one who works on military projects but he's worried about us!"

Chauncey smiled. "He was concerned that with all of the anti-Muslim sentiment happening right now, you might be in danger. I'm an expert in teaching people to protect themselves, so he wanted me to check out your house and see if you'd like some training."

Rather than respond to Chauncey's offer, the imam gave a quick, cautious look around the room. He then silently indicated that there were listening devices.

"No worries about that," said Chauncey. He pulled out a small device that was the size of a walkie-talkie. It had three, stubby antennas sticking out from the top. "I've jammed all the wireless video and audio devices that are in here. They can't hear a word we say for up to 30 meters around this unit."

"That is most comforting," said Imam Ayman. "I think I may look into purchasing one of those. Please stay for some tea. We would like to hear about our adopted son."

"Love to," said Chauncey. "Especially if it's that wonderful chai that he makes. I'm sorry about the lights and startling you. I had to do it that way because, well, just because."

"We understand," said the Imam.

Claudia moved to the kitchen, flipped on the lights then went to put on a pot of hot water.

"Come in, please," she said. "And tell me all about Armi. I haven't heard from him in months. Is he eating? Is he sleeping? How did you two meet?"

Chauncey smiled at her warmth and followed into the kitchen. He sat at the small four-person dinner table as the imam followed and sat across from him.

Still holding the NVGs to his eyes, Aberbach described the situation to Breskin. He wasn't sure how, but he'd been spot-on about the kitchen.

"There are now three targets in the location — the primary plus the inhabitants. Is that who you were expecting?"

Breskin didn't honor the question with an answer. Instead, he simply said, "Proceed. And make sure they are all included."

"Fina-fuckingly," said Hammer and began the sequence of arming the hummingbird.

"Can you hear what they're saying?" asked Breskin.

"Not a word. He's jamming every wireless signal you've got set up. No wifi, Bluetooth, or RF," said Aberbach.

It was the first time he'd heard any discomfort from Breskin. He wasn't sure if Breskin wanted to know because he was really curious about what they were saying, or if he wanted to know because he didn't want Aberbach and Hammer to hear something they shouldn't.

Breskin replied stoically, "Should've figured that."

Hammer nodded that all was ready and carefully took hold of the NAV. He crawled out from their cover to hold it aloft for takeoff. Aberbach was about to remove the NVGs and grab the iPad controller but stopped.

"Wait," he said. "One of them is moving."

Hammer quickly shimmied his way back into cover.

Imam Ayman stood up from the table and looked first at his wife, then at Chauncey. He was acting a bit paranoid from Chauncey's perspective, but then again, being under surveillance for as long as he must have been could be nerve-wracking.

"I am happy that Armagan is concerned for our safety," he said to Chauncey. "But I am even more concerned about his. How familiar are you with his past?"

"I know about the attack on his village and that the government brought him here to be raised. Bit of a publicity stunt, but it seems to have worked out okay," said Chauncey.

"So you are not connected with the men who brought him to the States?"

Chauncey shook his head. "Not that I know of," he said.

"May I show you something?" asked the imam and beckoned Chauncey to follow him. The two men walked out of the room just as Claudia took the whistling pot off the stove and poured it over the tea leaves to steep.

The imam and Chauncey walked down the hall, the flowery aroma from the tea following them. They passed the imam's office and entered the bedroom where Armagan had apparently grown up. Chauncey immediately noticed they hadn't changed a thing. Probably hadn't touched anything since the day their adopted son had left for college.

Not surprisingly, Armagan's bedroom wasn't like the room of a typical American boy. The linen on the twin-size bed was solid burgundy with a plain white comforter. There was a heavy wooden computer desk with mathematics and engineering books neatly lined on an attached hutch. Chauncey smiled that there were several meticulously constructed and painted models of vehicles from *Star Wars, Bladerunner, I Robot"* and other science-fiction movies.

Everything seemed pretty normal except for the single poster on the wall. Prominently displayed across the room from the bed hung a large-format, blown-up satellite image of Armagan's village. Chauncey had no idea where he'd gotten it, but the image was of his village just moments after the attack had taken place. The grainy black-and-white photograph showed dead bodies and turned-over vehicles. The UGVs that had perpetrated the massacre were in plain sight. GIs in desert gear stood in various positions.

Chauncey was stupefied. How in God's name had Armagan gotten hold of such highly classified GEOINT? And why would he have even wanted it? From everything he'd told Chauncey, Armagan had left the past behind him. Yet here it was right in his face.

As Chauncey turned to ask Imam Ayman what it was about, the imam handed him some hand-drawn illustrations. They were incredibly detailed, gruesome cartoons of locusts crawling on men in the desert. Many of the insects were bombs, and the drawings showed body parts blown off and explosive-induced craters in their bodies. Chauncey immediately thought about the scorpion bots that had nearly killed him. The imam noticed Chauncey's fixation and offered what little explanation he could.

"As you can imagine, when they brought Armagan to us, he was a very troubled young boy. At first he was simply confused, which made sense. We did our best to make him happy and to help him deal with the trauma he'd endured."

He pointed to the drawings. "Armagan drew these all throughout his childhood. We were told that it was cathartic. That it was his way of acting out anger. So we never tried to stop him. He rebelled against us, me especially, for being the cause of his agony. He hated religion. He hated the world. But not his mother. She represented the West. It was always confusing for him that she would marry an imam, but he loved her nonetheless. I never felt the same love, but I would read to him passages from the Koran on mercy and forgiveness until one night I found him burning one in the yard, so I stopped.

"It took many years, but as time passed he seemed to grow more accepting. Yet as much as he knew he was loved, he could never get past the well of deep anger. He had an unstated need for revenge. And as hard as I tried, I always felt that Captain Breskin was working at cross-purposes to ours."

Taken off guard by hearing Breskin's name mentioned in this context, Chauncey tensed up. He didn't reveal his concern, however, and gazed more intently at the imam as he continued.

"On one level we should be grateful as it was Captain Breskin's idea to bring Armagan to the United States," Imam Ayman said. "But on another level, I think in some way he kept the fire burning. Maybe even stoked it. He would come to visit once a month, and they would have private conversations. He introduced him to robotics and nurtured his interest in engineering. Every time he left, Armagan's anger seemed to grow. Claudia hated him."

Chauncey checked his initial response that it was the same Breskin he knew. After all, it was a fairly common name. And it was a very big army. Maybe it was another Breskin.

"Do you have any pictures of Breskin?" Chauncey asked.

The imam pulled a framed photo out from between a pair of the books on Armagan's desk and handed it to Chauncey. It was a picture of a much younger Douglas Breskin standing beside Armagan as a teenager. Chauncey was instantly on edge.

"So I am worried that my son was somehow involved in some of the bad things that are happening. I don't know why. Call it my inner voice, my

Nafs-e-Lawwâmah, praise be to Allah, but I never trusted this man. Have you ever noticed anything in your dealings with my son that would make you concerned?"

It was as if a tidal wave of blood had deluged Chauncey's brain. His senses screamed "Code Red." They were in danger. He knew immediately that he had to get himself and the Aymans out of the house.

From the bushes, Aberbach watched the two men returning from the back of the house to the kitchen. He wasn't going to miss an opportunity for a third time by waiting. He nodded to Hammer who then crawled back onto the lawn to hold the Hummingbird up for launch. Aberbach immediately took up the controller.

Once in position, Hammer looked back over his shoulder and nodded. On command, the biological bird's wings sprang to life, fluttering up and down over twenty-five times per second. The NAV gracefully rose into the air, and Aberbach guided it toward the house.

Chauncey and Imam Ayman arrived back in the kitchen as Claudia was placing the cups of tea on the table.

"Claudia, we must leave," the imam said firmly.

"But we haven't had our tea yet," she said. "And I want to ask Chauncey about Armagan, and —" She stopped her sentence, noticing the hummingbird that was now hovering outside the kitchen window. "That's odd. I didn't know hummingbirds flew at night?"

Chauncey looked up. In an instant he recognized the bird as the same one he'd seen in the glass case of Armagan's office.

"They don't!" shouted Chauncey from the doorway. "Get down!"

Chauncey dove back into the living room as Aberbach pressed the detonator. The Semtex in the bird went off immediately. The concussive blow shattered the kitchen window, sending shards of glass into Claudia's face. They penetrated her eye and shredded her brain in an instant. The explosion-propelled window frame knocked the imam to the ground at the same time the shrapnel from the bird and the house pulverized his head. The kitchen wall buckled and the ceiling fell on them both, crushing their already dead bodies.

In spite of his sudden loss of hearing and copious amounts of airborne debris, Chauncey quick-crawled into the entrance to the kitchen. He saw the imam and Claudia lying dead in the rubble. There was nothing he could do except get out fast. He stumbled his way to the front door and ran out just as Aberbach and Hammer ran in though the demolished side of the house, machine guns at the ready.

Chapter Thirty

Chauncey lay still in the way back of Aberbach's Suburban as it sped away from the imam's house. He'd been conscious for about thirty minutes, but rather than alert his captors of that fact, he calmly, quietly assessed his situation. The first question that had occurred to him was why he was still alive. He'd clearly survived the explosion, although his hearing was still somewhat impaired. Why hadn't Aberbach just put a bullet in his head and been done with it?

He dismissed the question almost at the same time it had occurred to him. There was zero sense in focusing on things that couldn't be answered. Instead, he turned his senses to figuring out where he was and how he could escape. He was lying on his right side in the back of a large SUV. Based on the smoothness of the ride and the easy sound of the tires beneath him, he surmised they were on a freeway doing about sixty-five miles per hour. Which direction they were headed he didn't yet know.

His hands were tightly bound behind his back, and with his fingers Chauncey determined that he'd been shackled with a pair of high-end police handcuffs. His elbows and knees were cinched together with what was probably duct tape. Based on the tight, thinness of his ankle restraints, he correctly reasoned they must have been zip-tied. Aberbach and Hammer had also, it seemed, connected the handcuffs to the zip-ties on Chauncey's ankles with another length of zip-tie. If he'd been a calf in a rodeo, they would have won the blue ribbon for hog-tying.

So that he wouldn't be seen by anyone looking into the vehicle, they'd covered Chauncey with some kind of dirty canvas tarp. From its musty smell and feel, it wasn't exactly dry-cleaned before they'd put it on him. To cap it off, just in case he'd miraculously managed to push off the covering, his head had been covered with a sack that was tied on around his neck. Beneath the sack, his mouth was gagged.

In spite of himself, he recalled the joke he and his mates had told about a "double-bagger." He couldn't remember the exact words but it went something like, "How many bags do you need when you sleep with an ugly woman? Two: one bag to put over her head, and one to put over yours in case hers slipped off." He shook off the soothing image of him and his mates laughing and returned to the present.

The first order of business was to slip the handcuffs. There was nothing he'd be able to do if he remained hogtied. Once they were off, he'd be able to focus on where they were and determine his next move. Picking the cuffs was one of the first and most basic skills you learned in Chauncey's line of work. When he'd been on active duty he'd always carried keys in his wallet, or even in his mouth. Unfortunately, one of his abductors had taken his wallet and he'd decided not to chew any metal during his meeting with Armagan's adopted father.

Like most well-trained and paranoid spooks, Chauncey had sewn open paper clips into the seams of all his pant cuffs, shirt collars and even the folded seams of his back pockets. Within a few seconds, he'd pulled the metal piece out of his back left pocket and picked open the left handcuff. Luckily, they hadn't threaded the zip-tie through the handcuff links so he was able to easily feed the loose cuff out of the zip-tie's loop. He allowed himself the luxury of straightening up slightly. He would have liked to straighten completely, but there was only one seat between him and his assailants. Rather than risk their scrutiny, he would wait. The longer they believed he was unconscious, the better.

The canvas bag over his head was itchy and hot. Perspiration dripped onto the down side of the bag. He wondered why it was so hot. There was a no way these guys were going to drive around without air conditioning. Then it dawned on him that they were probably headed back out to the desert. The heat from the road was emanating upward.

Even though the sweat was irritating his cheek, he resisted the urge to adjust. He kept his movements as conservative as possible. Now somewhat free, albeit still uncomfortable as hell, he turned his thoughts elsewhere. He knew nothing would happen as long as they were on the freeway. He wouldn't need to escape until they arrived wherever they were going.

As he listened hard to the two men's muffled conversation his thoughts reverted to the other questions he'd ignored. How had they known he'd be there? Only Armagan had known that. So either Armagan had set him up, or his house had been bugged when he'd asked Chauncey to warn his parents.

While he wished the answer was the latter, the photograph of Breskin with Armagan tied the two together. So Armagan had set him up; that was the most likely truth. And even though his personal desire for his new friend's innocence pressed against him, the armed Hummingbird drone was the clincher. He recalled seeing the NAV beneath the glass case in Armagan's GA office. Armagan had said it was a gift from AeroVironment to remind him of what he was passing up.

Was Armagan responsible for the scorpion bots also? Carby had told him that he'd been working on biomimetic bots, and even though Chauncey didn't like it, the answer was fairly obvious. Armagan had tried to kill him. Twice. Maybe Green had somehow forced him to assassinate Chauncey against his will. Yet he'd had another perfect opportunity the other night. Armagan had held a loaded AA-12 in his face. He could have blown him away and said it was self-defense. Nobody would have questioned it. And what the hell was with Breskin? Could Green have ordered Armagan to kill him without Breskin's knowledge?

"Enough!" he said to himself. "First things first. I need to get my ass out of this."

Chauncey felt the Suburban slow a bit, then steer slightly to the right. He figured they'd gotten off the freeway. The SUV came to a stop then turned left. With the bumpier and slower ride, he determined they were on a local road. It was a town of some kind and they made frequent stops without turning. Probably stoplights or stop signs. Either way they were most likely getting closer to their destination.

Aberbach and Hammer were talking more now. Although Chauncey still couldn't make out what they were saying, the increased chatter confirmed in his mind that they were getting closer and were now discussing what to do when they got there. Making use of their conversation, Chauncey slowly reached his left hand up to feel the back of the partition. He found the top of the thick, plastic knob that would release the back seat and pulled it up until it clicked. The seatback gave way, signaling that it could now easily be folded down.

The SUV stopped again. They turned left and the ground became rougher. Based on the road surface and the even slower speed, Chauncey knew they had gone off the main route. They made several more turns. He wished he could hear or smell the outside to get a better sense of where they were, but the men had kept the windows closed. It was a smart move, he thought, because he could have started screaming at a stop to alert someone of his presence in the back.

Chauncey went over his plan. He had to be lightning-quick, he had to make his move before they stopped again, and his attack had to be lethal. Piece of cake. He tensed up, ready to pounce when Aberbach's cellphone rang.

"Yeah?" he heard Aberbach's still muffled, although much louder voice, say.

"What's your twenty?" asked the voice of Breskin over the vehicle's Bluetooth phone system. The conversation was over the car's speaker system so Chauncey could hear every word. They were either convinced that he was either still unconscious or that he didn't present a threat.

"We'll be there in two minutes," said Aberbach. "I still don't know why we didn't finish him off at the towel-head's house. Going back to his place is ridiculous."

Chauncey patted himself on the back. He'd been right in guessing they were back in Adelanto. It made a lot of sense to off him at his own place. They'd already picked it apart looking for clues, so the likelihood of any further investigation was thin. Not to mention that Breskin had probably called off the entire investigation anyway.

Breskin's rebuke was sharp as he responded to Aberbach's question. "Because you failed to kill him with the explosion. You would have had to shoot him, and then there would have been multiple methods of death. Too many loose ends. Anyway, I have my reasons, just do it."

"There," said Hammer's voice. Although he couldn't see anything, Chauncey figured Hammer was indicating their final stop. Knowing they were going to his old house, he recounted the turns they'd taken since getting off the freeway. He knew they were about to turn into one of the three entrances to his driveway and that he didn't have any time left. He fleetingly wished he could see, but given that the hood was shackled around his neck with zip-tie, he resigned himself to doing it blind.

As the Suburban slowed to what was potentially the last turn of his life, Chauncey sprang into action. Lunging forward, his body rammed down the rear seat. Using the handcuffs as a garrote, he jammed his hands around Hammer's neck and pulled back with a huge tug. The chain links and metal sides of the cuffs sliced into Hammer's soft neck, severing his carotid artery. Chauncey couldn't see it, but blood spurted against the inside of the windshield.

"What the hell was that?!" demanded Breskin's voice, hearing the sudden violence.

Keeping his left hand on the steering wheel, Aberbach ignored Breskin and elbowed Chauncey in the head. He then reached across to his left side to grab his holstered firearm. Before he could get it free, Chauncey blindly swung his still-handcuffed left arm crosswise. The metal fork of the loose cuff entered Aberbach's right eye like a hook. And like a deep sea fisherman landing a marlin, Chauncey yanked his arm back as hard as he could. The prong tightened against the inside of Aberbach's eye socket. He screamed in agony and fell back, his foot pressing the accelerator, his hands letting go of the wheel. The SUV turned, flipped on its side and slid to a stop.

"Hello? Hello? What's going on?" Breskin's voice barked through the car's speakers.

Chauncey laid there, twisted and covered in the blood of the two men he'd just killed. He panted a moment, then shimmed off the zip-tie that held his hood in place. He pulled off the hood and yelled back at Breskin.

"What happened is that you just signed your death warrant, mate. Your boys are history. I know what's going on, and now I'm going to end you like I ended them."

"Is that so?" Breskin responded feigning fear. "What are you going to do? Rat me out to the media again? They didn't believe you the first time, and you ended up in prison. You almost took that slut with you. Besides, how are you going to come after me when every law enforcement agent in Southern California is going to be hunting you for murdering the imam and his lovely bride?"

Chauncey fell silent. His nostrils flared, filling his chest with air as he focused on catching his breath. He realized that by surviving the blast and being captured, he'd allowed for the possibility of being set up. He also knew that Breskin wasn't through, so he just waited for the other shoe to drop.

"Yeah," Breskin continued. "That's right, *mate*. We have Predator footage of you entering the house thirty minutes prior to the explosion. But there's no footage of your leaving. And yet, you're alive."

"Why, Grandma, what big eyes you have," Chauncey replied, not quite sure what else to say. But he knew that Breskin probably wasn't making it up. He was tied in with the dronecos and they wanted him dead. They also knew where he was right now. Debating with Breskin was no longer in his best interest.

"Yeah, well you'd better pray to the spirit of Joseph Smith that I don't find you," Chauncey said. "Thanks for the ride home, dickhead. There's some stuff I forgot to grab the first time you failed to kill me."

"We're coming for you," Breskin taunted. Then the line went dead.

Chauncey kicked out the windshield and slithered his way out of the car. He freed his legs then jogged up the center driveway.

Chapter Thirty-One

Breskin clicked the red *end* button on his phone and shook his head. He wondered for a quick moment whether Chauncey was that good or if the men he'd sent were just that bad. Ultimately, it didn't matter because in a few short minutes the abilities of men like Aberbach and Hammer would be far less important when it came to these types of missions. Unmanned aerial, ground, and marine vehicles were much better suited for surveillance and incapacitating targets than human beings.

Besides removing the element of human error from the equation, automated law enforcement drones were faster and more powerful. They could access, process, and analyze data in an instant. Their targeting algorithms provided much higher Pk, so the potential for collateral damage was decreased exponentially. Not to mention that if for some unforeseen and miraculous reason the perpetrator destroyed the drone, nobody really gave a damn if a robot got killed.

That stopped him. "Killed," he thought. They can't be killed because they're not alive. The heavenly father would be smiling at the respect this showed for the sanctity of his children. It was the moral thing to do. It was also one of the biggest reasons that Bush's war in the Middle East had lasted so long. Casualties had been mostly limited to equipment and heathens. Our Predators and Reapers had been used to pile bodies high and wide by trigger-pressing pilots safely sitting a half world away.

Sure, war would always be about killing the enemy; the more you killed the greater the victory. But people didn't like it when their own side suffered casualties. So if you could substitute machines for men the only ones who would care were the losers, the engineers, and the bleeding heart liberals who warned about the dangers of perpetual war and a "Skynet" world filled with terminators.

Perhaps they were right to a certain degree. Without body bags and television footage of flag-draped coffins coming home with our dead sons and daughters, nobody really noticed anymore. Breskin reasoned that the same went for law enforcement. The public wanted to be kept safe. They just wanted the tactics used to keep them safe to be neat and tidy. Follow a few simple rules and you could do just about anything: Keep the good humans safe. Don't hurt children. Don't get caught on camera shooting a defenseless suspect.

Not that Breskin really had a problem with any of those things happening in the name of law and order, it was simply bad PR when they did. And bad press caused demotions. If you asked a hundred people whether they'd give up their personal freedom to be safe, ninety would say "yes," nine would say "within reason," and one would say "no." The one who said no would be the person everyone needed protection from. In any event, majority ruled. The within-reason risk takers could move to the West Bank of Israel if they wanted a thrill ride.

Twenty-first century Americans were soft. The age-old adage, "no pain, no gain," was something now reserved for athletes alone. Even then, the difficult and excruciating exercise required to increase strength and endurance had been shortcut through the use of chemicals. Everyone wanted to get without giving. To succeed without sacrificing. To reap without sowing.

Today's children received trophies for merely showing up; it didn't matter if they tried, improved, excelled, or won. As a matter of fact, winning had been diminished and supplanted by the false notion that making an effort was all that counted. It would prove to be calamitous because everyone knew the world didn't function that way. There were winners and there were losers. That this didn't matter was a modern-day fairytale created by Pollyanna-types to spare the feelings of losers. And it took away the desire to strive and value hard-earned success.

American parents were now raising a second generation of children who couldn't cope with conflict. Because of that, for years to come it would be the inheritors and the immigrants who got the spoils. They would be the ones with the money, the power, the mansions, and the fancy cars. But Breskin would be the one with the most advanced and lethal weapons; the ultimate winner was always the ultimate predator.

Chauncey had mocked Breskin with his, "Why, Grandma, what big eyes you have," quip. What he didn't know was how right he'd been. And not only did Grandma have big eyes, big flying, all-seeing, all-knowing, all-recording digital eyes, she also had big teeth. Big, sharp, robotic teeth that were about the change the way Americans viewed the world. Oh, yes, they would finally get the safety they craved. They would get the gain without the pain; unless you considered 24/7 surveillance, continuous analysis of your every move, and automatic, algorithmically induced arrests by drones to be painful.

The light on Breskin's landline flashed three times, signaling that all was ready. He lifted the lid of his etched, lead crystal candy dish and scooped up a handful of hard candies. Stuffing them into his pocket, he strode out of his office and down the sterile hallway of FBI headquarters. He passed framed photographs of previous FBI directors, each one responsible for gaining a little bit more access to private lives. He passed the open doors of data analysts, soon-to-be unemployed. And he passed the secretaries who would lose their jobs and become baristas or housewives. Or maybe, if all went well, part of the tragically diminished religious flock that needed new blood.

He turned the corner and opened a set of double-doors, revealing the Los Angeles FBI headquarters command center. The walls were covered with a dozen, high-resolution video monitors. The large, polished oak conference table with pitchers of water and glasses in front of every high-priced Herman Miller chair was full. Seated around the table were the CEOs of General Atomics, AeroVironment, and iRobot, the new stewards of air and land. Also present were Senator Stevens from the drone caucus, Jim Sorrentino of the AUVSI and now General Brewster, the biggest military advocate of robot war in the Pentagon. Rounding out the group was Armagan, the wonder child. The gift.

That they were all sitting in this room together was a testament to the greed for power. These three competing DoD contractors had blood-derived trade secrets learned in Afghanistan, Pakistan, Iraq, Yemen, Syria, and other Middle East conflict zones in order to create the integrated software and hardware that were about to subdue the mastermind behind the massacres and tortures that had terrorized their employees and the US population for the past nine months. And once their convergent technology was proven safe and successful, it would disrupt the way things worked for centuries to come. As far as defense contract size was concerned, these three men weren't the largest, but based on ability, they were about to be the kings.

On two of the monitors were live video images of Tom Carby's house in La Jolla. One of the feeds was from a camera held by Agent Zellner who was standing outside the house. Breskin had reinstated Zellner after he'd completed a drug rehabilitation program. Not only was he now clean and sober, but he was as loyal to Breskin as a Pekingese lapdog. The other feed was being broadcast live from a Predator drone that was circling the area from 20,000 feet above the house. The resolution from the drone's five-megapixel cameras was astoundingly clear. Not only could you see the color variations of the Mexican adobe tiles covering Carby's roof, you could see decayed and stuck leaves that had been blown into the wavy, clay roof over the years.

Breskin spoke to Zellner through a conference call hub on the table. "All set to begin?"

Zellner's voice came back, "Roger that. Just say the word."

The mission was simple in its goal: to apprehend Thomas Carby without harm to property, FBI agents, or Carby himself. The skies above and the neighborhood below had been evacuated over the last several hours as the mission was set up. They knew that Carby was home because the Predator had initiated a tactic used in the warzone through which it could imitate cell towers. The unmanned bird had activated Carby's phone, turned on its location settings, and confirmed that it was inside the house. His movements were clear and voice analysis had positively identified his throat-clearing as him. So they were certain he was there with his phone.

Carby had become the prime suspect as they'd pieced together his movements over the past nine months through his emails, cellphone calls, texts, credit card charges, and CCTV camera footage taken from various locales. License plate readers had identified his car as being parked at the Rose Bowl on the "day of the drones," as it had become labeled. Facial recognition software taken inside the stadium had placed him at the event when it happened. Cameras posted around the Hotel del Coronado had captured him on his dinghy just off the coast when the explosion took place; not to mention that cellphone calls had been placed between him and DJ Soli for several months leading up to the massacre. Last, but not least, emails between Carby and Doctor Kay Adams were found, showing that he'd had contacts with her just prior to her horrific sarin gas attack at the Sherwood Country Club.

In the face of overwhelming evidence, Breskin had submitted for and easily obtained a warrant for Carby's arrest. However, because he'd presented such an unorthodox procedure for the takedown, it had required the intervention of Senator Stevens to get permission from the FAA and Homeland, both of which were watching the proceedings offsite with a mix of curiosity, dread, and excitement.

Breskin had argued that the radical departure from protocol and iffy legal procedures were necessary in order to protect agents from harm. Carby was known to have an arsenal of potentially armed and dangerous security drones around his house. Given the tragic results of the standoffs at Ruby Ridge and Waco, nobody wanted to risk another black eye. Especially since he lived in a wealthy, high-density area. If Breskin had it his way, the circling Predator would have just launched a Hellfire missile and spared the taxpayers the expense of a trial and costly lifetime incarceration of a domestic terrorist.

Breskin, Green, Paulson, and Peter Engeler, the CEO of iRobot, had presented the results of test missions they'd conducted with their new automated detection and apprehension system at March Air Force Base in Adelanto. They'd secretly been working on it for years and had copious amounts of data and video footage to prove its effectiveness. Given the current climate of fear, the potential danger that Carby presented to

American citizens, and the possibility of FBI casualties, the green light had been granted.

"Have you attempted to have Carby give himself up?" Breskin asked Zellner.

"Yes, sir. He knows we're here and is ignoring my call for his surrender."

Breskin looked around the room. "Okay then, initiate the LEAD."

A drone pilot at GA's La Mirage airfield switched his circling Predator into autonomous mode. From here on, the drone would be making all of the decisions. The LEAD, or "Lead Enforcement Aerial Director" algorithm on the Predator, signaled a dozen of AeroVironment's Qube MAVs to launch. Although the ultimate plan was to one day have them stationed in charging ports every quarter mile in cities and every three miles in the suburbs, tonight they were sitting on the ground by Zellner and a half-dozen other blue-slickered agents stationed outside of Carby's house. The sophisticated quadcopters spun up and rose into the air in concert. Directed by the LEAD, the Qubes flew into Carby's yard and took up strategic positions around the house. A dozen floating, buzzing, staring eyes scanned the house with IR cameras and located an individual inside.

Zellner narrated the sequence as if it were a sporting event. "Qubes in position. Defenses not coming online. Wait. There they go."

As he finished his last word, the gathered men could see on the monitors that Carby's defensive drones had activated. The quadcopters that had blocked Chauncey's path barely a week ago now positioned themselves in between the house and the Qubes. Every window and door to the house was covered. The sound of the ninety-six rapidly spinning propellers drowned out the more soothing sound of waves crashing against the cliffs behind the house. It was like a swarm of warring insects in some Amazon rain forest.

For a moment nothing happened, other than a flurry of unseen, uplink and downlink activity. The sensors on the Qubes were recording the obstructions, sending the information to the LEAD, and waiting for its next instructions. Sensing no weapon systems in Carby's drones, the LEAD autonomously issued a simple command. It directed each of the Qubes to lock onto individual drones and emit multiple GPS spoofing signals. Losing their technological homing signals, Carby's quads jiggled and swerved as they tried to regain their geobearings. Unable to do so, some of them flew off the cliff. Others flipped over and fell to the ground, their propellers snapping on impact and spraying dirt and grass into the night air.

Carby's aerial defenses now gone, the LEAD issued a command to a pair of iRobot UGVs. Similar to the UGVs that had decimated Armagan's village, these were smaller and more elegant. They were, however, by no means less lethal. Each of the dual-tracked units had multiple sensors, high-resolution infrared cameras, grenade launchers, laser-sighted M240 7.62 mm mounts, and articulated arms with pneumatic hammers. The iRobot Enforcers, as they were being called, nimbly rolled into the yard and headed for the front and back doors.

At once a pair of Carby's newly replaced Rotundus ground bots rolled out of hiding and blocked their paths. The Enforcers stopped. The UGVs scanned each other in what seemed to be a techno-stalemate. As the Enforcers sent signals to the LEAD, a second pair of unanticipated ground bots emerged from the bushes. Each of them rolled furiously toward the Enforcers. Although one of the Enforcers was fast enough to dodge the Rotundus, the other one received a savage ram that bowled it over. The powerful orbs retreated and set up to attack again.

"Oh my God! Did you see that?" yelled Zellner. "That was amazing. Should we move in?"

"No," Breskin replied. "Tonight, and possibly for the rest of your career, you're just a bot-sitter."

As Zellner contemplated telling Breskin where to shove it, the Qubes sent information about the orbs to the LEAD. Using that data, the LEAD triangulated the locations and possible paths of the orbs, then transmitted the data to the still-standing Enforcer. Implementing the targeting signal it received, the unit's turrets instantly turned and fired-off three 7.62 mm rounds. Three of the four Rotunduses were blown to metallic bits. The fourth orb spun back on itself and began a death-roll toward the Enforcer. Before it could strike, the prone Enforcer used its articulated arm to right itself and fired off a round. The blast hit the orb, sending it to the same robot hell as its fallen comrades.

Now unobstructed, the Enforcers rolled to Carby's front and back doors. The Qubes flew into position behind the bot, as the UGVs easily climbed the stairs. The LEAD sent signals to both of the ground drones. Responding without question, the Enforcers activated their articulated arms like battering rams and splintered the doors.

"Doors are down," reported Zellner, unnecessarily, because the assembled men had watched it breathlessly from the room. "Shall we move in to apprehend Carby?"

"Stand down!" said Breskin. "This is not your op. All you need to do is sit back and watch how things will be done from now on."

Before Zellner could ask how they would get Carby out of the house, four of the Qubes opened hinges in their bellies releasing a swarm of bees. Only these bees were NAVs, biomimetic nano-arial vehicles that had been engineered by Armagan. Directed by the LEAD, the tiny bee drones flew past the Enforcers through the demolished doorways and into the house.

On screen in the conference room, Breskin, et al., watched camera feeds from the bees' eyes on screen. They buzzed through the house looking for Carby. Using the heat sensors in their tiny robotic bodies, they quickly found the temperature scent and flew through the kitchen. They banked left in the living room and found Carby sitting at his dining room table.

Wearing a closed, purple kimono and casually sipping a cup of steaming saki, he lifted his middle finger to the bugs as they sent his facial scans to the LEAD. In less than a second, the LEAD cross-referenced the information with the FBI's Guardian and the NSA's Utah-based facial recognition databases, positively identifying the subject as Carby. As one, the bees swarmed over Carby, much like the locusts in Armagan's nightmare had done to al-Wahiri and his mujahedeen in the Afghan fields.

Completely covering his head, the bees emitted a collective electrical current that shocked Carby into unconsciousness. He crumpled to the ground like 208-pound sack of Idaho russets.

In a rare show of emotion, the men in the conference room were on their feet, applauding and whistling their approval. Hands were shaken and backs slapped gregariously. It felt as if Peyton Manning had thrown the game-winning touchdown pass of his career to finally win a decent Super Bowl.

As the Enforcers rolled back to the FBI equipment van, the bees returned to the Qubes, and the Qubes returned to their cases. The now retreating LEAD sent a text to Zellner's iPhone. It read, "You may go in and see how things are supposed to be done."

Chapter Thirty-Two

Marcella gazed across the rickety, knife-gouged table at the man she'd practically ruined her career trying to help. Whether she'd made the attempt because she loved him or believed his story was something she'd never sorted out. After reporting Chauncey's story that blew the whistle on America's torture tactics, she'd not only lost any chance she ever had at network news, but the DOJ had threatened to send her to prison for revealing state secrets. When it was all said and done, though, she was happy with her decision and would have done it again.

It had been five years since last she'd seen Chauncey, but he looked like it had been twice that long. She looked past his dirty and disheveled appearance into his red, tired eyes. They were eyes that had once been kind, gentle, and loving. Eyes she'd spent hours staring into, mesmerized by their pain, vulnerability, and intelligence. Eyes that were now filled with rage, fear, and a spirit near the breaking point.

She didn't kid herself; she knew that Chauncey had always been a dangerous man. He'd taught torture and killed men in ways she could never imagine. Not that Marcella had ever felt threatened by him in any way. In all their time together he'd always made her feel safe and protected.

His normally neat and well-combed hair was now matted and dirty. She correctly surmised it was because of the motorcycle helmet that sat on the chair beside him. His eyebrows were askew, his hands were smudged with oil, and his wrists had deep, red cuts from being handcuffed. He looked even more desperate now than on the day they'd led him away from their condo to go to prison.

Marcella thought she'd gotten over the anger, confusion, and disappointment she'd felt at his refusals to take her calls or visits while in jail. These feelings that seeing him in the flesh had aroused surprised her. In the time they'd been apart she'd played out what she would say to him if they ever met again, most of it harsh and accusing. Seeing him this way, the only thing she felt was concern. Her resentment evaporated, and had circumstances been different she would have taken him into her arms to take away the pain he was obviously feeling.

Carlos Menendez, the owner of the Whipple Tree restaurant, walked over and set down two plates of fish tacos. Their delicious and familiar aroma rose from the chipped and faded, powder blue plates into both Marcella's and Chauncey's nostrils.

"It's nice to see you again, my friends. It has been a very long time," said Carlos with a thick, Mexican accent. "I know you didn't order anything, but I remember this was your favorite."

"Thank you, Carlos," said Marcella. "They smell delicious as always."

"Gracias, amigo," Chauncey replied. "It's nice to see you as well."

Carlos nodded and receded back to his place behind the bar to take care of his other early-morning patrons.

Even though it was only ten o'clock in the morning, the tiny restaurant was beginning to get stuffy. A pair of old metallic fans clanked and feebly regurgitated the musty air across the faces of the men at the bar. A half-dozen ageless, Latino men, quietly sipped cold cerveza. Some of them were about to legally cross the Mexican border to bring their families the few dollars they'd earned as day laborers. Others were coyotes, human smugglers, who'd just sold their chattel to the fields sown by American corporations. Both sets of men knew that when it came to such things, Carlos was Switzerland. Completely neutral.

The Whipple Tree, or "The Whip," as Chauncey called it, was the last restaurant in San Diego before the Mexican border. A small taqueria located beneath the Fifteen freeway, it was hardly on the Zagat's list of fine Mexican eating establishments. But those with a sense of adventure were rewarded by the most authentic tacos north of the border.

Chauncey had brought Marcella here the first time they'd met because he knew it was below the radar. For the powers that be, it didn't even exist. It was one of the few places left in the country where you could talk without fear of being seen or overheard. So for Captain Charles Paunce, the whistleblower, and Marcella Kraner, the investigative journalist, it was both a smart and sexy choice. And since Carlos arguably made the best fish tacos on either side of the border, it had also become one of their favorite date places.

Chauncey gulped down his third glass of water, and then looked at Marcella's untouched glass. She nodded. Chauncey sucked it down in a single sip. She watched him as he practically inhaled his fish tacos without even seeming to chew. Although his frame of mind was miles away from wanting food, Chauncey's training had taught him to get nourishment whenever it was available. Especially when he had no idea when or even *if* his next meal might be.

After he'd dispatched Aberbach and Hammer, Chauncey had called Killa to come get him. Killa had given Chauncey the stay away code, indicating that it wasn't safe for him there. He'd gotten the same warnings from both Diddy and Phil. Having nowhere else to turn, he'd called Marcella and asked her to meet him at the Whip.

He'd offered her no apologies or explanations, just said that he needed help. He'd also asked if she still had his old car. When he'd gone to prison, he'd left her with the keys and location of his 1998 Olds Cutlass. Not only did he need transportation, but he needed the evasion and escape kit that he'd stowed in the trunk. She agreed to meet him at ten in the morning.

Chauncey had then stolen a motorcycle from one of his ex-neighbors and driven from Adelanto to San Ysidro. In order to make sure he wasn't followed, he'd stuck to local streets, backtracked a dozen times, and swapped out one stolen motorcycle for another along the way. The normally two-and-half-hour drive had taken him nearly ten hours. He was trashed.

After polishing off his own fish tacos, Chauncey finished off Marcella's, then sucked down his last swallow of water. He wiped his hands and mouth on a rough, brown paper napkin, then looked around at the people in the Whip and finally back at Marcella. There was so much he wanted to say. He wanted to say he was sorry for endangering her career and her life. For cutting off contact without explanation. Even for loving her. She was strong, smart, and independent, everything he wanted in a woman. And although he still cared for her deeply, he knew it wasn't in the cards.

"So will you help me?"

Marcella blew out a breath and reached across the table to take his hands. The familiar warmth of her touch calmed him and instantly lit up his tender feelings. He softened slightly.

"I don't know what to say," she answered. "I haven't seen you in five years, and when I finally do, you ask me to risk what's left of my career and probably my life again by reporting what I can only say sounds — insane."

Chauncey wet his lips with his tongue. No matter how much water he drank, the ten-hour ride had made them dry and chapped.

"I know I cut you off," he said. "It was the only way I could survive. I'm sorry. Hopefully one day you'll forgive me. And I know that what I just told you sounds crazy. But it's true. You didn't believe me when I told you about Gitmo and Abu Ghraib either, but those proved out in the long run."

"Yes, but they didn't seem so far-fetched. This is entirely different. You sit there looking like a maniac, saying you were hired by the FBI to kidnap and torture the CEOs of the country's top military contractors, and now they want you dead because you did what they asked?"

"No. They want me dead because of this Panopticon thing."

"I understand. Under torture, they divulged some top secret conspiracy that you don't even know what it is. I thought you always said that torture doesn't give reliable information."

"Not directly. Sometimes people say things and they don't even realize. Like when a drunk is honest because his defenses are down. And I said I didn't know what it was 'yet.' But what I am telling you is true. Breskin is involved. He's the one who brought me into it. He's the one who's trying to kill me. He brought Armagan here. He got him into MIT, introduced him to the defense engineering community, and I don't know what else. I know it sounds nuts, but Armagan is the key. He's the only one capable of creating the bots that tried to kill me. And Breskin is his handler."

"How do you know that? Where's your proof? You have no reliable information."

"I saw the drawings in his house. His father showed me."

"I know," Marcella said, withdrawing her hands. "Right before the hummingbird drone blew up and killed his parents. But they were drawings made by a little boy whose family had been killed with robots. It's textbook catharsis. Is that it? Is that your proof? Do you really expect me to report this on air? And even if I did who would believe it?"

"Don't turn me into some Cassandra. He works for General Atomics, the Hummingbird is an AeroVironment drone. Not to mention that GA makes air drones and the scorpions are ground. They don't do that technology. Somehow they're all working together."

Chauncey realized he was babbling. He knew that what he was saying must have sounded insane, but it was true. He knew to the core of his being that he needed to convince her to wake up the American public that had clearly fallen back into its lethargic stupor.

"And Tom Carby told me," he added, hoping that would make Marcella believe him.

"Carby?" said Marcella, surprised to hear his name. "Now you really do sound crazy. Carby was just arrested for being involved in the massacres and tortures of those engineers and their families."

Chauncey felt the blood drain from his face. He opened his mouth to say something, but nothing came out. Seeing his confusion, Marcella explained.

"It happened last night. I guess you were still, escaping. They apparently used some kind of FBI drone team to arrest him. Said they had to do it that way because his house was a bot-protected fortress. It sounded far-fetched, but after your story maybe not."

Chauncey's mind reeled. He knew from personal experience about Carby's defenses, but to arrest someone using robots? Was the technology that developed? Had it been approved right under everyone's noses?

"I can't imagine Carby was involved," he said. "I knew the man in Afghanistan. He was a great roboticist. Fixed and modified hundreds of EOD bots." Struggling to piece his memories back together, he added, "They had him working on this robotic enhanced interrogation program, but he walked off the project. Burned his files and any computers that had any data on them. He abhors torture. There's no way in hell he would do that."

Marcella studied him hard. She was growing more concerned by the moment.

"A robot torturer? Charles, do you know how that sounds?"

"Forget that. It's in the past. The project was shelved after he walked and threatened to go public."

"Well, the FBI said he's involved. He's in the Colorado Supermax penitentiary waiting for his trial."

Chauncey wanted to tear the skin off of his own body. He forced himself to calm down and looked intently at Marcella. The ferocity of his gaze forced her back in her seat.

"It wasn't Carby, do you understand me?" he said with intensity. "It was Breskin. Breskin. He's the one in those tapes."

"No," said Marcella. "He's not."

"He is!" screamed Chauncey, slamming his fist down on the table. "I watched those YouTube videos a hundred times. I know him. I've seen his sick, sadistic techniques. I saw them at SERE, I saw them in Bahrain, and I damn well saw them in Morocco. Carby is not a torturer."

Marcella looked around, concerned that Chauncey's outburst would attract too much attention. None of the men at the bar had even flinched. Even if they had heard him, they weren't the types of men to get involved in arguments that didn't concern them.

"They didn't say he was the torturer," Marcella said. "They said he was the architect."

"Then who are they saying did the tortures?"

Marcella looked away again. This time it wasn't to see if they were being overheard. It was to gather herself. She looked back at Chauncey.

"You. They said you were working with Carby. That you were bitter for being thrown in prison, and that you were trying to get revenge."

Chauncey didn't react. He didn't freeze up. He didn't even breathe as the words slipped from Marcella's mouth. He simply asked, "Marcy, are you sure you weren't followed?"

Before she could answer, a .50 caliber sniper bullet entered Marcella's right ear. Her head literally exploded, covering him with a spray of her blood, brains, and hair. More bullets pounded the Whip from outside. Several of the men at the bar fell off their stools to the ground, dead. To Chauncey it was a surreal, slow-motion moment. Instinctively, he dove to the floor.

While his body reacted, his mind raced. Of course they'd pinned it on him. He'd been such an idiot. Breskin had found him at the bottom of the well and offered him a second chance. A way back into the life he'd know. But he'd been a patsy. And because of his desperation, the only woman he'd ever loved had just been murdered. Rage, not fear, bubbled through his body. It oozed out of his pores like hot sweat.

The hail of bullets increased their tempo. Bottles of tequila, glasses, and furniture splintered and shattered from the assault. Chauncey looked across the floor toward the back of the restaurant for an escape path but bullets punched through the back door as well.

"Senor Chauncey!" screamed Carlos, peeking out from around the base of the bar. "This way. Rapido!"

Chauncey fast-crawled through the broken glass, liquor, and blood to where Carlos was lying. Carlos pointed behind the bar to an open trapdoor where the last of the surviving patrons were disappearing.

"Go!"

Before Chauncey could say thank you a bullet ripped through the bar and into Carlos' chest. Chauncey dove for the trap door and pulled it down behind him. He ran through a dark tunnel toward wherever it led. As he raced, he silently pledged to take matters into his own hand. If he lived, that is.

Chapter Thirty-Three

Breskin hacked at the tall grass with his three wood, hoping to chop away enough rough to expose his miss-hit, red, Calloway One. After the five-plus minutes he'd been hunting, the ferocity of his swipes now mirrored his frustration.

"This is ridiculous!" he spat. "Golf balls don't just disappear. It came down right here. We all saw it."

Nels Green, General Brewster, and Senator Stevens, the other members of the golf foursome, just smiled and chuckled. Green, about two yards from Breskin, was poking around the base of an oak tree trying to find the ball.

"That's what you said on the sixth hole," said Green.

"And on the fifth," tossed in General Brewster as he walked out of the rough, apparently abandoning the search. He walked to his cart on the edge of the fairway and relit his cigar.

Senator Stevens, far less concerned about Breskin's missing ball than pissing off possible constituents, looked back at the foursome that was anxiously waiting to tee off behind them.

"Come on, Doug," pleaded Stevens. "You've already looked for more than five minutes. Drop a ball and take a double penalty. Those are the rules."

Breskin ignored him and kept on swinging and kicking through the four-inch high grass.

"Not on your life," Breskin replied. "I'm just a low-paid federal employee. I should never have agreed to play for fifty dollars a hole. You one-percenters can just wait."

"Well, we never should have agreed to play on a public course. Even if it is Torrey Pines," Green chimed in.

Rated as one of the top ten municipal courses in the country, Torrey Pines had a pair of magnificent, eighteen-hole courses. Lined with treacherous bunkers, canyons, eucalyptus, oak trees, Torrey pines, and high grass, both the North and South courses were challenging. The South course, the one they were currently playing, was the more difficult of the two. Both courses were positioned along the cliffs of La Jolla, which provided some spectacular views of the Pacific Ocean, paragliders, and even, for some golfers, a perfect view of the famous "Blacks Beach," a private nude beach.

Admittedly not a good golfer, Breskin couldn't have cared less about the South course being redesigned by the fabled Rees Jones. Nor did he give a crap that it was where Tiger Woods had won the 2008 US Open. And even though they were only on the seventh hole, he was already sick of hearing about how the legendary golfer had tackled each shot. Not to mention he was going on his fifth lost ball.

"Woods played this one by hitting to the left side of the fairway," Stevens had advised. "His shot landed about five yards off the bend then just rolled into the middle. It was magical. So stay away from the right side where it doglegs," he'd cautioned Breskin before his tee shot. "If your ball goes into the rough, you may as well kiss it goodbye."

Apparently Breskin's ball hadn't listened to Stevens' advice, which is why he was getting grass stains on the bottom of his khaki pants right now.

"I picked a 'public' course because it has less surveillance," Breskin informed Green, a bit peevishly. "Your hoity-toity private courses have cameras at every hole. I assume it's because you guys cheat so much, but I still wanted to be cautious. So let's just forget the golf lessons and the Tiger Woods admiration society stuff and get to business."

Green sighed and nodded. "Okay, Doug. You're right. What did you want to talk about?"

As Senator Stevens and General Brewster walked back toward the rough for a more private conversation, one of the men at the waiting tee box screamed at them.

"Hey, assholes! Move it along! People are waiting!"

Not one to take orders from others, especially civilians, Sunday golfers playing at a public golf course, Brewster spun back and faced the men.

"Shut your goddamned pie-holes, you pukes! We'll move on when we're goddamned ready to move on!"

Senator Stevens paled. "Jesus Christ, Don, you can't say that." Then back to the waiting men, "We'll just be a moment! Thanks for your patience." He turned to Breskin, twirling his hand in a hurry-up motion, "Let's move this along, shall we?"

"I'll start," said Brewster. "I'm not so convinced about your plan, Doug. I still think having Carby arrested before I brought the system to the Joint Chiefs and Homeland was a bad idea. And now that the public feels safe because the boogieman is gone, the pressure's off. We'll need to build the momentum all over again."

Green chimed in, "And somehow, the FAA got a copy of the arrest feed. Now they've slapped us with an injunction for flying weaponized UAVs in the NAS. They've pulled our COAs and are threatening some hefty fines. Not to mention that I'm getting calls from the DHS science and technology director, pissed that he didn't know about Nightshade."

"How in God's name did the FAA get a hold of the video feed?" asked Brewster with some concern.

"I leaked the information to the FAA and the media," said Stevens.

Green turned to him, his anger apparent. "And why the hell would you do that?"

"First of all, mind your tone," Stevens replied to Green. "And second of all, I did it because Agent Arnold Palmer here told me to," he said, indicating Breskin.

Without warning, a ball came flying down the fairway accompanied by a barely audible cry of "Fore!" Evidently tired of waiting, the man who'd complained about the holdup had decided to tee off as an attempt to force some action.

General Brewster looked at the ball and snarled. "Not acceptable."

Before Stevens could stop him, Brewster stomped onto the fairway and dropped three balls on the close-cropped grass. He then hit each one, in succession, back at the tee box. The waiting men screamed and dove for cover as the speeding balls careened off trees, a bench, and the ball washer.

Brewster casually returned to his associates. "That'll buy us a few minutes. But I really do think we should get moving."

"All of you just need to calm down," said Breskin, still apparently looking for his ball. "Your problem is that you have no faith that the government and the media will act as they always do. You need to look at the world the way it works. We've done our job, now we just have to let things play out. Mark my words, within the next two weeks, the FAA ban will be lifted, Carby will be released, and the plan will move full steam ahead."

Green cut in, "What about your pal, Chauncey? He's still out there and has enough information to put us all in some pretty hot water. Why the hell can't you take him out?"

Breskin put up his hand, palm facing Green. "Not to worry. Not only did we get rid of Marcella Kraner, his whistleblowing outlet, but now he's on our most-wanted list as an accomplice to Carby. He hightailed it to Mexico like a scared Chihuahua. We've seen the last of him, trust me."

"Setting aside the fact that I never trust people who say 'trust me,' you'd better be sure as shit about that," said Green.

No longer listening to him, Breskin looked down. "Ha! Found it!"

He reached down and picked up his ball with a smile. He then tossed it right into the center of the fairway for a perfect lie.

"Shall we?" Breskin asked his compadres, then headed to his cart to switch clubs.

"You can't do that!" protested Stevens, following. "That's a penalty stroke. This is a gentlemen's game. There are rules you know."

Chapter Thirty-Four

Chauncey crouched in the corner of the dive motel where he'd holed up to catch his breath. Naked, he rocked back and forth, arms around his knees, staring at the crucifix on the wall above the bed. As soon as he and the others had emerged from the tunnel into Mexico, he'd stumbled to the closest and worst place he could find. As soon as he'd checked in, he'd ripped off his clothes and begun pacing through the room. Like a macabre farmer's tan, once he'd removed his shirt, his arms and neck were painted red with Marcella's dried remains, which had splashed all over him when she'd been shot.

He hadn't eaten, slept, or even washed in two days. The only stench he recognized, even worse than the substandard plumbing of the establishment, was the smell of his shame.

On a small television that sat on the dilapidated dresser, a FOX news broadcast played loud in English. He wasn't paying any attention to the spinning, no-spin talking head that was blathering anti-President Obama rhetoric. Chauncey didn't even recall turning the set on, although he'd done it to cover up the sounds of his destruction of the room. The lamps had been thrown against the walls, the desk chair lay splintered on the floor, and several broken drawers sat in the sink and on the countertop below the shattered bathroom mirror.

He also had no idea how long he'd been staring at the mass-produced replica of the Savior. They all looked the same, he thought, as he leaned his head left, then right, surveying the plastic idol.

It was a simple, thorny crown-wearing Jesus Christ nailed to a miniature crucifix, the same kind that hung in thousands of motels around the world. Small dabs of silk-screened gray paint represented the Roman nails that had been hammered into his outstretched hands and crossed feet. Tiny dots of red paint spilled around the edges to simulate blood. Chauncey fixated on the Savior's facial expression. He hardly believed that the artist had captured the true anguish of being hammered to a ten-foot cross, much less that of carrying around all of mankind's sins.

A fleeting part of Chauncey wished he was a member of the God club, if for no other reason so he could pray for Marcella's eternal soul. But she'd been a card-carrying atheist, and he figured his prayers wouldn't make one bit of difference to the salvation of her eternal soul anyway. If there was a hell, she was there. The small, plastic figurine gave him no sense of hope or faith or love. He wondered if the fact that he was as close to the bottom of his existence and that the figure's grimace hadn't changed him somehow proved that he was genetically tainted.

The tiny room was a sauna. It was sweltering in part because there was no air conditioning and in part because the windows were painted shut. Beneath the slick coating of perspiration that covered him from head to toe, his entire body shivered as if he were outside on a frigid, wintery day. It had started as he raced through the tunnel away from the taqueria. For some reason his mind had transported itself twenty years backward to the day he and three strangers had attempted the first-ever, four-way group skydive over Antarctica.

Because of their lack of preparedness, his jumpmates' canopies hadn't opened on time. Tragically, when they stepped from the plane they were closer to the ground than they'd thought. Since Chauncey was the only one with a Cypres automatic activation device, his comrades had deployed mere feet above the ground. Rather than pop the chute to slow their descents, the impact into the 1.5-million year-old ice had crushed every bone in their bodies.

On that day, Chauncey, the sole survivor, had trekked nearly two miles over the frigid continent to find help. When he was picked up by a rescue snowmobile, his tongue was swollen, and he was nearly catatonic because of hypothermia. With every step he'd wondered why he'd survived. He wondered the same thing now. Unfortunately for him, the wall-mounted Jesus had no answers.

As he stared at the crucifix, his state of shock protecting him from reality, his shivering body attempting to keep him alive, the words from the television broadcast drifted into his ears.

"Breaking news," hissed the familiar voice of Sean Hannity. "The FBI agent who is credited with the arrest of the worst domestic terrorist in US history has been suspended. Special Agent Douglas Breskin, an expert in anti-terrorism and interrogation has been placed on temporary suspension by the director of the FBI. The suspension is pending an investigation of unapproved, dangerous, and possibly illegal tactics used in the arrest of Thomas Carby, the engineer executioner."

Upon hearing the name Breskin, Chauncey switched his gaze from the Savior to the television. Sean Hannity, the conservative FOX news anchor, sat behind his signature glass broadcast desk. Playing on a monitor over his shoulder was a loop of the leaked Carby arrest with a superimposed graphic that read, "American Engineers Saved."

Hannity continued, "Just two days after the daring takedown of the alleged mastermind of the murders, torture, and terrorizing of American engineers and their families, the man who planned and executed that letter-perfect arrest has been stripped of his power."

The graphic changed from "American Engineers Saved," to "An American Hero Deposed."

"According to our exclusive sources high up at the Department of Justice, Special Agent Breskin used a highly classified integrated drone system that was never approved, potentially represented a risk to ordinary citizens and, according to some, was a violation of Carby's constitutional rights. To discuss the development, we have with us the esteemed senator and chairman of the Senate Drone Caucus, the Honorable Todd Stevens from San Diego.

We're also joined by General Brewster, military drone expert. Lastly, we've got constitutional and privacy rights advocate and attorney, Steven Posner.

The screen split vertically to reveal the three men in separate, stacked frames on the right. Hannity remained in the left side of the screen. Chauncey pulled the blanket from the bed and wrapped it around himself to stop the continuous chills that he was now feeling. The image of General Brewster made every sinew in his body tighten to the painful point. The last time he'd seen the man was when he'd been asked to consult in a bat-shit crazy automated interrogation project.

General Brewster, at the time Colonel Brewster, had been the head of robotic warfare in Afghanistan. He'd apparently concocted a project that basically created an interrobot. Unlike the shiny, black interrogation drones dreamed up by George Lucas in the Star Wars saga, this was an inelegant table that was wired to detect whether a detainee was telling the truth and mete out torture until he broke. It was also set to monitor a person's vital signs so that he or she remained alive and that no vital organ failures occurred. He'd apparently dreamed it up because torturing people the old-fashioned way was too traumatic for his own men.

Chauncey had taken one look at the project and called it immoral and illegal. It so trumped everything he'd seen that he could hardly believe it had gotten as far as it had. He'd immediately threatened to resign his commission as an officer if they continued the research. The last he'd heard they'd defunded the program. Not because it had killed every subject that the table had interrogated, but because the American public had lost its appetite for torture. Something that Chauncey felt he'd contributed to by revealing the truth about the enhanced interrogation tactics we were employing. It sickened him that a man like Brewster was still in the service, much less a general officer.

"Senator Stevens," Hannity said. "Let's begin with you. As chairman of the Senate Drone Caucus, you must have knowledge of most cutting edge robotic technology. Did you know about the system Breskin used?"

As Hannity asked, the leaked footage of the exterior drone battle sequence of Carby's arrest played.

"Of course we were aware of it," said the senator. "And it was developed by companies in San Diego. Companies I'm proud of. Because of FAA testing regulations, they developed the systems overseas rather than here, which could have meant lots of local jobs, I might add. It's an amazing bit of technology. I had no idea that Agent Breskin had proceeded without the proper authorization, of course, but rather than vilifying the man for demonstrating its effectiveness so successfully, we should be celebrating him as a hero."

Chauncey stood up and stared at the television. He couldn't believe what he was hearing.

"He's a criminal! A traitor to humanity! A goddamned murderous Mormon moron!" he screamed at the set. It was only because he wanted to hear more that Chauncey restrained himself from tearing the Jesus off the wall and stabbing it through the monitor.

Senator Stevens went on, "Southern California, specifically San Diego and San Bernardino, was sent into a state of panic by those ruthless attacks. Instead of calling foul, the FAA and the director of the FBI should be pinning a medal on Agent Breskin's chest."

Hannity feigned intelligence and probed, "But isn't it true that Agent Breskin not only used autonomous predators in the National Airspace for unauthorized surveillance, but he then used weaponized drones in a residential neighborhood to arrest an American citizen? Former Attorney General Holder said years ago that there would never be weaponized drones in the United States, did he not?"

"Yes, Sean, he did," Stevens answered. "But as you know, we live in dangerous times. The Islamic State is threatening to plant its flags in the Oval Office. So sometimes you have to do things that are out of the box to keep people safe. American citizens want to be protected."

Chauncey was on his feet. "They sure do! Protected from self-interested, powermongers like you!" he wailed.

General Brewster chimed in. "I couldn't agree with the senator more. We've used drones in Africa, the Middle East, Afghanistan, and Pakistan for years. They've proven to not only be incredibly powerful tools, but they are superb at keeping our men and women safe. Given the nature of the threat to this country from both outside and in, it would be irresponsible of us to not give these tools to law enforcement."

He continued, "These engineers that were being targeted by Carby are a vital national security interest. Since these cowardly attacks began, over 150,000 of the nearly one and a half million engineers in our country have refused to go to work until their protection and that of their families can be ensured. And I can't blame them. But we can't deploy the National Guard at each one of their homes. That would be an intrusion of their privacy. However, we damned sure can put a few drones in the skies above their cities to keep them safe. And I say we need those systems up there now. Right now. Everywhere. After all, without our engineers we'd fall behind the rest of the world more than we already have."

"The general and I are in complete agreement here, Sean," added Senator Stevens. "Just this morning we submitted the Stevens Bill. It calls for the immediate deployment of the system Breskin used over San Diego County. As a city, its infrastructure is vital to the security of this nation. Besides the military and aerospace presence, it has the fifth most engineers of any metropolitan area in the country."

"Military drones in America? Posse Comitatus! Posse Comitatus!" Chauncey railed at the set. The shock of his last encounter at the taqueria was quickly fading and he began to feel like his old self again. "Say something Hannity! You're supposed to be the uber-patriot!"

As if he'd heard Chauncey's protestations, Hannity replied "Drones in the sky? Sounds an awful lot like the NSA on steroids to me. I'm all for being safe, but that sounds very counter to our Constitution. What do you think, Mr. Posner? What are the legal implications of all this?"

"General Brewster is right," responded Posner. "But not about the technology part. Where we'd fall behind the rest of the world is in our freedom. Using drone surveillance and killing in a warzone is one thing, but turning these things loose to conduct unfettered spying and arrests in our own country is something entirely different."

Hannity turned on a dime with his follow-up. "So are you saying that they should have let Carby just kill more people because you don't like drones?"

Chauncey leapt onto the bed, his hands clenching into fists. "No mate! He said the good general is a paranoid puke." He began feverishly jumping up and down on the bed as the broadcast continued.

"I'm not sure where you got that, Sean," answered Posner. "Be that as it may, if the law enforcement community is going to start using military-grade equipment on American citizens in the continental United States, there needs to be a very serious debate on state and federal laws. Unfortunately, I'm dubious that it would be in time because as Posner's Law states: 'The law is always behind the technology it purports to protect.'"

"Well, as I've said many times," replied Hannity, donning a self-imposed pundit persona, "I for one am completely against a surveillance state. But more regulations? That's always the liberals' answer."

"Yeah, we do love our liberty. We're crazy that way," Posner quipped.

"Is that right? Unfettered regulation is your idea of liberty?" Hannity shot back.

"Unfettered, no. But enough to protect us from our government employing illegal, dangerous, and possibly biased over-policing to control us, yes."

"So you're saying that Carby should be set free?"

"Again, I have no idea where you're getting that because I didn't say it. Either way I don't think my opinion much matters. The entire arrest was shoddy and Carby will be released."

"Good!" blurted Chauncey throwing a pillow at the talking head. "It was obviously illegal surveillance. Improper procedure!"

Hannity mugged intensely, as if he'd just eaten a rotten piece of sushi. "How do you figure that? It would be a travesty to release this man."

"First off, from what I've seen on the tapes and read in the arrest reports, the surveillance methods used to get the warrant for Carby's arrest were illegal, and therefore the information cannot be used in court. And a FISA warrant doesn't even apply because not only was there no real tie to international terrorism, but the technology used isn't covered by FISA or, for that matter, Title 3."

Feeling clever, Hannity smiled and interjected, "See Posner's Law, right?"

"Very good," said Posner. "Secondly, the manner of Carby's arrest, a dogfight with robots in a residential neighborhood, followed by the violent arrest of Carby by unauthorized, unregulated, armed drones constitutes excessive force."

"I won't argue the law with you, Mr. Posner, but it seems to me that you would rather have risked the lives of our brave FBI agents and put the rights of this vicious domestic terrorist above all others."

Posner laughed and shook his head. "It's uncanny, Sean. You don't look anything like my wife, but just like her, you're excellent at saying I'm saying things I'm not saying."

Hannity, Stevens, and General Brewster all guffawed at the comment.

"For the record," continued Posner, "I'm glad that Carby, if he is indeed guilty, was arrested. I'm just dubious that the evidence gathered by the FBI, through illegal data collection methods, cellphone impersonation, license plate readers and stalking, armed drones, and excessive force will hold up in court. It would be a tragedy if he were released and more massacres happened, but because of the way he was arrested, I fear that is the case.

"I'm also afraid that if it does stand up in this Justices Scalia-Alito world we live in, it will open every square inch of this country to persistent, unwarranted surveillance from 20,000 feet above and below sea level. I have no desire to live in a panopticonic state where I have no idea who is watching me, where, when, and why."

Chauncey stopped jumping up and down and stared grimly at the television. Nothing that any of the men said beyond Posner's last statement registered in his brain as anything but white noise. It all became crystal clear. He knew what "Panopticon" was. He also knew his next move.

Chapter Thirty-Five

Most cutters were self-loathing types who sliced and hacked and mutilated themselves because of low self-esteem and self-hatred. They either learned about it from the movies, from other outcasts in school or by trolling suicide websites. The tragedy of it is that no matter how many times they cut, no matter how deep into their own flesh the blade went, no matter how much blood flowed from the self-induced gullies in their arms or legs, they could never cut out the source of the pain.

While that personality profile was certainly true for Armagan, he'd only started cutting after learning about the techniques used by medieval priests. They'd bleed their parishioners to release their demons: the demons that caused disease, psychosis, and sinful acts. His curiosity gave rise to his first attempt and, while his virgin bloodletting didn't release any demons that he could see, it gave Armagan a queer euphoria that instantly became an addiction.

Nobody in his private high school for gifted students had ever suspected he was a cutter. The signs were apparent though. He was a moody loner, and even though his school was situated in the extremely hot suburb of Irvine, he never wore short sleeves, not even in gym class. Rather, he would wear dark sweatshirts all the time to cover the blood which sometimes leaked out of the bandages.

Besides being the brilliant, infamous orphan of war and the adopted child of an influential imam, the faculty just assumed he was eccentric. Maybe if he'd hung out with the emos or goths they would have suspected something, but in all honesty it was much easier to just write him off as a quirky genius who had some emotional challenges based on his past.

He held his left arm up and forward with a slight bend at the elbow. His wrist, hand, and fingers drooped over a clear, glass teacup filled with steaming hot water. Mesmerized, he watched as the trickles of freshly freed blood ran from the cut in his wrist. It skittered across his downward facing palm, then across his ring and middle fingers. When the red rivulets reached his fingertips, they welled up into balls and dangled there. When they'd accumulated enough mass, the bloody orbs fell, like crimson tears into his cup.

The first few droplets struck the surface and exploded across the top of the hot water. As more and more drops fell, the color overcame the clear water. It became redder and redder. In short order it took on the color of the chai that he used to drink with his family after dinner.

One part of him felt indescribable relief. That only lasted for a few minutes before being replaced by guilt and shame. It's just the way the revolving door worked. What made this particular time worse was that he'd resisted cutting for nearly a year and considered this a relapse. The horrific acts he'd helped to orchestrate had apparently sated the need, although afterward, the urges to cut increased. He wondered why the sickness had overcome him this time. He'd been working alone in his robotics lab in the converted auditorium at March Air Force Base, preparing for the next event. The literal nature of the next plan came closer than any of the previous ones to a catharsis, so it mystified him why he'd felt the sudden and overpowering call to cut.

It reminded him of days when he'd be overcome with the urge during classes at MIT. Once school was over he would rush to the Crossroads Pharmacy on Massachusetts Avenue and buy a single Exacto knife, a bottle of hydrogen peroxide, a package of gauze, and a roll of first-aid tape. Like a cigarette smoker trying to quit would throw away the pack after having just one guilty smoke, Armagan always threw the contraband away after a session to make it harder to do again.

His body would tingle in anticipation as he placed the accoutrements in the blue plastic shopping basket at the store. He would tap his foot and crack his fingers while waiting in the checkout line. The closer he got to the register, the edgier he would become. After paying, he would exit the store and walk to his apartment at a slow gait. He never allowed himself to run because he wanted to stretch out the anticipation as long as possible. Once home he would spread out a red hand towel on the white porcelain sink, then methodically, ritualistically lay out the bandages. He sterilized the blade with peroxide then lay his arm, wrist up, on the towel.

He always wondered, as he began to trace the blade across his wrist, if there would ever a time when he'd have the nerve to sever an artery and bleed to death. He knew deep down that he would never do that because it would mean he wasn't a complete and utter failure. He'd successfully hidden his addiction from everyone he knew, except for one person.

Ignoring his bloody continuously bleeding wrist, Armagan picked up a spoon with his right hand and stirred the red water. He put down the spoon, then picked up the cup and toasted to empty air.

"Here's to the pain," he said to no one present, then gulped down the liquid without taking a breath.

"I thought you'd stopped that," said the unexpected voice of Breskin, who was standing in the doorway of Armagan's highly secure office.

"Apparently I have not."

The response wasn't nearly as taken aback as someone who'd just been caught self-mutilating. Rather than turning to face Breskin, Armagan simply opened the cap of hydrogen peroxide and began to pour it over his cut wrist. He poured over the garbage can so he wouldn't stain the office floor carpeting. He watched as the clear antiseptic mixed with the catalase of his blood and bubbled.

Breskin pocketed his key to Armagan's office and sat down in a chair beside the desk. He observed as Armagan expertly began to dress his wound. Disgusted, Breskin looked away. He took in the rows of high-tech computers, monitors, and 3-D printers and scanners that were placed in the office. The computers were where Armagan worked obsessively to create the algorithms used to connect the new Nightshade system. Breskin glanced out of the large, one-way glass window and saw the different sections of the converted gymnasium where they tested the drones and worked out their kinks. It had the most expensive and cutting-edge technology money could buy; a veritable Garden of Eden for AI and robotic creation.

"You know how unhealthy that is, don't you?" Breskin finally asked. "One day you could slip and cut an artery. Then what? Not to mention that defiling your body like this is an affront to the Heavenly Father."

Armagan finished wrapping a gauze bandage around his wrist and applied some white first-aid tape. He wordlessly offered his arm to Breskin, so he could tear off the tape from the roll. Breskin sighed and did as he'd done many times before. He then smoothed the tape down, making sure it held the gauze in place.

"Yes," replied Armagan. "We both have our poison don't we? Mine is cutting, yours is God. But you didn't come here to lecture me or to pretend that you care about my eternal soul, did you? You came to make sure everything was ready for the next slaughter."

Breskin took Armagan in with his eyes. He remembered the day he'd picked up the seven-year-old orphan in Kandahar to bring him to the United States. Even though he knew then that rather than saving a soul he was creating a golem, he'd felt a bit sorry for the boy. Over the years, as he'd given Armagan access to the greatest software, electrical, mechanical, and aeronautical, and robotic engineers in the world, all the while filling his head with hate and the desire for revenge, he'd felt something akin to pride. The pride of a creator. Even a monster's maker felt pride, didn't he?

The greatest sense of pride, almost that of a father for his son, had come on the day that Armagan graduated from MIT. As he sat in a metal, folding chair with parents, friends, and fellow students, the Charles River over his shoulder, Breskin had gotten teary when Armagan accepted his diploma.

Now, on the verge of completing their mission, his pride threatened to spill over.

Armagan despised Breskin. He'd always known what his purpose was. And while a small piece of himself was grateful for being given the opportunity to earn the highest degrees of robotics and engineering, even if it were to avenge his family's death, there was another part of him that wished he could severe the Pinocchio strings and live his own life. As the puppet he'd become, he didn't believe that his real mother or father would be proud of him.

Armagan abruptly stood up and tapped the window. He pointed to a vehicle parked by the facility's double-doors. Breskin rose and looked to where he was pointing. It looked like an over-sized, ride-on lawnmower. The kind that gardeners use on large lawns.

"The MAARS is there. Beneath the chassis. No one will suspect it's not a lawnmower until it's too late," said Armagan.

He was referring to the armed, Foster-Miller, unmanned ground vehicle. The MAARS, or Modular Advanced Armed Robotic System, was the next phase of the SWORDS bot that had destroyed his village. And while the firepower of the earlier version had evidently been enough to change his life forever, this one was even more lethal. The ground bot sported a remote-controlled M202A1 66mm FLAME rocket launcher, an M240 machine gun, and a six-barreled 40mm grenade launcher. It would do far more damage than the three bots that had changed his life fifteen years ago.

"You truly are a gift," Breskin said, invoking the meaning of his name. He wasn't being cruel, he was simply impressed and marveling at what Armagan had created. "It looks just like a lawnmower."

Armagan opened a drawer and pulled out a pair of remote controls that looked like they were for a Sony PlayStation. He handed them to Breskin.

"Give the black one to the gardener. Keep the white one for yourself just in case he gets shot or changes his mind. It's an override."

Before Breskin could say anything, Armagan continued:

"I wonder if maybe this one should be the last. With this machine and its target, I'll finally get some closure. And since Senator Stevens has already presented your bill, you've gotten what you want."

Breskin leaned his back against the glass window and folded his arms across his chest. "No matter how long you live in this country, you'll never understand Americans, will you? Carby's arrest has made them all feel safe again. It's made them lower their guard. That's the only reason this party wasn't cancelled."

He straightened up and walked around the office, taking in all of the equipment that Armagan used to make his magic. "But in order for all this to work," he continued, stretching out his arms to indicate everything in the office and beyond, "they need to feel they're still in danger. Thinking you've caught the boogieman, then realizing you haven't will push things closer to where we need them to be. Trust me."

Absent-mindedly fingering his bandage, Armagan said, "I do understand that. I guess I'm just tired of the horror. But," he said and then stopped.

"But what?" asked Breskin, growing a bit perturbed by Armagan's defiance?

"Why did you have to pin the rap on Mr. Chauncey? He seemed such a decent sort. He did everything you asked, and then you just destroyed his life."

"Chauncey? A decent sort? You meet the man three times, and all of a sudden you feel beholden enough to him that you text him a 'get away' message?"

Armagan drew a quick breath. He knew that they'd probably figure out he'd texted Chauncey to save his life, he just didn't realize they already had.

Breskin continued, "Let me tell you about your pal, Captain 'Chauncey' Paunce. He's not only a whistleblower, he's a coward and a traitor. He walked away from interrogating criminals in Iraq and Afghanistan, men who were murdering our servicemen and women. He refused to do his duty, and then he turned on those who were. Oh, no, Chauncey is getting precisely what he deserves. And besides," he added as he popped a candy into his mouth. "You asked him to go visit your adoptive parents? To warn them to keep their heads down? Well, he went to visit them all right. But he's the only one who walked out of that house alive."

Armagan stopped breathing. He hadn't heard from his adoptive parents in some time, but he figured it had been because he was busy.

"What are you talking about?" he asked, barely breathing.

"Chauncey went to visit them, per your request, but he really went to get information about you because he suspected you had something to do with this whole mess. When we found their bodies in the rubble, they'd both been tortured to death. Where do you think I learned it? Chauncey's the real expert at information extraction. So don't you start doubting me. I am the only family you have left."

Armagan fell to his knees. Real boy tears flowed down his cheeks. He knew in his heart that Chauncey wasn't the kind of man who would have done such an act. He knew that Breskin had somehow caused their murder. He also knew that short of cutting his wrists through and through, there wasn't a damned thing he could do about it.

Chapter Thirty-Six

Chauncey was in a major hurry to get back stateside. He instinctively knew that Breskin, Armagan, and whoever else was involved in Panopticon were going to escalate things fast. Breskin's suspension was probably planned to free him up to move around unfettered. The problem was that Chauncey's name was now on top of the FBI's Most Wanted list. He couldn't just saunter up to the customs and border patrol checkpoint and say, "Excuse me, mate, I've lost my passport, and I really need to get back to the states to bust up a conspiracy being pulled off by a rogue federal agent and an Afghan whiz kid."

He couldn't communicate with Killa, Diddy, or Phil either because they were, no doubt, being watched, and he had no desire to drag them into this anymore than he already had. Chauncey cracked an inward smile as he thought about what Killa would say to that. "Are you out of your damned mind? I haven't killed or maimed anyone since I got out of the service. That would be better therapy than any of that VA crap I get."

It was a sad truth that Spec Ops guys like Killa had not only been trained to be superior killers, but they now considered it a desirable career choice.

Even though Breskin had been suspended, Chauncey didn't fool himself for a second into believing that his face had been removed from the NSA, DHS, and FBI guardian databases. His own pasty-white, Irish mug could now be accessed and cross-referenced by every cop in the country. He didn't even trust that he could call the media. Other than Marcella, they were all a bunch of wanna-be personalities who parroted whatever their mogul puppetmasters told them. There was no way any of them would risk their careers for the truth if that truth put them in jeopardy.

His first task was to cross the border. And he had to do it immediately, without getting picked up by the CBP. It was always a big risk to cross into the states illegally, especially during the day, but the sad truth was that it wasn't all that difficult. Even though the borders were now being heavily watched to stop the flood of children from Central America who wanted to cross before the immigration laws changed, for a guy like Chauncey it was just a matter of finding the right spot. There were over 6,000 miles of border between the US and Mexico and not nearly enough agents, technology, or money allocated to watch every bit of it.

As much of a rush as Chauncey was in, he had to once again fight his desire to go fast. Not an easy task given that besides wanting to stop Breskin and Armagan because they were hurting America, he wanted to right some seriously personal wrongs. Marcella's bloody head hung like a gruesome painting in his mind. This was without a doubt the biggest shit storm he'd ever been in. He found it ironic that it was happening in his own country rather than in all of the danger zones he'd gone to while in the service.

It was now a matter of finding the right place to cross. It had to be a place without the high-resolution, tower-mounted FLIR cameras or buried ground sensors that would notify the CBP and prompt a rapid deployment of choppers, ATVs, and armed feds. He'd developed multiple cover stories to use in the event that he got stopped, but in truth, none of them would be useful if he were caught by federal agents.

If he'd had more time, he probably would have found a coyote and made him an offer he couldn't refuse, but Chauncey despised the human smugglers. He wasn't a big fan of illegal immigration and had no problem with strong tactics being used to stop them, but coyotes were scum. They exploited hope. They manipulated the poorest, most desperate human dross there was. Whether these people were illegals or not, they were just trying to make better lives for themselves. They certainly didn't deserve the rape, murder, and abandonment that often followed the high price they paid for help. And if Americans really wanted to stop illegal immigration, then they'd have to take crappy jobs and pay higher prices for their strawberries.

All these thoughts bounced through his mind, mimicking the hard hits of the Honda dirt bike he'd stolen from outside a bodega on the edge of Tijuana. He'd made his way east along Mexico 2, racing to get past the miles of border fence and find an opening, He figured he would find a spot to cross somewhere between Brown Station and Campo. Once the fence ended, he'd turned north off the road to ride along the border. He passed mile after mile of concrete, Normandy Beach-style barricades that had been placed as a barrier between countries after the steel fence ended. Well, those barricades may have been suitable to slow down human or drug smuggling cars, but it would do nada to stop him.

The dirt and exhaust from the long ride had coated Chauncey's arms and face with thick brown and black residue. His nostrils were so clogged that he could barely breathe. His forearms, neck, and back were cramping from holding onto the dirt bike through the unstable terrain. Yet in spite of those obstacles, he peered north through his sunglasses, looking for a place to jump the barricade.

Finally, his unwavering intensity paid off. About a quarter of a mile ahead, he saw the hulk of a rusted-out, bullet-ridden car sitting on the Mexico side of the barricade. The tires flat, the body of the abandoned car sat partially buried in the sandy ground. If he could get enough speed, and lift off at just the right time, he could use the car as a ramp and jump over the low border.

He continued riding north, past the car for another two miles, searching for any signs of border patrol vehicles or towers. Seeing nothing, he turned around and headed back toward the car. He passed it once again, riding two miles in the opposite direction to make sure he hadn't missed any signs of observation. Situational awareness was key to his success. He looked for dirt in the air, the telltale sign of moving vehicles. He even scanned for glints of light that might indicate the sun reflecting off of binocular lenses.

Confident enough that it was as safe as it was going to be, Chauncey spun the dirt bike 180 degrees and throttled up. As he charged toward the car ramp, the hot, desert wind whipped around his sunglasses, attacking his eyes. Loose rocks and sand launched upward, assaulting his clenched fists and face. When he reached the car's bumper, he pulled up the handlebars just enough to ride over the trunk, then launched skyward off the rear window. Feeling like Steve McQueen escaping from the Nazis in *The Great Escape*, he rose into the air, easily leaping across the barrier at a diagonal angle.

As he looked down to see where the tires would land, out of nowhere a shot rang out. The front tire's rubber disintegrated as it was hit with a bullet. Too late to do anything but try to avoid going headfirst over the handlebars, Chauncey shifted his weight to do a one-wheeled landing. He pulled back to force the brunt of the impact on the rear wheel when another shot rang out and pulverized that tire as well.

The ground was pure sand, and upon impact the rear rim was sucked into the earth. The bike instantly began toppling to the left. Pushing off the footstands, Chauncey propelled himself off the seat and hit the ground face first. If it hadn't been for a great deal of luck he would have been sent right, his unprotected head smashing into the concrete barricade.

As he laid there, his lungs burning from breathing in sand and heat, he wondered who was shooting at him, and so expertly. His answer arrived in the form of three camouflage-painted ATVs roaring up beside him.

"Yeehaw, boys!" screamed one of the drivers. "Score another one for the Campo Patriots!"

Chauncey remained still. He gathered his wits and flexed his muscles for any pain points that would indicate a broken bone, or worse, a gunshot wound. There was neither. Thank God for small favors, he thought. He didn't dare move until he knew who these guys were. And as bad as it was, he was grateful it wasn't the border patrol. These men, as undisciplined as he assumed they were, could probably be reasoned with.

One member of the posse, a muscular, black-bearded man nicknamed Hoss after the character in Bonanza, stayed farther back, a sniper rifle slung around his shoulder. "Must be ex-military," Chauncey decided instantly.

Another of the guys, a tall, skinny twenty-five-year-old who was aptly dubbed, "Ichabod Chicken Bones," jumped off his ATV and kicked Chauncey in the ribs. In spite of himself, Chauncey groaned and rolled over.

"Shit," called Ichabod, jumping back and drawing his .40 caliber. "This beaner's still breathing."

It took all of a second for Chauncey to realize that all the dirt and soot caked on his face and arms obscured the true, blue-blooded American that he was.

"I'm American," Chauncey coughed.

As soon as he'd raised his hand to wipe his face, he knew it was a mistake. Taking it to be a potentially threatening move, the three men cocked their weapons and aimed them at Chauncey. He froze.

"American, huh?" said Hoss, clearly the alpha of the pack. "We'll see about that. Don't you fucking move."

He removed the pale blue bandana from around his neck and poured a bit of water on it. He then tossed it to Ichabod Chicken Bones. Ichabod approached Chauncey, the bandana in one hand, the pistol in the other. He roughly wiped a small spot on Chauncey's forehead. The black and brown stubbornly gave way to the red, white, and blue whiteness hidden underneath.

"Sonnofabitch," the third man said. "He ain't lyin'."

This guy, Chauncey noted, was fat and had a scraggly unshaven face. He wore a deer hunting cap and a thick pair of prescription glasses held on by a green, neoprene, sport strap. Fat Ron, as his buddies called him, holstered his weapon, then took out his iPad and began taking pictures of the scene.

"Well, how about this?" said Ichabod, turning to Chauncey. "If you're American, how come you were sneaking across the border? You a drug dealer? Because even if you are a citizen, we don't like dealers, Mexican or not."

Chauncey blinked at the hot sun and shielded his eyes. He'd lost his sunglasses in the crash and the glare hurt. "Water," he croaked, coughing out some sand.

"First the story. If we believe you, then you can have water," said Hoss.

"My name's Rob Shriner. I'm a motorcycle dealer from Van Nuys." Chauncey began. It was a masterful performance deserving of an Oscar, a skill he'd developed while assuming the roles of foreign interrogators at SERE.

Chauncey continued his charade, getting more worked up as he went, "It's my birthday, and since my wife won't give me b'day BJs anymore, a couple of buddies and me cruised to Tijuana to get laid. Biggest fucking mistake of my life. The whore's wetback pimps rolled us and stole all of our money. They fucking shot my friends! They would've killed me, too, but I told them I could get them a lot of money if they let me live."

"Fucking beaners!" said Ichabod Chicken Bones, completely buying the story.

"So how'd you get away?" asked Fat Ron. He didn't even look up as he asked the question. Rather, he was intently focused on his iPad.

"They were so happy I was going to pay a ransom that they broke out some tequila and got shit-faced. Lucky for me, they couldn't hold their liquor. I got away after they passed out." Chauncey explained. "I stole this bike and tore ass out of town. I guess they didn't think I was worth following."

"Damn," said Ichabod, his exaggerated Adam's apple bobbing in and out. "I hope the poon was worth it. Though I gotta say I do love me some mamasita muff."

"Never again," said Chauncey, regaining his bearings enough to check out the distance between the men and trying to decide if he could get out of the jam should it be necessary. He figured he could at least rip out Ichabod's throat and grab his weapon. But they seemed to be buying his story, and he hoped that wouldn't be necessary.

"Never even got my dick wet," Chauncey said. "Bastards stole my wallet and my passport so I couldn't get through customs. I couldn't call my wife to come get me because, well, *because.*"

Hoss finally relaxed a bit and shook his head. "You're a damned idiot. And you're damned lucky to be alive." He patted his rifle. "I was a sniper in Iraq. I could've shot you in the head if I'd wanted to."

He tossed a liter bottle of Arrowhead water to Chauncey. As Chauncey gulped down several mouthfuls to cool his burning throat, Hoss asked, "So what are you gonna do now, playboy? You ain't got no wheels anymore, and it's miles to the nearest town."

"I don't suppose one of you guys could drive me to San Diego, could you?" Chauncey asked.

Ichabod answered. "Hell nope. We can't desert our post. We've got a sacred duty to perform here. Saving our country from the illegals. It's a goddamned war, you know? But Route 8's just on the other side of those sand dunes. You can try to hitch a ride."

"How about a cellphone, then?" asked Chauncey, pushing his luck. "I could call my brother to come down from the Valley."

"Well, okay." said Ichabod. "But make it fast, okay?"

Before he could give Chauncey the phone, Fat Ron interjected. "Hold up a second."

He held out his iPad and revealed a photo of Chauncey with the words "Fugitive. Extremely dangerous," written across the bottom.

"This guy's a liar. His real name's Captain Charles Paunce and he's a goddamned terrorist. And," he added with a smile to his friends, "they're offering a $100,000 reward for his traitorous ass."

"That a fact?" asked Hoss, pointing his rifle at Chauncey's head. "Dead or alive?"

As Chauncey wondered who the real dross at the border was, Ichabod Chicken Bones smashed him on the side of head with his pistol stock. Chauncey crumpled into the sand.

Chapter Thirty-Seven

Armagan had arrived at all of the other events early because it not only gave him enough time to find and lure away his marks, but it also gave him the pleasure of seeing the faces of the people who were about to be slaughtered. The unexpected and even less desired consequence of that strategy was that those faces now visited his dreams on a nightly basis. So today, in order to limit the time he socialized with victims, he'd decided to time his arrival to coincide with the gardener's.

With that in mind, he'd parked his gold Lincoln Town Car on Hillcrest Lane, about a half-block away from the house and waited. What he hadn't considered was that the other guests would be parking on the same street and walking right past him. "The best laid plans," he sighed to himself.

To his chagrin, Armagan saw people that he not only knew, but people with whom he'd shared ideas, meals, and even laughter. He saw Matt Anderle, one of the senior software engineers from Raytheon whom he'd met at several business lunches, and his wife pull up and walk to the house holding hands. Beth Miller, one of his classmates from MIT who now worked for Lockheed Martin, passed him and even waved when she noticed him sitting in his car. Andy Urban, an astrophysicist from Alameda Labs with whom he'd conferred on numerous occasions, shuffled toward the house with his characteristic slumped shoulders and depressed demeanor. Armagan couldn't help but notice that Urban's outward appearance revealed none of the warmth he exuded in person. In the hour that he sat in his car, Armagan saw nearly forty people pass. His nightmares would be crowded tonight.

The other thing Armagan hadn't anticipated was how many people would show up. After the first two massacres, parties with engineers and their families had pretty much stopped happening countrywide. People were understandably scared. He noted that Breskin had been right in predicting that Carby's arrest would make the community breathe a collective sigh of relief. Not to mention that in order to reinstill a sense of confidence, the directors of Homeland and the FBI, along with the president, had urged the public to return to their normal lives. It harkened to the days following America's financial collapse when President Bush directed Americans to go back to the shopping malls. This was one of the first parties since Carby's arrest, and the relieved geeks were out in force.

Armagan shrugged. He figured it was win-win. At least they'd be having fun before they died. Isn't that the best way to go? Isn't that how his family had died, in the middle of his sister's wedding? In the middle of their greatest joy?

As he watched the beige gardener's truck that held the disguised MAARS unit pull into the neighbor's driveway, Armagan drew a breath. The inevitable had arrived. A part of him wanted to drive away and suffer Breskin's wrath, but the anguished, ghostly screams of his father, his sister Lila, his best friend, Mahdi, and the disembodied head of his mother shouted that thought down. He grabbed the wrapped graduation gift from the passenger seat and made his way to the house.

Located in a quiet upscale neighborhood in Agoura Hills, California, the Scott house was just one of many nondescript McMansions. Situated on a perfectly manicured half-acre lot, the ten-thousand-square-foot tract home was as rich and opulent as it was bland and unoriginal. The interior was a mix of ticky-tacky marble floors, oak-paneled walls, and Restoration Hardware furniture.

He'd placed his gift alongside the others on a solid mahogany table in the foyer and followed the sounds of music and conversation to the backyard where the lawn party was happening. As soon as his feet stepped onto the gray flagstone patio a pretty, young member of the catering staff approached him, carrying a tray of prefilled champagne glasses. He politely declined a drink, and as she walked away, wondered if she would be among the dead or if she would escape it by being inside refilling glasses.

Armagan turned his attention to locating his mark. After finding him, he would have to lure him to his car where he would knock him out, shove him into the trunk, then drive to the nearby private airport where his plane was waiting. Getting a jump plane had been a stroke of genius. Again, a tribute to Breskin's well-developed military, decision–making skills. Because of Armagan's prosthetic leg, the oversized passenger door made it easier for him to load the body inside, then crawl over it to the cockpit.

Arriving late had ultimately turned out to be good thing. The guests had already filled their plates with food from the buffet and were sitting at tables placed on the sprawling lawn behind the house. Like most Southern California days in the spring, it was perfect. Besides just being comfortable, the lack of humidity or breeze meant that the targeting systems in their semi-automated weapons would work to perfection. An odd thing to appreciate, but many things had become odd in his life, so it rolled away with just a small notice.

He was grateful, but not surprised to see that the guest of honor, his mark, was not among the guests seated on the lawn. He was standing by himself, eating directly from the buffet. Armagan stared at their next victim and wondered how he'd hold up under Breskin's sadistic torture. Not well, he imagined.

As repulsed as he was by the young man's appearance, it wasn't all that alien to him. Many of the engineers he'd met over the years were just as fat, slovenly, and socially awkward as Tobor. His real name was Randy Scott, but because he loved the 1960s manga cartoon character, 8 Man, he'd chosen to be called Tobor. Tobor, or robot spelled backward, was a Saturday morning, cyborg crime-fighter from his dad's youth. The character would eventually become the inspiration for the movie, "Robocop," and for Tobor's career path.

Everything about Tobor screamed Comicon geek. If you judged him by his matted hair, bad teeth, and Hulk T-shirt, you would have thought he was just a harmless, goof-ball nerd. But that judgment would have been dangerously wrong. Tobor was a gifted computer hardware designer who'd just received his master's in engineering from Cornell Tech.

His parents, both highly successful engineers in their own right, were throwing a graduation party for him. Tobor hadn't asked for it, nor did he seem to be enjoying himself. Not that you could really tell because Tobor was as Asperger's as you got. At conception, he'd received a shotgun blast that contained DNA buckshot filled with all the mental illnesses that frequently accompanied genius. He was a high-functioning autistic, had obsessive-compulsive disorder, and even a bit of Tourette syndrome had been thrown his way for good measure. His tics weren't the vocal type, however. They were physical and caused him to crack his knuckles, stretch upward on his toes, and suck his snot continuously. Being around Tobor for any stretch of time was difficult at best.

It was hard to tell what Tobor really thought about the world at large because he had a tough time having a conversation about anything other than his work. If you asked him what he thought of the Dodgers or if he liked hiking on the beach, he would just look at you funny and say, "That's interesting." Then he would add, "Well, anyway," and launch into a lecture on some aspect of his work that had absolutely nothing to do with whatever you'd asked him.

The only real world issue he was able, or interested in articulating, was how much he thought the Arab countries, Russia and even China for that matter, needed to be wiped off the face of the planet.

"Nuke 'em," he'd say, then laugh an odd, high-pitched giggle. For most bigots, statements like that would just be seen as benign ignorance, but the frightening thing about Tobor was that he had the intellectual capacity and soon the mandate to harm the people he deemed vermin.

His work at Cornell Tech had been instrumental in the development of the IBM TrueNorth brainchip, a NexGen computing chip that was based on the way a mammalian brain functioned.

That work had landed him his first postgrad job at General Aeronautics, the subsidiary of General Atomics that was working on autonomous weapons systems. He would be applying his knowledge to adapting the brainchip's sophisticated sensing and processing capabilities into Reaper drones. The ultimate goal was to turn them into highly effective, lethal autonomous weapons systems despite knowing little about the world or the people in it, like most of his classmates, except from what they saw in the movies.

Armagan had met Tobor at a corporate meet-and-greet for new employees at General Atomics during the summer. He was confident that he'd be remembered because Tobor had made a joke about him. Tobor had said that because of Armagan's dead parents, his prosthetic leg, and his uncanny genius, he had the makings of a Marvel Comics supervillain. He'd even changed Armagan's real name to create his villain name, Armageddon.

Tobor looked up from the carving station where he was using his fat fingers to shove thick slices of roast beef into his mouth. He saw Armagan and with a look of glee, exclaimed, "Oh, no! Armageddon is here! It's the end of the world!" Then he giggled his distinctive sound and lifted himself onto his toes.

The inadvertent prescience not missed, Armagan smiled and walked over to Tobor. He didn't reach out to shake hands because he recalled that on Tobor's laundry list of DSM-5 conditions was germaphobia. He wouldn't shake hands with anyone.

"Greetings, Tobor," said Armagan. Then, going for the area he thought would set up an easy exit, nodded toward the gathered guests. "This is very nice. Your parents must be so proud of you."

"Whatever. They wanted to have a party. I'm just the excuse," Tobor snorted. Without looking around or even acknowledging what he'd said, he continued, "Anyway, I start work on Monday."

Armagan knew: his plan would work. It would take a minimal effort to get Tobor away from the party. In spite of himself, he looked across the seated guests, avoiding eye contact, but still desiring to see who was going to be killed. Through the tables, he noticed that the gardener was now standing on the neighbor's lawn surveying the Scott property. As he scanned, he absent-mindedly opened and closed a pair of garden sheers.

That wasn't a part of the plan. The gardener wasn't supposed to draw attention to himself. It was because of Armagan; he was supposed to be gone already. The gardener was a vet with traumatic brain injury and had limited cognitive abilities. The guy was probably anxious and getting impatient because he had to wait. Breskin was most likely anxious as well, wondering why he hadn't gotten the go signal. It was time.

"Tobor, I have a really awesome gift for you, but I left it in my car."

Armagan wasn't lying. Even though he'd brought a present into the house, he'd only done so to avoid suspicion. There was another surprise waiting for Tobor in the trunk of his car.

Armagan continued, "Can you tear yourself away from this party to get it? It's too heavy for me to carry with my leg."

"Too heavy, huh?" asked Tobor. "Must be a good present. What is it?!" he asked, without realizing he was being as rude as a ten-year-old.

"Let's just say it starts with the words, "First edition —"

Tobor didn't let Armagan finish because he already knew the rest of the sentence would be "comic books."

"Right on! Let's go," he said, wiping his greasy hands on his shirt.

Armagan was amused at how simple it was going to be. Tobor was such a child. But he reminded himself that children could be dangerous. All you had to do was look at the child guerillas in Senegal or Malaysia to know that innocence was easily corrupted.

As they turned to leave, from behind them they heard, "Well, hello there, Armagan. I didn't even see you come in."

Armagan and Tobor turned back to see Tobor's father, Alan Scott, approaching. He was just as short and dumpy as his son, but Scott had none of the mental illnesses. He was steady as a rock and typically engaging. Now retired and living off the ample residual income he received from patented algorithms he'd developed for the Warlock Red and Green, anti-IED systems, Alan Scott was an icon. One of the "good" engineers, as defined by Armagan, Scott had worked with EDO to develop the Counter Radio Electronic Warfare, CREW systems, that helped to detect and prevent IED deaths in Iraq and Afghanistan.

Touted as one of the most successful defensive technologies in the war, these CREW systems were responsible for saving hundreds, if not thousands of American troops. The government had paid billions. Much of it was apparently used to pay for this house, Armagan thought.

Armagan had hoped to avoid seeing the elder Scott because he was truly sorry that he'd been targeted. In his mind, while Tobor was a monster who had no problem creating conscienceless killer-bots and deserved his fate, his father did not. He'd even argued with Breskin. Killing men like Scott would reduce the crop of ethical engineers. Men like him hadn't killed Armagan's family. If anything, they'd strenuously argued against creating the technology that had. And given that the yard was filled with like-minded engineers and scientists, killing them was not what he'd agreed to. But Breskin said that it was the only way to get the gardener onboard. He had a vendetta against Scott and EDO and wouldn't fulfill his part unless that was part of the equation.

Scott had intentionally used his gifts to create defensive technologies. "I make shields, not swords," he was often quoted as saying. A member of the Association of Old Crows Society, he was known for giving speeches on the importance of applying a code of ethics to the Warcos. He had even established several curricula for engineering schools to help students connect the dots of their projects and hopefully steer clear of working on weapons whose sole intention was killing. This had placed him and his son on a clear collision path after Tobor had decided to work on lethal autonomous robots. But Tobor always said his father was weak and didn't have a firm grasp on reality. The irony was lost on no one.

"You can't take a human out of the loop," Scott would argue with Tobor. He was referring to keeping a human being involved in the ultimate decision of whether to kill someone. It was the key distinction between a LAR and a drone.

"Dad," said Tobor. "Armagan's got some first editions for me. I have to go help him. We'll be right back, okay? Please?"

"That's great, son," said Scott, like a father speaking to someone much younger than Tobor. "But it will still be there in a little while. I want to introduce Armagan to some of my friends. They're all anxious to meet him."

While Tobor sighed and pouted, Armagan tried to think of ways to get out. He then felt his phone vibrating in his pocket. Breskin was no doubt calling to see what was holding things up. He didn't need to think hard though, because at that very moment, the gardener had started his lawnmower and driven it to the edge of the property. The noisy engine made a racket that cut into the conversation. Armagan was alarmed. He hadn't given the signal that he was ready. If he didn't get out of there now, instead of being a part of the plan, he would be a part of the carnage.

"Now what's that all about?" asked Scott, turning to look at his neighbor's yard. "The Arnolds are out of town and they just had their lawn cut yesterday. Your mother considered that in her plans."

He turned to Armagan. "I have to see about this. Please make sure to come right back, okay?"

"Of course," said Armagan. Tobor squealed with joy, then grabbed his arm and practically dragged Armagan away.

Chapter Thirty-Eight

Judging by the sun's location, still directly overhead, Chauncey surmised he'd only been unconscious for about fifteen minutes. While that was certainly better than an hour, it was still time wasted. Time he didn't have. Upon coming to, he discovered himself sitting on the sand facing north. His hands were zip-tied behind his back through the barricade. Without any head cover, his face and neck were burning in the direct heat.

Chauncey noted that Hoss and Fat Ron had retreated slightly into the shade of some nearby scrub brush, but from there Hoss watched him like a hawk. Ichabod Chicken Bones was sitting, cross-legged about ten feet in front of him. As Ichabod listlessly stabbed the sand with a Buck knife, Chauncey correctly guessed he'd secured his pistol in the small of his back. He figured that Ichabod had been placed so close to keep a close guard. Or possibly because the guys just didn't like him that much.

Keeping his body completely still, Chauncey isolated his wrists and easily slipped the zip-ties. He considered making a dash back into Mexico, but given Hoss's skill with the rifle, he decided against risking a bullet in the back of his head. Figuring that the CBP would probably be there any minute, getting loose was his priority.

He set out to determine which man was the weak link. Maybe if he could figure that out, he could manipulate his way to freedom. It was a long shot, but since he needed information it was worth the try.

"Excuse me, mate," he called to Hoss. The men were surprised that he was awake. "May I please have a little water? This sun is killing me."

He squinted and lowered his head away from sun for effect.

Hoss was unimpressed. "You'll live," he said.

The response was exactly what Chauncey had expected. As a sniper, Hoss had to be a cool, patient, and disciplined man. Not a hint of emotion was apparent in his words. Just factual and final. Definitely not the guy to work on. Chauncey glanced over at Fat Ron, who still had his face glued the tablet.

"How are you getting a Wi-Fi signal all the way out here," Chauncey asked.

Only happy to speak geek with someone, Fat Ron looked up. He held up his iPhone.

"I got a hot spot on my phone. It's really cool. I can make this a Wi-Fi transmitter so the iPad or even my laptop can connect to it from anywhere. Even in the middle of nowhere. Of course you need to know the password. And nobody could ever figure mine out."

Ichabod snickered. "It's probably donut, you dork. You're such a friggin' Screech!" he said, referencing the infamous nerd from the television series, *Saved by the Bell*.

"Shut up you moron," Fat Ron spat at him.

Chauncey ignored Ichabod and continued, "Find out anything else about me? They say what I supposedly did?"

"Supposedly?" snapped Fat Ron. "Ha! There's more crap about you on the Internet than I could read in a year." He looked down at his device and started reciting the more exciting points. "You even have your own Wiki page. You ran the SERE program in Spokane, you're a convicted whistleblower who ratted out our own guys for supposedly torturing prisoners, and they say you were working with that guy Carby to kill all those engineers. Not to mention you just murdered your own girlfriend and shot up a restaurant in San Diego." Then, to his friends, "No wonder there's a bounty on his head."

"Your iPad says all that?" asked Ichabod, incredulous. "I'm gonna use some of my reward money to get one of those."

"You have to know how to read first, moron," said Fat Ron.

"Fuck you, you fat fuck," Ichabod shot back.

"Ooh, good comeback," laughed Fat Ron.

Chauncey noted the friction between the two men and tucked it into his pocket for potential future use. For the time being he stayed with Fat Ron.

"Is that all that you could dig up?" asked Chauncey. "There's got to be a lot more. Keep digging and you'll see that I'm worth more than a measly hundred g's."

He noticed that Ichabod had started paying more attention. He was now drawing dollar signs in the sand with his knife.

"I already tried," said Fat Ron. "A lot of stuff about you is either redacted or the Web pages have been removed."

"What's that mean?" asked Ichabod.

"It means that you should just shut up."

"Yeah, well maybe it means that you suck with that thing."

Ichabod pointed his knife at Chauncey. Like an artist surveying a canvas with a brush, he pantomimed cutting out his eye. "Maybe we should just torture this guy to find out what he's talking about. I sure could use more money."

Hoss, who until now had just been quietly watching, chimed in. "Can it, you two. He's playing you idiots. Now stop talking to him until Sarge gets here." He checked his wristwatch. "Should be here any minute."

"I don't know why we didn't just call the feds," complained Ichabod. "Now we have to split the reward with one more person."

"Goddamnit, shut the hell up!" said Hoss, realizing that they'd just given Chauncey information he didn't have before.

Chauncey breathed an unnoticed sigh of relief. They hadn't called the border patrol, which meant he still had a chance. But as he didn't know who this Sarge guy was, he figured he needed to step up the pace. He focused on Ichabod who had just begun playing a simple-minded game with an unwitting scorpion. The scorpion was walking across the sand in front of Ichabod. Before it could get too far, he stabbed his knife into the ground to block the arachnid's path. The scorpion stopped, then turned around, and skittered in the opposite direction. Ichabod stabbed the sand, blocking its route once again.

"You ought to be careful with those things," said Chauncey. He recalled the bots that had nearly wiped him off the planet. "They've got a pretty explosive sting."

"What, these?" said Ichabod. "What's the matter, Captain?" Then, ala Tweety Bird, said, "Is da' big bad tewwoist afwaid of a widdy, biddy spider?"

Not completely full of it, Chauncey showed some discomfort. He shifted his weight back. "Let's just say I had a really bad experience with them."

"That so?" said Ichabod.

He grabbed the scorpion's torso just behind its pincers and held it up. The scorpion snapped and tried its best to sting him. Ichabod stood up and slowly walked toward Chauncey. As he approached, his open knife held loosely in one hand, the scorpion extended toward Chauncey, he taunted.

"How about you tell us what else they want you for so we can get a bigger reward."

Chauncey pressed his back into the barricade, feigning fear. He pulled his heels back and bent his legs at the knees, readying to pounce. He was about to launch at Ichabod, when Hoss shot the scorpion out of his fingers. Everyone, including Chauncey, was completely surprised. Ichabod spun back to Hoss, pissed.

"What the fuck?!" he screamed. "You could have shot my hand off!"

"I told you to sit down and shut up," said Hoss, matter of fact.

Seizing the opportunity, Chauncey leapt to his feet. He grabbed Ichabod in a chokehold with his left arm and grabbed the Buck knife. As he pulled Ichabod back toward himself, Chauncey threw the knife at Fat Ron, sinking it deep into his leg. Fat Ron shrieked in pain and fell off his ATV. Chauncey yanked the .40 cal out of Ichabod's pants and placed it against his temple.

"Fuck!" screamed Ichabod to Hoss. "Do something!"

Chauncey pulled his forearm tight around Ichabod's scrawny throat, increasing the pressure on his Adam's apple. As Fat Ron was rolling on the sand, screaming, Hoss jumped to his feet, aiming his rifle at the two men.

"Okay, mate," said Chauncey. "Here's how this'll go down. You're going to place your weapon on the ground. Then you and Mr. Hot Spot over there are going to lie face-first in the sand."

As the men stood there sizing one another up, an old red Ford pickup barreled up and stopped. The driver's door opened and Sarge got out. Using the door for cover, he aimed a .45 cal Berretta through the open window.

"Chauncey!" the man called from behind the open door. "You probably don't remember me, but I'm here to help."

"What?!" squealed Ichabod before Chauncey squeezed away his ability to speak again.

"My name's Jake Samuels. Staff Sergeant Jake Samuels, former Green Beret with The Unit. I went through SV-93 with you back during Desert Storm. Your training saved my life."

Chauncey didn't move or loosen his grip on his human shield one bit. He tracked through his memory, trying to pull the name from the thousands of troops he'd trained at SERE. Sergeant Jake Samuels didn't stand out.

"If that's true, then lower your weapon," said Chauncey. "And tell American Sniper over there to do the same."

Samuels slowly stood up from his crouched position behind the door. He held his hands in the air. In his late forties, he had a full, black beard and a large barrel chest that showed the maintained physique of a special operations soldier. He cautiously moved into the open. Keeping one hand raised and a constant eye on Chauncey, he lowered his weapon and placed it on the ground.

"Hoss, lower your rifle," Sarge ordered.

Hoss did as he was told without question. He then raised his hands into the air. Chauncey remained on the ready, but lowered his pistol to his waist, muzzle down, and released Ichabod. He looked intently at Samuels, and then said something that seemed complete gibberish to the others. For Samuels, it was a sword of interruption, something Chauncey had taught everyone who'd gone through his program. Sarge's response would reveal if what he'd said was true.

"I've just crossed the border, mate, and I really need to find the flight surgeon."

Without hesitation, Sarge replied, "Absolutely, Captain. Are we A1?"

"Roger that. A1 on a national level." Chauncey replied. He let the pistol hang on his finger to show that he was now comfortable. He continued, "I need to E&E pronto. Can you assist?"

Staff Sergeant Samuels indicated his pickup truck. "The keys are in the ignition. I recommend you scramble now. The CBP is en route and their birds are in the air. The whole damn border patrol is on the lookout for you, sir."

Chauncey approached the truck. Keeping the pistol at ready position, he did a quick pat-down of Samuels. He then turned his attention to the truck. Looking for any signs of GPS tracking devices or wireless mics, he looked all through the cab and in the engine compartment. Satisfied that Sarge's story was true, he reached out to shake the man's hand.

"I apologize for these men," said Sarge. "Only Hoss is ex-military, the others are just patriots. But they really do believe in what they're doing." Samuels then turned to the others. He nodded toward Chauncey. "This guy is no traitor. He's one of the truest Americans you'll ever meet. And because of his training, when I got nabbed by an Iraqi patrol, I was able to keep my shit together until my unit got me out."

"Glad to be of service, mate," said Chauncey.

"No, thank *you*, sir," snapped Samuels. "Now I'd recommend that you evac right away." Then, to Ichabod, "Give him your water. He needs it more than you do."

Sarge then reached into his pocket. Alarmed, Chauncey leveled his weapon.

"I just want to give you some money. This is all I have," said Sarge. He pulled out a wad of about $200.

Chauncey nodded and gratefully accepted the green. He hoped his good fortune would hold up for a bit longer.

Chapter Thirty-Nine

The gardener, aka PFC Hymie Peralta, watched as Scott trudged toward him across the lawn. He noticed how fat the man was and wondered how much of the food he'd eaten to stretch his pregnant belly had come from making the device that had destroyed his life. He watched the grass disappear and get crushed with each step that Scott took. In stark contrast to the stillness of his body, Hymie's eye twitched uncontrollably.

He'd never met Scott, but Hymie despised the man. For the past twelve years he'd felt a generalized hatred of the world, so this was one of the rare moments when that hatred became focused on something concrete. To finally have it come to a point like this was indescribable. He thought that once Scott was taken out, all the hatred would be gone, and he would find peace.

On some level, Hymie knew he hadn't always felt this angry. His wife, parents, and friends had constantly reminded him of that. But he couldn't hold it. He couldn't access the thoughts or the memories of what they told him. He'd looked at the beaming face that had once been his in the puffy, light blue baby book his mother had kept. He'd watched the videos of himself growing up and playing with friends. Even photographs and letters he'd sent home from Iraq that showed him grinning with his squad didn't seem to register as him. Those were images of someone else. Someone who no longer existed.

Before she'd died, his therapist, Doc Adams, had tried to teach him that his anger was displaced; many vets had suffered wounds like this. She tried to help him realize that because he still had all of his limbs, there was something to be grateful for. But Hymie had lost his mind and he would have gladly spent the rest of his life in a wheelchair if it meant he'd be rid of the tinnitus, the constant migraines, the memory loss, and more.

In the early days of his rehabilitation, Hymie had told himself that he'd be slightly okay with his traumatic brain injury if he could just regain some semblance of his life before the blast. Instead of his service earning him the money to get an MBA in hospitality management, then buying his father's restaurant, he was now washing the dishes he'd hoped to own. Rather than being the hostess at their own place, his wife, Yolanda, couldn't work because she had to play wet nurse to him.

She had to set his phone so he knew when to eat, when to take meds, and other trivial tasks. He had high levels of anxiety, sensitivity to light and loud sounds, and the ever-present anger. He was always so angry. Some distant inkling told him that Yolanda might be wondering where he was right now, hoping that he was okay and that he'd remembered to take his meds.

He silently thanked God for introducing him to Agent Breskin. He was the best shrink he'd had because he'd figured out the source of Hymie's rage.

"It's those smug engineers," Breskin had told him. "They think they know everything, and they care more about money than making you safe. They should have to test the equipment they build to make sure it really works. They should be the ones who die when it fails."

Hymie had nodded furiously, and over time, the plan had emerged. He now envisioned Scott trying to squeeze his huge ass into the up-armored M1114 HMMWV where he'd been a gunner on the day that ended life as he knew it. Only in that way could Scott have understood the need for what he was making. He would have felt the buildup of nausea and anxiety as he tried to watch for enemy ambushes or IEDs hidden along Route Irish. He would have had to deal with the constant crackling of the Warlock Green's giant antenna buzzing by his head, then endured the weeklong migraines that its radio waves had caused.

How would Scott have dealt with living inside the hellishness caused by hoping that the Warlock would block just the right radio frequency the IED makers had wired into the detonator? Hoping, praying it was within the narrow range being sent out.

Hymie had been twenty years old when he'd gotten deployed to Bagdad. IED attacks were rampant. His first time on patrol had been May 1, 2005, the one-year anniversary of President Bush's announcement that major combat operations had ceased. But the killing hadn't ended. In the year he spent there, IED attacks in Iraq swelled to thirty per day, bringing the number of his comrades either killed or injured by this heinous tactic to nearly 6,000.

The bombs had evolved from pressure plate detonators to radio frequency triggers. That meant an insurgent could stay away and click a key fob or a garage door opener to set them off. So the engineers, this engineer, had developed the Warlock Force Protection System. The Warlock Green, the one Hymie had used, represented the first generation. It was a programmable, passive IED jammer. It worked by scanning a series of target frequency bands, then transmitting a signal upon detection of activity in that band. The 25-watt signal it sent out would presumably fake out the bomb detonator so that it never received the order to trigger the device.

Sometimes it worked great. It was saving hundreds of GIs, and the Pentagon began ordering them in truckloads. Unfortunately, it had some serious drawbacks that made it like playing Russian roulette every time Hymie's squad went out on patrol. Besides the obvious drawback, that it didn't detect all of the needed radio frequencies, there was the issue of electronic fratricide.

The strong signal that the Warlock sent out to block the IED from going off could also block the communication devices that the soldiers had to use. It could completely shut out the instructions being sent out to the disarming bots or even the drones they needed to target the enemy. Nobody expects perfection in any war, but this just seemed like some really basic "duh" shit that should have been worked out before being deployed.

The day it had ended for Hymie, they'd been driving the deadly route from Baghdad Airport to the city to clear IEDs. Three M1114's that should have been spaced fifty meters apart drove ass to ass because the center vehicle had the Warlock. If it worked, they all wanted to be in its protective electronic bubble. They should have been spaced out farther to prevent them from getting caught in daisy chain multi-IED attacks, or being blow up by a mortar round, but hell, one cause of fear at a time, right?

As they approached a tunnel, the armored Humvees slowed down, and the men scanned for bombs. Hymie spotted one off the right side of his vehicle, the center one with the Warlock. It hadn't detonated so either the Warlock CREW system had worked or the low-tech bomb was broken. Hymie's driver had radioed the lead vehicle over the comm unit to tell the CO and find out if they should pull over to disarm it. The radio just crackled in return.

Realizing that they were trying to communicate but couldn't, the lead vehicle stopped. The hatch popped open and their sergeant carefully pushed his head up, holding up the handpiece to the vehicle-to-vehicle comm unit. He pointed to it to Hymie, signaling that they should try talking to him. Hymie yelled that there was an IED and pointed off to a dead dog's body that was hiding the bomb. He signaled that they should continue moving forward to get away from it. Once out of the kill zone they could send in a Talon UGV to destroy it.

The radios crackled, frustrating everyone, and the tension mounted. That's when they started taking enemy fire. Hymie looked upward at the overpass and spotted a couple of Iraqis firing. They weren't even shooting at them. They were aiming at the IED to try setting it off with bullets. Hymie returned fire and yelled down to his driver.

"Go around!" Hymie screamed. "The Sarge can't hear us and they're trying to light up the bomb. I think it's because of this goddamned Warlock."

Unfortunately for everyone, including the men on the bridge, the driver thought Hymie had told him to turn off the Warlock so they could end the signal interference. It was the last thing the driver had ever done.

"How could you not have known that would happen?" Hymie screamed at the nearly arrived Scott. The screams were only in his head because that day in Iraq was the last time he'd spoken a word.

"Excuse me, sir," Scott said to Hymie, in a friendly tone. "I think there must be a scheduling mix-up because someone was here yesterday."

He pointed to the neighbor's close-cut lawn to make his point.

Hymie's response was to pull out a Glock and point it at the man's face. The look of fear that his action provoked in Scott was sheer bliss, and Hymie wished he could have shot him right there and then. That, however, was not the plan.

Scott opened his eyes wide and immediately raised his flabby arms. His intelligence all but evaporated in his terror.

"Wh-wh-what do you want?" he asked, his voice and arms quivering.

Hymie said nothing. He just stared at Scott without any emotion. Scott didn't move a muscle. With his free hand, Hymie handed Scott a Motorola XTS 3000 handheld radio. It was the exact same model that Hymie's unit had tried using that day in Iraq.

"He wants revenge, Mr. Scott," a digitally modified voice of Breskin responded over the comm unit.

Scott looked at Hymie, puzzled. He took the radio and pressed the talk button. In an extremely shaky voice he asked, "Revenge for what? I've never seen this man in my life."

"That's true," responded the unknown man. "But due to the failure of your Warlock, this man has joined the thousands of veterans with traumatic brain injury, and he's just a little pissed."

Scott was incredulous. His look was that of someone who had been accused of doing something he never knew had happened, much less being responsible. He stammered, unable to articulate a response. Finally, he managed a feeble, "What are you going to do?"

As Hymie kept his pistol trained on Scott, he pressed a button that released the fake sides of the lawnmower. They fell away, revealing the MAARS. The compact, repurposed unit had been equipped with a pair of mounted 7.62 mm M240 machine guns. Fully loaded, with belts snaking over them, each of the guns could shoot 950 rounds per minute. The articulated robot arm jumped upward, its forward-looking infrared camera pointing toward the Scott backyard.

Breskin continued, "This is a semiautonomous robot. It is currently calibrating its motion sensors. In thirty seconds it will begin scanning. Once it begins, if you or any of your guests so much as blinks, they will be shot.

"You may also notice that on the rear of the vehicle we've placed a Warlock Green. So in addition to the motion sensor, the unit has been equipped with a radio-controlled trigger. If activated, the MAARS will become fully autonomous and shoot anything with a body temperature above ninety degrees Fahrenheit."

Even though he had no spit, Scott gulped. While he didn't grasp the *why* of what was happening, the *what* was clear. Breskin continued as Scott turned to look over his shoulder. Most of the guests were still seated and the catering staff was beginning to clear away the dishes. His wife was now at the bar with Matt Anderle and Beth Miller. Not realizing anything was wrong, she gave him a smile and wave, then held up her glass. She was signaling that it was nearly time to toast Tobor. Scanning the guests, Scott realized his son wasn't there.

In that instant, Scott understood the *why*. This was being orchestrated by the terrorists who'd committed the other attacks. And if Tobor was gone, it meant only one thing.

"You're wasting time, Mr. Scott."

Although terrified, he now had knowledge. And for men like Scott, that was comfort. He responded. "What do you want me to do? If you're who I think you are, then there's nothing I can do to stop you from killing us."

"Your fate is not sealed. Right now you need to make sure nobody moves."

Hymie handed Scott a bullhorn. Without being told, he understood what to do. Turning to the guests, Hymie's gun now at his back, he raised the megaphone to his mouth. He pressed the wrong button and the unit emitted a piercing screech. Everyone from the lawn suddenly stopped talking and looked toward him.

Seeing their friend in what was clearly a compromised position, the guests did exactly the opposite of what he was supposed to tell them. They stood up and began a motion forward. At that moment, the MAARS unit emitted a loud click that signaled its arming sequence had completed. It began to move on its treads from where Scott stood toward a preprogrammed GPS coordinate that would have it stop right in the center of the party.

Scott immediately pressed the correct button. As he watched the MAARS move across the lawn toward his wife and friends, he practically yelled into the mouthpiece.

"Nobody move!" he shrieked. "If you're sitting, don't stand up. If you're standing, don't sit. Don't even take a sip of your drink!"

Sweat coated his face. It dripped down his bloated cheeks and fell into the folds of his chin and neck. He struggled, not knowing what to say as the MAARS continued its slow and ominous approach.

"We're all in danger," he barked. "That thing has a motion detector. It's programmed to shoot anything that moves."

Rather than raising objections, his guests immediately grasped the situation. They were all employed by DoD contractors and realized their lives were in danger. Ironically, many of them had worked on various components on the MAARS and they knew that it would do what it was supposed to do. The catering staff, however, wasn't privy to semi-autonomous robots equipped with machine guns and motion and heat sensors. The pretty gal who'd offered Armagan a glass of champagne took a step toward the house with a tray of empty glasses.

The response from the MAARS was instantaneous. The green lawn silence was torn apart by a loud burst of machine gun fire. Her body was riddled with bullets and she fell to the ground. The empty glasses shattered on the flagstone all around her. Everyone screamed in horror but miraculously remained still. Anyone who'd been looking in her direction dared not turn their heads for fear of getting shot. They merely closed their eyes to avoid watching her body twitch.

Breskin's voice came from the Motorola again. "Okay, Mr. Scott, now we're going to play a little game that I call 'electronic fratricide.' The gardener is going to remotely turn on the Warlock that's attached to the MAARS. Once the unit is on, you'll all be safe inside the jamming bubble. Then there are only two possibilities, and the gardener is holding them both."

Unseen by Scott, who didn't dare turn his head for fear that even a slight motion would be detected, Hymie had put away his weapon and taken out a pair of radio controllers. One of them was a key fob, the electric part of a car door key. The other was a garage door opener. Both of the devices were the types that had been used to detonate IEDs in Iraq. They were what the Warlock Green had been invented to combat.

"He's only going to press one of these buttons. That's good because the Warlock is only programmed to work against one of them. But this man wants you dead. He really, really wants to press them both. In spite of your immorality in deploying such an ineffective system, he's only going to press one. Now here's the important part. I know which one works and which one doesn't. I will tell him to press the safe one."

Neither Scott nor Hymie could believe what they'd just heard. Why would he tell Hymie to press the one that the Warlock was programmed to defend against?

"Because the Warlock has been known to interfere with communication devices, once it's on, he may not hear me. You know why, don't you? You saw the results of the testing in Yuma. The testing that showed the Warlock Green interfered with radios, but was still sent to squads that used those units. Who knows, maybe you'll get lucky and it won't affect this one. If it does, this man will choose which one to press on his own. I guess then you'll have the same chance he did in Iraq."

The Warlock Green activated and the air was filled with electricity as it emitted signals in every direction. Everyone could hear the low hum and buzz as if a small power generator had been turned on. Hymie closed his eyes for a moment as it brought back sense memory. Fear gripped him as well. A fear that had been conditioned by continuous use. At the same time, the comm unit emitted a stream of useless static, just as it had done to Hymie's unit so many years ago.

"Please!" Scott cried to Hymie. "We didn't know about it until it was too late. We begged them not to put them in the field. They told us it was good enough. I'm not who you should hate. I was trying to save you. To protect you. Please don't do this. Please!"

Hymie didn't move. He seemed confused. Maybe he'd forgotten why he was there, maybe he reconsidered what he was doing, but for a moment he just stared blankly at the two devices in his hands. Lost in a fog, he did nothing. Scott pleaded and cried for mercy as the MAARS sat, waiting among the guests, its antenna humming.

Hymie's cellphone beeped. It wasn't a call, though. It was the alarm Yolanda had programmed into it to tell Hymie it was time to take his meds. He dropped the R/F devices and reached into his pocket to withdraw the phone and turn off the alarm. Having been shielded by the sizable Scott, his small motion went undetected, but when he reflexively took a step to go to the truck where his medicine was, the MAARS unit's twin M240's pivoted and mowed him down like the blades of grass on which he stood. Scott, in the line of fire, was gunned down as well. Tragically, as he fell, his palm landed on the garage door opener. It was the wrong one.

Chapter Forty

Armagan and Breskin had wasted no time with Tobor. After Armagan landed his jump plane in his yard, he'd taxied as close to the house as he could. There would be no problem with the police or the FAA because they were aware of his commuting situation. His property had been cleared for daytime takeoffs and landings.

As soon as the modified jump plane stopped bumping its way over the dirt and rocks, Breskin, wearing his Dick Cheney mask, had opened the jump door and yanked out the blubbering, petrified young engineer. Still groggy from the shot of PAVA spray he'd received at Armagan's car, Tobor had begun rolling around on the ground, wailing for his father to save him. Breskin pulled out his pistol, and as he aimed it at the floundering engineer, yelled for Armagan. He appeared a moment later wearing his George W. Bush mask.

From his perch nearly a mile away, Chauncey couldn't hear what Breskin had yelled, but based on Armagan's quick response, he assumed it was an order to hurry the hell up. Chauncey had arrived in Shadow Mountain about an hour prior to their landing. Armed with Ichabod's Colt and a pair of high-powered Zeiss binoculars he'd gotten from Sergeant Samuels, he'd ditched the truck and settled into a rock outcropping to survey Armagan's house. When he'd arrived, Breskin was already there, pacing.

Resisting the urge to rush in, Chauncey had maintained his position to gain some situational awareness. It had taken all of his self-control to not just move in and rid the world and himself of Breskin. Now, seeing what they were up to, he hoped he could make it to the house before they executed the hostage.

Through the binoculars, which had been so effective at spotting illegal immigrants crossing the border, Chauncey had watched as Breskin savagely kicked Tobor in the stomach. He'd then yelled at him and gestured to the cellar door on the side of the house. Tobor had risen and staggered to the house, falling after each pair of steps. Once there, Armagan had gone down to open the door and Breskin shoved Tobor down the stairs. After a quick look over his shoulder, Breskin had made his way down.

Under normal circumstances, Chauncey would have called the police and let them handle things. But with his newly minted status on the FBI's Most Wanted list, he wasn't confident it would end with an arrest. Not to mention that this was personal.

He waited another ten minutes to make sure nobody else would show up. Satisfied that it was clear, Chauncey began a low, slow zigzag across the barren dirt that lay between him and Armagan's house. Twenty minutes later, Chauncey stood at the top of the stairs that led to Armagan's basement. He'd been correct that there were no additional unfriendlies at the house. The two men were currently working alone. To be sure, he did a quick recon of the airplane and made a loop of the other side of the house. As he did, he considered his assault.

Slowly, careful not to make a sound, Chauncey took out his weapon and started down the stairs. The wood was old and prone to creaking, so he made sure to place his feet as close to where the step met the frame as possible. Halfway down, he hit a board that groaned. He froze, pointing his weapon at the door, waiting to see if he'd been heard. Luckily, the sound baffling that Breskin had used to keep the screams of his victims inside the room also had the effect of keeping the sounds of Chauncey's approach out.

When he'd reached the bottom, he met a heavy metal door. He placed his ear against its smooth, cold surface, but couldn't hear anything from the other side. Backing away a small step, he gripped the doorknob and slowly turned it. It wasn't locked. He was grateful because it wasn't his style to blast his way into a situation like Diddy or Phil.

Visualizing what he'd seen of the room in the torture videos, Chauncey figured Tobor would be against the far wall. He had no idea what shape the poor bastard would be in, but he'd been in there for nearly an hour, and based on what they'd done to others, he prepared for the worst. Breskin would probably be to the left, on the close side of the door. Armagan would either be by their prisoner or directly in front of the door. If that were the case, Chauncey would shove it open hard in order to jolt Armagan forward and hopefully knock him to the ground.

He grasped his gun tight and turned the doorknob once again. When he felt it click open, he pushed it forward with all his might.

"Nobody move!" Chauncey yelled, launching into the room.

He pivoted his weapon from side to side, making sure that anything in front of him was a target. He'd been correct. Breskin was to his left and Armagan was in the back of the room with Tobor. Both of the men were wearing the political masks that had come to terrorize Americans over the past few months. Breskin was sitting behind the table, a manila folder in front him. Armagan stood beside Tobor, holding a bloody scalpel.

The scene was beyond anything he'd imagined. Apparently, they'd decided to waste no time with this victim. Tobor had been stripped naked, his hands bound behind his back. The zip-ties had been connected to a rope tied to the water pipe running across the ceiling. It was a form of self-inflicted torture. The victim is told that if he remains on his tiptoes, he'll be fine. If he sags, his arms will lift backward behind his body. If he sags enough, they will eventually dislocate from the shoulders.

As an enhanced interrogation technique, it's done to make the interrogated feel responsible for his own pain. "Confess and we'll let you go free. Don't confess, and the pain will continue. But since nobody is touching you, it's your own fault." Given Breskin's historic goals, it was only being used to inflict pain.

Due to Tobor's overweight, out-of-shape frame, he'd dropped to his knees immediately. His arms were no longer even connected to his skeleton. They were simply held there by muscle and skin. At least, one of them was. Armagan had used the scalpel to cut the tissues connecting Tobor's left arm to his body. By the looks of it he'd gotten about a third of the way through. Now Tobor just sagged, moaned, twitched, and sucked his snot continuously.

"It's over!" yelled Chauncey. Then to Armagan he barked, "Cut him down."

"Kill him," said Breskin. "He's already confessed."

"Don't do it!" said Chauncey. "You're finished. You've gotten what you wanted. It's over, Armagan."

Upon hearing the name, Tobor began to wail, "Armageddon! Armageddon! Oh, no, it's the end of the world!"

"Shut up you idiot!" Armagan yelled at Tobor. But Tobor didn't stop. His Tourette's had been intensified by the pain and anxiety, and he was unable to control himself.

"Armageddon! Armageddon! Armageddon!" he continued. He moaned louder and his legs twitched. His feet pointed and flexed constantly.

"Kill him!" yelled Breskin again. "The people need the execution."

Chauncey slapped Breskin across the face with his weapon. "Shut it, mate!" he yelled over Tobor's caterwauling. Breskin's Cheney mask split in two, the pieces falling to either side.

Keeping his gun trained on Breskin, Chauncey addressed Armagan. The fact that he hadn't killed Tobor revealed his ambivalence.

"Enough people have died," said Chauncey. "You've gotten your revenge. Your rage is understandable. But this isn't the answer. This won't bring your family back."

Tearing off his mask, Armagan glared at Chauncey.

"What do you know?! You may as well just shoot me now because it's the only thing that will stop me!" he said.

Armagan dropped behind Tobor, using him as a human shield. He pulled Tobor's head back and placed the scalpel to his throat.

"You want it to end," said Chauncey. "You don't want this anymore. That's why you texted me to get away from my house. And you sent me to your adoptive parents so I would see your bedroom. So I would understand what was happening."

"You're no different than anyone else," screamed Armagan. "I thought you were. But you're an American. All you understand is lying and killing. You dishonored our friendship. You killed them."

"Is that what he told you?" asked Chauncey, indicating Breskin with the muzzle of his pistol. "It's not true. I tried to save them. Breskin knew you sent me and set a trap. He wants you to believe I killed them so you won't trust me."

"Shut up!" Armagan yelled. "Breskin is my father. My only father. He saved me!"

"That's right," Breskin chimed. "Don't listen to him. This man is a trained deceiver and a traitor. He is countryless, friendless, godless! Now kill that immoral, fat blob. Slit his throat like the repugnant pig that he is."

Chauncey turned to Breskin. He pointed the pistol in between his eyes. "Tell him the truth, you son of a bitch."

As Chauncey's focus was fixed on Breskin, Armagan stood and threw the scalpel. It spun through the air, then sunk into Chauncey's forearm. Chauncey dropped the pistol and without missing a beat, Breskin snatched it up. He savagely pistol-whipped Chauncey across the face, splitting his lip and sending him sprawling against the concrete wall.

Breskin turned and shoved the muzzle against Chauncey's cheek. He moved it and pressed it against his forehead. He switched to his eye, pressing the muzzle into the socket.

His face oozing intensity, Breskin asked, "You couldn't just stay in Mexico, could you? No, you had to come back and try to stop us. God, I hate you."

Chauncey stared at Breskin as he started to pull the trigger. Before the weapon fired, he turned and shot a single round at Tobor. The bullet split his head open and he slumped forward. Having extinguished Tobor's moans and screams, the room fell into a silence that was quieter than a buried coffin.

Stepping back a pace, Breskin aimed the weapon at Chauncey again.

"I won't kill you yet. I need something first." He turned to Armagan and ordered, "Tie him up."

"Yes, Father," said Armagan.

As he rose to his feet and approached Chauncey, Breskin soothed him.

"That's right, Army. You're my son — my one man army. And your mother, God rest her soul, was right. You are a gift, a gift the Heavenly Father delivered to me so I could repair this broken world."

Breskin's insanity coming to full bloom, Chauncey allowed Armagan to lead him across the room. Armagan shoved him down on the chair beside Tobor's corpse.

"You don't want to do this," Chauncey said to Armagan. "I'm not your enemy. I'm your friend. This man has brainwashed you, used you. He used the death of your family to –"

"Shut it, mate!'" Armagan mocked. He slapped Chauncey in the face and tugged his arms behind his back. To Chauncey's surprise, Armagan only tied one of his hands to the chair. He then stood back to let Breskin approach.

Believing that Chauncey was fully secured, Breskin placed the Colt on the table. He picked up a sharp, ultrathin, pearl-handled knife. He waved it at Chauncey like it was a precious gem.

"Do you see this?" asked Breskin. "It's a flaying knife. A specially engineered device whose sole purpose is to skin a human being. Just another fine torture tool developed by the great minds brought to you by the human race. We were going to slice away pieces of fat boy until we reached his morality. I suspect we never would have. But maybe I can slice away some chunks of your head until I find out where you squirreled away those recordings."

Chauncey stared at the knife. He knew what it was. He'd seen its results on murdered and tortured victims of al-Qaeda. He'd seen strips of flesh cut from women's breasts and men's genitals. Nothing left but the red, exposed tissues beneath. Once he'd seen a man's torso flayed completely around his body, then the skin had been tied in a knot and wrapped around his neck. It was one of the most sadistic and painful things a person could have done because it wasn't fatal. It caused pure and intense anguish.

Rather than resist, Chauncey gave way instantly. His fear overflowed. "Don't do that, Breskin. God, please don't. I'll tell you whatever you want to know. Just ask. Just don't use that thing on me."

Breskin put down the paring knife and laughed.

"Well, look at this. Complete compliance and all I had to do was threaten you. I'd really expected more from the SERE King. But I guess it's true what they say 'those that can't do, teach.'"

He snatched up the knife once again and took a step toward Chauncey. Chauncey licked his lips and murmured something to himself. It was barely perceptible. Breskin ignored him.

"So? Where are they? On a server somewhere?" he asked.

"No, sir," said Chauncey. "I'm not a cloud guy. I used cassette tapes."

"Wow! Quite the Luddite, aren't we? Well, where are the cassettes?!"

"I'll tell you, but first I need to know why you want them. Will your bosses kill you unless you return them?"

"My bosses?" said Breskin. "If you're referring to the men I'm working with, then know that they are not in charge. Not yet, at any rate. As of now they still need me. They needed me to bring Armagan here to raise as my own. They got him into the best schools while I found mentally disabled veterans who would give anything to end their own pain. Using lifestyle events was a bit of romantic irony we threw in for Armagan. So we all got something out of it. And it's almost over. That's why I want the tapes. In the next few days the president and Congress will get so much pressure from the DoD, Homeland, the FBI, and the American people, that they will amend the Patriot Act to open the national airspace to unfettered drone surveillance. Predators, Ravens, and swarms of minidrones dispersing smart dust like clouds will fly and crawl through this country like a pestilence. You won't be able to take a piss without them knowing. But the poor, scared people will be safe! Nobody will hurt them. Society will become compliant because its citizens will never know if they're being watched. It will mark the total annihilation of the great city of light on the hill."

"What do you get out of it?" asked Chauncey.

"Once I have those tapes, I'll get enough money to fall off the grid forever."

Chauncey nodded toward Armagan. "So all of this? Bringing Armagan here and brainwashing him to hate us? All of the torture and the massacres were just for money?"

A look of consternation crossed Armagan's face.

"No," said Armagan. "It was not for money. It was because America is broken. It needed its soul rebuilt. *Tikkun Olam.* You said they would thank us after they'd realized the error of their way."

"They will, Army. Only I still need to get something out of it."

Armagan stiffened in shock. The full realization of Breskin's immorality awed him. He took a step toward him.

"All of this was so you could get rich?"

Breskin picked up the Colt pistol and took a step back.

"Easy there. I gave you what you wanted. Vengeance is normally reserved for the Almighty, but He has given you that power to restore your soul. You can be at peace."

"This is not what you taught me. This is not why you told me we did these things. Money? You're as bad as the rest of them. I absolutely was a gift! A gift to get you rich!"

Seeing what was about to happen, Chauncey yelled, "Armagan, don't!" He jumped out of the chair to try grabbing him, but it was too late. Breskin fired. Red spread across Armagan's shirt and he fell to the ground, gasping.

Breskin pointed the weapon at Chauncey again.

"Where are those damned tapes? Tell me or I'll blow a hole in your head. You may be able to save him after I'm gone, but the longer you wait, the less likely that becomes."

Glaring at Breskin he said, "They're in a tunnel just to the side of my house. There's a large rock covering the entrance."

"You're a resourceful man, Paunce. I'll give you that. But how do I know you're telling the truth?"

"You don't," said Chauncey. "It's one of the key failings to torture. You never know if the person says the truth or lies just to stop the pain."

"Well, then, if it turns out to be a lie, I'll be back. And if I do come back, there will be no end to your pain."

Breskin grabbed the video camera that had stood capturing the entire scene and backed out of the room. All Chauncey heard was the locking of the metal door from outside.

Chapter Forty-One

The pain was more intense than Armagan ever imagined pain could be. On a scale of one to ten it was 10,000. And it wasn't just the agony of the bullet that had pierced his sternum, and shattered his rib cage, lungs, and organs. It was a sabotage of his senses, and rather than distinct memories of his life flashing through his mind, Armagan was drowning inside the most excruciating emotions he'd ever experienced.

He heard a symphony of shrieks from not only his victims, but of his parents and friends in his village. They pierced his eardrums like tiny razor-sharp pitchforks. Staccato, metallic bursts of machine guns and grenade explosions mixed with the begging, pleading moans and screams of those he'd helped to torture, now tortured him. Beneath those sounds the voice of Breskin played on a loop, "We'll fix them. We'll fix them all." The ghosts ruled the day.

His nostrils became stuffed with the stench of blood, sweat, and sulfur. They filled his sinuses like solid chunks, constricting his ability to breathe. Opening his mouth fared no better. Every labored breath he drew brought with it the taste of sand and locusts. They raced down his throat, choking him, gagging him.

Jump cut, hiccup, gulps of reality trickled and danced around his periphery, though he didn't know what they meant. He was too far gone. Too close to dying. He stretched his eyes open wide, hoping, through them, to suck in some oxygen. They bulged and he made no sense of what he saw. A man. Chauncey, tearing a corroded water pipe down from a ceiling. Unthreading it from a dead man's shackles then racing, ramming, jamming it through a wall. A wall beside a door. Then light. But not "the light." Not the tunnel. Not salvation.

Whether his eyes were open or shut tight, he still saw things. Images projected through the eye holes of a plastic Halloween mask. Hazy and unfocused, through thick air he saw his mother's head flying through the sky. Red, liquid ribbons rained from her neck. He saw the slices cut into his wrists, lifting from his body. They putrefied in midair. Swarms of insects, thick as cold tar, infested the wounds, entering him and racing through his veins toward his heart.

A fat laser beam of intense heat severed his leg. Melted it. Stretched and ripped it apart and off him. He flew through the air and landed on rocks, smashing his head. His brain slammed against the inside of his skull over and over, as if it were today. Now. Tomorrow.

Then up. He rose. His eight-year-old body, hemorrhaging from the femoral artery, lifted from the dirt and placed in a chopper.

"We'll fix you," the soldier said.

He fell to the ground, his body unaccustomed to a metallic, strapped-on appendage.

"I'll fix you. We'll fix them." Breskin said, lifting him to his feet.

His weightless newness rose and flew through the air. He was upstairs in a house, lying on a bed.

"Armagan, can you hear me? Can you hear me, mate?" he heard.

Armagan opened his eyes and saw Chauncey standing over him. The agony faded a bit, but stayed close, lurking behind a nearby corner. Somehow he was in his house, on his own bed. The memory of Breskin shooting him sped back into his eyes with a flash of blinding speed. He knew where he was. And with that realization came a new kind of pain.

"I can't stop the bleeding," said Chauncey. "I'm sorry."

Chauncey sat beside Armagan, sweating and covered in blood. Armagan tried to speak but choked. He coughed and blood escaped his mouth. His pain was gone. But he knew inside that it would return, and he needed to hurry.

"I'm sorry," he said, tears flowing from his eyes. "I'm a monster."

Chauncey was overcome with compassion and pity. No apologies could ever make up for the horrors Armagan had committed, yet what the man was saying was true. Yes, he was a murderer. But it wasn't his fault. His true nature had been erased and overwritten by a master of coercion and cruelty. A master that Chauncey had taught.

"How many more?" Chauncey asked. "How do I stop him?"

It took a moment for Armagan to comprehend that Chauncey was asking about Panopticon. He closed his eyes and fought off the reapproaching sensory barrage.

"One," he said. "No, two," he corrected himself, struggling to stay present. "They were lifestyle events. To punish them for destroying my family on the day of Lila's wedding. First a bat mitzvah, then an Eagle Scout ceremony, next a college graduation. A wedding. A wedding is next."

"Whose wedding? Where?" asked Chauncey with urgency.

"I don't remember. It doesn't matter. Without me it can't happen. Without the house. My bots. The basement." He closed his eyes and winced as razor blades spun inside his body. Then he continued, "But it's too late. Not necessary. The panic will force their hand."

"Whose hand?"

"There's another one. A final one." said Armagan.

"A final what?"

"Massacre."

"Where? When?"

"They didn't tell me. They were going to kill me before it happened. I'm sure of it."

"What is it?"

Armagan glazed over and shook his head sadly. "It's a double. A birth and a funeral."

Chauncey saw that Armagan was fading. His blood covered the bed now. It had seeped into the sheets and was now dripping onto the ground, filling the tiny spaces between the wooden floorboards. His eyes flickered as he licked his lips and shivered.

"How do I stop him? How do I stop Breskin?" Chauncey urged.

"He's not who you need to stop. Someone else is in charge."

Chauncey stood up and grasped Armagan's shoulders in a firm but gentle grip. He had to keep him alive for just a bit longer.

"Who?" yelled Chauncey, trying to keep Armagan's from falling unconscious. "Green? Paulson? One of the other CEOs?"

"No. You know him. From before."

Armagan stopped and stared at Chauncey hard. He lifted himself onto his elbows and whispered.

"Forgive me, Chauncey. Please. You're a good man. A friend. I'm sorry for everything. Please."

Chauncey looked at Armagan and saw the man with whom he'd shared more than tea. He was guilty. He was culpable. But he was not responsible.

"I forgive you," he said.

Armagan's body bucked upward in spasms. His senses overtook him again. Only this time, instead of the acrid, sour odor of evil, he smelled spices and felt the arms of his mother and father lifting him. They whispered in his ears, "You are our gift."

Chapter Forty-Two

Senator Stevens and General Brewster sat in the Senator's DC office savoring the smoky peat of the $600 bottle of 40-year-old Laphroaig. Other than wanting to tie Green to a chair so he would stop pacing and touching every single thing in Steven's office, they were in extraordinarily good moods. By the smug expressions on their faces, one would have thought they'd just won the Powerball jackpot. And in a sense, they were about to. The fact that they'd rigged the game in their favor didn't seem to bother them at all.

Brewster turned to Stevens and indicated the pacing Green with his glass of neat amber liquor.

"He didn't hear a goddamned thing you just said, Todd," the general said.

Stevens shrugged helplessly. He didn't need a video playback, much less Brewster to see the obvious. He'd been watching Green pace and fidget for nearly an hour. He turned toward his longtime benefactor, "What's going on, Nels?" asked Stevens. "You're really wound up."

"I'm fine," Green snapped, clearly not fine. He snatched a letter opener from Steven's desk and touched the point to see how sharp it was.

"Please be careful with that," Stevens warned. "It came directly from Ronald Reagan's Oval Office desk."

Green didn't even acknowledge the statement or the obvious reverence with which Stevens held the silver and mahogany, White House seal-emblazoned idol. He just waved it like a conductor's baton and kept moving. Had it been anyone other than Green, Stevens would have erupted. But the elder senator's temper, it seems, was reserved for people who weren't the CEOs of companies that created and funded PACs intended to keep him in office. The general, however, was not beholden to Green. Of course, very soon Stevens wouldn't be either. That reality just hadn't quite set in.

"For Christ's sake," barked Brewster. "Sit the hell down and enjoy the moment, will you? And put that fucking letter opener down."

Without warning, Green threw the prized letter opener across the room. It hit the window and ricocheted back, nearly hitting the general in the eye. Brewster was instantly on his feet, fists clenched. His reflexes may have slowed somewhat since he was in his prime, but his muscle memory and ferocity hadn't ebbed one bit.

"What the hell is wrong with you?!" Brewster snapped.

Green squared off with him. "What? Aren't you happy? I put it down. You sound like my wife." Then, speaking in an exaggerated female voice, "Are you okay? What's wrong, honey?" He finished it off by looking back and forth between Brewster and Stevens, "I told you and I told her; I'm fine."

"Oh," said Brewster in monotone voice. Then after shooting a "this guy's a lunatic look" to Stevens, added, "Since you put it *that* way, I'm convinced."

The general grabbed the letter opener, mumbling something about "shove" and "up ass," then sat back down. He shot a quick look at Stevens that belied his concern. It wasn't really concern over his own safety, but rather, worry that one of their partners might be having a nervous breakdown at zero hour. Stevens, who knew Green much longer, got up and walked over to him. He placed a calming hand on the agitated man's shoulder.

"Nels, relax will you? We're nearly there. The bill is on its way to the president as we speak. And with all the chaos that's going on after the last event, there's no question that he's going to sign it. I mean, I've never seen a bill get passed so fast. This sucker went through both houses faster than you can say 9/11."

Stevens was referring to S.9250 - *The Total Information Awareness Bill,* which he'd written over a year ago and submitted to the Senate two days ago. Its passage into law was the culmination of their plan. The bill not only broadened the FBI's ability to track the domestic phone calls of all American citizens no matter where they were made to or from, but made it an act of treason for goliath companies like Google, Facebook, Yahoo, LinkedIn, and the major ISPs to refuse turning over the actual content of emails, chat, and IM session transcripts, and user IDs and passwords when instructed to do so. No court order was necessary under the bill. All that would be necessary was the assertion that there was reasonable suspicion of domestic terrorism.

For the men in the room, the most important part of the bill had less to do with privacy rights. They knew that even now the NSA had the ability, albeit not the legal authority, to collect pretty much whatever it wanted. It was the method of data collection they were focused on. The part of the bill they cared about was Section Three. That part of the bill authorized the DOJ and local law enforcement to deploy drones, both large and small, anywhere they deemed fit. The FAA would have to accept it and The Reauthorization Act that governed their regulation of the national airspace would be burned in the fire of new regulations. In the new world era, commercial aviation in the national air space would be flying coach.

Green's company, would be selling over 10,000 Nightshade-equipped Predators to the government. They would fly continuous surveillance missions over every inch of the country's border, watching every piece of critical infrastructure, every major and minor American city, and every citizen who was deemed a potential threat to the homeland. In addition to selling the planes, GA would be contracted to operate them and collect the data. Paulson's AeroVironment would be supplying the state and local police forces with hundreds of thousands of quadcopters and iRobot's UGVs to monitor their jurisdictions. Smart Dust, license plate readers, facial recognition software, and retinal scan technology would be ubiquitous and would track and log the comings and goings of people 24/7. The cameras that the police had now been ordered to wear would lead drones like Dobermans on leashes.

In these men's minds, such Orwellian action was the only reasonable thing to do in an increasingly dangerous world. People who know they're being watched behave better. It doesn't even matter if they really are or aren't being observed. For most of them just the fact that they think they're being watched is enough to make them behave. Prisons had used circular, panopticonic guard towers with one-way glass for years. Inmates, not knowing if a guard is watching, don't cause as many problems.

Even though he'd helped to cause them, Stevens rationalized his culpability in the deaths of so many innocent people by convincing himself that this was the best answer to the rise in domestic terrorism. So when the FBI did stop the current wave, which was pretty much the plan, everyone knew that al-Qaeda, the Islamic State, the Taliban, and other radical Muslim extremists would be visiting an American mall soon. The media would broadcast that message over and over again.

To be sure groups like the ACLU, EFF, and others would sue the government over the law's constitutionality, but that would take years. And Stevens knew from polls that while a significant percentage of the population would be against it, the vast majority would gladly give up their privacy to be kept safe. That the current danger had been completely manufactured was beside the point. His fuzzy logic concluded that eventually it wouldn't be, so why wait?

What had really helped to push the barrel over the edge so quickly was that this law was the only way to protect the now, "on strike" community of defense-contracting engineers. The massacre of Tobor's family had played out perfectly and represented the tipping point for which they'd planned. After the footage of the lawn party went viral, every single engineer and scientist in the country packed up their white boards and went home. Boeing, Lockheed Martin, L3, Raytheon, and more were shut down. Their paid representatives had put more pressure on them to pass the legislation than ever before. Cries of "Chinese supremacy," "weak military," and "lost jobs!" echoed predictably through the Capitol's cavernous marbled walls.

"It's a goddamned great bill," Brewster said to Green and Stevens. "Long overdue. And other than a few dead Arabs from scared folks here and there, and a slight backlash against vets because they're the ones committing these massacres, this thing has played out perfectly. Now we can get the country back to its ignorant bliss and enjoy our rightful place at the top of the food chain." Then, switching gears, he levied a rare compliment. "And I have to hand it to Breskin. The guy pulled it off magnificently. He was amazing in the sandbox, but that was only his first act."

While Brewster used the Reagan letter opener to conduct an unheard, John Philip Sousa march, Stevens lifted his glass in an air toast. At the mention of Breskin, Green became more agitated. He apparently didn't share the love.

"Breskin?" Green scoffed as if even shaping the sound caused painful sores to form inside his mouth. "Where the hell is he anyway?"

Stevens replied, "After the last event, the FBI reinstated him. The first thing he did was to order Carby's release. He's on his way to Colorado right now to ask Carby some questions about Paunce before the media finds out."

"Another stroke of genius," said Brewster. "By releasing the boogieman, the public will stay scared and increase the pressure on our stubborn president to sign the bill. Ha! The man is brilliant, I tell you!"

"He's garbage," spat Green. "We should have done it without him. And when it's all over he and his buddy Chauncey are getting a pair of Hellfire enemas."

Brewster was taken aback at the mention of Chauncey. It was true that the man had become an irritating fly and needed to be swatted, but there was no way he could prevent their success now. He could be dealt with later. A small piece of the general admired Chauncey for having gotten this far. It was, after all, military training that had given him the skills, and he took some pride in that. Yet now, as he looked at Green he began to see what his behavior meant.

"That right?" asked Brewster. "Does any of this have anything to do with your 'treatment' by Paunce?"

Green stared out the window, lost in himself. He wondered for the millionth time what he would have done had Breskin warned him about Chauncey's concerns over running nonmilitary personnel through his intensive training. He thought he would probably have gone through it anyway. He probably would have told Breskin that he could take anything Paunce could throw at him. And he probably would have labeled anyone who'd failed at the training or suffered lifelong trauma from it a weak link. Probably.

In part, Green felt that way because he was one of the people who believed enhanced interrogation wasn't torture. He agreed with the definition made in the torture memos that "to constitute torture, 'severe pain' must rise to a level that would ordinarily be associated with a physical condition or injury sufficiently serious that it would result in death, organ failure, or serious impairment of body functions."

Green also felt that way because of hubris. He was a great man. A captain of the new millennia. He was in the one percent of the one percent. And why not? Since the War on Terror had begun, his technology had changed the world. His high-flying robotic planes had even changed the way wars were conducted. Not to mention they had made him insanely wealthy. In addition to the upcoming contracts with the DHS, he'd correctly predicted that the events of Panopticon would *not* cause the stock market to crash. After studying the effects of terrorism on the stock market since 9/11, he knew which stocks would go up.

After the 17 percent, one-day drop just following the World Trade Center attacks, the market had rebounded within a month. And not all stocks had been hurt. While hospitality and travel had taken big hits, war contractors, security, and surveillance stocks had performed incredibly well. Investors like him had surfed in the wake of disaster and become savvy at navigating the volatile world of terrorism. It was the new normal. His net worth increased with every Panopticon attack that happened.

Green's ego could only allow him to associate his recent bouts of nausea, panic attacks, flashbacks to the ice truck, and threats to his wife and daughter as the culmination of the stress of orchestrating Panopticon. There was no way he would allow even the slightest possibility that his lapses in focus and short fuse had been caused by someone like Chauncey.

"Probablies" aside, the fact was that Breskin hadn't told Green about the high incidence of PTSD associated with Chauncey's particular brand of SERE training. Even the abridged and watered-down version Green and his cronies had experienced could cause trauma. And General Brewster knew that. As he'd risen through the ranks of the U.S. Army, he'd seen many strong, steely, and emotionally stable men from both sides lose their minds after being subjected to or subjecting others to torture. So as he sat in Senator Steven's office watching Green's agitation and hatred for Breskin and Paunce, Brewster knew what he saw. It had taken a few months, but Green was suffering from severe PTSD, and obviously it concerned him greatly.

Brewster stood up and took a $50 swig of his single malt.

"Green," he said. "You're a brilliant man. You've got everything you want. A beautiful home, a great family, and an amazing future. Unfortunately, I'm afraid you've also got a raging case of PTSD."

Green turned from the window and looked at Brewster. "Is that so?" he asked. "So you're a psychiatrist all of a sudden?"

"Don't need to be," said Brewster. "I've seen it enough to know it. The kind of intense training that Paunce put you through can send SEALs, Rangers, Green Berets, Air Commandos and other Spec Ops troops into a dark place. And they're prepared for it, more or less."

"So what do you suggest?" asked Green, unimpressed. "Therapy?"

Brewster laughed and shook his head. "Nope. The chinks in your armor are never going away. Nick Rowe's never did. Mine never did after Vietnam.

That loony McCain's never did either. Just call it battle scars and move on. My suggestion would be to get yourself a prescription for Xanax, wash it down with a case of single malt, then take it out on your wife like the rest of us do."

Chapter Forty-Three

As Breskin pulled his Jag out of the prison and made a right turn onto Colorado Route 67, he studied Carby's face through the rearview mirror. He'd only been inside ADX Florence for three weeks, yet he looked like he'd aged by a dozen years. His once bald head had a thin layer of gray and red curls, and his once neatly cropped goatee was now a coarse beard with flecks of white. His eyes, which had always been keen and laser-focused, somehow seemed to have receded deeper into his skull, much like a mammal's scrotum contracts to protect it from injury. Breskin understood, though. He knew what the federal Supermax prison did to a man.

"Those guards hate you, Tom," said Breskin, continuing to look at him through the silvered glass. "It seemed to me that they would rather see you dead than get freed."

"Yeah, well after a while, forcing people to live in holes would fill even Gandhi with loathing," said Carby.

"Are you saying they don't deserve it?" asked Breskin. "That it's okay to send bombs in the mail and sell secrets to the Russians?"

Carby didn't respond. He just gazed out the window, attempting to let the majesty of the world rejuvenate him. As he looked at the snow-peaked Rocky Mountains, he noted how perverse it was that mankind had sullied one of the most beautiful places on earth with a place like the one he'd just left.

Until his arrest, only two other men had ever been held in the most secure section of Colorado's ADX Supermax called Range 13. Unseen by the media, the special section with just four cells also held Tommy Silverstein, a member of the Aryan Brotherhood who killed a prison guard at the federal pen in Marion, and Ramzi Yousef, the man responsible for the first World Trade Center bombing in 1993.

Appropriately dubbed "The Alcatraz of the Rockies," the Supermax prison was the most secure detention facility in the world. The complex had five prisons in all, ranging from a lower security work farm where the likes of disgraced Illinois politician Rod Blagojevich would spend his days going gray, all the way to the most heinous pits of despair ever created by mankind.

At any given time, 80,000 men in the US prison system were held in solitary confinement, ten times that of any other civilized country. Most confinement cells were housed in buildings where the cell doors had thin windows to see the outside world or patrolling guards. The cells were also adjacent to one another, so other prisoners could be heard, and conversations could be had through the doors.

By design, ADX Florence made those solitary confinement prisons look like quilting clubs. Only 490 cells were in this prison. The most secure were underground. They were designed to hold the worst of the worst in a manmade hell where they would never see or even have the hope of seeing another human being again. Men like Ted Kaczynski, Richard Reid, and Timothy McVeigh's accomplice, Terry Nichols, would spend the rest of their lives locked away from the rest of humanity.

For the past twenty-one days, Carby had spent twenty-three hours a day in a seven-foot by ten-foot cell. The sterile, claustrophobic room was continuously saturated with artificial light, so he wouldn't know if it was day or night, and his natural rhythms became fogged. Video cameras stared at him like unblinking mechanical sentries as he slept on his poured concrete bed, wrote on his concrete desk, and sat on his concrete stool. Besides the inhuman furnishings, each cell had a toilet and a shower so the men wouldn't have to leave for any reason. He ate his meals in his room and saw no other human beings besides his attorney.

The only time he was allowed out of his cell was once per day to exercise. The double doors would unlock, and the voice of a guard would instruct him to walk down the hall to the yard. But this yard wasn't outside. Nor did it have the grass, trees, or other things usually associated with a yard. It was a small concrete chamber that resembled a sunken swimming pool. All a man could do here was to pace an extra ten feet in each direction.

The isolation and sensory deprivation, or "administrative segregation" as they called it to whitewash its true nature, was intentional. And in spite of multiple lawsuits proving that it violated the US Constitution's Eighth Amendment banning cruel and unusual punishment, it flourished nationwide. The fact that in the early 1900s the increased incidence of insanity and suicide caused by prolonged solitary confinement had been forgotten, the practice re-emerged and proliferated over the past forty years.

Word of Carby's release hadn't been announced prior to today. Mostly it was due to the incredibly speedy and top-secret manner in which it had been approved. So when Special Agent Breskin, newly rehired and dubbed as the domestic counterterrorism czar, showed up to fetch him, the warden and the guards were in a complete and utter state of surprise.

Although the DOJ knew that releasing Carby now would increase America's already cresting panic, they had no choice. In a nation that still had a few laws, arrests had to be conducted in a specific manner that protected the civil and constitutional rights of all citizens. Carby's celebrity attorney had proven in a federal court that his arrest had constituted excessive force.

Video reviewed by the court showed that on the day of his arrest, Carby had been found passively sitting at his dining room table. He'd offered nor threatened any resistance. Still, the bots employed by Agent Zellner at the scene, had violently shocked him into unconsciousness. The shocks had caused a neurological injury that now caused his left eye to twitch. He'd had no weapons and presented no threat, so it had been a clear violation of procedural law and was enough to have a federal circuit judge toss the arrest.

When Warden Michael Cline had challenged the decision to drop the charges, Breskin had agreed. He'd shared the warden's outrage, but said there was nothing he could do about it. The only solace the warden got was when Breskin hinted that he'd be "interviewing" Carby before he "dropped him off" at the Pueblo bus station. Knowing Breskin's reputation, the warden walked away to get Carby from his cell, satisfied in his heart that justice would be done outside of the usual channels.

Carby looked back at Breskin's eyes in the rearview mirror. "That place is the culmination of our failure as human beings," he stated. "It's a clean version of hell."

"And that, my friend," said Breskin, "is just another reason they are being punished."

Carby sighed and looked back out the window. His eyes tracked the upward and downward slope of the tall white-capped mountains. "I suppose it is. But it still saddens me that we do what we do with these big brains of ours. It makes me question the real concept of evolution."

"You mean the theory," Breskin corrected.

"Whatever," Carby replied. He then resumed his attempt to merge himself with the exquisite horizon.

"Where's the turnoff, Tom?" Breskin asked, breaking Carby's reverie. "It's somewhere up here, isn't it?"

Carby leaned forward, casually crossing his arms and laying them on the top of the seat. He looked out the front of the car.

"Just ahead," he said pointing. "Turn right at the Sumo Valley Estates sign. Then drive up past the golf course and follow the dirt road."

Breskin turned east off of Route 67 and wound through a small, residential neighborhood. As he passed a pink tricycle with powder blue handlebars, it struck him as odd that children were playing in the shadow of the prison. That their parents would allow them to jump rope or play patty cake while living so close to the most dangerous, corrupted men on Earth was tragic.

He continued driving, and as they passed the Sumo Valley golf course, the eastern perimeter of the prison appeared on their right. The two most secure complexes were now visible. Each trapezoid-shaped compound was surrounded by double fences of razor wire and massive, modernist-brutalist guard towers that sprang from the ground like tall mushrooms. At the base of each tower was a pickup truck that belonged to the guards who had 360-degree views of the prison and the surrounding area. Along the perimeter fencing and perched atop each tower were high-powered cameras that ingested everything in sight, just in case the guards blinked.

When Breskin was parallel to the backside of the building where Carby had been held, he pulled over and stopped.

"So you're certain you got the recordings from Chauncey?" asked Carby.

"Yes, I listened to them all. And I'll tell you what: I understand why Green and the others want them destroyed. Truth or no, Paunce got them to admit to some incredibly dark things."

Carby pursed his lips and nodded his understanding. He didn't need to know specifics; his imagination was more than enough.

"Then I guess Chauncey really earned his money, huh?" said Carby.

"He earned a lot more than that," Breskin said, the threat in his statement apparent.

"Yeah, he definitely has been a pain in the ass. But you have to hand it to the guy. Even back in Afghanistan, do you remember how disgusted he was when he found out about the MAID? I swear, if we hadn't Shanghaied his ass and sent him back stateside, he would have burned the project to the ground by himself. Kind of a shame nobody listened to him. Who knows, if they had, maybe none of this would have been necessary. Bottom line, he's a better man than us."

Breskin grudgingly agreed, although he wouldn't allow himself to admit it outright. "Guess we'll never know," is all he said.

Carby continued with his melancholy. Maybe he wanted to keep talking because after so many days of isolation he finally had someone there to listen; maybe it was to purge himself. Whatever the reason, it didn't matter. "And it's a real shame about Armagan. He was one of the good ones. Though he likely would have offed himself over it sooner or later."

"Maybe," said Breskin. "That's for the heavenly father to sort out, Tom."

Carby rolled his eyes and sighed. He didn't agree with Breskin's faith or anyone else's for that matter. He was a man of science to the core, and it irked him that a prehistoric concept like religion still held men's belief systems in such a tight noose. For now he kept it to himself. Over the past few years he and Breskin had argued many times over religion. And while they'd usually been respectful and had logical debates that Carby always thought he'd won, Breskin always ended them with the statement, "You just have to have faith." Five aces could not beat the faith card.

The men sat in the parked car looking right, toward the prison. They were each lost in their own thoughts and didn't say a word to reveal their content.

After a bit, Carby said, "Okay, let's do this thang, Doug."

Without a word, Breskin passed his Glock to the backseat. Carby hefted it a couple of times, then jumped out of the car. He yanked open Breskin's door and savagely pulled him from the driver's seat, throwing him to the dirt road. Breskin slowly rose, his hands in the air, fear on his face. He circled the car, backing away from Carby to its prison-facing side. As he moved, Carby followed him, the pistol aimed at his heart.

"See you on the other side," said Carby. He pulled the trigger and Breskin lurched backward like a ragdoll and crumpled to the ground. Carby put the gun in his pocket and checked Breskin's pulse. Satisfied with his findings, he dragged Breskin's limp body to the trunk and threw him inside.

He strode back to the driver's side, but before he got in, he looked directly at one of the prison's surveillance cameras and raised his middle finger. He then jumped back into the car and peeled out, leaving ADX and the Rocky Mountains behind.

Two hours later, from inside the prison, Warden Cline looked up from the video playback monitor. He stood in the prison's main security room, surrounded by guards. His normally pink-faced complexion was devoid of any color whatsoever.

"Holy fuck," he said.

Andy Reed, the security guard who'd noticed the feed and frantically called the warden, responded with a simple, "Yeah."

Had any of the guards been watching the video feeds that monitored the massive prison's perimeter when it happened, they might have seen the execution and escape. They could have alerted the FBI and state police immediately. They didn't know how Carby had gotten the gun from Breskin, or why they'd parked behind the prison. The only thing they knew was that the most dangerous man on Earth had a two-hour head start.

"Holy fuck," the warden repeated.

Chapter Forty-Four

Abdullah Habibi, MAID Subject #16, sat upright, strapped to the table which was now bent on hinges, forming a cold, uncomfortable metallic chair. His fat, hairy arms and legs were secured by clamps that prevented him from moving or standing. His head was held firm at the sides, forcing his gaze forward. He wore the familiar purple fMRI cap, as well as having a blood pressure band around his right bicep and a blood-oxygen clamp clipped to his index finger, all of which were intended to monitor his vital signs for deceptions and possibly near-death situations during the interrogation session.

Although he lacked a beard typically grown by of al-Qaeda or Taliban followers, that didn't mean #16 still wasn't a fanatic. Many terrorists shaved their beards before missions in order to appear normal, and #16 was quite capable of growing one. That much was evident as a thick, dark stubble had formed on his face from the last seventy-two hours he'd spent in a dark cell, hanging from the ceiling by his wrists. He coldly stared straight ahead at the MAID, waiting for the interrogation unit to turn on and begin the session.

From #16's vantage point, the MAID, an acronym for "Multifunctional Automated Interrogation Device" was a freestanding, oak-paneled kiosk with a video monitor. His interrogators would appear on screen and attempt to establish a buddy-buddy relationship with him in order to get answers to their questions. Except that the interrogators were not human. They were a collection of high-resolution, computer-generated avatars that would have made George Lucas envious.

At the start of his interrogations, he'd mused to himself how silly a charade the contraption was. The idea of a robotic interrogator was preposterous. And he would know. He was an eleventh grade science teacher at the Kabul HS for gifted boys. He'd taught the sons of Afghani dignitaries, politicians, and artists. He was a brilliant mind in the service of his country, and one day he would be hailed as a national treasure.

Believing that such a device could be effective on people like him was akin to those insipid American movies that showed explorers giving fire to ignorant, primitive savages as a display of omnipotence. Well, he would neither quake nor be impressed. It was laughable. And to be honest, for a man like #16, it was a bit insulting. Yet he'd decided to play along for as long as the Americans wanted. After all, they'd caught him red-handed making IEDs, so he wasn't going anywhere anytime soon. Possibly, never.

As #16 gazed at the blank monitor of the MAID, its embedded sensors gazed back at him. The unit's interrogation algorithms patiently waited for certain physiological changes that would indicate he was at the proper point to begin. Through its electronic eyes and wires feeding it the data collected by the table's inputs, it silently and darkly monitored #16's pulse, blood pressure, blood-oxygen levels, body temperature, heart rate, respiration, and brain activity, looking for some increased signs of stress. The only sound in the cold room was the unit's soft hum and #16's breathing.

This part of the session was the cyberversion of the silent treatment and had been especially planned for this man. Not only did the MAID's artificial intelligence programming understand how #16 would respond, it was vastly more patient than any subject it encountered.

Three days ago, after #16 had been captured making IEDs in a small bombed-out warehouse just outside of the city, it had used its screening algorithm to obtain basic biographical data, areas of general knowledge, source cooperation, and vulnerability. The goal of this process was to select approach techniques and identify knowledge of critical intelligence tasks. After determining that #16 was likely to have information of value, it ran its "Type of Sources Algorithm" to determine if he was likely to cooperate.

Once his bona fides had been verified through networked Afghan and Pakistani intelligence databases, the MAID set out to create a personalized, noncoercive interrogation plan. It accessed techniques found in preprogrammed counterintelligence interrogation sources like the CIA's KUBARK Counterintelligence Interrogation Manual, the REID Interrogation Manual, Human Resource Exploitation Training Manual, Army Field Manual FM-34-52, KGB Interrogation & Punishment documents, Chinese Interrogation and Indoctrination Processes, and Biderman's voluminous collection of human behavior. From its initial screening and rapport-based conversations, the MAID knew what types of biases and phobias #16 had, and therefore, what types of interrogator avatars he would respond to during interrogations.

At first #16 had been confused by the unorthodox interrogation. He'd known the risks of using his knowledge to make bombs and had been trained by his al-Qaeda handlers in ways to resist the Americans if caught. He'd been extremely well-coached, and in spite of the obvious fears that any man would have in the face of possible torture, had handled himself well. He had, however, been confused by the kiosk and its cartoon questioners. Initially, he'd refused to discuss even the most basic information about himself, but that didn't matter because after a fingerprint scan, the MAID knew his name, profession, salary, spending habits, home address, lineage, religious background, political affiliations, and more. DNA analysis had even determined his current and potential future medical conditions.

#16 had somewhat enjoyed the American "game," and as most of the other subjects had done, tried to outwit the MAID. He'd spoken French, Farsi, Russian, German, and several other languages he knew fluently. The MAID spoke every language he threw at it. At one point he even remarked, "Very clever, Americans. You have a team of interpreters hiding behind your Wizard of Oz curtain."

Although not a devout Shiite like many Afghan men, #16 had read the holy Koran hundreds of times throughout his life. He, however, had only read it so that he could say he'd done so to impress people with his abilities to quote the holy book. He threw bogus passages at the MAID to pierce its supposed omnipotence. Each time he did, the MAID would correct the verse, then attempt to have a discussion of its meaning.

"I see that you have Islamic scholars behind the curtain as well," he said while contemplating his next way to unmask the machine's vulnerabilities.

The interrogation sessions had been conducted by an avatar that resembled #16's favorite college professor. The avatar was dressed in stereotypical American academic garb, complete with a pipe. Even though #16 knew it wasn't really his professor, in spite of himself, a part of him related to the avatar as if it was. And a subliminal part of himself regarded the professor as if he were real and was to be envied. Even still, being the superior intellect that he was, #16 had thrown out questions about cosmology, religion, politics, culture, and more at the professor. Whether the conversation was fluid or required the unit to say "let me think about that" as it accessed the correct information, each time it was able to conduct a stimulating and interesting conversation with no perceptible pause.

After several hours of testing, #16 had become amused. "This isn't so bad," #16 laughed. "If I'm going to be interrogated at least I have someone that is nearly as smart as I."

While #16 laughed, the MAID learned. The table sensors had measured baseline levels in his vital signs, and the MAID's monitor had recorded his visual responses of body language, pupil dilation/constriction, and speeds of reaction, the MAID's professor avatar laughed in agreement. Once rapport had been established and the MAID understood the type of man it was interrogating, it changed its tactics and set out to get the information it needed. Specifically, who else was involved in #16's bomb-making activities? Throughout each session, the MAID's constantly working daemons cross-referenced the information through its internal databases, local intelligence sources, and the NSA's forensic metadata centers in Australia, New Zealand, the UK, and Utah. Although it had its interrogation plan in place, the system was constantly evolving and matching the subject's personality with the most appropriate tactics.

The MAID project was being run through the Science Applications International Corporation and headed by a top SERE psychologist and a master roboticist with a PhD in artificial intelligence, yet it was still subject to some of the same challenges as its human counterparts, albeit less so. The most difficult thing for any interrogator, human, or otherwise, was detecting the truthfulness of a subject who was a good liar. While language, biases, personal desires, and cultural references had been programmed into the MAID, and its sensors were the most sophisticated deception detectors known to man, it wasn't perfect. Especially with a man like #16.

His combination of personality traits made #16 one of the best liars in the animal kingdom. And for those times when false statements slipped through the MAID's cybercracks, it could almost always learn the truth through fact-checking. When those failed to yield the veracity it sought, the device would simply switch to its Coercive Interrogation algorithm. That would determine whether deprivation of sensory stimuli, threats and fear, debility, pain or what combination and duration of enhanced techniques should be utilized.

Before applying any of the EITs, the MAID would run them through the databases of its allowable methods as proscribed by the War Crimes Act, the Torture Victims Protection act of 1991, Common Article 3 of the Geneva Conventions, the Detainee Treatment Act of 2005, The Torture Convention Implementation Act of 1994, the Magna Carta, and even The Bill of Rights. As its final step before choosing a course of action, the MAID would do one last check by applying the "Cheney Algorithm." This program utilized the Torture Memos by Yoo and Gonzalez and then applied Cheney's Law of Interrogation which stated, "Do whatever is legal, but with the caveat that letting innocent detainees die is more acceptable than letting guilty detainees free."

During testing, there had been a steep learning curve for the MAID's programmers. Several detainees had died, and some had become psychotic. But that was the hidden beauty of the device. From a legal perspective, vital organ failures, death, nor insanity could be directly attributed to any man. Therefore the MAID alone was at fault. And since it was a machine, the worst that would happen was that those involved would have to endure a bit of bad press. No doctors or psychiatrists would lose their licenses. No intelligence agents would be prosecuted. And no interrogators would get PTSD.

Not to mention that the deaths showed proper adherence to the Cheney Doctrine, so that logic had been proven. In short, while there would always be bugs in any system, the MAID had acceptable risks. As the grunts who led the detainees in and out of their sessions liked to say, "The MAID ain't perfect, but she always cleans up the trash."

The kiosk silently monitored #16, waiting for some change in his vital signs to indicate growing stress. During the last session, over seventy-two hours ago, the MAID, seemingly getting tired of #16's evasive answers and refusals to give names, had finally threatened him with sensory deprivation. It knew that pain was not a motivator for his personality profile and statistically might strengthen his resolve, but it took into account that he was ego-driven and liked an audience to hear him opine about his brilliance. It concluded that the fear of isolation might loosen his tongue. The kind of isolation, he knew, that would dull his genius by taking away his ability to prove it to people.

The threat had worked. He'd relented and revealed the location and name of his al-Qaeda contact's apartment. #16's ability to control his heart rate and convince himself that he was being truthful had led the MAID to send his intel to a nearby US Marine base. They'd put together a squad to raid the location, but it turned out to be a ruse. In answer to his lie, #16 had spent the last seventy-two hours in a cold, dark cell, hanging from the ceiling, shitting, and pissing on himself.

After over an hour of staring at the silent, blank screen of the MAID kiosk, #16 finally spoke.

"Are you going to talk, or has someone forgotten to plug you in today?" he asked.

The MAID switched itself out of observation mode and the professor avatar appeared. He sat behind a large elegant desk. A bookcase with the Koran, the Hadith, and various academic texts, the titles of which were chosen to impress #16, stood behind him. He tapped his pipe into a heavy glass ashtray, then methodically refilled it with fresh tobacco and tamped it down. After a moment he looked up at #16. He smiled, sympathetically.

"Tsk, tsk, you look awful," said the professor in flawless Farsi. "A man of your prestige deserves better. I suppose it must have been terribly difficult for you to get any sleep."

"You know it was," came the weary response.

"I can only imagine. I felt terrible about ordering it. But you were warned."

#16 shook his head. "You cannot FEEL anything about it. You are not real."

"I suppose not, but your pain is real. I know that you miss conversing with others. You may have that after you've cooperated."

"But I have told you the truth."

"No. You lied. I transmitted your information, and it was proven to be false. Several men nearly died in the mission. It seems that besides being smart, you are very good liar."

#16 was unmoved, though he still loved the compliment. The MAID's sensors could detect no physiological changes to indicate any emotion whatsoever.

"Oh, well," responded #16. "So what does that mean for me? More torture? No more human contact ever?"

The professor mirrored #16's nonchalance. He picked up a solid gold Zippo lighter and flipped open the lid. He effortlessly flicked the wheel and lit the wick. As he looked up at #16, he placed the pipe in his mouth and slowly drew in a breath. The light was pulled toward the tobacco, and puffs of smoke came from his mouth. If #16 hadn't known any better, he would have sworn the professor was real and that he could smell the aromatic, burning tobacco.

"What it means," said the professor, leaning back in his comfortable, brown-leather desk chair, "is that we've blown up your house."

He exhaled a digital cloud as a smaller video box appeared in the lower quarter of the monitor. The MAID's monitors watched #16 as #16 watched a Predator video feed showing his house on Drachma Road. Through the grainy borders of an onboard camera, he could see his simple house situated along the pitted road. The house was larger than the others in the neighborhood, a symbol of #16's prominence as a highly respected professor. After a moment, a Hellfire missile cruised into the frame, causing a strobe of bright, greenish light that momentarily distorted the image. The dust and smoke slowly settled, finally revealing that his house had been reduced to nothing.

The MAID's sensors detected a tightening of #16's jaw and a slight increase in his respiration, but that was the only response. His verbal reaction, however, the volume and speed of his words did not match that finding. He yelled and pulled at his bonds.

"Oh, no! You animals! Was anyone at home? My family? Was my family home?"

"I'm not prepared to answer that right now. But would you care?"

"Of course I would care! They are my family. And you are a failure. If you've killed them you've taken away any motivation I had for telling you anything."

"Telling us what? You've told us you don't know anything. You said that you were making bombs as a hobby and had no idea where the material came from or where the IEDs went after you'd finished making them. Tsk, tsk, such a story," said the professor.

The MAID noted that #16's levels were normalizing. He was clearly in control of himself. The Interrogation Plan algorithm updated instantly as the MAID attempted another gambit. The avatar of the professor gave way to one of #16's wife. Wounded, she sat in the rubble of their home, holding the body of their dead and bloodied son. She looked up, a desperate, forlorn expression on her face. Her voice, while not that of his real wife, was feminine and had the right dialect.

"I understand that you made the bombs because they threatened to kill us if you didn't. I also understand that you won't tell them the truth because they threatened to kill us if you didn't," she cried. She then fell dead on top of their son.

#16 had no reaction over their apparent deaths. He responded to the avatar's words that she "understood." But he spoke to the MAID, not her fiction.

"You understand much."

The avatar switched back to the professor.

"We also understand that you hate the men you are protecting. So why not let us punish them for you?"

"Because I hate the Americans more. I am a Muslim and will not turn on my own people. All of this is your fault."

The professor gave way to another avatar. This time it was #16's imam. Younger than most, the imam kneeled on a prayer rug before the mihrab in a CG version of his mosque. He looked up at #16 and spoke sternly.

"You are also a Shiite and the men you protect are Sunni — not even Afghan. They see you as an infidel. To them you are a dog and they would kill you. Why do you protect them? You would not be welcome in their caliphate."

While momentarily shaken at the appearance of his spiritual leader, #16 quickly regained his composure and disregarded the avatar. He spoke to the room. To the men he presumed were behind the curtain.

"It is true that the Sunni are disrespectable vermin and not of the true faith. They distort the true teachings of Allah, praise be He who is merciful. All of this is moot since you have apparently already killed my family."

The professor appeared on the monitor once again.

"What if we hadn't? What if we could guarantee their safety? Fly them to wherever you want and give them a new life? Would you tell us the name of the men you work for then?"

#16 paused and considered the question for a moment. "Yes," he finally said.

The MAID detected no changes that would verify deception. It was, for lack of a better word, confused.

"Are you telling the truth?" asked the professor avatar.

"No," said #16.

"Are you telling the truth, now? Your answers are contradictory. I know that you are guilty. You will never be freed. So what is the point of being uncooperative? Don't force us to really kill your family."

"You must do as you will," he said.

Beyond that statement, #16 remained unresponsive. Based on the disparity between his words and his physiological response to the video, the MAID was 87.3 percent certain that both the "love of family" and "loyalty to faith" gambits were deadends. #16 cared about neither. The program searched for new potential ways to motivate #16. Although fear of pain was not one of the response points of his personality types, perhaps fear of something else would work.

"This is incidental," said the professor. "We will tell them that you told us what we wanted to know and render all of this useless."

"But I have told you nothing."

Again, a quarter-screen frame appeared on the lower right portion of the monitor. This time, in the frame was #16 himself. He was seated comfortably, as he'd been during the screening portion of his detention.

From off-screen came the voice of the professor.

"Do you work for al-Qaeda?"

"Yes," said #16.

"Do you know the names of the men you work for?"

"Yes. The Sunni are disrespectable vermin and not of the true faith."

"Then you will help us to stop them?"

"Yes."

"Is Kalid Wali Bin Hussein your handler and the man who forced you to make bombs?"

"Yes."

#16 knew that the recording was a fabrication. It was a propaganda piece edited together from pieces of his interrogation to make it look as if he'd turned in his handlers.

"You will kill my family with this falsehood?" he asked.

"Not me. You," replied the professor. "You have all the power here. Just tell us the truth. Save your reputation."

Against his own will, #16's mouth grew dry and his pupils constricted. At the same time, he swallowed harder than normal. The MAID picked up on the changes and pressed. The word "reputation" had triggered the response, so it focused on that aspect of his personality. And since his reputation was based on being a teacher, the MAID looked for the true source of his pride. The monitor filled with a montage of images of dead Afghani teens. The background played audio of youthful screams and explosions. The MAID's professor voice played over the images.

"These could be your students," it said. "Your class at Kabul High. Can you imagine if your peers discovered that you'd withheld information that could save their lives? It would show that you only pretend to care. That you have used your position as a shield and that you are nothing but a selfish, despicable poser who only cares about himself — not jihad. You will be disgraced."

One of the photographs showed Kabul HS in ruins. #16's blood pressure ticked upward. Noting this, the MAID played footage of the blast that had torn it apart. #16 worked his hardest to conceal his emotion. The MAID pressed. It displayed a photo of #16's class that Marines had found in his home after they'd arrested him. It showed all nineteen of his current students smiling and wearing white shirts and ties. His BP and respiration continued to rise.

Like a hunter closing in on its prey, the MAID zoomed in onto the individual faces of the students. #16's vitals slowed a bit as he attempted to fight for self-control. The MAID panned from student to student. When it reached the face of Fatima, #16's student-teacher, suddenly he spiked. The MAID stopped. It slowly zoomed in on her pretty, smiling face. #16's vital signs were going crazy, and the MAID knew the key to his getting his information was close at hand.

"Who is she?" asked the professor.

As the avatar asked, it simultaneously scanned the school's records and found her identity. The MAID cross-referenced her information across all of its networks and found her driver's license. She was Fatima Kashmir, a 27-year old graduate of Kabul University with a master's in engineering. She was unmarried. It displayed her driver's license, circling her address as evidence that it knew where she lived.

"You seem to care about this woman more than either your family or your faith," said the Professor. "Are you having a relationship with her? Tsk, tsk, if that was to get out, it would ruin you, wouldn't it? It would destroy your marriage, you would be disgraced and —"

#16 cut the professor off. He screamed. Tears rolled down his cheeks. "Leave her alone! She is innocent! They will kill her, they have already taken her as a hostage! Oh my god. Oh my Allah, please, please leave her alone!"

At this juncture, whether the interrogator had been human or not, the truth was apparent and the proverbial scent of blood permeated the session. The difference was in understanding. A human being, endowed with a sense of compassion and biological kinship, might have employed a tactic of compassion and tried to use understanding. #16 had gotten himself into a bind. He'd cheated on his wife and been caught by al-Qaeda. If exposed, not only would his beloved mistress be killed, his reputation would be destroyed. And a human who understood that #16 would rather save his reputation more than Fatima might have used her in a different way.

The MAID, however, could never understand this. For all of its algorithms, it would never be able to read the nuances of human behavior. It simply judged him against facts and networks, and databases. It didn't understand that he would give up his beloved Fatima, his family, and anything else to preserve his reputation. So when the professor focused on the girl, promising to protect her, it didn't understand that while his family lived, exposing the truth about Fatima would ruin his reputation. He'd wanted the Americans to kill his family. He'd withheld the truth, hoping they would truly fulfill their threat to kill them if he continued to lie.

"Tell us who they are," the professor asked again. *"We will find her and kill them for you. We will return her to safety and let everyone know that it was your bravery that did this."*

#16 struggled with his own morality. He fought his soul to find the humanity he once had, but it had drowned in his own ego a long time ago. He could not save Fatima or his family if it meant ruining himself.

"I can't," he said.

The MAID knew the truth was there. It was just below surface. All he needed was some coercion. It sent instructions to the table, which responded by straightening. It then lifted #16's arms upward and freed his feet. #16 dangled from his wrists, his toes barely touching the ground.

"Who is your handler?" the professor asked.

"I don't know," #16 cried, still clinging to his primary motivation.

The MAID sent another instruction to the table. It lifted #16 higher, then dropped him violently while keeping his wrists trapped. His arms dislocated from his shoulders. He screamed in pain as the table lifted him again. The avatar of his wife appeared.

"What is the next target?" she asked.

"I don't know," he cried.

Clamps regrabbed #16's ankles to hold him firmly again. The table pushed outward, off its base and began to spin. Turning faster and faster, it spun #16 in a dizzying ride. The MAID became psychotic, changing from avatar to avatar. It was another tactic.

"Tell them what you know," the professor asked.

"You are a dog!" screamed his wife.

"You deserve to die!" said the newly created avatar of Fatima.

As the table continued to spin, #16's vital signs increased. They were off the charts. And, evidencing just one more shortcoming of technology, the MAID's DNA scan had not suggested #16's congenital heart condition. He went into cardiac arrest, then flat-lined. The MAID continued spinning, but applied electrical shocks through the platform in order to revive him. It didn't work.

Slowly, the MAID stopped and reset itself so that #16 could be removed from the table for whatever fate his body had in store. As it waited for the next detainee, it noted in its interrogation log that a guilty man had not gone free.

Chapter Forty-Five

Old school to the core, Chauncey placed a half-gram cube of Lebanese Blonde hash onto a pin he'd shoved through Killa's vintage vinyl Pink Floyd's *The Wall* album cover. Killa had nearly cried as the single pinprick through the white cardboard cover reduced its eBay value by over $500. But Chauncey had paid him $1,000 from his newly acquired riches and said, "Screw those vaporizer pens. This is the best way to smoke hash. Besides, Roger Waters would've approved."

Killa, Diddy, and Phil stood around the Drop Zone's hangar and watched Chauncey light the hash with a wooden match so that it became engulfed in flame. After a moment, he placed a glass upside down over the burning cube and held it flush against the album cover. The lack of oxygen slowly choked out the fire, replacing it with a thin, grayish-white wisp of smoke. The stream rose from the hash to escape but was turned back, trapped by the bottom of the glass. It swirled sideways then rolled down, fogging the inside completely. Once the cube stopped smoking, Chauncey placed his lips at the edge of the glass and tipped it up slightly. Through the gap, he sucked all of the smoke into his lungs.

The THC-infused cloud expanded in his chest, punching at his lungs to escape. Even though it burned, Chauncey held it in. It hurt, but not nearly as much as the past ten years and ten months of his life had. His honesty had cost him his reputation and position with the JPRA, where he'd helped the likes of Killa, Diddy, Phil, and hundreds of others to survive torture with honor and dignity. He'd unwittingly helped Breskin to advance whatever his plan was. Worst of all, he'd lost Marcella. And it was his fault.

Like the smoke, his thoughts expanded and pressed hard against the inside of his mind, attempting to escape. But he held them in and dealt with the pain like he always had.

He wondered if he deserved the pain. If he were being punished by some unseen force for making wrong choices. For being uncompromising with his values and his morality and for being prideful of that. He considered himself to be a good man. His decisions had been made for love of family, for comrades, for honor. Look where it had gotten him. Maybe he was full of shit. Maybe he just lied to himself about his motivation. Had he used principle as an excuse to make himself feel superior or was it simply that the world was just too damned hard for a good man to stay good? And who's to say what good was anyway?

He knew that this mind-fucking was his Achilles heel. His Winston weakness. If he'd ever been captured and tortured they could have subjected him to as much physical stress and pain as they'd wanted. He never would have cracked. For Chauncey, it was the psychological pain that would have broken him. And the older he got and the more failures he experienced, the more vulnerable he became. If you wanted to break Captain Charles Paunce, you'd only have to shove the bamboo shoots beneath his self-doubts. Breskin had known that. He'd tried to break him without direct torture, and it had nearly worked.

When he couldn't take the pressure in his lungs any longer, Chauncey exhaled. He blew out fast and hard, trying to purge both his chest and his mind. Most of the smoke had absorbed into his body so little came out. The self-doubt and frustration, however, emerged as violent coughing.

His friends didn't see the psychic smoke coming out of Chauncey's mouth. They only saw a man getting wasted. They didn't realize that he'd become wasted a long time ago. Wasted in a much larger sense.

The hash did its work. The buzz smoothed the jagged edges off Chauncey's turmoil and he sat back with a melancholy grin that looked like contentment.

"Goddamn," Chauncey finally said after he stopped hacking up a lung. "I needed that."

"Amazing," said Phil. "The world is falling apart and you're getting baked."

"Can't say I blame him," said Diddy. "If the guy who'd fucked up my life got offed by something other than one of my hollow-points, I'd be camped out in a bottle of Hornitos."

Chauncey didn't respond. He knew they meant well. They had his back no matter what. After he'd gone to Killa's Drop Zone and told him about Armagan, Killa had rallied the troops. Diddy and Phil drove to the desert like madmen to see how they could help their brother. They were horrified to hear about Marcella and even more shocked after hearing how Breskin and Carby had not only orchestrated the massacres and tortures, but had used mentally disabled vets to help. You just didn't do that. It was an unforgivable crime. Above all, they were appalled that Breskin had been killed by someone other than Chauncey. There was no justice in that.

Not wanting to be exposed to whatever satellites or drones that were probably looking for him, Chauncey had opted to stay inside Killa's private hangar. So the guys had lit a grill and made brats while they sat on lawn chairs and listened to Chauncey's story.

Two cases of beer and a liter of Kentucky sour mash later, Diddy was still agitated. "After what that bastard Breskin did to you and all of our brothers, I'd have taken revenge to a new level, amigo. I would have shot an AT-4 at his ass from 400 meters and left him in hot lumpy pieces."

Phil laughed and snorted, "Yaa!"

Killa shook his head in disapproval. "Like that's plausible. You're just gonna walk up to a guy in broad daylight with an Anti-Armor bazooka? Why don't you just order an ACME guided missile and set the selector on 'Ass Hole'? I'd be much more subtle. What was that movie where that Rutger dude shoved a frag grenade in Gene Simmon's mouth while he was tied up and pulled the pin?"

Phil answered, "It's *Wanted Dead or Alive* and the guy was Rutger Hauer."

"That's it! *Wanted Dead or Alive*. BOOM!" said Killa.

Killa and Diddy exchanged a high-five and yelled out, "Hell, yeah!"

"You guys have no imagination," said Phil. "A sicko like Breskin deserved a truly distressful way to die. I would've crawled up to his house at 0300, cut all his power, jammed his cellphone signal, ninja'd my ass to his bedroom with NVGs, zip-tied him, then dragged him outside to raise him on his own flagpole and flame-throwered him head to toe till he was a crispy critter. Then, I would've roasted a marshmallow on his flaming, screaming ass and enjoyed a hot fucking s'more on my way home."

The full visual of Phil's vengeance played out in the men's minds. As one, they bellowed out, "Hooyah!"

"Damn," said Chauncey. "What a buzz-kill. Remind me to never piss off any of you guys."

Chauncey knew they were trying to make him feel better over his now obliterated opportunity to exact revenge on Breskin. And if anyone had a right and sufficient cause to want vengeance, it was him. It just wasn't in his DNA. Not murder as revenge, that is.

"I'm not saying I didn't want to get all *Game of Thrones* on the guy," said Chauncey, "But killing someone you hate to get revenge isn't the best way to get revenge. The desire for vengeance is powerful, and I was using that power as motivation to stop him from whatever he was doing. Well, my motivation is even stronger now. Breskin may be dead, but my true revenge will be to make sure he died in vain."

"Well you'd better hurry up because after what Armagan told you and what's happening out there, it be coming to a head right now," said Phil.

Phil was referring to the riots that had broken out in the hours following the news broadcast of Carby's escape. The footage of Breskin's execution had been leaked to every news channel. The pent-up fear and anxiety resulting from Armagan and Breskin's nine-month terror spree had suddenly erupted. The public just didn't know that Breskin was behind the terror. To the nation, the boogieman had escaped and killed the man trying to protect them.

Mob mentality ruled. It had taken hours for Diddy and Phil to get across the Coronado Bridge because of protesting and cops. Students from UCSD were getting unruly in Balboa Park. From what they heard on the car radio, someone had even blown up the fountain. Besides the few peaceful protests, anyone who wanted an excuse to loot and burn now had one. It was like the sixties on steroids but without a noble cause.

The National Guard and police departments were dressed in riot gear and using their army surplus weaponry to subdue the masses any way they could. In many instances that meant Tasers, batons, and rubber bullets. The president appeared in an effort to restore confidence. He said that people needed to stay calm or he would have to impose martial law. Nobody cared. It was stupid. No matter how good your speechwriters are, you can't allay fears with words.

Even the president's announcement that in order to protect Americans he was going to sign a bill that would give broad powers of surveillance to the nation's peacekeepers didn't help. If anything, it made things worse. The big IT firms became belligerent, and the anarchists and violent liberal fringe joined the fracas. They smashed CCTV cameras on traffic lights, in subways, on banks, and everywhere else they could, all while screaming, "Down with Big Brother! Down with the Police State!"

It was even worse than the days following 9/11. Phil was right in saying that they had to act fast. Breskin and Carby had apparently succeeded in breaking the country. Unfortunately, in order to fix it, Chauncey needed information. His gut told him that if he could decipher what Armagan had told him, he could stop the madness.

Because he blamed himself for helping Breskin, he felt that he had to stop it himself. He was just getting a final buzz and summoning his energy to beat down the demons for one last great charge. He had the skills, God knows he had the motivation, now he just needed the plan.

Before dying, Armagan had told Chauncey that two more lifestyle event massacres had been planned: a birth and a funeral. Those were the culmination of the twisted plan. Chauncey and his buds had discussed the possibilities for hours.

"Those massacres had to have taken months, maybe even years of planning," said Killa. "And you can't plan a funeral that far ahead of time because you don't know the exact date and time someone's going to die."

"Unless you're terminally ill," added Phil.

"Or it's going to be a murder," said Diddy. "Then you can plan it down to the second."

Chauncey stopped them. "There are too many engineers to be able to figure it out that way. A birth and a funeral? Who's pregnant? What's the due date? Who would they murder? Impossible! Besides, without Breskin and Armagan, the torture element is gone. The fear element isn't necessary anymore because the country's already going berserk, which is what they wanted. The plan was called Panopticon. That's a theory that says you can get complete social obedience through pervasive surveillance. General Atomics, AeroVironment, i-Robot, the bill the president just mentioned. The plan was to terrorize the country enough that they would give anything, including their freedom, to be protected."

"If that's the case, those CEO friends of yours are about to become the most powerful men on the planet," said Killa. "Let's grab them and have Chauncey make 'em spill their guts."

"How are you going to grab the guys who control the cameras?" asked Phil.

"Even if you did, you guys know that I won't torture them," said Chauncey. "First of all, it's immoral. Secondly, it doesn't work. And third, after what I taught them, Breskin could return from the grave and they'd be able to resist until it's too late."

The guys fell silent. None of them liked what was happening, but none of them knew what to do. They each contemplated the new America in which they were about to live. They'd each dedicated their lives and fought for freedom. Everything they'd risked life and limb to protect was about to be eradicated.

"If their goal was terror, then why aren't they done?" asked Killa.

"Obviously, that wasn't the end game," said Diddy.

"Yeah, well, we can't just ask Breskin or Armagan," said Phil. "Dead men tell no tales."

The room became quiet again. The silence was ended a moment later by the sound of Chauncey's cellphone as it began to vibrate and skitter across a table. Since everyone who had his private number was here, he had no idea who it was. Until he looked at the screen.

"Maybe dead men do tell tales," Chauncey grinned. "I put a kinetic GPS micro transmitter in the audio tapes of my sessions with the CEOs. Whenever the tape moves, it activates the transmitter."

"And they're moving?" asked Killa.

"Yup. Someone is playing them right now. At Armagan's lab."

Chapter Forty-Six

In spite of the Army's policy against sending condolence letters to the next of kin on behalf of soldiers who had committed suicide, three of the five sealed envelopes sitting on Colonel Brewster's desk were just that. Even though it wasn't true, he'd penned them to say the men had died bravely, that they'd been killed in action while defending Camp Omega from a Taliban raid. On the one hand, he'd lied to spare the families undue grief and to ensure they'd receive the death benefits due to every fallen soldier no matter what the cause of death. On the other hand, he'd written them in order to circumvent any official investigations that would have revealed the true cause of their passing.

Captain Thomas Carby and Douglas Breskin, PhD, sat in front of the colonel's desk, somber and silent. They looked at the stack of envelopes and sadly remembered the faces of the men whose lives had been reduced to some ink on letterhead. They realized their families would never know the truth. Four of the soldiers had served as detainee and gate guards, the fifth had been a lieutenant who had created the artificial intelligence portion of the MAID's algorithms. Neither Carby nor Breskin envied Brewster the task of writing the letters, but both of them agreed with what he'd said.

For a time, nobody spoke. All were steeped in the merciless silence of their own guilt. As senior members of the team, Brewster had brought them in to tell them that the deaths had marked the end of this phase of the MAID project. Even though the end of the project represented an authentic "too little, too late" scenario, Breskin and Carby were relieved beyond words that it was over.

At first they'd all been gung-ho about the MAID. Breskin, because it allowed him to create the perfect interrogator, one that was free of bias, human fallibility, and indecisiveness. He'd reverse-engineered the SERE tactics he'd perfected in Spokane with Chauncey and been given the opportunity to show the world how enhanced interrogation, when properly employed, could be effective in getting actionable intelligence that would save lives and not cost any in the offing. Carby's participation hadn't been for nearly as lofty a reason. He'd been brought in because of his engineering and robotics brilliance. It represented a once in a lifetime chance to develop something cutting edge and that was, in his words, "fuckin' cool, man." For Colonel Brewster, it had been a chance to spare American soldiers the trauma of torturing the enemy, even if they did deserve it. He'd seen interrogators, interpreters, and guards alike suffer gravely from what he'd deemed a necessary, albeit regrettable, practice. Whatever their reasons, all three of them now knew they'd been horribly, tragically, deathly wrong.

Everyone who'd been a part of the MAID program had undergone psychological evaluations by Breskin to make sure they not only shared the philosophical belief that these tactics were morally and ethically correct, but that they had the intestinal fortitude to endure the impending brutality that the project comprised. Only true patriots had been accepted through the gates of the black operations site, Camp Omega. For God and country was the mantra they'd all subscribed to at the start. At the end, there was no honor for any of them.

As the MAID began filling body bags with corpses that had produced no reliable information, it became clear that all they had created was an elaborate system for murdering Muslims. Even Brewster's original assertion that in the face of failure nobody would be to blame was now exposed as preposterous claptrap. They were all culpable. Machines serve their masters and do their bidding no matter what anyone said. If a nuke was launched in error because of a computer algorithm, it was the fault of those who'd created and given the computer the power. This was no different.

Brewster, Carby, Breskin, and Lieutenant Brooks had sincerely believed the project just needed some tweaks. Brewster had reported the casualties and promised better results for the first three months. He then barked at Breskin and Lieutenant Brooks to make the fucking thing work. They worked long hours, searching every brain cell they had in order to improve those results.

When it became clear to them and to the soldiers tasked with leading prisoners, at first to and from their cages to the MAID, then, from the MAID to shallow, limestone-lined graves, that the project was just a sophisticated and Kafkaesque guillotine, they'd implored Brewster to end it. It had taken Carby just six deaths to break, Breskin ten, and Brewster a cool dozen to finally admit its monstrous futility. Brewster had ruefully requested to his CO that they end the project, but was rebuffed., "POTUS wants results. We need information. Our boys are dying," was the response. They were stuck in a nightmarish quagmire from which the only escape was a court-martial.

So they'd kept going and with each additional death or MAID-induced insanity, they worked harder to make it succeed. Their motivation morphed from getting intelligence that would save the lives of Americans to saving the lives of the detainees. It became a battle to save their own psyches. A battle they had lost.

Carby had been the first to crack. It had happened when the blood from one of the dead detainees had spurted into the kiosk and fried some of its sensors. As he cleaned circuits and replaced hardware, his hands shook. He muttered to himself and begged the MAID to work. For Breskin it had been when one of the detainees had shrieked that they were not God. It was true that they'd all said it. But there was something about having an imam say it that shook him to his core. It was the first Muslim cleric he'd ever really listened to, and he knew that what he said was true. Colonel Brewster, a career soldier whose blood flowed red, white, and blue, had remained dogged until he'd had finished writing the five letters that now sat on his desk.

The official story, the one that would cloak the truth forever, was that three nights ago, after the MAID accidentally killed Detainee #16, Sergeants Fussell and Kennis had heard a gunshot from Lieutenant Brooks' office. Racing to the sound, weapons drawn, they'd found him slumped over his computer with a six-inch crater in the back of his head. Just before pulling the trigger of his service weapon, he'd sent an email to someone that said, "I'm a monster. I'm sorry. I love you."

Rather than follow protocol and report the incident to Colonel Brewster, the men were shattered. It was the final straw in a two-year nightmare that pushed them far beyond the edge of their ability to cope. They immediately went to the detainee cellblock and led two of the surviving prisoners to the front gate to set them free. They didn't care if the men were terrorists or goat herders. They didn't care if they came back the next day and blew Camp Omega to kingdom come. They couldn't deal with the guilt anymore. Depression, rage and PTSD had gotten the better of them both. Before they could set the men free, two of the guards at the gate confronted them. At gunpoint, they ordered Fussell and Kennis to return the men to their cages. They'd refused and opened fire on their comrades instead.

When Colonel Brewster had been summoned to the gate moments later, he found six dead men. The detainees lay face down, apparently shot by the gate guards. The gate guards had been killed by Kennis and Fussell. Kennis and Fussell had died the same way Brooks had. Brewster no longer had any separation between the hell of being awake and being asleep.

"We're done here, gentlemen," Colonel Brewster finally said to Carby and Breskin. "The powers that be have pulled the plug on MAID."

Breskin and Carby nodded, silently digesting the meaning of the words. After two years of pain, it was finally over. Over in the physical sense, that is. They would no longer have to hurt and kill on a daily basis. They knew, however, that the pain inside would never go away. The blood, the deaths, and the sounds of the detainees screaming and begging for mercy, spitting and accusing, hating, would follow them to their graves.

"Thank God it's over," said Breskin in an uncharacteristic display of surrender.

"You'll be happy to know that there won't be an investigation. As far as the world knows, none of this ever happened," Brewster added.

Carby instinctively snorted. "Big whoop," he said.

Brewster looked up. "Carby, you're being reassigned to a robotics unit in Kabul. They're working on some autonomous UGVs called MULEs. They can apparently move into small towns and take out unfriendlies; supposedly they can tell the good guys from the bad all by themselves. Breskin, since you're a private *contractor, consider this the end of your contract. Your plane leaves at 0600. I hope you enjoy the money."*

"What about you?" asked Carby.

"I'm getting a promotion and heading stateside to head up the next phase of the MAID project. It's DoD, but being championed by Senator Stevens, the head of the US Senate Select Committee on Intelligence."

The statement hung in the air like the thick, gray cloud that surrounds an evil Tolkien mountain. Each man knew what it meant. In spite of the wake of dead bodies and shattered souls the MAID had left behind, the government thought it was worth pursuing. Lost in their own miserable thoughts, they each saw dead Muslims, Russians, North Koreans, Chinese, and even Americans hanging limp from the straps on the stainless steel table.

"But it doesn't work," said Breskin. "We did all we could. A machine can't determine the truth any better than a human. And even if it could, it doesn't have the capacity of mercy. And I was wrong about EITs. They don't work either. We didn't produce one shred of good intel here. Not only was it a disaster, but it was an affront to the Lord. How can they continue? Didn't we send enough poor souls to the hereafter proving that?"

"Apparently not," said Brewster. "I tried to tell them. I even declined the promotion. But they've already sent out RFPs and have them coming out of the yin-yang from bot companies and universities. Seems that everyone's got a hard-on to do this. Like we did."

"We have to stop them. They're going to destroy some great young minds," said Carby, his rage stirring just below the surface. "I fucked up. I thought it was cool. No. Strike that. I didn't think at all. I betrayed my intelligence. You have to think about what your work is going to do. You have to connect the dots. Even if they aren't obvious, you've got to make 'em up and follow the invisible threads, then refuse if it leads to the dark side. This can't happen, Colonel. It has to be stopped."

"Don't you think I know that? I've committed more than murder here. I've destroyed my men. Men who trusted me. And when I reported it, the brass didn't care. Soldiers are just cogs in the machine. Me included." He took a breath then said, "I'm not going to do it. I'm going to resign my commission."

"It's against God's will," said Breskin, agreeing with Carby and Brewster, but for different reasons. "We've helped to break the world by bringing this Frankenstein into existence. We need to repair it."

Carby was suddenly on his feet. He towered over Breskin, his fists clenched in rage. He spit in Breskin's face with his words. "What the hell do you know about broken?! It was your fucking idea! You were the one who said it was possible. You wrote that goddamned paper! The one everyone believed. Mr. Big-Fucking SERE man. We believed you! And I brought in Brooks!"

He fell back to his seat, all of the hate gone, replaced with sagging, empty eyes. "My poor, brilliant Brooks. Every time one of those poor bastards died because the MAID couldn't decipher the truth, he blamed himself. He was too fragile for this. He'd weep every night. 'I'm not asking the right questions,' he'd say. Over and over and over." Carby spun back to Breskin, "You killed him, you smug fuck! You killed my Michael. That fucking email he sent was to me!"

Breskin and Brewster didn't know what to say. They'd suspected that Carby and Lieutenant Brooks had been lovers, but they'd never understood the truth of it. The depth of it. They felt beyond dreadful.

"Colonel, you can't resign," said Breskin. "We have to stop them. We have to repair the damage we've done. For your men, for Brooks, for God. But I'll need your help."

Chapter Forty-Seven

Although Chauncey normally won arguments with his buddies, after about thirty minutes it had been clear he was going down on this one. If he wanted their help to raid Armagan's lab, it was going to be their way or the highway. They'd all agreed that whoever was playing the tapes needed to be grabbed, but, to a man, they all said Chauncey wasn't participating in the takedown.

"We're SEALs, pal. It's what we were trained to do," Killa explained.

"Well, technically, it's what we *did* about ten years ago," added Phil, for accuracy. That comment prompted a stereo punch in the shoulders from both Diddy and Killa.

Chauncey had tried argument after argument, but no matter what gambit he chose they wouldn't budge. When he got desperate, he'd even tried the ridiculous ploy they used in lame movies by calling them a bunch of losers whom he didn't even like, so they should just go away. That was met with a couple of mock tears and sad, hound-dog howls from Diddy. But this wasn't a movie. It was as real as life got, and few men were ever this close to the nerve that ran down its spine. Finally, he'd told them the truth. That he loved them like brothers and didn't want them to risk their lives on his behalf.

"Listen, bud," said Killa. "We respect that you don't want us dragged into this any further, but besides being your friends, some bastards used our brothers to get what they wanted. Well, I'm using my desire for revenge as motivation to take down whoever it was."

Chauncey couldn't argue with that logic. He'd simply nodded and said, "Gear up."

The booze and the hash had been put away, strong coffee brewed, and they'd all started rummaging through Killa's treasure trove of sophisticated, stolen equipment. Like kids in a lethal candy shop, they pulled out amazing gear. As they did, their plan emerged. Fifteen minutes later, they'd devised a way to approach the lab and grab whoever it was that was playing the tapes. Chauncey had explained everything he knew about Armagan and the lethal robots that had attacked his home. He'd told them about the drones at Carby's house and how he'd beaten them.

Chauncey knew he was damned lucky to have them. In their prime, they'd been some of the finest Spec Ops troops in the game. And even though they were out of the game, not one of them had lost the fire in the belly. He knew deep down that their expertise and experience in missions like this were far superior to his. Their mutual admiration and respect for one another was only to be found in men who'd served together.

In the end, their preparations for sophisticated defenses hadn't mattered. When they'd arrived at Armagan's lab, they'd used an L3-made Ranger-R handheld radar sensor to determine how many people were in the building. Its radar waves had penetrated the building and bounced back, revealing only one person inside. As luck is always a welcome member of any team, the guy apparently had finished his work and was headed to the exit door. Phil was there, waiting with a Taser, a pair of zip-ties, and a hood.

Nobody had wasted any time trying to see who the guy was. They'd simply tossed his limp body into Chauncey's ice truck and hightailed it out of there. As they drove, Chauncey and Killa pulled off the hood and revealed Tom Carby's unconscious body. It was the last thing that Chauncey had expected, but it did clear up a host of questions.

Carby couldn't have known about the tapes unless Breskin had told him. Breskin's murder must have been planned, and Carby was a part of Panopticon. Probably the other guy Armagan had mentioned. As Chauncey considered the myriad possibilities that this represented, Killa had secured Carby to a chair bolted to the floor of truck.

Once they'd put some respectable distance between themselves and the lab, Killa banged on the side of the truck. Diddy pulled over to let Killa out, then continued driving. Chauncey remained, leaning against the back wall of the truck contemplating Carby's still unconscious body. He considered as many explanations as he could think of as to why, rather than going into hiding, Carby had been in the lab mucking with the tapes. Ultimately, he knew that only Carby held the answer to that and his other questions.

Chauncey listened to Carby's breathing and felt the road passing beneath the truck's tires as he waited for the man to regain consciousness. He didn't know exactly what information the tall man sitting there would give up or how hard he'd have to push, but Chauncey was sure it would lead him to the culmination of the most heinous rampages he'd ever seen. A rushing river of questions flooded his mind, and like a gold miner standing in turbulent water, he panned for the best nuggets. He calmed himself and formulated a hasty interrogation plan. Just as he thought of his open, Carby stirred.

His eyes opened slowly and he blinked a few times. He groaned and rolled his neck. As he drew a long breath through his nose, Carby tried to lift his hands but couldn't because they were tied behind his back. The fog of a thousand volts evaporated and his eyes jolted open. He stared around the dark truck trying to understand where he was. Providing him with a silent answer, Chauncey flicked on a lamp that sat beside him. The directed floodlight bathed Carby in a harsh white beam. He straightened and brought his shoulders back, defensively.

"Good morning, Sleeping Beauty," Chauncey said.

Carby squinted and looked through the beam of light to see who'd spoken. In spite of his clearly disadvantaged position, he smirked.

"Chauncey," he said. "How are you, man?"

Chauncey took in Carby's nonchalance. "I'm good, Tom. Nice to see you."

"Ditto there," Carby said. His voice was filled with what seemed to be great relief.

"Yeah," said Chauncey. "Better me than the police, huh?"

Carby looked around the truck, surreptitiously tugging at his bonds to test their strength. "Where are we?" he asked. "This your new home since yours got blown up? It's good you got something with A/C," he added attesting to the cold temperature.

"Just an old ice truck. I like my beer really cold, mate, and out here in the desert you can never count on finding one when the mood hits."

"That's nice," Carby replied, not responding to Chauncey's attempt at humor. "So what are we doing here? Why am I tied up in your mobile fridge?"

"Well, Tom," said Chauncey, matching Carby's condescending tone with a bit of sarcasm, "I have a few questions I'd like to ask. Do you mind?"

Carby pulled back the corners of his mouth and sucked in a breath. He shrugged then said, "Yeah. Sure thing. Whatever you want. I mean, you're clearly in charge, amigo."

Rather than ask anything, Chauncey silently studied Carby. The longer he watched, the more uncomfortable Carby became. His eyes moved left and right and he drew his knees tightly together. His mouth was rigid. The silence continued. All either of them could hear was the wheels on the road.

Carby rolled his head around, trying to loosen himself. He cracked his neck to both sides. Chauncey noted that he was clearly stressed but trying to appear calm. He watched him for as long as it took Carby to reach the end of his fidgeting and look forward again.

"Well?" Carby asked, a bit irritated.

"Well, what?" asked Chauncey.

"Questions. You said you had some questions."

"I do. But not all questions are verbal."

"Ah, checking my body language," said Carby. "I forgot. You're the Grand Inquisitor, ain't you? Quasimodo or some shit?"

"Torquemada," Chauncey corrected. "And, no. I'm definitely not him. He was a really, really bad guy. You don't want me to be him."

Carby sighed loudly. "Whatever."

"You seem uncomfortable, Tom. You okay?"

"Of course I'm fucking uncomfortable. I'm doing some work, and when I go to leave I get zapped by a Taser or something, then I wake up in the back of a truck tied to a shit chair with a goddamned nail or something poking me in my ass. What's that, some interrogator trick to keep me off balance?"

"Actually, it is," said Chauncey. "All of this, the chair, the light in your face, the cold, the nail; it's all intended to make you feel stressed. But you know that. You know a lot about interrogation, Tom. Especially the 'enhanced' kind. I think you even know it's not Quasimodo, don't you, you crazy joker you?"

Now it was Carby's turn to stay quiet. He knew who Chauncey was, and since he knew he wouldn't be tortured, that worry was out of the equation. In spite of that knowledge, he still felt vulnerable and, if he were being honest with himself, a bit afraid. Chauncey was looking right through him, past him, and out the front of the truck. It was the same thing that Breskin could do, but even better. He didn't see any advantage to going against him. Not yet, at any rate.

After what seemed like hours Carby was unable to bear the silence.

"So where are we headed?" he asked. "You taking me back to prison so they can stick me in that Gitmo-style isolation cell? I sure hope you don't drive through San Diego. I hear they're rioting in the streets."

"They're rioting in the streets all over the country, Tom. Thanks to you and Breskin. The president declared martial law and governors deployed the National Guard everywhere. So, no, we're not going into any densely populated areas. Just driving around the desert. There are miles and miles of desolate, unpatrolled roads out here. Not too much civil unrest to worry about. And you should be happy we're in an ice truck. It's much cooler in here."

"Yeah," said Carby. "Lucky me."

Chauncey had spoken the truth. They were driving around the desert. And it was much cooler in the truck. But in spite of the temperature being a cool sixty-eight degrees Fahrenheit, Carby had begun perspiring. It was precisely what Chauncey had been waiting for.

"Why'd you want me to find you, Tom?" Chauncey asked.

"Pardon?" said Carby.

"You're one of the smartest men I've ever met. There's no way you didn't know those tapes had transmitters in them. I may have fooled Breskin because he's not that technical. Well, not in that way at any rate."

Carby let out a laugh and nodded his head furiously. "Yeah, he's a bit of a fuck-tard when it comes to scientific stuff. But you're clearly not so technical yourself. They were pretty easy to spot. So let's just say you were right. I'd rather it was you that picked me up and not the police."

"Why is that?"

Carby snorted derisively. He then sucked a large wad of snot from him nose and spat it on the floor of the truck.

"I sure hope you guys got a lot of gas because we're going to be driving around for a lonnng time."

"Really?" asked Chauncey. "I don't think so."

"It's a free country. Think whatever you want, while you still can," Carby said.

"I don't think this is going to take that much time. You wanted me to find you because you want to tell me something. You probably don't even realize it."

"Whoo-wee!" Carby suddenly yelled out like was at a rodeo. "You really are a great interrogator there, Chauncey. You got me figured out better than a Texas whore knows a horny senator."

"Well, I'm sure as hell a better interrogator than you are an engineer. How'd that torture table you jimmied up work? I mean the one that *didn't* work. The one that killed everyone you strapped to it."

Carby's mood shifted to something soft. His bravado faded and he glared toward Chauncey. "You don't know shit," he said quietly.

"I know a lot more than you think. I know that torture breaks more than one person; it also breaks the torturer. And just looking at you, sitting there with a fake, smug expression, fidgety, shifty-eyed, sweaty, I know it shattered you. I know it's why you killed those engineers. I know it's why Breskin tortured and executed them." He paused for a moment, then added, "I know it's what killed your boyfriend, Brooks."

"Shut the fuck up!," Carby screamed at the mention of Brooks. "You don't know squat! You left. You left because you couldn't do what had to be done!"

Chauncey ignored Carby's attempt to get him riled. There was no way he was going to be dragged into an argument.

"Relax, Tom," he said. "We're just having a friendly chat. Don't get yourself all worked up." Then, without missing a beat, Chauncey completely shifted the conversation.

"After you digitized those audio tapes, who'd you email them to?"

Carby was thrown by the sudden change of direction. Before he could adjust, Chauncey changed it again.

"What's the final lifestyle event, Tom?! Why'd you keep me alive?! I know it was you, not Armagan. Why'd you want me to pick you up?!"

Needing something to grab, Carby seized the last question. He didn't even think about what he was saying. It just came out.

"Because I need to know why it didn't work. Why couldn't that goddamned MAID tell the truth from a lie."

It was the question Carby had been asking himself for the past ten years. It was the question that Brooks had asked before he shot himself. The question Carby had alluded to when he saw Marcella during the protest at General Atomics. It was the question that he couldn't answer, no matter how much he studied or thought or contemplated, and the lack of an answer was tearing him up inside.

Chauncey pursed his lips and sat back. He understood the question. He understood that to an empirical man like Carby, a man who believed that science held the answers to every question, the fact that he'd failed so miserably was destroying him. He wasn't an evil man. He meant good. He'd just made a horrible decision for all the wrong reasons, and it had destroyed him along with everyone else in the process.

"I'll make a deal with you, Tom," Chauncey said. "I'll tell you why the MAID didn't work if you tell me where and when the funeral and the birth are going to take place."

There was a decided shift in Carby's demeanor. A mellowness came over him. His body and his face became smooth and still. His shoulders relaxed. But it was his eyes that Chauncey noticed most. They looked straight ahead, no quivering or darting. Behind them was a blankness, a void that revealed a disconnection with reality. It took Chauncey's breath away.

"Okay," said Carby in a chilling voice. "But let's add something to your dealio. You have to torture the truth out of me. And you have to torture me really bad. Push me to the edge, then shove me over the side. Break me, Chauncey. Break me or you'll never find out the truth."

Chauncey looked straight ahead, considering what Carby was asking.

"It's the ticking time bomb scenario, brutha," Carby continued. "Over there we never knew if they really had information. Most of them didn't. We just used that excuse because 'maybe it was.' Maybe. Well, there's no maybe here, kemosabe. It's no bueno. It's the real deal. This is GW's wet dream."

His eyes began to roll around in unison with his head as he kept going.

"Something bad's about to go down and I know what it is. The shooter's in the mall. An Ebola bomb's in the White House! There's a nuke in Times Square! Beware! Beware! Now torture me, fucker! Torture the shit out of me!"

Chauncey was stunned. The brilliant, charming, personable man he'd known in Afghanistan had been so destroyed by what he'd done that he was asking to be tortured. He wanted to be punished and was asking Chauncey to do it. Yet Chauncey knew there was another reason. Carby wanted to be punished, but it couldn't be by just anyone. It had to be Chauncey. He had to have another man trade his morality like he had. The act wouldn't change anything. It wouldn't heal Carby, but in some dark part of himself, he hoped it would make him just a little bit less weak.

Though there wasn't a snowball's chance in Afghanistan of it happening, Chauncey considered the request. Carby was evil and deserved to be in pain. He even deserved to die. There were so many reasons to do it. He'd helped to corrupt and cause the death of Armagan. He'd been complicit in the death of Marcella. He'd killed and tortured hundreds of Muslims and now Americans, and he'd used innocent, mentally ill veterans to help.

Chauncey shook his head, slowly. He wasn't going to torture anyone. Not for Carby. Not for Marcella. Not for anything.

"No deal, Tom," he said. "My morality doesn't have a price tag."

"It had to be done! And you were a coward for leaving," Carby said, desperately trying to reinforce the rickety justifications he knew had never worked.

Chauncey was disgusted. "Is that how you justify it? By saying it had to be done? Give me a break, Tom. You did it because it was cool. You knew it was wrong but you still did it. You said, 'If I don't do it they'll just get someone else to do it,' right? And because you lacked the strength of your convictions you've pretended to be this ethical, moral guy, and you've been punishing engineers for your own failing. Well, I left and I told you not to do it. I wasn't a coward, Tom. I came back here and told everyone that would listen. I spent two years in jail for being a whistleblower. But nobody listened to me. And after that congressional torture report came out, nobody called to say they were wrong. Well, you were wrong, Tom. You killed the man you loved. Brooks only did it because you asked him to."

He paused for a moment, watching Carby. He was as rigid as a tree and listening intently.

"Is my morality the only thing you're willing to accept in exchange for doing the right thing?" Chauncey went on. "You've already killed the engineers to scare them. You already took Brooks' morality, didn't you? You already took another man's soul for the sake of your narcissism. Was it worth it?"

The question dangled there for a moment. Then Chauncey continued, "What if I had something else to wager? Say I could get you out of the country and satisfy your curiosity at the same time?"

Carby stared at Chauncey with an intensity that hurt. His nostrils flared as his breaths pushed them in and out.

"I'm listening," he said.

"I've got some mates I worked with in Australia that own a bit of land in Malaysia. It's on the coast and they've got armed mercs all over the place to keep out the Kumpulan Mujahidin, so it's next to paradise. What if I could arrange for you to go there and live out the rest of your life? The water's warm and blue, the trees are lush and green, and there's thousands of pretty, young island boys just waiting for a man like you to take care of them."

Ignoring the swipe, Carby asked, "And if I don't agree?"

"Then I don't answer the question you need answered and you end up in a hole ten feet deeper than Ramzi Yousef's, mind-fucking yourself twenty-four seven, times the rest of your life."

Chauncey could see Carby struggling with his offer. He wanted to take it, but he was afraid. Unsure. Chauncey pushed a bit harder.

"Come on, Tom. Dig deep. Find the logic. What's the best possible scenario if you don't do this?"

"You could just kill me," said Carby.

"Not gonna happen, mate."

Carby was silent. He thought about his choices, not only in this moment, but over the last twelve years of his life. He only saw more pain and he didn't want it.

"Okay," said Carby. "You got a deal."

"Good. Now tell me about the final events."

"It's not two events, it's one," Carby said. "It's a birth and a funeral at the same time. Monday night, at ten Eastern Time, the president's going to sign that new surveillance bill on national television. Senator Stevens of the CEOs involved in Panopticon will be watching at Steven's house. Just as they toast the birth of their newer, greater surveillance state, they're going to be executed."

"By who?" Chauncey asked.

"General Brewster," said Carby.

Chauncey disguised his surprise. This changed a lot of things. As an adversary in the mind, Breskin was formidable. But as an enemy in the physical sense, Brewster was worse. He had a lot other questions, but given the information he'd just gotten, he had enough.

"Thanks, Tom," is all that Chauncey said.

Carby nodded, then said, "Now what's the answer? Why didn't the MAID work? The AI was perfect. Why couldn't it tell the difference between the truth and a lie? What were we missing?"

Chauncey banged on the side of the truck with his fist. Understanding that was the signal to pull over, Diddy stopped the truck.

"What's the answer, Chauncey? We had a deal?"

The door to the rear compartment opened, flooding the truck with light. Chauncey got up and went to the door.

"What's the fucking answer?! Tell me! What the fuck did we do wrong?" Carby shrieked.

Chauncey shook his head, sadly. "Everything," he said.

He turned to Phil, whose head appeared from outside. "We need to move."

Chauncey jumped out of the truck and closed the door. From inside the truck, he heard Carby's muffled screams and his head banging against the wall.

Chapter Forty-Eight

It had taken all of a second for Chauncey to figure out that Green and the others were going to be executed because of their connection to the MAID project. They were the reason it had been kept alive. They'd used their connections to Senator Stevens in both the Armed Services Committee and the Drone Caucus to make sure it continued being funded, even though General, then Colonel, Brewster had requested it be stopped. Considering the deaths it had caused, it should have been canned and swept under a Snowden-proof carpet, but given who the players were and what they were after, it made sense.

Whether Panopticon had been the brainchild of Brewster, Carby, or Breskin, Chauncey didn't know and, frankly he didn't care. As powerful and driven as the co-conspirators were, they'd joined on with a group of seriously demented men who'd been planning their revenge from the day Brooks had committed suicide and the men at the gate had butchered each other.

In their own twisted way, the trio had tried to warn the country. Carby had tried to scare engineers away from taking military contracts and to become more ethical. Breskin and Armagan had thrown the brutality of murder and torture in the face of America. And they'd tried to show the dangers from the new tools of surveillance. Chauncey wondered if they would have pulled the plug if the country had responded with outrage rather than fear. He doubted it, but he also knew that it never would have happened. The country had been driven by fear since 9/11 and the government, the media, and anyone who stood to gain financially, fanned the fire.

Whether the MAID program had continued or not, Breskin, Carby, and Brewster were hell bent on retribution. They must have known that their massacre spree wouldn't stop the project. Chauncey didn't know whether his own part in the plan was there from the start or was an afterthought. Given how important the tapes were and how well he knew Breskin's mind, he assumed it was set up from the beginning. He still didn't know how those tapes would be used. Maybe they were made to help inform the American public after the fact. He only knew what was on them.

The CEOs had told Chauncey their secrets before the sessions, so he could teach them how to shield them. The reasoning was that if they ever got captured and tortured to reveal state secrets, these would be the things the "bad guys" would try to exploit. Mostly, the secrets had been about deep fears, phobias, crimes they'd committed and, for a couple, admissions of sexual indiscretions. But it had been a ruse. Breskin hadn't wanted to teach them resistance techniques at all. He'd just wanted to know their secrets. Now General Brewster had them.

The more Chauncey thought about it, the more frightening the scenario was. Once the new surveillance bill was signed into law, the men who owned the systems would have a 360-degree view of everything. It wasn't that Chauncey was naïve. He knew the technology for persistent surveillance had been around for a long time. Traffic cameras, CCTVs mounted on and inside buildings, license plate readers at overpasses and lights, and more were rampant. That, coupled with the NSA's Total Information Awareness Program, PRISM, and the electronic surveillance of cellphones and the Internet, already meant that American citizens were being digitally tagged and tracked like cattle.

For the powers that be, that apparently wasn't enough. Drones represented the final chapter. Helicopters and satellites were expensive and clunky compared to them; drones were not only cheap, but they were nimble and could follow people wherever they went. It was a fringe benefit that they could carry all the sophisticated surveillance technology the government or corporations could dream up.

Drones may not have been the actual surveillance technology, but they sure as shit were the most effective delivery system for it that existed. Not only would the watchers know where and when people went, what they said, and with whom they associated, but with the implementation of a MAID-like system, they would also know what people felt. After that it was a hop, skip, and a jump to what they were thinking and planning.

They would now be watched from above, below, and all around by moving, hovering, slithering eyes. With a chill, Chauncey imagined a swarm of AeroVironment, CUBE quadcopters surrounding a person and asking questions. As he answered, the onboard MAID would be scanning his face, voice, and posture for micro expressions, reading body temperature and blood pressure for indications of lies. If the answers were judged by the bot to be against the state or the corporations, the person would be detained until the authorities arrived. It was the Panopticon turned inside out. People would be afraid to even think wrong thoughts.

It was a nightmare that went against the basic tenets of America to be the home of the free and the brave. Because of the chilling effects driven by fear, even the brave would be squashed. Artists, activists, journalists, whistleblowers, and dissidents would be rendered inert. Even if they weren't being watched, they would be in constant fear that they were. Fear of being labeled as an enemy of orthodoxy just for thinking about a better, more creative way to live would rule the day. It would be a prison of the mind.

As much as it chafed his hide, Chauncey knew he needed to save the lives of the CEOs and Senator Stevens. It wasn't because he thought they deserved to be saved. As far as he was concerned they were mass murderers, traitors, and war profiteers, yet this was still a nation of laws so they needed to be tried and hopefully sentenced to spend the rest of their lives being watched in prison. They'd conspired to burn the Constitution for nothing more than money and power. The only way they could be punished properly was for Chauncey to save their miserable lives and then turn them over to the FBI. Although only God knew what the feds would do with them.

At his core he was a realist. But the part of him that still held to some ideals and optimism — the part of him that Marcella had loved — still had hope, which is probably why he cared and why he was planning to do something rather than go live out his days in a comfortable Malaysian hut. He wondered how this state of affairs had even happened. How the government had sanctioned torture and assassination of its own citizens? Had the whole concept of American "leadership" failed itself?

The National Security Strategy of the United States says that it's a leadership model. To Chauncey it wasn't. Rather than being still based on a "we the people" philosophy of public good, it had morphed into "enlightened self-interest" under President Obama. Money and power trumped God and country. He shook his head recalling how Breskin had asked the engineers who was their sovereign. In a way, it made sense. It was all about self-interest. You could see it in the way that the rich were abandoning equality, disassembling collective bargaining, and moving their assets out of the country to avoid paying taxes. It was toxic, and like a noxious weed had festered and to choke the life out of the country.

"It's a goddamned cancer," said Chauncey to himself.

"What's a cancer?!" yelled Killa, over the drone of the Dehavilland Twin Otter's engines.

Chauncey looked up, returning to reality. He was sitting on a bench inside the jump plane, in full gear. Beside him were Killa and Diddy. They were flying southwest from El Mirage to Rancho Sante Fe, waiting to jump in and attack the senator's house. It was cold, dark, and noisy inside the plane, so he realized he must have spoken pretty loud.

"Oh, sorry. Did I say that out loud?" Chauncey asked.

Killa and Diddy exchanged a look and rolled their eyes.

"Sorry, mate, just lost in thought," Chauncey added. "This whole thing is kind of nuts, you know?"

"Yeah," said Diddy. "But nuts or not, you'd better be with us because we're about ten minutes out."

Chauncey nodded, then looked out the window of the small jump plane. It was dark outside and they were flying low to avoid radar as long as possible. The FAA had issued a no-fly order along with the president's declaration of a curfew. If they were noticed before they hit the jump's exit spot, they would have gotten a curt warning, followed by an F-18 escort to prison. As it was, the pilot, Jim Stellini, knew he would be arrested after he dropped the men off. But he was an ex-comrade in arms and a good friend of Killa's, so he accepted the risk. It was an ethos they all shared. Like the German underground poet Bukowski said, "I'd rather have death tremble to take me! Fuck you, death!"

After they'd learned about the assassination plot from Carby, they'd spent the next day developing an assault plan to stop General Brewster. It was going to happen at Senator Stevens' home in Rancho Sante Fe. It was going to happen right after the president finished his speech and signed the bill on prime-time television. And unfortunately, there was an extremely high probability that they would fail. The only thing they had going for them was the element of surprise.

Chauncey pushed his helmet back and checked his watch. The president was scheduled to start his speech in ten minutes. He would talk for a half-hour, which gave them forty minutes to complete the mission. He considered going over the plan with Killa and Diddy one more time, but knew they'd just tell him they had it and to let them get into their warrior mindset. Compulsively, however, he reviewed the plan to himself for the umpteenth time.

He visualized the senator's house. Recalling with precision the information he'd collected from Google Earth, French L'images Radar, and Multispectralimage satellite sources. He saw the power lines, trees, roads, and the above-ground vents that told him there was a tunnel of some kind running from the senator's house to a nearby hillside. Going back to his boyhood trick of being a Native American hunting buffalo, he mentally ran his hand over the topography, felt the hardness of the ground, and smelled the foliage.

Senator Stevens was living fat and happy in Rancho Santa Fe. Located a few miles north of downtown San Diego, six miles east of the Pacific coastline, Rancho Santa Fe was the next best thing to having a So Cal beach home. The typical property was 4,000 to 9,000 square feet, had six beds, eight baths and was priced from $1.5 million to $5 million. The senator's neighbors included a congressman, a few athletes from the Chargers and Padres, and CEOs of local Fortune 500 companies. However, what people remembered most about Rancho Santa Fe was the famed Heaven's Gate cult and their mass suicide of thirty-nine followers as they tried to hitch a ride with a UFO on the occasion of Comet Hale-Bopp's Earth flyby in 1997.

The senator's home was a huge Tuscan-styled villa located at the end of a long winding road. It was more than the senator and his wife would ever need, but status is status and the senator had it all. It boasted two levels, a four-car garage, a pool, an attached guest house and a long, horseshoe-type drive up to the home. Opposite the front of the house, the other three sides were clear of any other home, street, or building. The western and southern sides of the property ended at a steep slope. On the west-facing side, the hill dropped some one hundred feet and emptied into a valley with an unpaved road used by occasional joggers, dog walkers, and kids on their dirt bikes.

The slope stopped within one hundred yards of the house and one hundred feet below. It then became part of a dry river bed, or *waddie* as they are called in Afghanistan, that once fed a stream from the nearby mountains to the ocean. What made this home unique from the senator's neighbors was that it had a SCIF, a secure room below the house with two-foot-thick concrete walls and accessed by an elevator inside the home.

Phase one of the plan required that when the plane was a thousand yards from the senator's house, Stellini would rapidly ascend to 12,500 feet. Fighting the g-forces and nausea, when they hit the high mark, Chauncey, Killa and Diddy would take the leap. Because they wore wing suits, they would fly down in a "V" formation at close to 200 mph. At that speed they would make up the distance to the house in minutes. The off-mark jump was their best chance of going unnoticed.

For guidance, Phil, who had driven to the neighborhood in the ice truck, now disguised as an overnight delivery service, would watch the jump from the ground. He would observe the team's descent from a nearby neighborhood ridgeline where they could also watch the back of the house and sit sniper watch. Once the guys were under parachute canopy, Phil would signal with a hand-held IR laser and vertically lasso small circles that would only be seen by their IR capable NVGs.

The guys would drop in behind the base of the slope 500 feet directly behind the house and 100 feet below house level. Once the assault team had landed, Phil would aim sniper rifles through the back of a cracked door 600 yards away and keep cover as they approached the house.

With secure text messages on iPhones, Chauncey would signal code for "we are safe, gear stashed." Next text would be, "movement to fence," next, "over the fence." Next text: "prepare to breach," next, "all secure inside home." At that point, Phil would stow his rifle and park within four homes from the senator's home. From there he would text, "we are here" and stand by for their exfil. The only texts other than these that the overnight delivery man could expect from Chauncey and would be either: "help-help-help," which means mission compromised, come in, pull our butts out now, or, "bingo," meaning "we have them, we are coming out with the mission element. Move to secure your loose gear, fire up the truck and stand by to grab bodies and split."

To Chauncey, "help-help-help" was never going to happen.

The only part of the plan that was up in the air, so to speak, was how to deal with outside defenses. That's because they had no idea what to expect. They knew that General Brewster was formidable. He'd joined the service in 1972 and had served as assistant chief of staff for operations and deputy commander, Eighth US Army in Korea. Before he'd come up with the MAID project, he'd been the assistant commander, JTF-Afghanistan, where he'd overseen military intelligence and military police functions. In short, he was a seasoned officer and knew how to set up a perimeter. The odd thing was that according to the satellite imagery Chauncey had gathered, there were barely any warm bodies outside of the home. That meant they were either unprepared, which was highly unlikely, or that before they'd nabbed Carby, he'd helped to set up a robotic defense like the one he'd had at his house.

Chauncey smiled to himself. If that was the case, they were ready.

Chapter Forty-Nine

When Breskin had first proposed his plan to Brewster and Carby, they'd thought it was impossible. Setting aside that their first thoughts were along the lines of feasibility, without even a hint of "holy cow, are you out of your mind?" they thought there was no way the heads of high-tech, scientific, engineering firms would agree to let their brain trusts get butchered like sheep. Scientists and engineers weren't a dime a dozen and they knew the inner-workings of their inventions better than their employers. Killing them would hurt profits, and replacing them wouldn't be as simple as slapping a job posting on Monster.com.

It was a real concern. The fact was that America had fallen behind the rest of the industrialized world in terms of generating intelligent, well-educated scientists, technology professionals, engineers, and mathematicians. Some people believed that most American-born engineers competed on the level of Third World countries.

While killing and terrorizing the current crop into leaving their jobs or scaring wanna-be geeks into pursuing more authentically, pacifist fields might push the government to authorize a domestic drone protection act, the lull would cause the erosion of productivity and profit. It also might seriously curtail the ability to create new and innovative, military technology. Setting aside their utilitarian concerns, Breskin realized he could convince them by exploiting their gargantuan egos and beliefs in their overstated value proposition.

These people were uber-capitalists, pure and simple. They believed that they were the only ones in society who contributed any value. They'd revolutionized technology. Their creations had "won the wars" in Iraq and Afghanistan. Robotics was the future. Not only the future of warfare and law enforcement, but of good governance. They were better than everyone else and not only did they deserve to be in charge, they deserved to be revered.

They all believed that democracy was a joke. Dinner conversations were often political and frequently devolved into outrage over why the hell American idiots got to vote? How could the opinion, if you could call it that, of a Walmart cashier be as valuable as that of those well-educated people who'd made the country what it was? Where was the equity in that? They even went as far as to believe they should pay zero taxes. Society should simply be grateful to them and do their jobs. Jobs that they'd created.

To Breskin, Brewster, and Carby's demented delight, the cabal, along with Senator Stevens, agreed. While they knew they'd need to replace their intellectual assets, they didn't care where they came from. Fifty-percent of the workforce at that level was already comprised of Chinese, Indian, and other foreign-borns. So in terms of getting a new crop of engineers, they realized it was an opportunity to finally get rid of the H1-B visa cap, which prevented them from hiring whomever they pleased by limiting the number of non-US employees they could get. Not only would eliminating the cap get them more talent, it would get them less "entitled" American workers.

To a man, they adored what they called the "Genius Visa." Not only would it bolster their own futures and take the best minds away from China and India, but it would finally destroy the American middle class. They would be the men on the hill, as was their right as innovators and producers of value, and the country would be beholden to them. Enlightened self-interest would see its day.

Over the past nine months, while Breskin and his team riled up fear and dissent, Stevens and the others had lobbied hard. And they'd won. The faster the country unraveled, the faster they got what they'd wanted. The pressure was intense. Engineers, who felt targeted, demanded protection or walked off the job. American honor students graduating from high school applied for hospitality management degrees. While the country became unhinged, Homeland, the FBI, DOD, and local law pressed harder for drones in order to protect the citizens. Colleges wanted students that would pay for eight and twelve years of tuition, and they didn't care what country they called home.

And these men wanted to control the new dragnet society from their John Galt place inside of the tower. They would be the watchers, the listeners, the punishers, and because of that, the deciders.

Privacy and freedom were misguided values that defied common sense. Science, innovation, and profit were the engine of prosperity. Anything or anyone who got in their way was just another person who'd joined the country's rising stupidity index. Nobody was going to miss it anyway. Americans had willingly given away their privacy and through that their freedom by adopting the Internet's social platforms and wireless tracking devices, and by re-electing representatives who passed and reauthorized legislation like The Patriot Act and the USA Freedom Acts.

In a way, people would feel lonely and alienated if nobody responded to their mindless Facebook postings, or had targeted pop-ups remind them what they liked to eat and that true love tasted like a can of Coke. They'd been fed fear by the corporate media for so long that they'd forgotten what privacy tasted like. They'd forgotten how hard people had fought to get rid of government surveillance and unwarranted wiretaps long ago. Now they just craved protection.

"Please keep us safe!" was the clarion whine of the masses. "We don't care if you listen to our phone calls or read our emails, just make sure we don't get hurt by the men with bombs!"

This was the day of reckoning. Americans would get what they wanted. They would be treated like children by the power elite who would finally be in complete control.

Paulson was as excited at the closeness of the moment as an expectant father whose wife was in the delivery room. More so, actually. He'd missed the birth of his own three children because he'd either been at meetings, out of the country, or playing golf. But he sure as hell wasn't going to miss this one. Besides his enthusiasm over having his small UAVs be the exclusive recipient of government contracts, he looked forward to the other benefits of omnipresent surveillance. He indulged in a fantasy about creating bots to follow employees who claimed workers comp to prove they were freeloading maggots.

Green, now on the high-side of his bipolarity's nine-month journey, had thoughts about tracking people from the moment they left their home until the moment they returned. He would be able to show how the supposed poor really went to bowling alleys and restaurants for fun. If they truly were so goddamned poor, how did they have money for such extravagances?

Engeler was chomping at the bit to launch a line of advanced biomimetic pets. Dander-free robotic dogs, birds, and kittens would replace messy, high-maintenance bio-pets in order to gather information about the children. They would record and uplink the children's intellectual and emotional proclivities, and because children say things to pets that mommy and daddy never hear, they would make a bundle selling their wants to marketing firms. Plus, if a child showed personality traits of anger, the police and FBI would keep a closer eye on the child as he or she grew up. He imagined the Supreme Court ruling that since the family brought the bot into their homes willingly, they had no reasonable expectation of privacy.

Additionally to what would mark his entry into the Trillionaire's Club, Stevens had visions of the presidency, or whatever it would be called once he was in charge. Out of habit, he liked to kid himself that he would use the collection, storage, and analysis of intelligence in a benevolent way. Citizens wouldn't have to worry that they were being watched so long as they weren't doing anything wrong. That is to say, nothing that was criminal. That was only proper. He smiled, thinking of what his idol, Frank Underwood, would do with such power. If these tools and laws had been in place years ago, 9/11, the Boston Marathon bombing, Edward Snowden's treason, the Occupy Wall Street movement, and the dissident unrest in Ferguson and Baltimore never would have happened. Life would be safe and simple. The masses would be happy.

Of course, none of these thoughts had been shared around the table where they all currently sat, waiting to toast the birth of their new order. That table, an opulent, twelve-foot, oak and mahogany Ethan Allan conference table, was in the basement SCIF of Steven's home. Everyone was assembled with the best champagne, scotch, and Cuban cigars that money could buy. Their personal security guards were upstairs, forbidden from knowing what was happening. For as much as any of the new watchers wanted to preach that privacy was only an issue for the guilty, they all owned homes that sat on acres and acres of land and were hidden behind guarded gates so that no snooping reporters or corporate competitors could get near them. They all had SCIFs and secure satellite phones and their passwords had passwords. The locks on their offices and homes were the highest end retinal technologies money could buy.

If you'd asked them, the reasoning would have been that they weren't doing anything criminal. Only that they were preventing their ideas from falling into the hands of those who would abuse them and use them to do wrong. They needed secrecy in order to protect the people from the *other* people who wanted to hurt them.

The self-love fest ended abruptly when Senator Stevens rose and clinked his glass of Isabella's Islay with his Chippendale lobster fork.

"My friends," he said looking around the room with exaltation. "We are about to witness the greatest moment in the history of the world. The moment when the right people will finally be in charge. The moment when the world will understand that the brilliant words of our founding fathers, 'We the people,' referred to us. Because truly, *we* are those people."

Everyone stood up and clapped. General Brewster gulped down his bourbon and stepped in front of the 100-inch Sony monitor. He blocked the talking heads that were blathering inane conjecture ahead of the president's upcoming speech.

"I'll put the president's speech on in a moment, but before we do, I think we need to pay tribute to the genius who brought us to this momentous occasion. Without his vision, planning, and perfect execution we wouldn't be here. Friends, colleagues, may I present, back from the dead, Douglas Myles Breskin."

A hidden door to the right of the monitor that led to Steven's tunnel opened. To everyone — except Brewster's — surprise, Breskin entered the room.

From behind Breskin, led by Agent Zellner, a half-dozen, heavily armed men entered and spread around the room. Each man took a position behind someone different at the table and placed a Glock by their head.

Stevens was as outraged as he was shocked. "What the hell is the meaning of this?!" he yelled, leaping to his feet.

Breskin answered his question with a stinging pistol slap to the senator's head. "Filibuster that, Senator," he said, as Steven's body crumpled to the floor.

The room fell silent. Nobody moved a muscle.

Breskin looked at Zellner. "Take care of their security," he said.

Zellner nodded and crossed the room to summon the elevator that led up to the house. The door opened, and he, along with four of the other men, filed out.

Chapter Fifty

Stellini throttled up and pulled back on the stick, forcing the twin-engine Otter into a steep and speedy ascent. In spite of their extensive experience in flying, all four of the small plane's passengers felt the discomforting effects of the increased g-forces. Fighting the flip-flops in their stomachs, Chauncey, Diddy, and Killa got up. Crouching because of the low ceiling, they duck-walked their way toward the now open jump door.

As soon as they were at 12,500 feet above, and a hundred yards due north of the exit point, Stellini yelled, "Exit, exit, exit!"

With no hesitation, the three men wordlessly dove, headfirst, into the cool, dark night air. Wearing wing suits for speed, NVG-fitted comm helmets, and certain pieces of preselected arms and equipment secured in the smalls of their backs and thigh holsters, they shot downward, quickly reaching a speed of 100 mph. Because he was the heaviest of the group, Diddy maintained the lead. They plummeted through the sky, the wind tearing past their clothing, scanning the darkness for traces of the infrared laser lasso from Phil, signaling his place on the ground. At approximately 10,000 feet, they spotted it.

Diddy adjusted slightly to his left, followed closely by Chauncey and Killa. None of them knew what to expect when they landed. They had roughly thirty minutes to get past the senator's exterior security, into the house, then down to his secure basement. But how much security was around the house? Preliminary recon had revealed zero human assets around the exterior, which served to confirm Chauncey's suspicion that, like Carby's house, the perimeter was guarded by some kind of automated defense system. And given who was in the house, it was a good guess. They'd planned for multiple contingencies and now that they'd deployed, hoped they'd allowed for all, or at least enough, possibilities.

As they sped closer to the ground, the red lasso narrowed. It then became a straight beam that pointed to a single spot on the ground. Chauncey spread his arms and used the birdlike construction of his wing suit to move to Diddy's right. Killa did the same, but positioned himself left. At 2,000 feet, they deployed their parachutes, cutting their speed and allowing them to prepare a landing on the hard, loose-dirt, sloped hillside that lay above the ravine 500 feet south and 100 feet below the level of the senator's property.

Chauncey hit the ground at an easy trot. But because of the pitched landing site, his feet angled downward to the left. He continued running a few more feet as he slid on the loose dirt. Nearly falling, he adjusted his posture and regained balance. He quickly removed his gear and rolled it into a tight pack. He then ran down the rest of the hill to the bottom, and together with Diddy and Killa, they stashed their chutes in the shrubs.

Silent thumbs-ups from all three to indicate no twisted ankles or other possible injuries meant step one was complete. Chauncey sent a quick text to Phil as the three looked up toward the top of the rise.

Led by Chauncey, with Diddy and Killa flanking him on both sides, they crept up the hill. When they reached the midway point, Chauncey stopped and pointed to several mounds of dried slash that had been cut and piled up in neat stacks. He and the guys cautiously made their way around the piles and found an old, iron door surrounded by 2-foot-thick, concrete walls. Chauncey had indications of the door on satellite, and based on certain air vents going across Steven's lawn, figured it was the exit to a tunnel that led to and from the senator's basement.

Kicking aside a few empty beer cans probably left by local teenagers using the place for secret parties, Chauncey inspected the door carefully. The displaced dirt and lack of cobwebs covering the door seals meant it had recently been opened. He looked to either side, at his mates, silently communicating that he was going to try opening it. Killa and Diddy both drew their H&K Mark 23 SOCOM pistols from their thigh holsters and held them at the ready.

Drawing a slight breath, Chauncey gripped the handle and yanked on the door. It was locked. Whoever had used it, whenever they'd used it, had secured the door behind themselves. Chauncey made a circle in the air with his hand, then pointed up the hill, signaling that they needed to get into the house via the back door as planned. Diddy and Killa nodded in understanding and holstered their weapons. The three of them crept stealthily to the top.

Like most of the homes in Rancho Sante Fe, Senator Steven's property was surrounded by a six-foot-tall, extremely expensive and sturdy, black wrought iron fence. Each eight-foot-wide section of fencing was bolted to a two-foot-square by seven-foot-high column of stone-inlayed concrete. The tips of each thin metal fence post were pointed and presented the risk of impalement for anyone attempting a clumsy climb over.

Chauncey and Killa, though clearly not in their prime anymore, were still in fairly decent shape. Diddy, on the other hand, had packed on a few beer and sausage pounds. So while vaulting a fence like this for him twenty years ago would have been a breeze, today the wind was still.

They belly-crawled the six feet from the edge of the hill to the fence. Lying face-down in the dirt, Chauncey pulled out a pair of IR binoculars and scanned the yard through the fence posts. In front of them was a well-watered, perfectly manicured, wide-open lawn that was about one hundred feet long by fifty feet wide. To the right of the grass was a red brick path that made a loop from the front of the house around a small grove of a dozen citrus trees. A three-foot-high hedge of bushes ran along both sides of the path. The trees were perfectly spaced, and circular, red mulched areas surrounded each one. Several new small trees had been planted close to the bushes and were being supported by metal stakes until their roots took hold.

To the left of the lawn was a large, kidney-shaped swimming pool surrounded by a flagstone patio. On the opposite long side of the pool was a large redwood gazebo with a concrete-encased grill and a full-sized, Subzero refrigerator. About twenty feet beyond that was a section of French doors that led into the house. Those doors were their way in.

Chauncey scanned the yard several more times, looking for any signs of guards. There were none. Either the senator had an overly confident sense of his own security, or there were some surprises waiting. Chauncey figured it was the latter and packed away his binoculars. He made a zero with his fingers followed by a finger gun, indicating that there were no sentries.

The three men stood up, careful to remain hidden behind the thick, stone columns as best as they could. Diddy stepped in between Chauncey and Killa, and they strenuously boosted him over the top. Once Diddy was on the other side, Chauncey and Killa scrambled up the stone columns and dropped onto the lawn.

Before they could even exchange a glance, the air filled with a thunderous buzzing as if a thousand flying insects had suddenly swarmed to them. Looking toward the house through the eerie green-tinted NVGs, they saw that a barrier of black, AV Cube quadcopters had formed and was now hovering just twenty feet before them. Besides the obvious speed with which the drones had detected and deployed, the mere sight of it was something none of them was likely to forget.

Altogether, there were twenty-four 18-inch square quads. They were perfectly spaced in a formation that was six drones wide and four drones high. Each column of four UAVs maintained a perfect distance of three feet between each unit. Up and down, the space in between them measured two feet. Speechless, the guys just stared at the hovering, buzzing, floating wall.

Not allowing himself to be intimidated, Chauncey motioned to Diddy and Killa with his head to shift right. As one, the men stepped to their right. As one, the buzzing barrier moved with them. They then moved to their left. The swarm followed again. Chauncey tilted his head, left then right, indicating that Diddy and Killa should move in opposite directions. As they did, the drones separated slightly to cover the spread.

Although he'd gotten a taste of drone swarms both at his house and while trying to get to Carby two months ago, Chauncey was still astonished. Diddy and Killa, however, had never seen anything like this. Not up close and personal, that is. Diddy still did some work with DARPA on demolitions, and Killa tried to stay up to date by reading military publications and websites, but that was the extent of it. Of course, they'd also just read about the Navy's recent unmanned surface vehicle operation. Even five years ago the idea of using swarms of robotic boats was pure science fiction. Now it was reality.

Over the din of ninety-six propellers spinning at 5,000 rpm, a speaker in one of the quadcopters barked a warning. It was the prerecorded Texas twang of none other than Thomas Carby.

"Hey there, trespassers. You're standing on private property and that's no bueno. Your mugshots have been recorded and transmitted to the local federales who are currently en route to bring you to the hoosegow. Now put your hands up in the air like you just don't care!"

It was disquieting to hear such a colloquial warning coming from the flying wall, and the fact that it was Carby's voice made it almost comical. But only almost. Because the "most" part of that was clear and present danger. Unsure of what would happen if they didn't comply, all three of them slowly raised their hands.

Figuring that the UAVs were maintaining their synchronicity by way of radio frequencies, Chauncey decided he'd risk lowering his hands to grab the jamming device he had in his backpack. Once engaged, the hand-held unit, like the older Warlock Green, would emit jamming signals on a number of random frequencies with the goal of throwing off the UAVs communication with each other. Unfortunately, he didn't get a chance to find out because as soon as he'd lowered his hands, the top left drone, swooped down at him, nearly smashing him in the head. Startled, he dropped the unit to the ground. When he leaned over to try grabbing it back, another drone swooped down at him.

Chauncey fell back to the ground and Diddy went for the jammer. As he did, a third quadcopter swooped down at him, then pulled up at the last second. It was like a flock of robotic, Hitchcockian crows were attacking a predator. It reminded Chauncey of a time when as a kid he'd watched a group of magpies terrorizing a hawk. He'd stared, mesmerized, as the much smaller birds, all perched in a nearby tree, had swooped and dive-bombed the much larger bird until it flew away. With no seeming rhyme or reason, individual quadcopters were now dive-bombing and "pecking" at the men. When one drone finished its attack and returned to the pack, another would swoop down. The quads kept coming at them. Sometimes one at a time, sometimes two or three at a time. The trio slowly got backed up to the fence.

"Screw this," yelled Killa. "I'm not getting beat by a bunch of bot birds!"

He reached into the small of his back and pulled out a Salvo 12, suppressed sound, 12 gauge shotgun.

"Hold it," said Chauncey. "Move closer together, first."

The men moved shoulder-to-shoulder. Predictably, the quad crows crowded in on one another. The distance between columns was now just one foot.

"Pull!" screamed Killa. He blasted a shot that contained a dozen 000 buckshot pellets that Diddy had prepped for their mission. He'd aimed toward the center of the swarm, and the spread of .36–inch metal balls struck four of the drones, blasting them out of the sky. The drones automatically regrouped, and Killa fired off a second shot, shattering another four with it. Chauncey pulled out his shotgun and joined Killa, taking out three drones with his first shot.

Rather than draw his own weapon, Diddy whipped out an aluminum baseball bat that he'd brought along with him. Besides it being his good luck charm, his reasoning was that if there were quads, he'd be able to practice his swing. While Chauncey and Killa took shot after shot at the now shrinking wall, Diddy stepped to his left and swung at the swooping drones. Every time one of the bots dive-bombed him, he'd swing. Three minutes and a grand slam later, all twenty-four of the bots lay on the lawn in scraps.

The guys exchanged a quick look of satisfaction.

"Goddamned Babe Ruth, I am," said Diddy, resting his bat on his shoulder.

"Damn lucky those suckers didn't have bombs in 'em," replied Killa.

Realizing the truth of that statement, Diddy turned a little pale. "Yeah, I guess so," he agreed.

"Moving on, mates," said Chauncey. "This is just the first inning."

He leaned over and went for the jammer just as another quadcopter raced at him from the darkness. This quad was different than the others. It was faster and had a lower buzz. It also came much closer and as it turned, it made a gash in Chauncey's sleeve. As it took up a menacing hover position ten feet in front of the group, they saw that it was indeed larger. It was over three feet square, with 15-inch props, spinning at 7,000 rpm. The blades were made of highly sharpened, carbon fiber and if they hit you, could cut off a limb as easy as a steak knife through butter.

Another drone shot out from nowhere and swooped at Killa. Proving the danger of its rotors, the drone tore a gash in his shoulder.

"Motherfucker!" he screamed and grabbed his arm. As the drone that sliced him took position beside the first one, he stared down at his and Chauncey's shotguns that now lay on the ground. The jammer's antenna had broken off and was rendered useless. They were contemplating how to retrieve their weapons without inviting another attack, when they heard a third quad whizzing toward them from the darkness.

Diddy leaped out in front of the guys with his bat and set for a huge swing. Even the Babe would have missed this pitch. It came in straight and low. And rather than flying in propellers flat, straight and even, like most quads, it was spinning on a horizontal axis like a top. The quad flew at Diddy and before he could even set, the unit banked and tilted. Its hard rotors hit their mark, slicing through his wrist, and completely severing his hand. The bat, still clenched in his closed fist, fell to the grass. Blood spurted from his radial artery in pulses.

Killa knocked Diddy to the ground in a fierce tackle just as another kamikaze drone attacked. It barely missed Killa's neck as they sunk below its blades.

"Bushes," shouted Chauncey, and the three of them quick-crawled ten feet to the right side of the lawn and hid behind the three-foot hedge that bordered the brick path. Killa tore off part of his pants and began to make a tourniquet for Diddy as Chauncey sent a frantic text to Phil, back at the truck.

"Man down," the text read.

"Holy shit," said Killa, "You expect that?"

"Not on your life, mate," said Chauncey. "You okay, Diddy?"

Diddy could barely speak, but he managed a "fucking crows," before passing out. Killa finished the tourniquet to stop the bleeding, but they both knew their friend wasn't going to be any help from here on.

"Crap," said Chauncey. "Crap! Crap! Crap! I knew I should've gone solo on this one."

"None of that, Paunce," said Killa. "You don't have a monopoly on being patriotic. We knew the risk, now stay focused and figure out how to get us out of this."

Chauncey took a deep breath and turned his attention back to the space between themselves, the still hovering drones, and the house. Sending the text would get Phil mobilized and into the yard fast. And based on Carby's announcement from the drones, the police were on their way. Even if the message had been a ploy, their shotgun blasts would have caused neighbors to call 9-1-1. Time was running out. The president was probably halfway through his speech, which meant that they had fifteen minutes to get into the house and down to the senator's basement.

"The first group had to be self-organized," Chauncey said to Killa. "And since they didn't hit us, their targeting sensors weren't nearly as good as these flying ninjas. There has to be some kind of laser sighting system out there. They wouldn't have put it on the quads because the extra weight would slow them down."

He flipped up his NVGs and pulled out his binoculars to scan the area again. What had he missed? Just beyond them were the three hovering drones. Their props were spinning so fast that it looked as if they were just floating in space. He scanned the drones for any sign of a protrusion that could be a LIDAR sensor. Nothing. There had to be one somewhere. But where?

He moved the lenses to the house and scanned the eaves and the corners. Nada. Tracking left, Chauncey focused on the gazebo by the swimming pool. On one of the edges beneath its roof, he saw a darkened round dome. It was the same kind of dome that covered CCTV cameras. That had to be it. Just before he could put down the binoculars, he saw an IR beam shoot out from the cover toward the fence line.

"Damn," he thought. "That's got to be Phil."

As Chauncey shifted his gaze left, a pair of even larger quads darted out from behind the gazebo. They sped across the pool and into the open space between where he, Killa, and Diddy were laid up. He helplessly watched the drones as they found and targeted Phil, who'd just climbed over the fence. Before he was even aware of them, the drones sprayed him with tiny electrical fragments. As the particles landed on him, they reacted with his perspiration and emitted an electrical shot that knocked him unconscious. He dropped to the ground like a stone.

"Phil's down," Chauncey reported to Killa.

"Damn," said Killa. "No wonder they didn't have any security in the yard. This is like ADT on steroids. Who the hell needs humans anymore?!"

"Well, if we don't get inside, this is just a small taste of what the world's going to be like," said Chauncey. "We need to get to that gazebo," he continued. "That's where the targeting laser is."

"Let's just take it out," said Killa, pulling out his pistol.

"It's too far with a pistol," said Chauncey. "I think I have a better idea."

He handed Killa his binoculars to look at the three UAVs that were holding their position to keep the men at bay.

"See that wobble?" Chauncey asked.

"Yeah," said Killa after he noticed the quads go from perfectly level to a slight bob, then back to level.

"Gyros are magnetic," explained Chauncey. "I think I know how to mess them up. If it works, it should give us enough time to get to the house."

"What's the plan?" asked Killa, checking on Diddy who was still out cold.

Chauncey stayed low and reached to his right. He grabbed a garden hose with a pistol grip sprayer that had been left at the edge of a mound of mulch.

"I want you to spray water at the LIDAR," he continued. "That will screw up the targeting beam long enough for me to reach the gazebo. Once I'm there, I'm going to try something. If it works you'll be able to knock those three suckers out with Diddy's bat."

Killa looked out to where the bat was lying on the lawn. Diddy's severed hand was still wrapped around the handle. Killa arched his eyebrows and blew out a breath.

"You da' boss," he said. "Let's do it."

As Killa turned on the above-ground spigot to open the water flow into the hose, Chauncey reached behind himself and yanked a long, green, metal spike from the ground. The small sapling that was attached to it for strength listed sideways. The two men exchanged a look, then nodded at the same time.

Killa aimed the pistol sprayer at the LIDAR and unleashed a strong, steady stream of water. As Chauncey launched from the brush, the motion detector portion of the LIDAR spotted him and attempted to paint him up to give the drones a target. But the water served to refract the beam so that it couldn't project a strong enough light on his body. The drones flew around aimlessly. Chauncey sprinted as fast as he could, ducking beneath another pair of UAVs that were scattering across the yard attempting to hit targets that weren't there.

He reached the flagstone patio around the pool, then raced to the gazebo. He found the refrigerator's power plug and tore it from the receptacle. Using his knife, he quickly cut away the thick, rubber insulation from the outside of the chord. He then wrapped the inner wires around the metal post several times. Once done, Chauncey plugged the chord back in and began waving the post in the air from side to side.

As he waved what was essentially a homemade electromagnet in the air, the tiny magnometers in the UAVs lost their ability to send adjusting signals to the internal gyros. The net result was that the slight wobble they'd seen became more pronounced and, at least for a short bit, the drones didn't know where they were. They were unstable and didn't know north from south, or east from west. They began moving in what could only be described as a sluggish, drunken state.

Killa saw the reaction immediately. He raced from the bushes and picked up Diddy's bat. The water now off, the LIDAR reacquired him and painted his body for the attack drones. But the quads couldn't respond properly. They moved slowly, in circles, unsure of where to go. Killa easily smashed to bits the three kamikaze drones that had attacked them.

Breathless, Killa joined Chauncey at the gazebo.

"You're like a friggin' MacGyver," he smiled.

"Just trying to survive, mate," said Chauncey.

The approaching sirens told them they had no time to rest on their laurels. They looked back toward the fence, hoping that Phil's man would somehow be able to stall them. To their happy surprise, they saw Phil running toward them. He hadn't been killed by the shock, just knocked out for a bit.

"What if there are more of those things inside?" asked Killa.

"No worries, mate," said Chauncey racing for the French doors. "We only needed to get here. The inside's already taken care of, I hope."

Leaving the still unconscious Diddy hidden by the hedgerow, Killa and Phil joined Chauncey, pistols drawn. Chauncey knocked three short raps on the door. A moment later Agent Zellner opened the door.

"For a minute there, I didn't think you guys were going to make it," said Zellner. "Let's move. They're all in the basement. Nothing between us now but a set of stairs and a door."

Chapter Fifty-One

In stark contrast to the cacophony of explosions, buzzing drones and audibly increased heartbeats coming from outside of the senator's house, the sounds coming from his basement were mostly internal. But they were just as loud. As the CEOs and the senator, his head bleeding copiously all over his Armani shirt, sat around the table watching the president's speech, their minds screamed with fear and confusion. All but Green, that is.

Green stared slack-jawed at the president's lean face and short, tightly curled, graying hair. He wasn't listening to the words escaping the walnut-colored man's face, because there were none. Instead, he heard a recording of his own voice being played over the speakers. It was like when you hear music in a car while it's raining outside, and every now and then the windshield wipers sync with the song's tempo. But mostly, they don't. Mostly, they maintain two different beats that are difficult to track at the same time.

If the underground office had been a passenger-filled car driving through a storm, and in a way it was, the only sounds that would have been heard would have been the music's downbeat and the click-clack, click-clack of the wiper blades. In this case, it was Green's voice that was on top of the music. His voice playing over the president's moving lips.

General Brewster stood on the left side of the table brandishing his MP5. He stared at each man with complete ease, but utter disdain. Breskin's remaining agent stood posted beside the elevator in a similar posture, watching the goings on with obedient attentiveness. Breskin was farther removed. He sat on the floor, leaning against the paneled section of wall that led to the tunnel. He balanced his weapon on his bent knees, and with closed eyes listened to the terror he was causing.

Rather than hearing the president informing the country that he'd signed a bill that would decimate freedom and justice; that he'd done so only after great deliberation and with the utmost reservations and knowledge of the repercussions; that it was necessary; that it was responsible; that it was his job to keep the nation safe; and that it was the only patriotic thing to do in an increasingly dangerous world, Breskin had plugged in an iPhone playing the digitized audio from Chauncey's SERE sessions with each of the CEOs.

Green sat in the center seat on the long side of the conference table, staring straight ahead. The fingers of his hands were interlaced in front of him and resting on the table top. The only betrayal of his casual exterior was the whiteness of his knuckles as they clenched one another like a vice.

"What was your meeting about? Did you discuss killing more of my people? You're a murderer, Mr. Green," said the Arab-inflected voice of Chauncey, the faux interrogator.

"What? I, who are your people?" Green asked in his recorded response.

"The people you kill with your drones. Your robotic, flying assassins."

"I don't kill people," replied Green.

In the here and now, Green licked his lips. He remembered what came next. Even though it had been an exercise, it had been one of, if not the most harrowing experiences of his life. Just hearing it caused his mind to race backward into that room with Chauncey. Backward to the one time, until this time, that he felt out of control. He smelled his own sweat and rising panic.

"Of course you do. And you started a long time ago. In Nicaragua, yes?" asked Chauncey's voice.

Green cringed as the moment approached. He hated himself for it even now. Not a day had passed that he hadn't cursed his weakness.

"Nicaragua?" repeated Green on the audio, his voice genuinely confused.

"Yes. Long ago. Before you bought General Atomics. When you were building your fortune on the backs of peasants on your Nicaraguan cocoa and banana plantations."

"What about —?" asked Green, completely taken off guard by the sudden change of direction, and nearly stepping outside of the circle that Chauncey had taught him to never leave. He recovered. "I don't recall," he answered, not as convincingly as he would have liked.

"You don't recall Olga Sacasa? The poor thirteen-year-old girl that you raped, got pregnant, and then had your despot friend, General Samoza, murder?"

At this point, everyone around the table leaned in with rapt attention. They'd all gone through the same thing, reliving their SV-93 sessions with Chauncey and the nightmares that had plagued them ever since. Like hyenas smelling weakness, they lusted to hear more. To have Green be worse than they were. But only Green knew it was a lie. He'd been in Nicaragua, yes. He'd made his first fortune there. The labor had been so cheap. But there was no Olga Sacasa. He'd raped no one. He'd had nobody murdered.

"I just make drones," Green said. "The military orders them. I create jobs."

"It is your company that makes them so you are responsible for the deaths they cause!"

"I don't know about that. I just sign checks is all. That's all I do. I sign the checks."

Green braced for it. Without thinking, he put his hands over his ears. Not so much to block out the sound, but to block the memory of how he'd been duped into believing that his family had been abducted. That Chauncey made him believe they'd been kidnapped and were tied by men holding sharpened machetes to their throats. He remembered his wife and daughter's screams. Their fear. It had been real. So real.

"Shall I kill them?" Chauncey's voice asked in the past, as the real-time president accentuated some point by punching the air with his fist. It was coincidentally in sync with the question: Click-clack, click-clack.

In Farsi, Chauncey's voice then yelled, "Kill them now!"

"No, I did! I did!" yelled Green.

"Did what?"

"Everything you said. I built unmanned assassins. I paid politicians to keep the war going. The meeting was about Panopticon!"

"And what about Olga Sacasa?"

"Yes. I raped her. I had her killed so that nobody would find out. I'm a murderer."

The audio stopped there. Nothing in the room moved except for the president, who evidently had finished his speech. He soberly took up a $350 Cross Townsend pen and signed the bill. He then looked back at the camera and mouthed the words, "God bless, America." The monitor went dark as General Brewster clicked it off with the remote.

Green moved his hands behind his head. He stared down to the table, concealing his expression.

"I lied," he said to the table. Then he looked up. He turned to everyone there. "It wasn't true. I said it to save my family. I was being tortured for God's sake. You all admitted things to make him stop!" He was half pleading, half ordering them to believe him. "They made it up! I never killed anyone. There was no Olga Sacasa. I would have said I was Adolf Hitler to make him stop!"

Seeing Green's anguish, and remembering his own incriminating admissions after having a heart attack, Paulson looked up. "Dammit, Breskin! What's your game here? What do you want? More money? Is this some kind of elaborate shakedown?"

Breskin looked up and smiled. It wasn't a happy smile. It was the kind of smile that a parent shows a child experiencing deep pain for the first time. It was a smile of understanding and compassion. And it was a smile that sent chills down everyone's spines. Breskin ignored Paulson and spoke to Green.

"Sadly, Nels, I'm not so sure your wife and daughter will believe you're not lying," he said. "Especially after all the years of your telling them and anyone else who would listen that torture works. Besides, you really were in Nicaragua. A girl named Olga Sacasa was found dead. She was pregnant and you were in the village when it happened."

Taking his time, Breskin stood up. He stretched his head to the left and to the right. Like a cat waking from a long, luxurious sleep, he calmly stretched each of his limbs.

"You're all in the same boat," he announced. "As we heard, each one of you admitted on tape to doing something monstrous. Something criminal that, if it ever became public knowledge, would cause you a great deal of professional harm. Not to mention crushing your loved ones."

He nodded to his agent, who moved his weapon to hang around his shoulder. He opened the briefcase they'd carried into the room and pulled out a plain, manila file folder. From inside the folder, the agent handed a single piece of paper and a cheap, plastic pen, to each person. As they read, confused, Breskin paced.

"None of you are leaving this room tonight. I'm afraid that that the birth of your power will also be your funeral." he said.

In spite of his head wound, Senator Stevens jumped to his feet.

"What the hell are you talking about, Doug?! Are you insane?"

In answer to his outburst, General Brewster smashed Stevens in the back of his head again with the butt of his MP5. Stevens crumpled in pain, the head wound he'd received earlier gushing once more. No one moved to help him.

Indicating the papers now before them, Breskin said, "These are your confessions. They say that you are all traitors. And you are. You are traitors not only to your country and to humanity, but to the Heavenly Father. It says that you are guilty of hubris. That you are usurpers who dare to think themselves demigods and have no sovereign but the false idols of greed and power."

If it hadn't been such a strange night already, most everyone would have burst out laughing. Instead, they just exchanged a look. It was the same look. It said, "My God, we are with a madman." Without even noticing, Breskin continued.

"You have all become obscenely wealthy from war, spying, and torture. But now that the wars are over, you want more. You want to turn those machines onto the very people who helped you develop and perfect them. You want to continue profiting by turning that omniscient Panopticon on the very people who with their money, their lives, and their very souls made it possible.

"It's not only an affront to their country but an insult to the Almighty. For only God, who is all-knowing and all-merciful, who truly understands the souls of his children, can know and judge them. It's bad enough that you want to know what every human being on the planet is doing and saying every minute of every day, but the MAID project is the ultimate in hubris. That you would mass produce it and put them on your flying eyes in order to know the souls of man is an insult to God. For while it is his will that his flock be watched, he is the Shepherd. God is the watcher! Not you!"

Engeler became enraged. "That's enough! You're not only a raving lunatic, you're a total hypocrite. You made $42 million dollars for creating and implementing your torture plan in Afghanistan and Iraq. Not to mention how many millions more you've made from our rising stock prices."

"That's true," said Breskin. "I needed that money to finance the final event. As we speak, my men are moving in on all the other guilty people. Because it's not just you that must be purged; it's those who adopted and implemented the morally bankrupt system we currently live under. Within the next ten minutes, every man and woman who had anything to do with the authorization, implementation, and cover-up of torture, regrettably many of them are members of my own church, will be executed by drone."

Green scoffed. "He who casts the first stone."

"The difference is that I live in torment and you sleep at night. I take pills to help me, I pray to the Lord to take my life for my sins, while you lie at peace. But the Lord has a plan for me. He showed me the error of my ways and chose me to seek his vengeance. Now you will die in order to cleanse the moral stain you've left on mankind.

"All you pray to is money and power. So now, on the birth of your accomplishment you will die on top of that slag heap you've amassed. The only question is will you be so selfish as to destroy your families with the revelations of your sins, or will you admit your wrongs to the Lord before you meet him?"

The assemblage stared at Breskin in complete and utter distress. They didn't know what to do. They looked at him, then at the documents before them on the table. They understood the choice they had to make. If they signed, the audio records of them admitting to committing horrendous acts would be destroyed. If they didn't, Breskin would release them to the world. Either way, they were going to die.

"What will this accomplish, Breskin?" asked Green in a final plea. The bill is signed. It's the law. With us or without us, the Panopticon is here. Killing us won't change that."

"Maybe not," said Breskin. "But at least you won't be one of the watchers."

He turned to the general and said, "You, too, Brewster." He nodded to his agent, who passed the final confession to him.

"What the hell are you talking about? We were in this together," Brewster said. "We were all screwed up by making that fucking MAID. *They* kept it going, not me. This wasn't part of the deal."

"My deal is with the Lord," said Breskin.

"That's horseshit," said Brewster who moved the safety of his weapon to fire and aimed it at Breskin. "If I go, you're coming with me, you goddamned lunatic."

"I don't think so," said Breskin and leveled his own weapon at Brewster.

Brewster pulled the trigger of his MP5 but nothing happened. He pulled it again with the same lack of response.

"No firing pin, General. But I guess I have your answer."

Breskin fired off a burst from his submachine gun at Brewster. The flurry of bullets ripped open his chest and knocked him backward. He slid down to the ground, leaving a streak of blood against the wall.

The room fell silent again as everyone watched, in shock, as the life ebbed from the general's limp body. Green looked at his fellow captains of the military industrial complex, his fellow kings of mankind, then defiantly put down his pen, refusing to sign the confession.

"I won't play your game," he said.

All of the others followed suit, refusing to sign. Breskin merely shook his head at their continued hubris. He stood back and pointed his weapon at them.

"Sign it!" he screamed. "Sign it or be damned!"

Nobody moved. Nobody breathed. If they could have stopped their hearts from beating and still lived, they would have done so. All of them, save for Green, closed their eyes waiting. He stared at Breskin hard, his nostrils flaring with defiance. The thickness of the moment was suddenly cut by the low, mechanical hum of the approaching elevator.

For a moment, thoughts of salvation, true salvation, spread through the room. As the doors opened and Zellner stepped out, those hopes crumbled.

"The house is secure," said Zellner.

"Good," said Breskin, turning back to his flock. "Now help me finish this."

"I don't think so," shouted Chauncey as he, Phil, and Killa leapt out from the elevator.

Before he had a chance to react, Killa fired off a lethal headshot at Breskin's remaining agent. He fell to the floor with a thud.

Breskin reacted a thousand ways in less than a second's time. What was Chauncey doing here? How could he have known? How could he have gotten in?

Unable to accept the reality, Breskin screamed at Zellner, "Kill them!"

"I don't think so," Zellner said. "It's over, you crazy, fucking bastard. I called Chauncey. I told him what was going on. Your guys are out of commission. Now put down your weapon."

Breskin was stunned. He heard the words but couldn't fathom the betrayal. He slowly backed up to the wall, his MP5 aimed first at Zellner, then Chauncey, then Killa, then Phil.

"I saved you!" he spat at Zellner. "You Judas!"

He spun his submachine gun back at Zellner, but Chauncey jumped in front of him, blocking Breskin's line of sight.

"It's over, mate," said Chauncey. "It's time to get some help."

"I can't do that, Paunce. You above all should understand. These people are the reason you went to prison for telling the truth."

"That's true," said Chauncey. "These folks *are* the ones who destroyed my life. They labeled me a traitor in order to keep their empire, then threw me away like trash."

"That's right," said Breskin. "They're evil. But I can save their souls by releasing the divine spark that's trapped in their darkness."

"Yeah, well, I don't know about all that," said Chauncey. "All I know is that I have to save them from you, so the world can find out the truth. And if that means 'saving' you the same way you plan to 'save' them, so be it. Now stand down."

Chauncey held out his hand and took a step toward Breskin. As he approached, Breskin backed up all the way to the wall. He contemplated his situation, saw the overwhelming odds, but believing that he was indeed the chosen one, he rebelled.

"No!" he bellowed and unleashed a stream of bullets at the CEOs. Green and Paulson were hit. Everyone else in the room dove for cover. As they went down, Breskin punched the panel to open the tunnel door and ran inside. Chauncey lunged for the door just as it clicked closed and locked.

Chauncey spun back to the room and barked to Zellner, "Gun!"

Zellner tossed his MP5 sideways at Chauncey, who caught it on the run. He rushed to the elevator and hit the button. The door closed and the sleek machine quickly lifted him from the dark bowels of Steven's basement to the light of the surface. He lurched sideways, scraping his body through the doors before they'd fully opened and raced down the hall. He ran out of the French doors and onto the fine, taxpayer-financed, Italian flagstone patio. Adrenaline coursing through his arteries with tidal force, he sped across the lawn, his feet crunching the carcasses of the fallen drones they'd defeated. To the fence, the stone post. He vaulted up and over and ran to the edge of the hill.

Scanning the embankment, he saw Breskin appear from the hidden doorway of the tunnel and begin to make his way to the bottom. With a final, gravity-fed burst of speed, Chauncey powered down the hill. One step, two, then he launched himself toward his mark. Breskin heard Chauncey's feet thudding toward him and turned back, his weapon lifting to fire. There wasn't nearly enough time. Chauncey wrapped his arms around Breskin's waist and the two men tumbled down the rest of the hill. They came to a stop in the hard, dry riverbank, and were instantly separated by the impact. A second later, their weapons slid to a stop, nearby, but out of easy reach.

For a moment, neither man made a move to rise. They simply lay there, five feet apart, panting. Their chests heaved and their lungs stretched out for air. The pounding of their hearts and brains prevented either man from thinking.

"Why did you stop me, Paunce?" Breskin croaked through his gasps. "They are the traitors. You said it yourself at your trial."

"Maybe," Chauncey managed to choke out. "But it's not your place to be judge, jury, and executioner. We've had enough of that."

Breskin struggled to his knees. He looked up at the sky, his breathing coming under control. He wheezed, "I have to finish it."

"It's over," said Chauncey.

"No, it's not!" Breskin yelled. He stood up and pulled an iPhone from his pocket.

Breskin pressed the screen, activating an unseen app. The night silence was immediately interrupted by the eerie, distant echoing of what sounded like bats in a tunnel. Mere seconds later, 300 miniature black quadcopters burst outward from the entrance of the tunnel. The thick, flying mass hit the air and spiraled upward in a swirling tornado formation that stretched a hundred feet high.

"Armagan's finale!" Breskin shouted to Chauncey.

Not waiting to see what they were for, Chauncey took a step toward Breskin.

"Uh-uh," Breskin said, and pointed the iPhone at him.

An IR beam shot from the mobile device's modified flashlight and marked Chauncey's chest. The drones obediently screamed downward toward Chauncey and surrounded him. They imprisoned him inside a dense, pulsing tower of black.

"Most of these swarms are designed to incapacitate a person!" Breskin shouted against the noise. "But Armagan designed these guys to do more than that. Once enough of them touch their target, they emit a charge of ten amperes. You're surrounded by a flying, electric chair!"

"Killing me isn't the answer!" Chauncey shouted, trying to see where Breskin was. "The only answer is the truth. Show people the truth!"

"They've broken us! Both of us! We'll never be fixed." Breskin yelled.

From inside the eye of the drone helix, Chauncey struggled to stay calm. The wind from the blades was intense and lifted the dirt from the ground into his eyes. He knew that he had to respond to Breskin. Try to reach some part of the man that was still whole.

"It's true!" Chauncey shouted. "You're broken! The moral breach of doing violence on your fellow man has shattered you. But it did more than that. It broke the toxic leaders who justified what you did in the name of pleasure and self-interest — enlightened or not!

"Hubris breaks the system that chose those leaders and silently sits back condoning their actions," Chauncey screamed. "It breaks the world, mate. And you helped to get it this way. You helped to rip it apart. You don't get to break it, then all of a sudden decide you're the messiah so you can fix it. That's not how it works. You need to pay."

Breskin stepped around Chauncey, surveying the incredible sight as he went. "What, Paunce?! And let the laws that were created by the one-percent, the same laws that allowed torture, determine my fate?" he asked.

"Laws can be changed. What you've done has caused a revolution. They're rioting in the streets. People finally see. The soldiers who've been used and discarded see. Their families see. The voters see. The drones won't fly. Panopticon will not happen."

"You're naïve, Paunce!"

"I'm hopeful!"

"Clearly, the Lord wants you to live, Paunce," said Breskin. "So I won't defy his will. But his plans for me don't include staring at a prison wall for the rest of my life. He still has work for me to do."

With those words, Breskin looked upward. Chauncey followed his heavenly gaze, wondering if the man was so far gone that he was looking for angels to come for him. But it wasn't angels that he saw. It was the arrival of a Lockheed Martin K-Max, unmanned helicopter. With a 6,000-pound lift capacity, the brown, 5,100-pound, unmanned aerial truck, developed for behind the lines battlefield cargo resupply, hovered a hundred feet above Breskin's head. As Breskin punched a command into his hand-held control, a rope ladder began to lower from the helo.

Chauncey knew he had to do something but didn't know what. He was out of ideas. There were no more rabbits waiting to be pulled from his hat. Without considering that touching his swirling prison guards might kill him on contact, Chauncey reached out. Instead of being cut or shocked, the internal proximity sensors in the quadcopters responded. As designed to do, they moved away from his hand.

Focusing on the now arriving ladder, Breskin turned his gaze away from Chauncey and onto his now certain escape. He stepped onto the lowermost rung and checked his balance to make sure he could still control the ascent with his remote. He then signaled the UAV to bring him up.

For Chauncey it was now or never. He took a tentative step forward, and the entire drone formation moved with him. Against the updraft of debris still being pelted into his face, he willed himself to move slowly, purposefully forward.

Now rising toward his escape, Breskin looked down and saw Chauncey approaching.

"It's too late, Paunce! By the time you get here I'll be headed to freedom," he said.

Unable to hear what Breskin said due to the combined noise of the chopper and the quads that surrounded him, Chauncey continued forward at a steady pace. As he neared the spot where Breskin had been standing, the top of the quadcopters got close to the spinning rotors of the helicopter. The rotor wash pushed them back, but they persisted.

Seeing the approaching calamity, Breskin's eyes widened. He tried to order the quadcopters to collapse on Chauncey, but it was too late. The topmost quads made contact with the helicopter's rotors. While the velocity of rotation and powerful rotors tore the tiny drones apart like soft, low-flying geese, some of the shards got sucked into the engine.

The K-Max spit fire and smoke. Out of control, the UAV listed, then went into a counter-rotation death spin. It nosedived to the ground, crushing Breskin beneath its weight and shooting rocks and dirt in all directions as the main rotor disintegrated into the hillside.

The concussion of the crash sent Chauncey flying backward. The remaining quadcopters fell to the ground around him like robotic rain. In spite of injuries he'd gotten by the shrapnel launched by the helo's rotors hitting the ground, he immediately got to his knees and crawled to Breskin's pinned and completely broken body.

Breskin, still alive but just barely, whispered, "Did you know my church made me a bishop?! They made me a saint! Even after they knew what I'd done."

"Save your strength, mate," Chauncey said.

"I turned it down, Chauncey," Breskin said. "I turned it down. Even my faith is broken now."

As Breskin's eyes closed, Killa, Phil, Diddy, Zellner, and what seemed to be the entire police department raced down the hill.

"Chauncey! Are you alright? You okay?" yelled Killa.

Chauncey tilted his head back and closed his eyes, considering the question. Maybe he was naïve, but it didn't matter. After all he'd gone through, all that had happened, he was still hopeful. He was hopeful that his fellow soldiers who'd sacrificed their lives, their limbs, and their souls over a pack of lies would find peace. He was hopeful that the world would come to its senses and deplore torture so that the tortured and torturers alike would learn to forgive one another and themselves.

Maybe it would take a revolution, but he believed that ultimately, the country he cherished would wake up and find those other hopeful citizens and patriots who valued the many over the few, the selfless over the selfish, and meaning over power. Maybe they could save it before it was so broken that all the king's soldiers and all the engineers couldn't repair the damage done to our democratic ideals. After all, he thought, what's life without hope?

Chauncey opened his eyes to see what the new world looked like. The first thing he saw was his mates.

The drone that was patrolling the American sky four miles above him saw the same thing.

Afterword

Daniel Somers (January 14, 1983 – June 10, 2013) was part of the Tactical Human Intelligence Team (THT) in Baghdad, Iraq. While there he ran more than 400 combat missions as a machine gunner in the turret of a Humvee, interviewing countless Iraqis ranging from concerned citizens to community leaders and government officials. He interrogated dozens of insurgents and terrorist suspects. In 2006-2007, Somers worked with Joint Special Operations Command (JSOC) through his former unit in Mosul as a senior analyst for the Northern Iraq Intelligence Center.

Daniel suffered from severe PTSD, traumatic brain injury and several other war-related conditions. On June 10, 2013, Daniel wrote the following letter to his family before taking his life. He was only 30 years old. His wife, Angeline, and family have given permission to publish it as testimony that the words of this novel are founded on some of the sad and tragic realities now confronting our veterans and our nation.

I am sorry that it has come to this.

The fact is, for as long as I can remember my motivation for getting up every day has been so that you would not have to bury me. As things have continued to get worse, it has become clear that this alone is not a sufficient reason to carry on. The fact is, I am not getting better, I am not going to get better, and I will most certainly deteriorate further as time goes on. From a logical standpoint, it is better to simply end things quickly and let any repercussions from that play out in the short term than to drag things out into the long term.

You will perhaps be sad for a time, but over time you will forget and begin to carry on. Far better that than to inflict my growing misery upon you for years and decades to come, dragging you down with me. It is because I love you that I cannot do this to you. You will come to see that it is a far better thing as one day after another passes during which you do not have to worry about me or even give me a second thought. You will find that your world is better without me in it.

I really have been trying to hang on, for more than a decade now. Each day has been a testament to the extent to which I cared, suffering unspeakable horror as quietly as possible so that you could feel as though I was still here for you. In truth, I was nothing more than a prop, filling space so that my absence would not be noted. In truth, I have already been absent for a long, long time.

My body has become nothing but a cage, a source of pain and constant problems. The illness I have has caused me pain that not even the strongest medicines could dull, and there is no cure. All day, every day a screaming agony in every nerve ending in my body. It is nothing short of torture. My mind is a wasteland, filled with visions of incredible horror, unceasing depression, and crippling anxiety, even with all of the medications the doctors dare give. Simple things that everyone else takes for granted are nearly impossible for me. I cannot laugh or cry. I can barely leave the house. I derive no pleasure from any activity. Everything simply comes down to passing time until I can sleep again. Now, to sleep forever seems to be the most merciful thing.

You must not blame yourself. The simple truth is this: During my first deployment, I was made to participate in things, the enormity of which is hard to describe. War crimes, crimes against humanity. Though I did not participate willingly, and made what I thought was my best effort to stop these events, there are some things that a person simply cannot come back from. I take some pride in that, as to move on in life after being part of such a thing would be the mark of a sociopath in my mind. These things go far beyond what most are even aware of.

To force me to do these things and then participate in the ensuing cover-up is more than any government has the right to demand. Then, the same government has turned around and abandoned me. They offer no help, and actively block the pursuit of gaining outside help via their corrupt agents at the DEA. Any blame rests with them.

Beyond that, there are the host of physical illnesses that have struck me down again and again, for which they also offer no help. There might be some progress by now if they had not spent nearly twenty years denying the illness that I and so many others were exposed to. Further complicating matters is the repeated and severe brain injuries to which I was subjected, which they also seem to be expending no effort into understanding. What is known is that each of these should have been cause enough for immediate medical attention, which was not rendered.

Lastly, the DEA enters the picture again as they have now managed to create such a culture of fear in the medical community that doctors are too scared to even take the necessary steps to control the symptoms. All under the guise of a completely manufactured "overprescribing epidemic," which stands in stark relief to all of the legitimate research, showing the opposite to be true. Perhaps, with the right medication at the right doses, I could have bought a couple of decent years, but even that is too much to ask from a regime built upon the idea that suffering is noble and relief is just for the weak.

However, when the challenges facing a person are already so great that all but the weakest would give up, these extra factors are enough to push a person over the edge.

Is it any wonder then that the latest figures show 22 veterans killing themselves each day? That is more veterans than children killed at Sandy Hook, every single day. Where are the huge policy initiatives? Why isn't the president standing with those families at the state of the union? Perhaps because we were not killed by a single lunatic, but rather by his own system of dehumanization, neglect, and indifference.

It leaves us to where all we have to look forward to is constant pain, misery, poverty, and dishonor. I assure you that, when the numbers do finally drop, it will merely be because those who were pushed the farthest are all already dead.

And for what? Bush's religious lunacy? Cheney's ever growing fortune and that of his corporate friends? Is this what we destroy lives for?

Since then, I have tried everything to fill the void. I tried to move into a position of greater power and influence to try and right some of the wrongs. I deployed again, where I put a huge emphasis on saving lives. The fact of the matter, though, is that any new lives saved do not replace those who were murdered. It is an exercise in futility.

Then, I pursued replacing destruction with creation. For a time this provided a distraction, but it could not last. The fact is that any kind of ordinary life is an insult to those who died at my hand. How can I possibly go around like everyone else while the widows and orphans I created continue to struggle? If they could see me sitting here in suburbia, in my comfortable home working on some music project they would be outraged, and rightfully so.

I thought perhaps I could make some headway with this film project, maybe even directly appealing to those I had wronged and exposing a greater truth, but that is also now being taken away from me. I fear that, just as with everything else that requires the involvement of people who cannot understand by virtue of never having been there, it is going to fall apart as careers get in the way.

The last thought that has occurred to me is one of some kind of final mission. It is true that I have found that I am capable of finding some kind of reprieve by doing things that are worthwhile on the scale of life and death. While it is a nice thought to consider doing some good with my skills, experience, and killer instinct, the truth is that it isn't realistic. First, there are the logistics of financing and equipping my own operation, then there is the near certainty of a grisly death, international incidents, and being branded a terrorist in the media that would follow. What is really stopping me, though, is that I simply am too sick to be effective in the field anymore. That, too, has been taken from me.

Thus, I am left with basically nothing. Too trapped in a war to be at peace, too damaged to be at war. Abandoned by those who would take the easy route, and a liability to those who stick it out—and thus deserve better. So you see, not only am I better off dead, but the world is better without me in it.

This is what brought me to my actual final mission. Not suicide, but a mercy killing. I know how to kill, and I know how to do it so that there is no pain whatsoever. It was quick, and I did not suffer. And above all, now I am free. I feel no more pain. I have no more nightmares or flashbacks or hallucinations. I am no longer constantly depressed or afraid or worried

I am free.

I ask that you be happy for me for that. It is perhaps the best break I could have hoped for. Please accept this and be glad for me.

Daniel Somers

Author Biographies

Michael S. Kearns

Michael S. "Kearnsey" Kearns is a retired Air Force Intelligence Officer, and former Master SERE instructor, who has been a vocal opponent of the Bush/Cheney torture program and the dark complexities of political war profiteering at the expense of the American people. He is the sole survivor of the world's first four-way skydive over the South Pole and the first person to have parachuted over all seven continents. As a patriot who has risked his life and lost too many of his fellow veterans, this novel is his dedication to the truth.

Ronald B. Solomon

Ronald B. Solomon has created, written, and run successful companies and products spanning television sitcoms, children's toys and games, and information technology. He is deeply concerned about the condition of our country and the negative effects of financial elitists and their government lapdogs on our citizenry. His extensive background as a television executive producer, head writer, and show creator has helped to give his first novel, "Broken!" its exciting, cinematic feeling. He lives at the top of a mountain near Denver, Colorado, with his wife, Iris and pet security drone.

24703148R00281

Made in the USA
Middletown, DE
04 October 2015